Mamma Mia!

SINNERS, SAINTS & ESCAPADES

Hair-Raising Adventures in Italy & Greece

Book Two in the Mamma Mia! Trilogy
Scandalous Situations with the Americans
Secrets in the Sistine Chapel & Michelangelo
Historical Tidbits of the Apostles
Two Greek Weddings in Greece

STEPHANIE CHANCE

Bestselling Author of
Mamma Mia, Americans Invade Italy!

Front Cover photo by Aleh Varanishcha/iStock

Back Cover photo by anneleven/iStock

Map of Italy by pavalena/iStock

Publisher: Verona Valentino Editoria (Italy)

ISBN-13: 978-0-578-62980-3

ITALY - ENGLAND - FRANCE - AUSTRALIA - USA

Dedicated to all of the adventurous Americans who hop aboard my European tours, year after year, as I lead and guide them to fairy-tale places throughout Italy and beyond. Thank you for giving me lifetime memories as you get into the most 'hair-raising' situations! Here's to another twenty years of zigzagging all over Europe with me and the Sicilians!

And to my only granddaughter, Kaitlyn Paige, I pray you always keep Jesus as your best friend and a calendar marked full of fun adventures!

And, a big shout out to Danny's beloved momma who was with us each day via telephone as her voice blasted across the pond from Oklahoma to Italy and Greece, expressing her dire concern for her son's marital status. "Momma doesn't acknowledge the seven-hour time difference between Europe and the States. So help me, Hannah, she called again last night, upset about Gerald being with me. Her breathing was so heavy that it nearly knocked me out for a few short seconds through the phone line." (Chapters 26 through Chapter 29)

Danny, your mom made our adventure so much fun, causing continuous laughter. We will never forget your dear momma, with her flowery pink cheeks ... the face of peach cobbler in the rosy sunshine, a beautiful olive-kissed Oklahoman lady who tracked your air flights on her laptop to make sure the plane didn't go down, a genuine jewel that continues to sparkle like a rare diamond among her family and friends. Thank you for sharing her with us. She will never be forgotten as she walks those beautiful streets of gold in her heavenly home. RIP, Momma, we love you! 07/29/18

CONTENTS

1. Bringing Americans to Italy!   1
2. Requesting a Monk!   7
3. Michelangelo   17
4. Mamma Mia! Where is Mr. Cheeks?   35
5. Driving Through Tuscany   45
6. Tell Us More of Pitigliano & Grab Your Testicles!   57
7. Rose Bushes in Italy   67
8. Serenade the Grapes   71
9. Abbey of Sant'Antimo   79
10. Mamma Mia, Where's the Toilet?   97
11. Mamma Mia, We're in Meteora, Greece!   107
12. Mamma Mia, We're in Greece! (Going to Skopelos)   111
13. Mamma Mia, We're in Greece! (Greek Bowling Bowls!)   123
14. Mamma Mia, We're in Greece! (Gathering Flowers)   133
15. Mamma Mia, We're in Greece! (Ride to Chapel)   147
16. Mamma Mia, We're in Greece! (Going to Get Married)   153
17. Hot Affair on the Isle of Capri   163
18. Too Much Excitement in the Mediterranean - Man Overboard!   185
19. Living La Dolce Vita - The Good Life   201
20. Dancing in the Cave - The Africana   209
21. Janice Gets Run Over in Amalfi   217
22. Sicily, Midnight Swim, & Hookers - Colpo d'Aria   235
23. Mamma Mia, I Have Sinned!   249
24. Midnight Run to Perugia   267
25. Napoli - Red Lips Meet Chanel   275
26. Going to the Chapel in Greece (Confessions on the Coach)   289
27. Going to the Chapel in Greece (Finding the Ring)   309
28. Going to the Chapel in Greece (Rehearsal Dinner)   317
29. Going to the Chapel in Greece (The Wedding)   327

Acknowledgments   349
About the Author   351

Chapter 1

BRINGING AMERICANS
TO ITALY!

From behind the windshield, I can see absolutely everything that moves in Tuscany. The sign three miles back read "Montalcino," and underneath its proclamation was an old, rickety square board with a black painted arrow on it that dangled upside down.

"I hope tourists aren't coming this way," I tell Nino, but he doesn't hear me. Two seconds later, we pass a walled hilltop village with no direction for how to enter and no signage about its famed history nor a welcoming marquee. I wonder how one would reach inside its walls; by parachute or climbing to its mysterious beauty?

As I turn back in my seat, I see another medieval hilltop town, sitting like a royal wedding cake with each layer ascending higher than the next, towering tall among rolling hills. To my right, a flock of woolly-white sheep stroll behind a modern-day shepherd, and I wonder if Moses will follow behind carrying the Ten Commandments. Straight ahead are lush vineyards, silvery olive groves, and Italian cypress trees leading to medieval villas.

Across the aisle from me, sitting in the driver's seat of our Mercedes-Benz coach, Nino continues tapping his left thumb against the steering wheel in rhythm with the Italian music on the radio. We're both also listening to Tony provide us all with an analysis of this year's olive oil harvest and its superb quality and tastiness. I sit with a microphone resting in my lap and glance between the Americans seated behind me and the rolling Toscana hills. The Italian lyrics continue to play through the speakers, but with the "oohing" and "ahhing" from the Americans and Tony's loud voice, the music is forgotten.

The Americans, whom we host for two to three European tours a year, always love the "Tony and Nino routine." Both men seem to exaggerate the act of their Sicilian drama parading across the stage of everyday life. The orchestrated duo rolls out more laughter in their mother tongue than any comedy show, and it's not pretense. No, it's natural, unrehearsed *Italiano* playing out in full force and guaranteeing laughter.

Tony and Nino are two happy faces that greet us in the Italian airports after our long flights from America. Their hands wave like colorful balloons as they gesture us over to the coach from the terminal. Their olive-kissed faces and arms reach over the banister announcing, "We are ready to entertain. We are your genies in a bottle; your wish is our command."

The similarities between Tony and Nino end with them both being Sicilian. Tony, the mirror-image of Rodney Dangerfield, is a tall, robust man and a natural-born comedian. He speaks seven languages and has the arms of an octopus as he conducts us across Italy, pointing out this turn, that turn, and oh, the exit over there. Tony is everything that comes to mind when thinking of Sicily and more. He's a tall stick of spaghetti pasta, flexible at every angle. He can bend and bounce and make the unobtainable happen with the snap of his fingers or the press of his phone. He's a spicy round meatball exploding with colorful flavors; his personality is magnetically charged—220 volts, electrifying and omnipresent throughout Europe. Who doesn't know Salvatore "Tony"? *Mamma Mia*, even the fish in the Mediterranean Sea hear his Sicilian thundering, his voice echoing across the sky and ricocheting into every known region.

Nino, "Our Little Bambino," is my devoted driver over whom American women regularly faint at the sight of his dreamy face. He stands out like a freshly baked chocolate pie adorned with golden meringue on top of his perfectly round, glazed head. His cheeks are brushed by God's own hand with ruby-red blush. A sudden bout of heart palpitations usually occurs when meeting him on our arrival. There's something about Nino's appearance and his sex appeal. With the flash of his smile, he's a natural pain reliever just as sex causes the release of endorphins to explode throughout the brain. I've witnessed the results of his countenance repeatedly with the ladies. There's a predictable glitch within the brains of American women as though it's a sudden memory loss of their marital status.

Nino cannot match Tony's physical size; however, his persona is a dynamite package with explosive ramifications. "Our Little Bambino" is Sicilian, an Italian pocket doll whom all of our American tour-guests want to take home as their personal playmate. Everyone wants a piece of him when seeing his European stance, standing beside Tony with his man-bag strapped perfectly around his colorful attire.

"*Mamma Mia, Stefania*. How many years do you bring the Americans to Italy? It must be twenty or more now." Tony chops his words in broken English, his tone soft as if he's reminiscing for a brief second before he directs Nino to take a sharp right turn.

"*Si, si*, Tony. Yes. Can you believe I started the European tours in May of 2000 when I brought my first group of Americans to Lake Como, Italy? And months later, practically the same group of people hopped aboard for a September tour. How quickly life rushes through the hourglass!"

"*Stefania*! There's no way to escape the memories, and I'm getting older by the day. You must tell the things that happened to us! When will you write another book? The longer you wait to put these truths into print, the more we accumulate. I'm certain there will be another story to tell before I rid myself of you and the *Americani*."

"It takes time to write," I reply. "I work all the time. I'm in Italy and all the other countries doing two and three tours a year with you. Then back in America, it starts all over again. You know I'm a one-woman cabaret, a live entertainer, presenting our Italy tours like a television commercial...the many fairy-tale places we take the people to, the way we share our passion. And then there's the shop, the house, the family, the husband, the girls, and jetting back and forth from this plane to that plane. My feet are never planted in one place very long. Still, I always have my laptop nearby, pecking away on the keyboard, telling the endless stories about us and the Americans, describing the hair-raising situations they get themselves into."

"You must calm down, relax a little, and tell the stories before the light flickers out on both of us. *Mamma Mia!* What is this fire within you that never ceases, never dwindles down?"

"There's no need to fret, Tony. I have practically every tour engraved within my mind, especially the unusual happenings, although you might say those are normal for us. How can one erase twenty years of what we've been through with the Americans?"

"*Stefania*, there is always one who makes me question my sanity. And you, your life has no recipe to follow, no normal way of living. You are too Americanized. You don't know how to stay still. You work too much. And it's usually you who seduces the people to do the crazy things they do. *Mamma Mia!* You have no boundaries when your feet hit Italian soil. Why is that?"

"That's not true, Tony. I'm Snow White, and I have no control over the Seven Dwarfs—the Americans."

My thoughts rushed back. The previous night the rain arrived, dancing on the villa's ceramic roof, but the storm drifted away by the time the windows were swung open, leading us out onto the iron balcony that overlooks the valley of Lucca, Italy.

As I looked over the balcony, I affectionately rubbed the arm of the antique, royal blue chair that I was sitting in and reminisced over the countless times we'd been here. From this old friend of a chair, the same scene still strikes me with wondrous awe. I never tire of viewing the rolling vineyards and the fragrant olive trees swishing in the breeze from a slow-moving thundercloud.

Yes, touring Italy and the other surrounding countries is a

fulfilling job for each of us, but creating off-the-beaten-path excursions to fairy-tale places is also something we are passionate about. Exploring Europe with Americans, who can get themselves in the most bizarre situations, never gets old.

Chapter 2

REQUESTING A MONK!

This morning we're on our way to another storybook village with sixteen Americans, including Dr. Jerry Raybay, who is from the oil-boom state of Texas. Months ago, before signing up for this tour, he asked if we'd go to a monastery with monks wearing the "long robes and sandals." That's all he requested from the tour—to experience medieval friars swaddled in hooded garments with gigantic crosses dangling about their waists on knotted ropes.

I remember the conversation as though it were yesterday—my mobile phone was glued to my ear for ninety-eight minutes.

"You do know the meaning of the customary attire and why they wear them, don't you? And the ropes tied about their waist, do you know the true meaning? You know, the Franciscan Monks in Assisi, Italy? I've read about the rope belt that's called a cincture. Do you know where to buy them?" Dr. Raybay interrogated me through the phone, never stopping or slowing for me to reply.

His questions were like a runaway train that is jumping too many tracks and zigzagging all over the place. Nonetheless, I tried to respond, determined to answer his questions that were slapping in my ear.

"Yes, I know the Franciscan Monks. We've been going to Assisi for over twenty years, and I must admit that I'm fascinated with them too. You asked about the belt. Ah, it has many meanings according to that sect of monks," I hurriedly answered, trying to explain before he started up again.

"When seeing them walking the streets in Assisi, my eyes always seem to race to the rope entwined about their waist. The three large knots are tied on one end and dangle down on the right side of their vestments. They signify their vows: poverty, chastity, and obedience. You will see them when we arrive in Umbria," I breathlessly explained, not giving him a chance to derail me again.

"That's exciting, Stephanie. Can you arrange for me to meet them in person and perhaps join them for a day's activity of whatever they do all day? And is it possible to hear them chant or say something of importance? Perhaps, help in their vineyards or..."

"Yes, I'll take you to the Abbey of Sant'Antimo," I told him with pleasure. "It's been in existence since the year 814. Not only will we see it but we're staying nearby in Assisi, Italy, the home of Saint Francis. You will be surrounded by the Franciscan monks with their brown robes and rope belts. Just wait until you experience it; you'll be in a monk's paradise."

"Stephanie, I have another question." Dr. Raybay cleared his throat, trying to regain his breath that should have been depleted by now. "It appears you know what you're talking about, and I've talked with many people who travel with you. They say you're not a normal tour guide, in fact, you're just the opposite. You're an American with French and Italian genes, and Tony is a Sicilian—you two are quite unusual. If we want to endure continuous laughter and end up in God-only-knows what places, well then, this is the tour for me. Oh, yes, there is always someone who gets into trouble, or should I say, a situation, and leaves lifelong memories carved into their hearts that are too scandalous to forget. That is what I've heard."

"Well then, you must hop aboard with us and experience some of these shenanigans. Who knows, you might be one of the Americans landing in my next book and making a chapter or two," I encouraged

Dr. Raybay. I recognized his hunger for an adventurous romp of medieval tomfoolery before his light is snuffed out forever.

"Isn't that what we all want—a fun time making lifetime memories and forever friends while traveling to the most beautiful places in Italy, perhaps even the world?" I asked Dr. Raybay. I had felt my own laughter rise up as he interrupted me again. He probably hadn't heard a word.

I had continued anyway by saying, "We laugh our way through Italy and beyond, traipsing all over the place. And upon our arrival, Tony and Nino will ask the same question as they have for years."

"What exactly do they ask? I can only imagine," Dr. Raybay responded, which confirmed he had been listening after all.

"They watch the Americans as they step through the double-wide doors at the airport, examining each one as though on an assembly line—inspecting their faces. Tony predicts which *Americana* will be the scandalous one. He possesses a supernatural ability in detecting such peculiar behaviors in others, especially Americans. You know, some Sicilians are especially gifted in that department. His decision can be prompted by many things, such as one's eyebrows being too thick and woolly or having none at all. Or it could be the lips being too thin, almost invisible, or plumped excessively large enough to be suctioned onto a refrigerator door. And then there's the nose—too long or too short. Or it could be the entire face or just the eyes. Oh, yes, the eyes. Tony says the eyes reveal everything about a person. It's the window to the soul and speaks loudly to the various emotions of a person. And if you go with us to Italy, the visual examination will be before you."

I pretended to joke, but I know it's true. Tony has predetermined results on each American, whether they'll be scandalously fun, or prim and proper like Queen Elizabeth, or inwardly reserved. Nonetheless, from experience, I know it's the shy ones that usually send the loudest shock waves racing throughout Italy and jolt its boot-shaped country to the core.

"Well, I do hope to be in your next book. I'm sure Tony will confirm my own natural comedic talents. Everyone thinks me to be a professional," Dr. Raybay bragged.

"Oh, it's not the Americans who purposely try to be comedians or deliberately create drama to get in the book. It's the unintentional acts, the naturally occurring situations. Trust me, I have experienced enough true stories to write an entire encyclopedia. This is my twentieth year of taking Americans to Italy and beyond, and there is always at least one American who gets into a situation, unintentionally, that is. If you're lucky, you'll hear Tony say his perpetual mantra. Just listen as you walk through the double doors at the airport as his words roll forth, saying, "*Mamma Mia, Stefania*, who will it be this time? Which *Americana* will create the laughter for us?"

"I'll take it all, whatever you and Tony have to offer me. I just want to be with the monks, to experience the medieval lifestyle that has continued uninterrupted since the last crusades," he told me. "And, you say Tony will speculate which one of us will create the drama, or, as you say, forever memories? Could this be theater for him, creating the fun?"

"There's no show with Tony; it's all natural. You must carefully observe as he and Nino stand side-by-side, examining each face while eagerly greeting you all," I speedily told Dr. Raybay again.

"Let's talk about your book, the continuation from the first one. I've heard there will be many stories, some shocking and unbelievable, to put into print. Nonetheless, they say you'll write about them anyway. Will you?"

Smiling within, I started to explain, but Dr. Raybay overtook me with his voice on steroids and growing louder.

"Why keep the juicy happenings a secret when the entire population of Italy has surely already heard through the proverbial grapevines? Or, as I can imagine, they're more likely to be the innocent victims, the local fatalities, right?"

"Not necessarily, but you're getting close. Things do happen."

"I can see it now: Italians enduring the loud and talkative American behavior that sends shockwaves rippling throughout the quaint Toscana hilltops."

"Don't blame it all on the Americans. Italians are loud too." I tried to defend.

"How is it that everyone knows you and Tony? You say it is nearly twenty years of taking Americans all over Italy and other countries. But how do you get into the monasteries, the hidden treasures, the abbeys, the convents, the nunneries, or whatever you call them? How do you get into the ones that are occupied and closed-off to the public?"

"We have connections and friends..." I start to answer, but Dr. Raybay cuts me off.

"My sister's friend, Connie, said you go to them, the hidden jewels, even spending the night in their tiny beds. And Tony's first cousin is Mother Superior at the convent right in the middle of renaissance Florence, not far from the Star of David Church in the famous square of leather and gold markets in Piazza Santa Croce," Dr. Raybay told me matter-of-factly, seeming to have read from a script or looked into a crystal ball.

"Yes, Tony's cousin is, indeed, Mother Superior, right in the renaissance of history. You call it the Star of David Church, but it's not," I corrected him while smiling widely. "It's the Basilica di Santa Croce (Basilica of the Holy Cross), the main Franciscan church in Florence, Italy. And yes, the Star of David is proudly carved into its façade in honor of Michelangelo, who is inside. Did you know the Basilica is the largest Franciscan church in the world? We'll go to the Piazza di Santa Croce, and you can see its beauty. Some of the gold and leather shop owners are Tony's lifelong friends. I'll take you, that is, if you go with us," I hurriedly replied. There were suddenly strange grunting commotions in the background. I had imagined it was him trying to restrain his tongue.

"Didn't you take the Americans there to stay a few nights upon a request from one of your passengers, another lady desiring to participate in their way of life, just like me? That is, at the convent where the Mother Superior lives." Dr. Raybay's tongue was released. His laughter roared like a lion, causing me to extend my phone in the air.

"I heard all about the huge rose garden behind its cloistered doors, the little cabana nestled within its secluded walls. It was the essence of an *Italiano pasticceria*, a bakery shop. She told me there were thousands of flowers."

"Yes! You heard correctly. The floral beauties are arrayed in cherry-cobbler reds, strawberry pinks, and sprinkles of lemon yellow, all popping up here and there within the canopy of Italian cypresses. And lots of fruit trees. Huge fuzzy balls of luscious peaches are suspended over the blessed Madonna, which is an old masterpiece of Carrara marble, a statue the size of a giant. And the enormous lemons that dangle heavily on the slim branches are surely offsprings from Sorrento, the land of gigantic vegetation. It's all in the volcanic soil, you know," I tell Dr. Raybay.

"I heard about thievery within the sacred convent? Who stripped the trees of its production?" Dr. Raybay asked.

"What?" I swallowed hard.

"As I was saying before, I've already heard all about your Italy adventures, and I did my homework on the historical background, you know, everything I just told you, which is another one of my talents, or you might say hobbies."

"What?" I was completely discombobulated. "How do you know all of this?" My head had spun from his overwhelming mental capacity that acted like a powerful memory chip lodged within his brain.

"It's true, not a piece of fruit left in sight. And yes, the Americans enjoyed themselves while pulling the fruit from its branches," I admitted to Dr. Raybay, defending their actions and almost tasting the succulent juices that had dripped down my face months ago.

"Oh, I've already heard all about it. The Americans assumed it was free for the taking. The various fruits were all gathered and stashed in big bags, and some loaded their luggage with the apricots and persimmons. Mother of God! What did they plan on doing with such confiscations? Sell it all on the street corners in Florence? You even went to mass the next morning with the sisters who experienced the thievery firsthand!"

My left hand flew to my mouth as I gasped at the truths. "I owe them." I tried to talk, but Dr. Raybay heard nothing.

"I laughed when I was told about the sparse breakfast the next morning. There was delicious homemade bread with nothing to smear on it. The sisters all gathered outside in search of the missing fruit. Of course, there was none in sight. The entire wealth of their yearly supply of fruit for marmalade had vanished. A thief in the night had climbed the walls, or was it aliens from afar, floating in midair with a large space-ship opening up and stripping the entire orchard. Most of the trees were left bare save for their green leaves. Afterward, the sisters scurried inside, shaking their heads, talking to the Madonna, crossing their chest with the sign of the cross." Dr. Raybay stops to catch his breath.

"Yes, it's all true. They are Catholic, as you know, and do talk to the Madonna about everything," I tell Dr. Raybay as I loop my fingers around my gold cross about my neck.

"Stephanie, this is unbelievable. Did this really happen? Connie said it did. I had to hear all of the details more than once. She replayed it all with such vocal animation. You should have been there to hear all the things she told us. My sister and I had never laughed so hard. Heck, with a few bags of popcorn and a cola, we were at the movies."

My thoughts quickly returned to the nunnery on that memorable morning. I will never forget the nuns' faces, and the questions left dangling in the air as they rushed around looking for answers.

What devastation had invaded their little piece of paradise, their solitude from the busy tourists and locals outside its walls on Number 15, Borgo Pinti? Was there sin in the camp? Suspicious minds raced around everyone, landing on none of the sweet Americans. Minutes later, after we had finished up every last morsel of bread and scraped the bottom of the glass jars containing their daily supply of jams, Mother Superior rang the bell, summoning us all to the chapel to pray.

"Stephanie, come on. Tell me the truth. Did you guys really take all of their fruit? I had to laugh when Connie mentioned aliens from a spaceship. She has a vivid imagination. Surely, you didn't steal the nuns' yearly supply of everything. Did you?"

My voice cracked as I asked, "How in the world do you know all of this?"

I was completely mystified by his never-ending report that included such details that one would expect from a woman or a news reporter. Was he truly looking into a crystal ball?

"Ha, I'm a good listener and have a photographic memory. And it seems to me that after one has traveled with you, they have much to say," Dr. Raybay says as he sparks my memory.

I can't erase the vivid details now flashing through my mind. I remember us leaving through the monastery's massive doors. All of us walked out onto the busy cobbled streets with the sisters passionately hugging and kissing each one of us while sincerely drawing the sign of the cross across their chests. They were asking God, the Madonna, and the long array of godly saints to bless us. Being Italian, Sister Annarosa had made her way up the cobblestones to purchase the morning's breakfast in an attempt to replace what was taken from their garden, knowing a guest can't possibly depart without a piece of bread or sack of fruit. Afterward, she hurriedly returned with a basket filled with fresh sweets from the farmers' market: succulent peaches, apricots, bananas, and dozens of red cherries, all for their newfound friends, the Americans.

"*Grazie, signora*," I told Sister Annarosa as I placed a white envelope inside her hand. "Can I let you in on a secret? The Americans harvested your fruit. I'm sorry, they took everything. They enjoyed themselves."

Sister Annarosa put her hand on her heart. "What do you mean? The people like?"

"*Si, si*, yes! They liked it very much. Inside this envelope is more than enough euros to replenish the fruit and a little extra for you and the sisters to go out and enjoy yourselves," I had told her as I bent down and kissed her cheek and squeezed the envelope already clutched in her hand.

Dr. Raybay breathes out a laugh. "Lord, have mercy. I guess a little adventure never hurts anyone, but you take it to another level. I anticipate visiting the monks and partaking in their daily chores. You can rest assured there will be no nonsense on my behalf. And I do want to visit the Church of the Holy Cross in Florence and hear more about Michelangelo and the Sistine Chapel. I know, without a doubt, all things are possible. And if it's true that this Tony you have is a genie in a bottle, then what else can he do for me?

Chapter 3

MICHELANGELO

I laughed again at his speculations and questions through the phone line while thinking that he would surely slow down for a breath of fresh air that would give me enough time to jump into the conversation. "Yes, we go to the convent when I have passengers who request it. And speaking of Santa Croce and the Church of the Holy Cross in Florence, did you know that Michelangelo is buried inside, along with Galileo Galilei?"

"Yes, I believe you mentioned that a few minutes ago. I've heard that you have a great love for Michelangelo and the Sistine Chapel. Why is that?"

"Oh, don't get me started. I've spent over twenty-five years going back and forth to the Vatican to visit the Sistine Chapel and study its mysterious beauty and Michelangelo's perspective of the biblical teachings from the Holy Scriptures from the King James Version. Every opportunity given to me, I gawk at the ceiling until my neck can't take the strain, then I gaze downward at the mosaic floor, which is another story within itself."

Dr. Raybay interjected, "I've heard you were given special privileges to be alone with Vatican officials in the sacred chapel. They were Tony's friends?"

"Yes."

"Tell me, Stephanie, who is this Tony I keep hearing about? He seems to pop out whenever the need arises. They say he's everywhere with you—here, there, this country, that country, and stays in your home every year for six to eight weeks, sometimes months. It's a family reunion when he lands in the states; the Americans who travel with you flock to your home to celebrate his triumphant arrival. They fly in just to be with you all for a few days. Many of them go on your tours, repeatedly."

"Yes! When Tony comes to visit, we have fun and visit friends from all over the United States. After being with the Americans for two weeks on tour, we develop close ties and make forever memories together. That's what the tours are all about to me: connecting people, showing them God's beautiful creations, sharing biblical history throughout Europe, and taking them to magical places off the normal tourist paths. Around the holidays, it's a huge reunion for all of us again. It's the people who travel with us on our Italian adventures who come to my home, and we go to—"

Dr. Raybay interrupted me. "There seems to be a buzz about you and your love for the biblical scriptures and King Solomon's temple. I can't recall the details from all the chatter. But, as you know, I'm more interested in the life of monks and a few highlights of Michelangelo and the Sistine Chapel."

"This insight you seem to have of me is quite impressive...either that, or you're looking into a crystal ball again. Occasionally, I do lie down on the cool tiles of the Sistine Chapel and zoom my camera lens up to focus on the tiniest paint strokes while contemplating the messages within its sacred beauty. However, those are rare moments when no one is inside, and I'm allowed alone time there to cherish and honor the reverence of its unexplainable splendor. This privilege is thanks to Tony. His friends work behind the walls of the smallest country in the world: the Vatican City. And, yes, I do love the scriptures and the prophet's predictions, especially concerning King Solomon's temple in Jerusalem and its future rebuilding.

"Did you know there are negotiations happening in Israel as we speak? A report came on the radio just weeks ago that a group of Jewish scholars is regularly meeting and preparing for the temple's third reconstruction. The Jewish people yearn for the temple to be restored, built again for the last time and—"

Dr. Raybay interrupted my thoughts again with his voice over-powering mine. "Refresh my memory, Stephanie. What happened to the original temple?"

"The Romans destroyed the second temple in 70 AD. Do you remember Emperor Titus? His soldiers captured thousands of Jews and took them back to Rome as slaves."

"Oh, yes. I remember now. But there's no need to tell me all of the history, not unless monks are involved, or Michelangelo did some-thing of importance beyond what I already know." Dr. Raybay's voice echoed through the phone line and disrupted my thoughts for a brief second. "Did you say Michelangelo's tomb has the Jewish Star of David on it? That's strange."

"No. Not his tomb. The star is on the outside of the basilica at the top. You can't miss it. Michelangelo died in Rome three weeks before reaching his eighty-ninth birthday. He'd been living in the Eternal City for three decades of his life, and it wasn't because he liked Rome. He was declared an enemy when he lived in Florence for a while. You might say there was a little crisis."

"Really? That's a news flash I wasn't expecting to hear." Dr. Raybay laughed. "What kind of crisis?"

I had flipped my legs over the arm of a chair, trying to comfort my numbing feet as the conversation seemed to never end, going from Dr. Raybay's favorite subject of monks to Michelangelo. I wanted to go backward and open the book and read the whole story, to tell everything stored within my brain, to connect the dots that were scat-tered around from his skipping to this and that. For one to under-stand the seemingly predestined life of Michelangelo and the biblical prophecy of King Solomon's temple, you need time to explain it in its entirety. Hopefully, the opportunity would arise, but not today.

"I had no idea Michelangelo died in Rome," Dr. Raybay flickered a spark of interest, and I took the bait.

"Yes. I believe it was Cosimo I de' Medici who heard about Michelangelo's death in Rome and wanted to honor him by returning him to his beloved Florence with a proper funeral and entombment. It was Michelangelo's nephew, Leonardo, who was given the task of organizing the return of his body. Did you know he had to steal his corpse and secretly place him in a large pile of clothes with other merchandise scattered around on a wooden cart? Can you imagine stuffing Michelangelo's lifeless body inside a towering mound of rags? Leonardo tricked the pope and the Romans who wanted the artist entombed in their town, not Florence, which is understandable. It could be equated to having Elvis' shrine within its city walls—what an honor."

"Michelangelo was probably spinning around inside his tomb while resting in Rome, eagerly anticipating his return to Florence." Dr. Raybay chimed in.

"Yes! It was a perfect plan. Who would ever think the world's most famous artist in the Roman Empire would be hidden within the fabrics of a cart? And what is this mindset of the Italians stealing bodies? Did you know that Saint Mark, the Apostle, was also stolen?" I offered more tidbits.

"Nope, I had no idea. I've never given it much thought as to where the apostles are buried. Why would I? My interest is with the monks and their lives in Italy and beyond. Nonetheless, it is intriguing as to why the apostles ended up in Italy. So, the Apostle Mark was stolen too? Hmm, that's interesting."

I sensed a slight green light flashing through the phone line, giving me the go-ahead to talk more and bypass the subject of monks for a few seconds.

"Yes! In 828 AD, Saint Mark's remains arrived in Venice, Italy, from Alexandria, Egypt. I presume it was two Venetians doing the thievery. I've visualized two or three sandaled men scurrying around with sweat dripping from their brows as they hurriedly pushed an old wooden cart towering high with wicker baskets, vegetables, and piles of meat hiding Mark's body inside. They hollered to the Islamic people that pork was coming through. Do you understand? Mark had been laid to rest in the land of Muslins, the religion of Islam. It was a brilliant plan for the thieves to know the locals would never touch the unclean swine. The ship awaited their return as they pushed, tugged, and rolled the cargo inside the hull to sail across the sea."

"Stephanie, I get the picture, but I want to know if the monks helped with returning Michelangelo's body to Florence? Did they? I'm having a hard enough time keeping up with you now that you've tossed Saint Mark into the mix." Dr. Raybay's thoughts never ceased from the monks, and I believed that he must be pacing back and forth with the phone glued to his ear and his eyes fixed on the ground as if the answer to his question could be found on the floor.

At Dr. Raybay's request, I jumped track and went back to his favorite subject. "I've not heard of any monks participating in the thievery, but there were two experienced bandits—if you want to call them that—who did steal the body of Michelangelo. Although, I doubt it was the brotherhood participating in the hijack, not under the circumstances."

"What circumstances?"

"That's another rabbit hole we'd have to run down to explain the trouble he created, or should I say he participated in, when politics escalated to explosive heights in Florence around 1530, which is the reason he escaped to Rome in the first place. I'm sure you remember the big ordeal that happened just five years after Michelangelo finished the Sistine Chapel. It's forever carved into the history books."

"I don't know what you're talking about, Stephanie. I haven't a clue. But please, don't leave me hanging after all of this information."

"All hell broke loose five years after Michelangelo wrapped up the Sistine Chapel. Remember the Catholic monk, Martin Luther, who wrote and nailed the Ninety-five Theses on the All Saints' Church in Wittenberg, Germany, on Halloween, 1517? He changed Christianity forever. He shocked the Christian world with his theory and sparked the Protestant Reformation. Martin Luther was an Augustinian monk, and his rivalry was the Dominican monks. Oh yes. You'll be excited to know that the monks were involved. The two secs of monks didn't see eye-to-eye on the scriptures."

"Good heavens! Are you serious? I had no idea that Martin Luther was a Catholic monk, absolutely no knowledge of that. And an Augustinian?" Dr. Raybay is listening with both ears.

I continued excitedly, "Nearly a decade later, German, Spanish, and Italian soldiers marched to Rome and slaughtered thousands in an effort to gain control of more religious territory. It was déjà vu all over again, just like the sack of King Solomon's Temple in Jerusalem. The Germans took everything of value: gold, bronze, jewels, everything. The Vatican was decimated and stripped clean of its belongings.

"Michelangelo had predicted this event. He agreed with Martin Luther's philosophies of the misguided direction of the Catholic Church at the time. You have to think back to him being on the scaffolding for four years inside the Sistine Chapel, hearing everything going on inside those walls and all the teachings he disagreed with. After Rome was sacked, a new group of freethinkers sprang up. And guess who was in that group?"

"Michelangelo!" Dr. Raybay said with force. "And they ran off the Medici family in Florence and took over the city. The Medici bunch ran like scared children. They were no match to the new freethinkers. Oh, yes! Now I remember tiny tidbits of what I'd read long ago. But I didn't know or realize Michelangelo was a Catholic monk and—"

I cut him off with excitement. "Yes! Michelangelo was on their side because he was disgusted with the Medici. However, the Medici family and the Vatican took back control again after a while. And guess what? Michelangelo was left holding the bag, so to speak. He tucked tail and ran away. That's why he ended up in Rome. The monks had to steal his body back to Florence for burial. Nonetheless, I see nothing wrong with the monks offering their assistance to fetch Michelangelo's body back to his beloved city. Do you?"

"I have no idea. I'm not sure if I know what we're talking about at this point." Dr. Raybay laughed.

"The thieves were honoring Michelangelo's last request: to be interred in Florence. And, if it makes you feel better, Michelangelo was the second of five brothers, and his oldest sibling did become a monk."

"Ah, now you're talking." Dr. Raybay became a bright light. I realized it was the mention of monks that flipped his switch. His voice revealed the enthusiasm within his soul. "Tell me more, Stephanie, more of Michelangelo and the monks."

"Well, you know that he was the greatest Italian Renaissance artist in the world. Can you imagine, at the age of fifteen, Michelangelo was already transforming a block of Carrara marble into a vivid masterpiece with such realistic features that one would think it was a living creation of mankind? He was a genius with a photographic memory, and he loved the Jewish people and the Hebrew Scriptures. I'd need a day or two to explain how he came to be living a life of luxury with the wealthiest clan of all in Europe: the Medici family."

"You should write a book. Tell it from your perspective. From what I've already heard, you love to talk in-depth about your infatuation with his life."

"Someday, perhaps, I shall. But, can you tell me, Dr. Raybay, where does your curiosity and intense yearning to be with the monks come from? I must say you are the first to request this."

"My grandmother's friend was a nun, and she fell in love with a monk who lived in a monastery in southern France. It's complicated and a long story but also fascinating. Her name was Maria Estella, and she reminds me of you—an adventurous soul who had few boundaries. To her, a stop sign was only a suggestion. Who lives like that?"

"Hmm, I know a few." Was Dr. Raybay still looking into a crystal ball? The question flashed before me as I saw myself through his description.

"She sucked in every ounce of life, living as though the clock would surely strike twelve on the midnight hour and end her enchanted life. Something within her fueled an intensity to fulfill her calling. She inhaled the scriptures and made bumbling efforts to love everyone before she turned into a puff of dust. She took her vows to join the sisterhood, but her soul yearned for a man and an intimate relationship like Romeo and Juliette. She told my grandmother all about the eccentric nuns and monks among them and the exploits of memorable characters in their long robes with knotted belts. Maria had zero constraints toward the end of her short-lived life. The flames of sexual desire finally got the best of her. She was excommunicated from the nunnery. Tossed out like a piece of day-old bread to the hungry birds."

"Wow! What a life! I'm not sure if that's a compliment to me or not."

"Don't be confused, Stephanie. The monastery life of that particular sect of monks was wonderful. They did great things for others. They lived on the land and provided everything with their own hands. The devotion to God was more than I can comprehend. Monks aren't saints but extraordinary human beings who commit their lives to the service of God and man, to be his hands extended to others in need. I want to experience a day with them to see how they live. I'd like to walk in their shoes and harvest grapes and olives and make marmalades from the fruit of their trees. Maybe observe their winemaking, too.

"Oh, besides the monks, I want to know how Michelangelo afforded his lifestyle. For some reason, he seemed to have it all, much different than the monks. Why do you place him above the monks? I know we're going in many directions with our conversation, but now you have me interested in several things."

I jumped in to clarify. "I don't place him above the monks. No, not at all. It was Cosimo I de' Medici who started building the fortune by lending money in Florence. He quickly took his family up the social ladder as a highfalutin businessman. They started the most prestigious bank in Europe and set the rules for all to follow. They were eventually bankers for the Vatican too. They started as wool dealers and ended up as Renaissance royalty. It was Lorenzo de' Medici who discovered the great talents of Michelangelo and took him in and raised him as his son.

"If that wasn't enough fame for one family, four of the Medicis eventually became popes. They held a lot of power in Florence, especially Pope Leo X. He, along with the other family members, loved art, and possessed exquisite taste. It was Pope Leo X who wanted to do great things with Saint Peter's Basilica. He wanted to rebuild and restructure to take it to bigger, more grandiose heights. There was just one problem: the Vatican needed more money. How would they pay for all the marble needed for the saintly sculptures, bronze statuaries, and the endless renovations of the Sistine Chapel? The list rolled on and on."

"Ah, don't we all need more money? I assume they got it; otherwise, there'd be no ornate Sistine Chapel with the famous painted ceiling by Michelangelo and all the other creations by his hands." Dr. Raybay said with directness.

"That's when the idea popped up. The pope created the outrageous idea of an 'indulgences' decree that declared—are you ready for this—if the people contributed money to the basilica, their sins would be forgiven, completely pardoned, thrown into the sea of forgetfulness, all in exchange for their coins. I remember my mother talking about this decree and the awakening of Martin Luther, who was already rising against the church." My heart started to beat fast. I didn't really want to talk about the past debaucheries.

"Your mother was living during that time?" Dr. Raybay joked.

I continue with my thoughts. "The Medicis had their hands in many things, going in all directions. Can you imagine ruling the bustling city of Florence during the great Renaissance era? The family loved art and had the greatest possession right before them: their adopted artist, Michelangelo. Since Florence was the hub for artists and had the most elite schools in the world, they commissioned works by some of the best and hobnobbed with the rising stars such as Donatello, Leonardo, and Botticelli. The Medicis hired Galileo to tutor some of the dukes.

"Imagine the power of the family who had four popes on the royal throne. When Martin Luther, a devoted Catholic, decided to post his Ninety-five Theses, which started the Protestant movement, it was a Medici who sat as pope. The list goes on and on. For Michelangelo, it was a love-hate relationship with the Medicis.

Remember when he spent four-and-a-half years on the freestanding, trapeze-like scaffolding made by his own hands, as he painted the Sistine Chapel and listened in irritation to the pope below?"

Dr. Raybay popped back in the conversation to go down another rabbit hole. "And don't forget it was Leonardo da Vinci who painted the Mona Lisa and the Last Supper. He, too, was one of the greatest painters of the Renaissance period. Mona Lisa was from Florence, right?"

"Yes. But Michelangelo possessed the longest list of talents that accelerated his accomplishments beyond the normal mind of a human being. He was a sculptor, painter, poet, engineer, and architect. He absorbed every Jewish symbol and mystical reference and the Hebrew language like a dry sponge. He was a genius with a photographic mind, a believer of Neoplatonism, Judaism, Talmud, Kabbalah—where does it stop? He loved the Jewish people. I've talked extensively with experts in Florence of his life."

"Michelangelo was a Jew? How did Michelangelo end up in Italy?"

"No. Michelangelo Buonarroti was Italian and Catholic, but remember when he arrived at the Medici palace to enter manhood, he was surrounded by the Jewish elite. In Jewish culture, boys acquire the religious responsibilities of an adult on their thirteenth birthday. Can you imagine?

"His father, Ludovico, purportedly beat Michelangelo unmercifully because he didn't have an interest in school to learn grammar and accounting to take on the Florence wool and silk leagues, a trade that he wanted his son to be in. He greatly opposed his son becoming an artist. To him, having a son dillydallying around with paints and plaster and chiseling away at a block of marble was the same as playing with women's handicrafts. Can you imagine being a government official in Florence, a proud administrator, and your son refusing to study in school to obtain a respectful position in the community? I'm sure Lodovico was worried about his social status and the wages Michelangelo would earn to help support the family and, of course, the pedigree of the Buonarroti family name. It turned out to be just the opposite, as we know."

"No, I don't know that much about Michelangelo, other than he was a painter and a sculptor, and he was mad as hell at the Medici pope at the time he painted the Sistine. He took his revenge out on the ceiling, so to speak, with all the turmoil within the church. Didn't he paint the face of Satan on one of the Vatican officials in the chapel, if my memory is correct?" Dr. Raybay shocked me with his knowledge of that tidbit.

"So I've heard. From my recollection, it was said that Biagio da Cesena criticized Michelangelo's nude paintings on the ceiling. He didn't approve. I guess the maestro, the genius, got the last word with that little jab. I must say, you are quite knowledgeable about Michelangelo."

"Gosh dang, Stephanie, I think you've covered everything pertinent to his life so far. There are only a few details that I seem to remember from my studies. But that was long ago. I do remember that Michelangelo was a body snatcher and a grave robber, stealing bodies to observe the muscles and anatomy. He and Leonardo da Vinci knew more about human anatomy than most doctors at that time."

Surprised, I continued this new line of thought. "Oh, yes. You're correct. Michelangelo traded his drawings and art for corpses. However, I don't think Michelangelo and Leonardo did the robbing. I think they paid real body snatchers under the table. That's how he learned about the human body as he dissected it before rigor mortis set in. Rumor has it that he and Leonardo frequently waited for the next warm corpse to be stolen. They were probably the only ones performing autopsies during the Renaissance era because it was illegal at that time. *Mamma Mia*, how did we get on this subject?"

"Heck, I don't remember now. Oh, you didn't say where Michelangelo was born. I presume Florence? You ought to toss that in as well since you feel the need to tell me his life story. I'm waiting to see where the monks fit into this history lesson." Dr. Raybay chuckled.

I laughed again. "You're the one who asked, correct?"

"Well...yes, I did. But—"

"Well, thank you very much. I will answer your question with pleasure. Michelangelo was born in 1475 in a little village called Caprese, a town in Tuscany, which is a forty-eight-minute drive from Arezzo. I go to that village, which is not far from Florence, every year in search of treasures for my shop. Coincidentally, his birth is the same year the renovation started on the Sistine Chapel."

"What's so surprising of him being born the same year as the Sistine Chapel renovation?" Dr. Raybay asked.

"Do you think it was a coincidence?"

"I don't know. I'm trying to remember back when I studied about his life and the Sistine Chapel in the Vatican. It was years ago. There are so many pieces of this puzzle. I believe without a doubt that God had a hand in Michelangelo's journey. How could one not see the writing on the wall? Or, in his case, the ceiling. Right? And with his endless education of the Hebrew language, the symbols, the Jewish people around him, teaching him? I studied—"

I cut him off in excitement. "Yes. Michelangelo's intellect was beyond the normal mind. Surely, he was guided by a higher power. God blessed him with more talent and wisdom than ten thousand scholars and artisans combined. Michelangelo had no choice but to emerge brighter than the day before he arrived at the Medici's door. He was already equipped with the brain cells of a genius. He created so many things. The list is endless.

"It seems that Michelangelo did get the last word through his paintings. His voice was loud and clear and defended the Jewish people and the word of God. Wouldn't you say that God directed Michelangelo as he does so many who are willing to be used for his glory, whether a sinner or a saint? Clearly, there are many not willing to be led by the Holy Spirit. They go kicking and screaming, refusing to walk through the doors that God has already opened. Think of the wicked city of Nineveh. God used Jonah, who didn't want to go, to preach to the sinful. Do you see the correlation with the two? Michelangelo didn't want to be painting in the Sistine Chapel. He wanted to be in Florence, doing what he loved: sculpting and chiseling away at the marble. His choice was either obey the pope and go to Rome or off with his head!"

Passionately, Dr. Raybay joined in. "Yes! And God used the great fish to get Jonah's attention when he refused to accept his divine mission. I see the correlation with the two. One would have to be stupid to not see how God used Michelangelo's talents to speak to the world, even though it took many years to see his paintings and messages after the ceiling was cleaned from the black smoke."

"Do you believe God knew us before we were born, and He has a plan for our lives?" I had to ask Dr. Raybay. "It's up to us to follow along and never let go of His hand and allow the Holy Spirit to lead and guide us. Of course, we're in a spiritual war, but we must walk through the opened doors."

"Yes, Stephanie. I agree. He gives us free will to do as we chose," Dr. Raybay shared more. "I love the types and shadows in the Bible and the comparisons and connections of allegories. The Holy Spirit is God's voice telling us what to do. It's that inner voice within us."

"Dr. Raybay, did you know that the Sistine Chapel in the Vatican is a replica of King Solomon's temple with the exact measurements that Samuel wrote in I Kings 6:2?"

"Yes. I heard all about it many years ago in a Bible study group where I thought we'd be learning about the monks. However, I do believe it to be true. Our class dissected many scriptures from the Old and New Testament and compared the measurements to the Sistine Chapel. We also reviewed his use of the Hebrew alphabet. I'm trying to remember the highlights that interested me back then. Who would've thought that years later, you'd reiterate the same story? I'd say you covered the last two thousand years! What's your take on it? You can't deny the evidence and the holy scriptures." Dr. Raybay kept going.

"Yes, you're correct. The evidence is there. It's history. And the writing is on the ceiling." I smiled, even though he couldn't see my face through the phone line.

"I agree. The Sistine Chapel was built to replace the original temple after the Romans destroyed it in Jerusalem." Dr. Raybay raised his voice with enthusiasm. "That's a no-brainer to me. I see a correlation between the Sistine and Solomon's temple."

"Yes! King Solomon's temple was the first temple ever built by the Israelites to worship God. What's interesting to me is that this beautiful temple was erected beside the king's palace. It was Israel's sparkling jewel and a glorious beacon of light for the world to see. It was King David, Solomon's father, who wanted to build the temple to house the Ark of the Covenant. I could talk all day about the Ark of the Covenant and the three things inside: the Ten Commandments, the golden pot that contained manna, and Aaron's rod."

"Peter was the first pope or bishop," Dr. Raybay announced. Nothing more or nothing less. He stated just one sentence with enough force that I knew he was eagerly listening, even if he did redirect the conversation again.

"Yes. The church took the scripture in Matthew 16:18 literally, where Jesus said to Peter, 'I say unto thee, that thou art Peter, and upon this rock I will build my church; and the gates of hell shall not prevail against it. And I will give unto thee the keys of the kingdom of heaven.'"

Dr. Raybay spoke with authority again, "That must have been a huge slap in the face to the Jews to have their temple destroyed and rebuilt in Rome. Now the Sistine Chapel is the holiest church in the world. I do know that much, Stephanie. And it's where the conclave to elect the next pope is conducted. Millions of visitors stare up at the paintings each year, trying to understand the mysteries and secret messages embedded by Michelangelo."

Dr. Raybay understood more than I gave him credit for ten hours ago. "How did Michelangelo get involved in all of this? I know the church had become corrupt. Didn't he want to condemn the church for failing to acknowledge the Jewish people, and—"

I interrupted. "He loved the Jewish people and the Midrash or biblical teachings. The Vatican preached loudly that the Jews had killed Jesus, which they had, and rejected his teaching. Therefore, they didn't deserve their Holy Temple, their homeland, or anything else in Jerusalem. Do you remember when the Sanhedrin brought

Jesus before the Roman governor, Pontius Pilate, and he couldn't find any fault in Jesus? It was the Jews who screamed, 'Crucify him and let his blood be on us and our children.'"

"Yes, of course I do. And I believe the Jews' proclamation came back to haunt them."

I was already talking before he ended his last sentence. "It's not over yet. The temple will be rebuilt again in Jerusalem on the holy Temple Mount according to biblical scriptures."

"Stephanie, you're losing me now."

"It's a long story and takes time to follow the scriptures and the correlation of God using Michelangelo. The first temple was built by King Solomon, the son of King David, and was destroyed by the Babylonians. This is the same David who is famous for killing Goliath, the giant, and who Michelangelo sculpted as his masterpiece inside the Accademia Gallery."

Dr. Raybay remembers. "Yes! It's the most famous Renaissance statue in the world!"

"Yes, absolutely! When we're in Florence and see Michelangelo's David inside the Accademia, I'll share some of the importance of his life before we go inside. It's necessary to stress who David is, especially when we have someone on the tour who has never heard of him. Can you believe I had one who didn't know David who killed Goliath in the Bible?" I repeated again for my own satisfaction.

"You have to use your imagination and think back to 70 AD when the Roman emperor Titus conquered Jerusalem, and his soldiers destroyed the second temple that the Israelites had built, and took thousands of Jewish captives back to Rome. They sacked King Solomon's temple and took everything. They loaded down the Jewish people like camels with gold, silver, precious stones, menorahs, and golden candlesticks. There were thousands and thousands of Jews: men, women, children, and their animals. They were paraded through the Roman Forum as trophies, loaded down with hundreds of pounds of anything of value. Afterward, Titus made the Jews build a huge arch called the Arch of Titus. It still stands in the Roman Forum and reveals the story of the Jews bringing the loot from their temple. I've walked underneath it a hundred times to explain it to the Americans."

"Did they bring the Ark of the Covenant back to Rome?" Dr. Raybay asked loudly.

"I suspect so, though I have no proof. I think the menorah was taken by the Romans when Emperor Titus sacked the temple." My thoughts quickly flashed to the towering Arch of Titus standing in the Roman Forum, which depicts the whole story of their triumphal entry into Rome carrying the loot from King Solomon's temple. My eyes have observed the carvings in the arch countless times, especially the part with the Romans carrying the huge menorah.

"Did you know that the menorah is over five feet tall and over one hundred and thirty pounds of solid gold? God told Moses the design plan for its creation in Exodus. I can talk all day about its symbolic—"

"Now that's interesting, Stephanie. You have to write a book about its meaning. I love the glowing candles in the churches. Do you think the menorah is inside the Vatican? Good gosh, that's a huge news flash. Shall we call the news stations?"

"Yes. Why would the Arch of Titus show its confiscation if not? That's a big debate, I know. The Ark of the Covenant was probably hidden right before the Babylonians sacked Jerusalem during the first temple destruction."

"Oh, my, Stephanie. You took me on a different road. Is there any stopping you? Where are the monks during all of this time? Were they kidnapped too? Do they still walk around in the long robes? I want to see them." Dr. Raybay has flipped the switch; he's no longer interested in Israel, Florence, or the hand of Michelangelo and the Sistine Chapel.

"Yes. I'll take you to see the monks for yourself." I stared at the floor, wishing he wanted to know more of what extended beyond the monks. I wanted to tell him about Constantine's mother, Saint Helena, who traveled to Israel and brought back to Rome everything connected to Jesus Christ, even the original cross.

"You'd do this for me?" Dr. Raybay sighed briefly.

"Yes. I can do that with pleasure." I visualized Dr. Raybay jump in excitement with the certainty of seeing things he'd only read about in history books and heard from his grandmother's lips. But as quickly as I had the visual of him, my mind remembered something else. I glimpsed at the luxurious, ruby-red, damask jacquard alter cloth resting on the arm of a chair that I'd found in Italy a few years ago. It reminded me of what I should've said earlier when I was discussing the chapel but forgot to.

I've always been intrigued by the Sistine Chapel being an exact replica of King Solomon's temple. When I step inside its majestic beauty, I gravitate toward the middle where the partition grill on each side is a dividing barrier that's parallel with seven marble cande-labras on top, mirroring the seven-branch menorah. I stand and visu-alize the heavy veil that would have hung in King Solomon's temple in Jerusalem, separating the holy temple from where the high priest would enter once a year on the Day of Atonement. It's the great divide wherein the process of ceremonial preparation took place before he entered into the Holy of Holies and the presence of God. Behind its thick fabric was the Ark of the Covenant and where the Holy Spirit dwelt inside. The high priest entered once a year to ask for forgive-ness for the people. I speculated again, would Dr. Raybay remember the three things within the ark?

Dr. Raybay's voice brings me back to the present as it echoes through the line. He's back to where we started nearly an hour ago. It's like he's completely disregarded our whole conversation about Michelangelo and the Sistine Chapel. His thoughts have returned to the beginning.

"Stephanie, can you tell me more about Tony? I hear the Sicilian is a theatrical comedy show and practically a godfather to Europe. Everyone seems to know him and you. How can this be? And this Nino they talk about—your driver who is your little bambino—they say he's Sicilian too," Dr. Raybay rambled on as he spilled out every-thing he'd heard, balling it up into one big meatball that was too large to devour.

Chapter 4

MAMMA MIA! WHERE IS MR. CHEEKS?

*M*y mind was spinning like a merry-go-round out of control as I listened to Dr. Raybay tell two and three stories at once. And when I believed he was nearing the end, it was just wishful thinking. He rambled more. He couldn't help himself.

"Oh, I remember this too. It was probably two months after arriving home from New York City that I met the lady who often travels with you. I believe her name is Millie, or it could have been Lilly. Does that name ring a bell?" Dr. Raybay asked, which caused the memories to rush in and spark my recollection of happenings from not so long ago. I knew exactly where this conversation was headed, and apparently, there was no detour in sight because he is a perpetual talker with more stored in his memory than the Smithsonian has in all of its buildings.

"She told me more about you and your shop, Decorate Ornate, and the Italy tours that you do twice a year. I laughed hard when I heard the story of Mr. Cheeks. Do you remember him? Never mind, that's a stupid question."

My heart dropped. "Yes. He's the man we left in the toilet while in Sicily. It's a long story."

"Oh, I've already heard all about it. You zoomed right off, forgetting about him. How in the world could you do such a thing? You are the tour leader, right? Didn't you do a head count before leaving each location? Heck, you need to install some kind of flashing-light device on them or come up with something accountable."

"Mr. Cheeks' wife didn't realize he wasn't on the coach until miles away. And when she finally realized her husband wasn't beside her, she hollered for Nino to stop the bus so he could turn it around to go search for him. Thank God for Jack, the nice man seated across the aisle from her, who remembered his whereabouts and volunteered to find him," I explain to Dr. Raybay.

"The Good Samaritan onboard your tour—what was his name?" Dr. Raybay asked but didn't stop talking long enough for my answer. "I heard he excitedly jumped off the bus and backtracked to the outdoor seating area in the—"

"Valley of the Temples and his name is Jack," my voice rolled out loudly and emphasized the place, not his name.

"Yes, that's it," Dr. Raybay speedily acknowledged. "This is unbelievable to me, leaving this poor man behind in such a desolate area. It's my understanding Jack jumped off the bus and found him. Good golly. Mr. Cheeks had never stepped foot on Sicilian soil before, and what do you do? You leave him alone—completely abandoned."

"Jack and his wife were seated across the aisle on the coach from Mr. and Mrs. Cheeks. And it was an accident. Mrs. Cheeks didn't mean to leave her husband in the toilet," I repeated, but he never acknowledged my words coming through the phone line.

"Jack recalled the urgency of a number two kicking in, a surprise bowel movement hitting Mr. Cheeks like a sudden bolt of lightning while they were seated at the restaurant. He said Mr. Cheeks' stomach was growling and rumbling minutes before the pasta arrived. The wife asked if he was okay when she heard the noise and saw the perspiration dotting his forehead. Even before he finished the meal, Mr. Cheeks had to excuse himself urgently in hot pursuit of a toilet.

"Gosh dang, Stephanie! You can't make this up. I'm not sure all the pieces are fitting together in this bizarre puzzle. I can't understand how his wife didn't know he wasn't on the bus, and like a sudden bolt of lightning, his stomach—"

I explained further, "Yes, it's all true. It was unexpected. They were seated together with their spouses while eating pasta and sipping wine. We had just finished the tour of Greek temples, after which we walked a few feet to the only restaurant in the middle of a UNESCO World Heritage Site. Minutes into the meal, Jack watched Mr. Cheeks dart around the back of the restaurant as he frantically searched for the toilet. That was his last remembrance of seeing Mr. Cheeks before we left."

Dr. Raybay interrupts again like a speeding train. "Millie rambled along with such graphic facts, laughing and snorting in between sentences and said his face was sweating profusely, dotted with large raindrops sprinkled all over his upper lip and forehead. The poor man was suffering from acute constipation, I guess. No, I mean diarrhea. Heck, I don't know what hit Mr. Cheeks. But Millie said it was as though a light switch flipped on within his stomach, causing severe urgency and panic to find a toilet. So, yes, all that you said is true, Millie said so!"

"It was an emergency. He knocked over several plastic chairs, bumped and bashed everything in sight, and scurried about like a man looking for a lifeboat. Can you imagine the panic of such a predicament?"

Dr. Raybay laughed out loud. "Yes. I'm sure we've all been in the same boat at least once in our lifetime."

"Thank God Jack finally found him after we backtracked," I told him.

"Millie spoke of the area surrounding that restaurant. Weren't you close to the famous Greek ruins? The archaeology site with ancient temples tagged as a UNESCO World Heritage Site? I watched a show about it on the Discovery Channel."

"Yes. We were in Agrigento in southern Sicily. The Valley of the Temples is beyond words, especially the Temple of the Concordia and Temple of Heracles and—"

Dr. Raybay interrupted me. "What about the green olives and

chocolatey carobs dangling on nearby tree branches? Millie said she picked a few olives and plopped them in her mouth. Her face scrunched like sour grapes. They were horrible, disgusting, bitter, and made her nauseous. Well, that's what she said, but not being there in person, I have no idea about the taste coming straight from the tree. That's where you were, right?"

"Yes, indeed," I sighed. I gave up trying to remember all of the questions he was asking and just waited for him to wind down.

"Millie said that when Jack finally found Mr. Cheeks behind the restaurant, the poor man seemed like a caged monkey; both hands were gripped around the tall square poles, and his eyes were swollen like large red apples."

"Well, he thought his wife had intentionally left him even though they'd been married over thirty years. The truth is, when he opened the toilet door, which was surrounded by a perfect iron square, he found that the restaurant employees had shut the gate, bolted the outside lock, called it a day, and headed for a nap. There was no way to escape."

"Why would they erect an enclosure around a toilet? Was the throne embossed with gold or sacred stones, or perhaps concealing the Ark of the Covenant?"

"The only way to escape was if he were a little bird with strong wings. The steel enclosure was topped with more iron bars. Can you imagine? It wouldn't have helped Mr. Cheeks to be a feathered parrot, either. No, not at all. Only a tiny flea could escape such an imprisonment." I try to paint a picture.

"Oh, I could visualize Mr. Cheeks running for the bus when finally freed from the toilet cage. Heck, you should have a reality television show; get someone to follow you around with a video camera while in Italy. His wife claimed she never knew her husband could run so fast as she watched his feet race toward the coach. That's what Millie told me."

I jump in, trying to cut him off from his continuous chatter. "Oh, yes. I will never forget how fast he ran. Afterward, he was permanently attached to his wife, stuck like glue throughout the rest of the tour. It nearly drove her crazy since she's overly independent and not used to having someone joined to her side like instant Siamese twins. Her defense was typical of a fast talker when she explained why she didn't notice he wasn't on the bus. Said she thought he was up in the front of the coach talking to Tony."

I take a sip of water, which gives Dr. Raybay the chance to start again.

"Millie said the wife laughed uncontrollably, giggling and snickering, not able to control herself—nervous guilt," Dr. Raybay spoke his verdict and paused again for more air.

Two seconds later, he continued. "It sounds to me like Mrs. Cheeks had her own agenda, and that was, well, I guess you'd say, she's a talker. How could she not know her husband wasn't on the bus? She thought the entire escapade was hilarious. Of course, I wasn't there, but I got the inside scoop from Millie."

"This happened over a year ago while we were in Sicily visiting the archaeological area known as the Valley of the Temples in Agrigento, Sicily. It's one of the most important archeological sites in the world and, yes, a UNESCO World Heritage Site. And as far as Mrs. Cheeks is concerned, she never once thought her husband was left in the toilet," I defended Mrs. Cheeks but was quickly derailed again as Dr. Raybay contradicted my words.

"Ha! Mr. Cheeks was too jolted to find humor in his imprisonment. Millie said his face reflected Casper the Friendly Ghost—white as cotton. That is until a few miles down the road when he finally let loose and burst out laughing."

I had to agree with Dr. Raybay. "Yes, Mr. Cheeks was white as snow, but you would be too if left in a foreign country by mistake. And it was a mistake!"

"Good golly, Stephanie. Millie said Mr. Cheeks babbled like a malfunctioning, battery-operated toy, shooting out all sorts of emotions."

"Yes, it took him forty-five minutes to retell the story from his perspective, which I'm sure is carved into his brain forever. How can you recover from the shock of being caged in Sicily, in the Valley of the Temples?"

"Man, oh man, that Millie was a talker. She even mentioned a flock of little feathered friends zooming over his head and flapping their colorful wings. Said they were no help at all; they were Sicilian, too," Dr. Raybay repeated everything he heard from Millie with more details than I knew even though I had been there.

Surely, he was looking into a crystal ball, or did he record every single word that Millie relayed to him? He must have one heck of a genius memory chip—a precise mechanism that's beyond my comprehension. How can one remember such details from an event when he was thousands of miles from the incident? The questions bombarded my mind but only for a split second. His voice traveled through the phone line again and crashed my eardrum with deafening giggles.

"Stephanie, I laughed even harder when I heard the recapped story of his release to freedom. Millie was giggling while telling me about the aftermath. She was on a roll revealing everything, and then her phone rang, and she took a long, fifteen-minute call from her momma."

Suddenly, Dr. Raybay was coughing and heaving in my ear as he slurped whatever he was nursing too fast. I held the phone away from me, thinking he might surely fall over dead from lack of oxygen, but miraculously, he bounced back and gained his composure enough to continue like nothing ever happened.

"Let's see, where were we? Oh, yes, when Millie finally returned her attention to me. Well, she started all over again and gave me more details than before. Millie said I needed to be there to get the full effect of how entertaining the whole event was. She emphasized how Mr. Cheeks grabbed his buttocks when he finally got back on the coach. Of course, that was after his release from the caged toilet and race to the bus as though a firing squad was shooting at his backside," Dr. Raybay laughed out loud.

"I don't remember that," I blurt. "If so, he was only joking, enhancing the theatrics of finally presenting himself on the coach after such a horrible ordeal." My mind quickly searches for the memory of the photographic visual, him grabbing his butt. The file comes up empty.

"Yes, the poor man thought he'd surely done a number two inside his trousers. Uh, of course, he was joking, thank God. Can you imagine if it were true?" Dr. Raybay asked, having no idea that I'd already experienced a real number two episode on our coach a few years ago.

"Okay, let me finish this story," Dr. Raybay declared, skipping every other word with a short, gurgling chuckle. "When he opened the toilet door into the sunlight, he saw the entrance of the iron enclosure bolted shut with a huge padlock dangling from its iron bars. He raced to the big gate, pushing and jingling it, looking up, down and all around. There was no one around only complete silence except for a little bird chirping in Italian."

"Yes, it's true. He hollered for his wife until his voice dwindled to a mere whimper. He even tried to climb the vertical rods, but what can a man do when his feet are the size of King Kong's? There was no way to shrink the size sixteen shoes. It was useless. There was no room between the narrow slats. All of his efforts of jamming and forcing those big feet into the narrow space were futile. He realized he was nothing more than a lonely caged monkey—abandoned—left in a foreign country, only fifty miles to Africa across the nearby sea," I try to finish the story.

"Stephanie, I'm repeating myself on the details, but Millie gave two different stories. The dang phone call interrupted her thoughts. But I'm glad now for the replay to get a clearer vision of this outlandish episode on your tour. Millie sure talked up a storm. It was nice meeting your faithful friend, who said she's been going on your tours for over eighteen years. She's better than a paid commercial, such a colorful character and chock full of information."

"Yes, she's a talker, but I had no idea she would remember so many details," I tell Dr. Raybay.

"She went from one story to the next and said her best friend goes with you for the laughter and food, not to mention the wine. Oh, she claims Tony is, indeed, your fairy godfather who waves his magic wand throughout Europe, always turning the impossible to the pleasurably possible. His favorite words are, '*No problema, Stefania. Si, si,* yes, we can do this with pleasure.' And he speaks seven languages and sings like an Italian operetta parrot. Yes, Millie told me everything from memory. She never once paused for thought. She tossed more information out to me than a library can hold," Dr. Raybay speedily told me through the phone lines, entertaining himself with laughter.

"Stephanie, do you remember Tony's legs doing the splits when he stepped off the coach and slipped on the wet street? Millie told me about that story too. Tony's legs went down like a Dallas Cowboy cheerleader, right there on the rainy cobblestones in Rome. I would have paid good money to see that. I bet his manly department has never been the same after such an intense stretch. Millie tried to reenact the performance, but there was no way she was going down like that. I mean, how can a lady that's 5'1" while standing on her tiptoes, with legs barely long enough to hold up socks, perform the splits?"

"I wrote about Tony's accident in my first book. It's all there."

"Well, that Millie is something else; she laughed more than she talked. And her vocabulary is—well, how can I say this without being judgmental. She's just downright funny, slinging this word and that word in the mix and never realizing it. She said Tony's legs shot out like someone tied a rope to each toe and pulled them hard in both directions, north to south. Ouch! I can feel the agony right now. God help his reproductive organs. I bet his testicles will never be the same," Dr. Raybay rambled on going from one episode of our adventures to the next one without any orderly fashion. He was enjoying his own comedy show.

"Well now, this is the tour for me. Yes, sign me up today!" Dr. Raybay declared as he took deep breaths to calm himself. "Oh, I nearly forgot. My wife will be joining me, too. Her name is Lizzy, and she has always wanted to experience Italy for the designer clothing. And the monks, well, she has no interest in them or the cloaked nuns.

But with your influence, Stephanie, I do request that you help her understand the sisterhood and brotherhood and bring her to a new realization and appreciation for both of them. I know you can enlighten her about the Old World.

"I believe it was Millie who was telling me about your obsession with anything pertaining to the church. She said you have a prayer room dripped and shrouded with ecclesiastical relics. And you probably have a monk or two hidden in there somewhere. She said she's been in your home many times, especially when Tony and his wife come to stay with you."

"Well, it's a good thing you remembered you have a wife." I laughed. "There are plenty of things Lizzy can do while you get acquainted with the monks. And yes, I love the biblical history in Italy, and I do collect many things for my prayer room. Did you know that many of the apostles are buried in Italy?"

"I think you've already told me a hundred times. But, excuse me, Stephanie, I have a few more questions. Is it possible for me to purchase a habit? I want the brown color, just like Saint Francis wore. I'm sure the price will be low since that's where the monks live."

"Ah, yes, absolutely. I know exactly where to take you to purchase the capuchin vestments. But as far as the price being cheap? No, it's just the opposite," I told him as he darted down another rabbit trail of questions, asking about the wine and stating his preferences for California reds.

Chapter 5

DRIVING THROUGH TUSCANY

*T*he memory from months ago of the power-packed telephone conversation with Dr. Raybay quickly fades as I glance back and notice him now leaning over the walkway to talk with Tom Littleworth about the best wines in the world. His voice carries down the aisle as though amplified by speakers as he brags about his expertise in *vino*.

"*Mamma Mia, Stefania*, we have a wine expert aboard," Tony tells me as he turns around in his seat to observe Dr. Raybay, who is speaking with professional authority and enlightening a fellow traveler about the finest wines in the world.

"Yes, Tom, I've traveled the world, and the best wines are from California," Dr. Raybay jokes. Yet he had never stepped off American soil until three days ago when he arrived in Italy with his carry-on luggage stuffed with his favorite snack: animal crackers. His wife, Lizzy, a professor of history at their local university, sits beside him, rolling her eyes. Her short, bobbed hairdo is flattened against the blue seat, and her feet barely dust the top of the floorboard. I watch as she lifts up her disposable camera while scrunching her face in disgust at her husband's braggadocio.

"They are all lies," she tells us thirty minutes later when we stop by a Tuscan field of velvety-red poppies for an impromptu photo shoot.

"Get your cameras," I tell the Americans. "The best photos of the poppies are up there at the top of the hill."

I point toward the rolling Toscana hills that are covered in a red carpet as Nino opens the door beside my seat.

Tom wags his finger in front of Dr. Raybay as he makes his way off the coach. "The best photos are beside the villa. I brought my Canon for this opportunity. I'll show you the simple techniques for shooting flowers and fading the background together."

Tom holds his camera up in the air in a proud moment to show off his favorite hobby: photography.

"Pull yourself together, Tom," Dr. Raybay laughs, tapping his fingers on his camera. "I'm walking to the top, over there."

Dr. Raybay waves his arm high in the air and accidentally hits Lizzy's head.

"Watch out!" Lizzy rubs her forehead and instinctively slaps his hand.

"Follow me. I'll show you around." I take Lizzy's arm and pull.

"Thank you, Stephanie!" Lizzy says then laughs. "I don't know what is wrong with my husband. But I think the fresh air will bring him back to his senses. We can only hope."

"What did he say?" I turn to Lizzy as we walk toward the colorful blooms.

"He's never been farther than the cowboy state of Texas except on our honeymoon. And that was only two hundred and seventy-six miles westward, barely making it into the state of New Mexico before he started receiving calls from patients. His partner, Dr. Leo, was covering for him, but that didn't stop the emergency calls from beeping through. Heck, he wanted to stay in Lubbock to watch the football game and eat Spanky's fried cheese sticks for breakfast. The next morning, he insisted we go to church, so we did without knowing anyone there.

"I'm exaggerating just a tad. We've traveled to a few other states, but you get my point. He's never been out of the United States. Not that we've wanted to go to other places, but his career has a tightrope around his neck. He never really gets any peace, except with a few of his hobbies," Lizzy speedily tells us, flashing a forced smile across her fifty-two-year-old face, which is perfectly round with no visible jaw-line. Her eyes—the size of tiny English peas—glance downward for a moment and display a colorful rainbow of eye shadow in pastel pink, blue, and creamy yellow, all blended together. When she looks up suddenly her eyebrows become pointed triangles, a permanent surprise tattooed in charcoal black.

"Why would he say California wines are the best?" Louise, from the potato state of Idaho, interrupts in her distinct voice, which reminds me of Marilyn Monroe singing "Happy birthday, Mr. President." Louise's eyes are shrouded behind two gigantic wheels—neon blue sunglasses with glossy black frames. Her silver-white hair is spiked with a lot of styling gel to hold the stiffness. She resembles Iris Apfel, the famous New York City fashionista, the geriatric starlet with her signature flying saucer glasses and fabulous designer labels.

"I'm certainly no expert on wines, but I can tell you anything you need to know about fashion. And I certainly didn't know the California wines are the best," Louise tells us, leaning in closer to hear more. Her six enormous bangle bracelets camouflage the silky flamingo-pink ruffle on her latest designer blouse—all different from yesterday's colorful assortment.

"Oh, my husband loves to joke. One will never know if he's joking or just downright lying. He's good at both," Lizzy conveys the secret knowledge with a booming laugh as she reaches for a pink rose blooming beside her leg.

"That reminds me of what my mother has always said about middle-aged men," Louise says with raised eyebrows.

"And what is that?" Lizzy asks.

"A man can easily tell a big fat lie with a straight face while never batting an eye," Louise echoes her mother's words in a serious tone.

"That's true for women too, don't you think?" Lizzy tells Louise.

"Sure, but I'm referring to men at the moment."

"Oh, he does like to stretch things, but we all do. And with us, we have different desires. He wants to take a risk with his life, and I don't. Coming to Italy is a huge..."

Lizzy throws the rose down before ending her words.

"Did you say that Italy is a risk?" Louise leans in closer. Her eyes are fast-moving pinballs as she absorbs this new information. Lizzy has her full attention now.

"Yes! It certainly is when your husband wants to be with a monk." Lizzy puts her hands around her head as though a headache is pounding. "I try not to think about it, but what can I do? I can't change the situation.

"What situation?" Louise is now face-to-face with Lizzy, with her gigantic glasses pushed up to her lashes.

"It's a long story. He likes monks. He wants to be with..."

"What? Who wants to be a monk in this modern-day age? In my professional opinion, he's not normal." Louise's diagnosis surprises those of us who are listening in. Did she just say Dr. Raybay "is not normal"?

"Oh, no. You have misunderstood. He's perfectly normal. He's just a doctor with a yearning to..."

"Change partners?" Louise interrupts with intense seriousness.

"Good Lord, have mercy! Absolutely not!" Lizzy forces a smile and begins to pace, going in circles. "My husband feels the calling of God upon his life. He wants to sell everything and retire from his medical practice in two years and probably join a monastery or some sort of ministry to help others. He loves gardening, making fruit jams, and messing around with this and that in the dirt. It's a hobby of his, and he gives the excess of tomatoes, peppers, strawberries, peaches, etc., to our neighbors and church people."

"Hmm...really?" Louise muses aloud. She can't hide her thoughts. Her theatrical facial expressions reveal everything within her mind. There's no camouflaging them.

"We are riding in two different boats, both going in opposite directions. I can't help that he didn't follow his heart when we were married. I'm not one to live life on a sparse supply like the missionaries do in foreign countries, if you know what I mean. That might be Jerry's calling, but certainly not mine!" Lizzy looked over at the medieval villa surrounded by red poppies and seemed to see through it.

Louise finally pipes in with her opinion. "I think it is all make-believe, fantasy, a phase of mid-life crisis. Men do that, you know. I've been through four husbands. Two died, one ended in divorce, and the other one, Larry, is at home with the cats and his golfing buddies. He'd rather play golf than spend time with me. He's a good man. He retired from banking three years ago and hasn't done much since except hit balls around.

"Still, I've heard all of my life and from professional experience, that when men reach retirement age, you better look out. It's all downhill from there. They get the itch to stray. Not all of them but many for sure. They want their cake and to eat it too, as the saying goes. You know, sex with whores who are half their age or younger. Yep, he desires a little romp in greener pastures, that's all. It will pass in time if you can hang on for the ride and let him be. He's using the monk story for a cover-up. I'm sure he already has another woman already. You know, a little candy on the side." Louise can't stop talking. She's giving the worse scenario of all: a cheating spouse.

"No. Absolutely not. Jerry Raybay is special, a good man. He's not like that at all, trust me." Lizzy is shocked at Louise's prediction. We all are.

"You say he's special? That's an understatement. They all are, if you ask me." Louise clicks her camera at a little donkey nearby. She's straight to the point and has a no-nonsense personality that fits her line of work of being a recently retired psychiatrist and marriage counselor. I think she retired just in time before mentally exploding from all the years in practice.

"He's a good man and makes a great living. But I'm not obsessed with all the bible history and Sunday school gatherings like he is. Jerry loves all of that, especially the classes, the discussions of this and that from long ago. Who cares?" Lizzy winked, or was it something in her eye?

"I do go to church with him sometimes to chitchat with the ladies. It gives me a chance to wear my latest fashions and connect for the holiday parties." Lizzy pulled a pink satin scarf from inside her blouse. My eyes focused on the double initials for Chanel in black.

"Excuse me, ladies," Carol from Dallas, Texas, pops over my shoulder. She has no idea about the conversation that's been going back and forth. "Isn't this a dream? Do you hear the faint chimes from afar? Look at the steeples over there. Are we really here in this beautiful spot? I can't believe we're standing so close to something that looks as if it was taken from a storybook. I love the pink stucco with sun-bleached green shutters and the ceramic roof tiles with ancient chimneys." Carol pulls out a photo from her bag. It's a beautiful, glossy picture from a travel magazine. "Look at this. Is this where we're at, the same villa? I can only imagine the inside! I see a marble staircase and sky blue ceilings with puffy white clouds. And it must have chandeliers dripping in colorful Murano glass with daggers piercing downward in all shapes and sizes."

"Yes! And don't forget the red damask curtains falling to the floor and the gorgeous array of antique chairs and divans in the finest Italian green velvets, everything swaddled with fabulous fabrics," I allow my mind to wander, forgetting about Lizzy's situation for a brief second and acknowledging the splendor we're truly experiencing in this very moment in time.

"I took on a second job and saved my hard-earned money for years. I had to make this dream come true, to be in Italy with you, Stephanie. Thank you for bringing me here and stopping to pick poppies and experience the ringing of medieval church bells. And the drive to the castle's hidden beauty. I can't believe Nino made the bus fit through the umbrella of trees and narrow pathways. He pushed us straight through. It was like going through a carwash with the gigantic strips swabbing the sides of the bus. Amazingly, there's not a single scratch on it. How can it be?"

"Nino can drive on a clothesline," I answer with one short statement.

"Stephanie, I can still visualize the feast inside the castle's majestic grandeur and see the hidden passageways within, and the wine cellar down inside the heart of the stones. I can't believe you opened the door, and there it was, a little chapel with medieval torches from long ago. We've already experienced a hundred history books within a few days. My mind is exploding.

"And now I understand how over fifty thousand Jews arrived in Italy and into the Roman Forum as slaves. I had no idea the Israelites revolted against the Romans and refused to worship their gods, which caused the short-lived war in Jerusalem when the Romans defeated them and destroyed their temple then forced them to build the Arch of Titus and the Colosseum. The Israelites came straight from Jerusalem into Rome. They were scattered into another world— a Roman world of pagans. It all fits together now with my grandfather's stories, how the Jews waited for nearly two thousand years for their return after World War II back to Israel. Oh, and the Jewish Ghetto in Rome where they were made to live like caged animals and the horrible slaughtering of Christians in the Colosseum. Yes, I understand it now." Carol's voice breaks as she begins to cry with tears streaming down her cheeks. "I've dreamed of seeing this place all of my life, the places where the apostles walked, the monks, the dedicated nuns, the..."

"Carol, it will take many trips to Italy with me to experience the many secrets behind the tourist sites. Remember, I've been bringing two or three groups of Americans here for over twenty years, studying its history and going into its mysteries. I will never accept the 'new age' uprising or the political correctness of refusing to acknowledge the brutal torture of Christians in the Colosseum and the unaccountable killing of innocent animals and followers of Christ. It's the politicians who want to bury the past history of debaucheries. But one can't wipe the slate clean. The blood is forever within the soil. History is history. It's not a blame game. It is facts. I don't understand the mindset of those who want to destroy the past or rewrite the books into a new memoir of fabled tales with no evidence of its truth."

My heart beats too fast. I know many would rather look through rose-colored glasses than know the truth.

Lizzy exhales slowly, making a noise of distraction. She smiles in awkward agreement and then says, "Yes, I agree with you, Stephanie."

The quick confessional discussion abruptly ends when Dr. Raybay walks up behind his chatty wife. His face is radiating beams of sunlight. I saw him coming toward us a few minutes ago with a fistful of flowers but didn't feel the need to interrupt Lizzy. She was on a roll and felt much better getting the truth out in her impromptu therapy session.

"That was a quick photo lesson," I tell Dr. Raybay, seeing his camera peeking out underneath the flowers.

"I'm no photographer like Tom. Let him enjoy himself with all of that camera jargon. He rolled out more words than my brain could comprehend: shutter speed, aperture, exposure, and heck, what else did he say?" Dr.Raybay kisses his wife on the cheek and then reaches into his pocket to retrieve the camera lens while trying to finagle as many flowers as possible with his other hand.

"Did you pluck and pull every living plant?" I ask Dr. Raybay while looking at the large bunch of petals smashed together in his fist.

"It was easier to pick flowers for Lizzy. I'm not interested in learning all of the details of a professional photographer as Tom seems to be," Dr. Raybay tells me.

"Do whatever you want." Lizzy stares at her husband with a smile.

"*Andiamo*! Let's go," I holler to the Americans, seeing their arms loaded with poppies. Behind them, the field is barren, plucked clean as though a lawnmower had followed their heels.

"Thank you for stopping in this picture-perfect setting!" I hear one of the Americans shout. I look back and see our group toting more than enough flowers, almost too many to fit inside the coach.

"You're welcome," I say, waving my arm in the air with my fingers pointing ahead.

Walking back to the coach with the Americans strolling behind me, I see Nino in the driver's seat. The words that Lizzy confessed to me minutes ago begin to roll around my mind.

Lizzy had rambled, "Italy was the number one priority on my bucket list. I've longed to buy Italian clothes, shoes, and designer leather bags. And, with much persuasion, my husband nearly convinced me that monks really do exist in Italy, and if he could only see them, well, he'd be the happiest man alive and forever grateful.

"He spends most of his time at the hospital, always working. And when he's not there, I find him pecking away on his laptop, researching his obsession with missionary work and the brotherhood of dedicated workers for the church. I wouldn't be surprised if he took his vows and moved right in with them. But here we are together. It's truly a miracle. I'm willing to see the monks with him and try to rekindle our love and hopefully prove my point. I know this all sounds ridiculously insane—the monks and his infatuation—but once he meets them, well, surely that will be the end of it? He'll be satisfied with this nonsense of the Old World that doesn't exist anymore. It's all fairytale rubbish."

Back on the coach, everyone is talking. There must be ten conversations going at once. The Americans are even more energized than before and ready for the next adventure. Everywhere we look is a postcard, a beautiful setting to capture.

I look straight ahead through the windshield and wonder if Lizzy even saw the beautiful poppies, which were the reason for our abrupt stop in the first place. Did she notice the rolling hills that resemble a giant mural painted with every color of the rainbow? Before my thoughts expand, I see a parade of a dozen or more medieval-looking people carrying big wicker baskets and pushing wooden carts loaded with vegetables. Where did they come from?

The closer the coach gets to them, I immediately realize what's before us.

"Look!" I shout as if Saint Peter had appeared before me. "Stop the bus!"

I'm in my seat with my face pressed to the windshield. Nino's foot slips off the accelerator.

"*Mamma Mia, Stefania!* What's the matter with you?" Tony jumps and hollers, too. We've only been back on the coach for less than ten minutes.

Out of nowhere, it's a pilgrimage of friars in their long brown robes and corded ropes about their waist with the three customary knots dangling down, representing poverty, chastity, and obedience. It's a brotherhood of Franciscan monks who live on the land in the nearby monastery, growing food and providing for themselves and the village people.

"The monks!" I shout louder as Nino slowly passes beside them. He can't stop the coach because we're sandwiched between a little farm truck and three scooters while navigating a sharp curve. But there we were in the Val d'Orcia region of Tuscany, south of Siena, driving alongside real monks.

I can't believe this. Just seconds ago, Lizzy walked to the front of the coach to get two bottles of water and lingered with Tony. And behold, there the monks appeared, a scene right out of a biblical storybook. How could this be? The perfect timing of divine intervention, Lizzy witnessing genuine monks doing what they've been doing for hundreds of years, tending the vineyards and growing their food with little or no modern equipment. I ponder our earlier conversation as I glance back to the luscious, pistachio-green patchwork fields undulating like a rollercoaster. The flowing hilltops run in different directions with threaded vegetation marching down the middle, appearing as though a professional seamstress had fashioned it. And if that isn't enough to cause one to take ten thousand photos, then the flock of wooly, white sheep dotting the land certainly is. Is this a serendipitous encounter? Yes! Oh, yes, indeed.

In that ecclesiastical moment when Dr. Raybay heard the word "'monks,'" he leaped across the aisle, banging his hand desperately against the window as though trapped inside a glass jar. In a second, he appears like a newborn baby with his lips suctioned to the window, struggling to drink in every ounce of medieval happenings before his star-struck eyes. The fast glimpse and the mouth-gaping stare made him shout, "Stop! Please! Stop the bus!"

Lizzy has the opposite reaction. In leisurely slow motion, she leans over Tony to see the flock of brown-hooded friars right before her eyes. The storybook setting moves before her as though she'd been sent back in time. She stares as though dumbstruck with her eyes bulging against the window. Was she stunned into silence?

Chapter 6

TELL US MORE OF PITIGLIANO & GRAB YOUR TESTICLES!

"*S*tephanie, tell us about Tony's fish around his neck," Rita reminds me again. She has a fascination with unusual jewelry.

"*Va bene.* Okay," I tell her as I reach for a bottle of water in the refrigerated compartment in front of me. "I'll get Tony to tell you," I say, but my voice is lost within the air.

Tony is quibbling with Nino in his animated Italian run-on sentences, hovering over him in a silk-threaded, long-sleeve, black shirt, which is unbuttoned at the top to reveal a gold chain with a large creature dangling about his neck. It was a gift from his wife, Pat, who felt it was time to replace the gold Star of David that he had worn for many years.

When looking at Tony, the first thing I see is the large fish around his neck. It proudly dangles four inches against his chest and shouts to the world, "I'm Sicilian!"

The gold showstopper swings back and forth as Tony theatrically oscillates his hands and arms above his head. When seeing the big eighteen-karat fish, I think of the catacombs in Rome, where it is carved into the tufa stone, deep inside the never-ending tunnels. It is one of the earliest Christian symbols.

During the reign of Nero, the cruel Emperor of Rome, the persecution of Christians was rampant, causing them to flee to the underground tunnels. It was there that they met in secret and were forced to use codes to communicate. Tony's gigantic fish doesn't have any outwardly visible symbols, but many of them do, such as IXOYE, which in Greek means Jesus Christ, Son of God, and Savior when turned into an anagram. The fish symbol was used because the first letters of each word: Jesus Christ, Son of God, Savior, did, in fact, spell fish in Greek. However, if one should ask Pat what the large creature about Tony's neck is, she would reply, "It's Pisces, Tony's zodiac sign, his birth symbol. People born on March seventeenth are talented, thoughtful, and have a deeply spiritual nature."

Several minutes later, Tony is still rambling about nothing of importance beyond the anticipated meal of pasta and sauce tonight. I watch him sit on the seat's edge with his knuckles, thick and robust, firmly gripped to the back of Nino's headrest. His right hand swirls in the air as though he's conducting an Italian operetta—free entertainment.

I sit in the passenger seat with my fingers tapping on the microphone that rests peacefully on my lap and stare through the gigantic windshield, knowing the privilege of my life. The countless times my eyes have beheld this place alone, or with Tony, Nino, and the Americans, are too many to recall. We've been all over Europe together, trekking up and down in our Mercedes-Benz coach. And when the blue seas refuse to part for our next journey to a bordering country, no problem. Nino drives the coach into the bottom of a floating ferry with the many other trucks hauling cargo from here and there.

We've been together on everything from planes, trains, cargo ships, luxury ships, river-boats, subways, taxis, cable lifts, scooters, ferries, funiculars, tiny cars, and fast-track luxury cars of the rich and famous. I've stood in sacred places that tourists will probably never see and mountainous terrain so high up that the air is crystal clear, and the heavens feel within my reach. While trekking through Meteora, Greece, I've looked upwards as far as my eyes can see, thinking that surely there must be astronauts floating around somewhere above my head.

We've taken the Americans off the beaten paths into many different countries, zigzagging throughout Budapest, Prague, Vienna, Slovakia, Bratislava, Bavaria, to name a few. The memories and adventures are endless, and many are too preposterous for one to believe. We've traipsed all over the hilly Czech countryside and the mysterious, green canopy of evergreens in the Black Forest of Germany. I had held the microphone to my red-painted lips, telling the Americans we were in Baden-Württemberg, which is in the southwestern part of Germany and is home to the beautiful, hand-crafted cuckoo clocks.

Today as Nino drives us through this beautiful place, my mind still rambles to the endless, hair-raising situations we've gotten ourselves into. And I still feel the urge to do more, to follow where God leads and take the Americans with me. At times when I have no one by my side, I hop aboard a scooter to reach the highest hills in pursuit of treasures for Decorate Ornate or to satisfy my own personal obsession.

Tony has taken me places where the ordinary man would never go, high up in the middle of nowhere.

"Hold your breath and stand up," Tony would say, knowing the tiny car would surely drag its undercarriage, and the little doors would crush inward from the narrow passageway of rocks. "If we stand up, the weight will surely lift from underneath."

We joked and laughed, knowing each other's thoughts. We were two wide-eyed faces—both different, but the same—one American and one Sicilian, both peering out the tiny windshield.

Going down memory lane, the thoughts refuse to stop. They play peek-a-boo in my mind, echoing the past as Nino makes a smooth curve by another Tuscan village nestled way above the vineyards. The sudden view causes an immediate reaction within me—an urgency to hurriedly reach for the microphone and start talking.

"Look, everyone! This is Pitigliano, also known as La Piccola Gerusalemme or Little Jerusalem."

"*Mamma Mia, Stefania*, we do not stop today!" Tony snaps out of his solo singing and turns off the switch on the microphone, which controls the stereo volume in the coach.

"We must get to the monks to hear them chant before it's too late," Tony tells me with deafening urgency. With the same breath, he hollers to Nino as though he's miles away and tells him to hurry faster. "Don't give *Stefania* the opportunity to jump off again and cause us to miss the monks."

I ignore him and continue, "Does Pitigliano remind you of something you must see? Can you envision the maze of streets twisting and turning and running upwards and around ancient buildings, revealing its Jewish past? Look at the houses perched within the tufa stone, one on top of another. I know it's just another medieval town in the Maremma area of Tuscany; however, there's something special up there. Did you know that Pitigliano welcomed the Jewish people long ago? There is a Jewish ghetto inside its walls. The last time I went up there, the Museum of Jewish Culture was closed, but one of the locals took me inside. The Jewish synagogue is there, too."

I roll out everything I know about this village in fast, run-on sentences as our coach zooms past the ancient beauty. Nino never looks its way.

"*Mamma Mia!* Now she starts with this bloody Pitigliano. Why this obsession with the Jewish people and the ghetto? The *Americani* didn't come to Italy to be sad, to hear of this catastrophe of Hitler," Tony tells Nino as though I'm invisible and deaf.

"Yes, they are interested," I tell Tony, defending my insistence on Pitigliano. "They've never seen such history and beauty. I know we don't have time to stop, but since we're passing by..."

Nino listens intensely, keeping his fingers gripped around the steering wheel, holding on as if letting go will surely draw us upward to the hilltop entrance.

Tony continues to dramatize the dire situation and advises Nino to look the other way. Melancholy waltzes in, consuming Tony and Nino's face. They remember the destruction of Hitler, and the horrible agony brought to this area. And just like that, Tony's words are magic. He undergoes a metamorphosis. The funny Rodney Dangerfield look-alike has left the building and is suddenly replaced with someone else. He is now an eye-popping, vein expanding, serious bodyguard who is alarming no one but him and Nino, the two Sicilians of great superstition. I laugh at his theatrical animation, his arms twirling and spinning like propellers above his head.

"*Mamma Mia, Stefania*," Nino mumbles in slow motion as he looks at me and reaches for my arm.

"*Stefania*, the *Americani* must hear and see nice things in Italy. You will bring us bad luck talking of such things. *Mamma Mia, Stefania. Basta*. Enough," Nino says in Italian, overdramatizing the mention of Pitigliano.

I watch him draw the sign of the cross upon his chest. Afterward, a slight smile peeps through then stretches across his olive-kissed Casanova face. He's Sicilian, too, I remind myself. He and Tony know me well. I'm not *permalosa*—overly sensitive, easily offended, thin-skinned. We say what we mean to each other with complete honesty and no hidden agendas. When Nino says, "*basta*," I take it with a grain of salt and usually with a roll of my eyes.

"Stephanie, are there any monks in Piglee—homa?" Dr. Raybay breaks into the drama before him. I turn around and see his face, stuffed with animal crackers.

"*Mamma Mia*, who is this speaking?" Tony jumps, not knowing anyone was listening to our chatter in the front of the coach. "What do you say, *dottore*?" Tony twists around in his seat and flashes a big smile while pointing in the opposite direction of Pitigliano, using his Sicilian trickery.

"Look to your left! Do you see the beautiful vineyards?" Tony shouts in electrifying haste, which makes me turn to see as well.

In whiplash speed, the passengers look in the opposite direction, away from Pitigliano, not knowing that Tony is joking. But to Tony's surprise, the Americans go crazy, whooping and hollering. They see the usual happenings of everyday life and an ancient farmhouse nestled in colorful strokes of a painter's brush.

As far as our eyes can see, we look upon a floral eruption like

Cleopatra's eyelids painted in exquisite hues or a royal bouquet bundled together as one. Before us are honeysuckles, peonies, red poppies, variegated roses, and colorful irises. *They have swallowed steroids through their Italian roots.* The thought races through my mind, determining it's the only possible explanation of such flowery flamboyance and magnificence.

Beyond this front row of splendor, the rolling waves of vineyards march perfectly up and down with jubilant explosions of silver leaves shimmering from the olive trees and leafy grapevines swaying in the gentle breeze. I see every shade of jadeite peeking out in such vibrancy. It's a painter's palette of variety, tossing out swirls of every known shade of green from vine-ripened avocados to splashes of key lime pie whipped in amongst the enticing foliage. And if that's not enough to cause one to take a thousand photos, then the abundance of purple grapes will.

"Look at the herbs growing wildly," Mary shouts, leaping across the aisle. She captures another photo of endless rows of thyme and rosemary.

"The cypress trees are over forty feet tall." Mary gives her news report of her Toscana sightings. "And the grapes! Oh, look at the grapes."

"*Mamma Mia*, what's the matter with them? Is it their first time to see the grapes?" Tony asks while gesturing wildly with his hands.

The Americans are pressed to the windows. Their lips suctioned against the glass, pointing at the unfamiliar happenings. To my right is a car loaded down with wicker baskets of vegetables towering on the rooftop with a little wire cage dangling on top.

I glance over to Tony. He is back to entertaining himself, singing to the Italian music that's coming through the speakers, and orchestrating his own symphony.

When traveling across the backroads in Italy or when going to eagles' nests on the edges of heaven, places unobtainable by most, there stand sites so magnificently created by God. I wonder if every ten thousand years, some new form of life arrives there—perhaps large, feathery friends equipped with wings of a jet. Or, knowing the greatness of God's creation, I think every now and then a little male sparrow with its gray head, white cheeks, and black bib must come to these places to chirp, build a nest, and look upon the splendor of the ancient rocks and caves.

The sporadic thoughts come and go within my mind as the breathtaking setting surrounding us unlocks the vault of my child-hood memories. Looking out over the silvery branches swooshing and swaying in the cool breeze, I glance to Nino, our little bambino, our beloved driver with the face of a creamy chocolate pie and enough sex appeal to ignite a bottle of iced water into burning flames. I think how much I love my life and the many paths God leads me on and how I want to bring Americans to Italy—more than I already do —to show them the hidden places and to let them sit at the tables of family and friends right here in this beautiful land of rolling hills and the Mediterranean Sea. I want them to see the places where the apos-tles are laid to rest and feel the history of the Bible coming to life. It's all still here, forever frozen in time and sprinkled all around.

My mind continues to reminisce as Nino turns off the main road to drive through an imaginative landscape of more rolling hilltop vineyards and ancient olive trees marching together in perfect coordi-nation, alongside towering Italian cypresses parading majestically as if painted on canvas. I look straight ahead through the gigantic wind-shield and marvel for the thousandth time. How can this land be so perfectly planted with each grain of dirt bedded underneath its canopy of foliage and topped with swooshing branches dancing in the gentle breeze? Did Walt Disney receive his inspiration right here in this rollercoaster of speckled vegetation that's deeply rooted in the Tuscan earth?

I'm quickly snapped back to reality as Nino hollers, "*Mamma Mia, Madonna!*"

Looking to my left side, I shout in surprise, too. The Americans lean into the aisle of the coach, stretching their necks to see. Have more monks appeared?

"Look! Look! It's a hearse!" My voice alerts the entire region of Tuscany as Nino hits the brakes and skids to the side of the road, causing gravel to pop and crackle underneath the gigantic tires. The long funeral carriage leisurely passes the coach on Tony and Nino's side.

Tony shouts louder than I've ever heard him yell before. In lightning speed, he twists around in the opposite direction of the hearse and roars hysterically, "*Mamma Mia, Madonna*! *Stefania*, is there a body inside?"

His eyes are rapidly ballooning, and sprinkles of sweat dot his brow as he refuses to look into the hearse.

Sicilian superstition states that one should never follow or look upon an empty hearse, *carro funebre*, because if you do, then you are riding at death's door, and something is bound to happen that won't be good. However, if the hearse is carrying a body, then you are safe and do not need to worry. I try to glimpse if there is any cargo inside.

"There's a body inside!" I shout, dropping back into my seat. My eyes fix on the bumper of the fading taillights as it slowly fades into the distance.

"Thank God the hearse wasn't empty," I say through the microphone. "If it had, gentlemen, you must immediately grab your testicles to save your life. And ladies, you must grab the testicles of any man in sight. Don't worry, though. You can give your apologies afterward. If you're squeezing the Italians, there's no need to fret; they'll understand and be greatly appreciative. And if you can't quite take the plunge to be so aggressive, do as the nuns do: cross yourself, grab the rosary, and call out to Jesus, the Madonna, and all of the holy saints for protection against the evil one. This would just be for starters. The continuous round-the-clock prayer vigil, conducted in shifts, for the next few days would follow. *Mamma Mia*, the things we do in Italy!"

Thirty minutes later, I stare ahead at the rolling vineyards and forget about the emergency with the hearse. The view ahead is beyond words. Against the kaleidoscopic sapphire blue sky with white cotton clouds, the medieval farm-houses cause one to believe in the enchantment of storybook legends. Everything blends in with the land. There's no beginning and no end.

Where is Aladdin? Surely, he is floating above, gliding on his magic carpet as Cinderella's Fairy Godmother swirls her wand through the aromatic air of ruby-red Sangiovese grapes. Will the heavens magically rain plump droplets of the famous Brunello di Montalcino, the finest wine in Europe? The thoughts race through my mind, shifting gears and flying in all directions. The microphone dangles in my hand for the voices within my head are loud, amplified, and blaring.

Nino stares ahead as he guides the coach around a sharp curve in rural Tuscany, the enchanting region of beauty, the Val d'Orcia.

I turn the music up and allow the Italian lyrics to fill the coach as we bump along to the next adventure.

Chapter 7

ROSE BUSHES IN ITALY

*I*nstead of pushing our sunglasses closer to our eyes in the brilliant sun, we pull them off to see the vivid colors rolling up and down in gentle waves. We're not on the Mediterranean Sea looking at the gentle waves of sparkling diamonds. No, the Italian Riviera is a few miles away. We're still in the countryside of Tuscany, bumping along underneath its sunny charm, hypnotized by acres of vines bursting forth with purply grapes nearly the size of ping-pong balls and statuesque rose bushes standing guard in front of each new row, adorned with vibrant blossoms.

"Stephanie, tell us why the roses stand at the beginning of every row. Is this only in Italy that farmers take the time to decorate the vineyards with beautiful flowers?" Bernie from New York City asks. His face is pressed against the glass window with his right hand gripping a honey-glazed roll from the morning's breakfast table. I stare at the homemade bread that's the size of a baseball. His accountant's fingers are wrapped around it as though it was a rare diamond. Suddenly, I become hungry even though breakfast was less than an hour ago.

"Bernie, the rosebushes are guardian angels, more or less," I tell him with an indulgent laugh. My eyes are still fixated on the luscious *cornetto*, the croissant.

"It's a medieval invention, alerting the farmers of the dreaded powdery mildew that can infect the grapes. It will first infect the petals of the roses. They are not only picturesque here but are also known as shepherds of the vineyards, leading the grapes to a bountiful harvest. The thorny green statues explode in colorful pinks and reds, standing tall, watchful to the danger of the disease," I continue as I point to the flowering beauties as we pass them.

"I had no idea there was such a thing, placing a rosebush in front of each row as a fungus detector. And if the powdery mildew is on the roses, then the farmer will know the vines are in danger of getting the same disease. That's a genius idea, and it works." Bernie turns to his wife, Kay Ann, continuing to chatter. Like a parrot, he repeats the same words and explains more of his discovery as I continue talking.

"And when they see the white, speckled fungus of the dreaded illness making landfall on the blooming petals, the farmers are alerted that the row of grapes is in grave danger of catching the disease. It's a domino effect—fleas jumping and spreading the disease, invading the whole line of luscious fruit balls, destroying them. At the first sign of white on the rose petals, the farmer takes immediate action to deter and kill the deadly infestation, typically by treating it with sulfur, which is a natural insecticide."

I spring up from my seat to demonstrate, pretending each person on the left and right side of me are rows of grapes and pointing to each imaginary rosebush on the outside walkway. I abruptly stop at the seat of Amy Krim from the trendy city of Sacramento, California.

"Hello, Amy. Do you have any white powdery mildew upon your rosy petals that could spread to your partner?" I joke, looking at Lindsey, who sits beside her and now represents the vines.

"*Mamma Mia*, what's the matter with you, *Stefania*? How do you know these things? Are you a winemaker? Why do you tell the Americans bad things today? You will bring us bad luck, talking of such devastation. And you saying the fleas invade the vineyards? *Mamma*

Mia, I do not want to hear any more of this talk. Bah! I do not understand why you bring sadness to our people. There are no fleas in Italy. Do you see any fleas in the vineyards we go to? Why do you tell such things? I will never understand this compulsion of yours to tell of such things. The *Americani* come to Italy to hear nice things, and look what you do to them. You make them sad," Tony exclaims as he gestures wildly.

Walking back to my seat, I bring the microphone up to my red-painted lips and continue the conversation while rolling my eyes and smiling at Tony. He knows me well enough to know that I pay no attention to his superstitious beliefs and never take them seriously.

"I love the ancient way of life in Italy as they detect the health of the succulent fruit like they did hundreds of years ago. And what is the saying around here in Tuscany, 'healthy vines are healthy grapes'? Isn't that what they say here in Montalcino, home to your favorite bottle of Brunello?" I ask Tony, but he doesn't hear me. His ear is glued to his phone again.

"I think we should propose a hardy toast to all of the hundreds of rose bushes right now." I pretend to salute everyone with an invisible wine glass by holding my fistful of nothing in the air.

"My friends, the next time you're sipping a glass of the red, the *vino*, remember the beautiful rose, its petals, and the representation of its protection against the evilness of this world," I tell everyone, shuffling my leather shoes on the black floorboard and swinging my marionette arms in the air while dancing and twirling around in the narrow aisle.

"*Mamma Mia, Madonna!*" Tony shouts as my elbow knocks his phone from his ear and sends it flying across Nino's golden bronzed head. His hair is almost gone, save the silvery-gray and black spikes germinating above his ears and around his head.

"*Mamma Mia, Madonna!*" Tony theatrically spews out the mantra again. I turn around and place the microphone back in its holder. I have become immune to those three Italian words since I hear them at least a thousand times per day. The same goes for Tony, who hears the Americans repeatedly saying, "Oh, my gosh." And today is no different from any other. The words fly in every direction and ricochet within the coach—like popcorn exploding in a bag.

Chapter 8

SERENADE THE GRAPES

"*Mamma Mia, Nino!* How many times do we come here with *Stefania* and the Americans seeing these rolling hills? She never gets fed-up, and she never sits in peace. This is the first time she talks of the rosebush so intensely, going into so many details. And I do not understand this obsession with the Abbey of Sant'Antimo, and why not the Brunello di Montalcino which has the best *vino* in the world. *Stefania* should talk more of its beauty, but the Americans have never heard of it. Did you hear the *Americano* seated behind us, *Dottore* Raybay?"

"*Si, si.*" Nino agrees.

"*Dottore* Raybay doesn't know the good *vino*, Nino! He said the California is the best! *Mamma Mia, Madonna.* He knows nothing of the grape. There is only one *Americano* who appreciates the Brunello di Montalcino as much as I do. It's Dee. *Si, si.* Yes, Dee Tullis knows the good *vino*. She brings me plenty of bottles when I arrive to *Stefania*'s home in America. Dee is very good. She knows the Brunello is the best."

Tony's blood pressure skyrockets his heart palpitations to a soaring speed, making them visible through the silkiness of his shirt and vibrating the dangling medallion about his neck.

"And Nino, you see how many *Americani* come back with *Stefania*, over and over, never tiring of Italy. And the music, "Tu Vuo' Fa L'Americano," that we sing too much."

Tony turns to me, his eyebrows knitted together on his forehead as he burps out another *"Mamma Mia."* I pretend to ignore him with an intentional smirk on my face while reaching for the stereo dial to turn up the music, blasting the lyrics through the speakers. The trumpets blow and crash hard against the interior of the coach. And just like that, Tony forcefully slams both hands against his airy white cotton pants, energetically playing an imaginary drum to the beat of the music while blurting out strange sounds like a donkey's bray. The Americans laugh hard, being pumped up by the energy in the coach.

We bump along the scenic stretch of the Val d'Orcia, a UNESCO World Heritage Site on SP146 road where the famous Vitaleta Chapel sits like a postcard of Tuscany, ready for its next photo. Regardless of the various personalities of the Americans on board this coach, they are of one accord, spellbound by the view and the church bells heard minutes ago ding-donging throughout the undulating land and clashing with the music blasting through the speakers. The velvety green flow of the hilltops covered with olive trees and rows of plump grapes are nothing but pastel-painted watercolors on a gigantic canvas. What we see now is no comparison to the quiet American vineyards. No, none. Before us are waves of hills painted as though Claude Monet stroked his brush across the earth of Tuscany. Even the sky is bluer, the stars are brighter, and the cypress trees are greener.

Thirty minutes later, leaving the fields of red poppies behind us, Nino brings the coach to a snail's crawl. He takes a left turn toward the medieval abbey in the valley of Montalcino, home to the famous Brunello di Montalcino wine, as Tony keeps reminding us. I hear the oohs and aahs as the passengers stare through the windows.

"Mamma Mia, what's the matter?" Tony jumps within his seat upon hearing the hair-raising scream. Looking back quickly, I see Lori Medley from Tennessee, who's seated three seats back behind Tony, yelling as if she's auditioning for an amateur soprano spot.

Nino's foot slips off the gas pedal, stalling the coach for a millisecond and causing him to turn around.

"*Stefania*, what's the matter with the *Americana*, Lori?" Tony asks as he hurriedly makes his way down the aisle, expecting a catastrophe of some sort.

"I'm sorry for disturbing everyone," Lori tells Tony, seemingly embarrassed by her sudden outburst. Her face turns crimson red as she quickly shifts her green eyes speckled with golden shards back to the window, and her slender body shrinks into a pile of flowery fabric.

I watch the ruckus and observe Tony in full Rodney Dangerfield animation. Such seriousness! His eyes protrude like large apples as Lori switches gears and takes Tony down a rabbit hole of make-believe.

"I've studied this monastery for many years, never dreaming I'd be here in person." Lori looks at him with a serious face. "I believe I was a monk in my former life. I've had many dreams about living in convents, but as a monk, not a nun."

"*Mamma Mia*, you must be joking?" Tony's eyes nearly pop out. "What do you mean your former life, and as a monk? Do you understand a monk is a man in Italy?" Tony asks. He slaps John's back, who sits alone in the seat in front of Lori.

"*Stefania*, you must come immediately," Tony calls out. His voice cracks with uncertainty, and his feet start to shuffle—either that or an army of ants has invaded his shoes.

"I'm joking, Tony," Lori laughs out loud. "I did, though, have a dream of being a monk, but Tony, it was a dream." Lori spins a long tale, seeing the shockwaves dance across Tony's face.

"No, no, you think you're a monk." Tony walks back to his seat, not believing it's a joke. His face is resigned and reveals his beliefs that another American has lost her sanity over Italy and lives in the fantasy of make-believe after reading too many books. Tony looks at me with seriousness. I already read his thoughts. They vividly dance across his face, telling me the same story as always when an American says something unbelievable.

He gets closer to me, then starts. "*Mamma Mia, Stefania*, where did you find this *Americana*?"

Nino drives the coach in, facing us toward the Abbey of Sant'Antimo, then he backs up and turns the coach in the opposite direction away from the local cemetery that's just down the road—another Sicilian superstition. The clicking of cameras starts, and the Americans join together again in perfect harmony, awe-struck and speechless at the intricately choreographed lines of vineyards that are patchworked in perfectly squared sections next to the medieval monastery.

"What kind of grapes are these?" someone in the back of the coach hollers out, forgetting we've already discussed the grapes.

"Purple grapes," Lizzy shouts, which causes a chorus of Americans to giggle with her.

"We're in the painting that's seen all over the world. The squares of candy-striped vineyards planted in Sangiovese grapevines that cover the hills of Montalcino," Dr. Raybay tells everyone.

Turning around to look behind me, I see Dr. Raybay's hand reaching down the long aisle as if Michelangelo's famous fresco painting of "The Creation" was coming alive and reaching toward me.

"Stephanie, can I talk?" Dr. Raybay's voice spills out from the back of the coach. His flour-white bald legs are thrust forward, jabbing everyone on the left and right side of the aisle. I think a bucking bronco could easily be wedged between them.

"I must tell the people about this area, Montalcino, and why the vineyards grow so beautifully." His voice echoes excitedly behind his waving hands, and his whiskey-brown-eyes declare, 'I can enlighten the Americans with my knowledge.'

"I know about the grapes in this area," Dr. Raybay repeats, as he makes his way to the front of the coach, his face trying to catch up with his stretched arms.

"*Mamma Mia*, what's the matter now?" Tony's eyes balloon, and his arms fly in the air as he leans into the aisle. "Ah, it's you, *Dottore*. You have a number two emergency?"

By now, everyone on the coach has leaned inward with their

fingers released from their cameras. They await the news of Dr. Raybay's emergency.

"I need the microphone." His silk white hands reach toward me again. I turn around and grab the mic, hurriedly extending it out to him before he speeds through the windshield.

"*Mamma Mia, Madonna*, what's the matter with you, *Dottore*? You want to sing?" Tony is confused, not understanding the sudden emergency of the *dottore's* hands speedily bypassing his face. Dr. Raybay raises his arms in the air, and just before speaking, he spins his body in an attempt at a graceful swirl but loses his balance and plunges onto Pat's lap. He's a ballerina gone wild.

Hysterical laughter erupts from Pat as she pushes him back into the aisle. "*Mamma Mia*, doctor," Pat exclaims in her Welsh accent.

"Ah, I love the way you talk so British." Dr. Raybay compliments Pat. Obliviously loving the attention, he takes it a step further. "Are you from Great Britain? Which island?"

"Yes, from Wales. I am Welsh," Pat tells him.

"It's confusing with the names in your country. You know, Great Britain is the name of the island containing England, Scotland, and Wales. And then you have the United Kingdom, which is England, Scotland, Wales and Northern Ireland. And to be more perplexing, there is just England, the part of the island that is nothing but England. It's total confusion for Lizzy. I had to draw a map for her a few years ago when we contemplated going to Ireland, which we never did. She asked if London is in England or the United Kingdom. That's a simple answer, or at least it was for me. Of course, we know it's in the United Kingdom. I can talk all day about your country, the United Kingdom of Great Britain, and its bundle of fabulous places. I assume you like Wales the best?"

"Of course," Pat responds with confusion across her face.

"I know better than to ask the silly question most Americans ask. Is Wales a part of England? Don't you just love that reference: Wales, England?"

"Wales is a country within its own right. We are part of Great

Britain." Pat tells him but is suddenly interrupted by her phone ringing in her black-leather Italian purse.

Dr. Raybay grabs the microphone from my hand and stretches the cord out too far, which makes Nino react instinctively. He immediately reaches out in midair and grabs the cable before it pops out of the socket. It is a big problem for the mic with its delicate connection, and it refuses to stay fastened when an American pulls and tugs on it as though it's a firehose.

"*Mamma Mia, Madonna,*" Tony hollers. He reaches out, too, trying to snatch the cord before it pops him in the head. Luckily, I grab it and place my fingers around its curlicue cord to keep enough slack to prevent it from springing out again.

"Hello, my friends. I'd like to tell you a little secret, a little something about this land and the soil." Dr. Raybay has the microphone glued to his mouth. His lips are suctioned to the round mesh, and it makes me think he's going to eat it like a lollipop.

"I read an article in a travel magazine that the grapes are serenaded all day, seven days a week, by classical music. These grapes, right here." Dr. Raybay shuffles his new leather loafers around on the floor of the coach while pointing his right index finger toward the window. As he does, he accidentally hits Tony's right eyebrow.

"*Mamma Mia, Madonna!*" Tony hollers out again. He tries to dodge the hit to his right eye, then immediately shifts just a smidgen and turns his face to the window, refusing to look my way.

"When will you learn to scoot over and lean closer to the window, away from flying arms?" I tell him, knowing it's just another normal occurrence on the coach—an American's adrenaline exploding and causing bizarre happenings when seeing magical sights through the window. It's the same as an American reading childhood books and seeing them come to life when they travel in Italy, with the pages turning right before their eyes. I look up and see Dr. Raybay proceeding as if nothing had happened, but perhaps motivated by the expression he's caused on Tony's face.

Dr. Raybay continues to talk. He stands in the morning sun,

showcased through the window like a theater stage-lit with flashing lights.

"Are there any more questions about the grapes and the effects of serenading them?"

"Take a breath!" Lizzy, his wife, shouts out, laughing hysterically at Gary's joke coming from the back of the coach. "Gary said he'd have to hire an Italian operetta singer for his grapes since they come from the local grocery store," Lizzy repeats the joke, but can't stop laughing enough to finish it.

Dr. Raybay runs his long fingers through his hair, which sprouts sparsely six inches from his forehead, as he continues to wait for questions from his audience.

"*Mamma Mia, Stefania!* Where do you find these people?" Tony laughs. "Let me guess, he read your book and discovered us."

With an amplified screech through the microphone, Dr. Raybay blows into the mic, alerting Tony he's not finished with the story.

"Yes, it's true," he starts with his voice intensifying through the mic as he disregards the chaotic frenzy of Tony's hands dancing in the air mere inches from him. "The property owner plays music to his grapes, broadcasting loud works of Mozart to the vineyard. It was published in detail about the tests performed on the purple fruit. Look at the rolling vineyard sections before us. The winemaker probably owns these. I imagine he compared the left square of land to the right partition, you know, one with music and the other without. The results were astounding and couldn't be denied. The local people surrounded this area and watched with their own eyes. The vines did, in fact, grow better. It was like gravity was pulling them to the speakers. The luscious fruit grew closer to the music and miraculously grew bigger—the whole plant, its green leaves, everything. They enjoyed the sound of Mozart. However, it wasn't just his music. No, the grapes loved all kinds of music."

Dr. Raybay sucks in air, which gives Tony the opportunity to cut in.

"*Mamma Mia*, this is true, but we already know this information," Tony says, not understanding Dr. Raybay's eagerness to report two-year-old news of Tuscany's happenings in the Brunello di Montalcino area.

Nino understands nothing being said with the loud whooping and hollering of the Americans as he opens the door of the coach for us to get out. We are yards away from the former Benedictine abbey, face to face to its fairy-tale setting with acres of silvery olive groves and purple-kissed vineyards exploding in mesmerizing shades. The rolling waves create the urge to dive deep into its secrets. Where is the crystal ball to tell us its mysteries, and where is Mozart's voice?

Chapter 9

ABBEY OF SANT'ANTIMO

From the coach, it takes us exactly forty-two minutes to walk to the back of the abbey and go inside. If we hadn't stopped for a million photos, we would have arrived at the entrance door within seconds. However, it's impossible to stroll up the long road at a steady pace and go straight in, as there is some type of supernatural force that pulls you aside, especially if you're an American visitor to this area.

We all pause to gawk at the twelfth-century, Romanesque Abbey of Sant'Antimo (home to French monks), and to stand in awe at the rolling vineyards and silvery olive trees, sectioned in perfect squares. It's a picturesque artisan's masterpiece, a painting worthy of a mass supply of Toscana postcards scattered throughout the world, showcased on beautiful coffee table books. I've been coming here nearly every year for over twenty years, and still, I stop and take endless photos, hoping to capture at least one that portrays the beauty. Nonetheless, it's a useless effort. How can a digital camera capture the intense creation of a Toscana grape dangling on its vine, magically perspiring and dotted with tiny speckles of dew?

As we scatter out along the road, I watch the Americans dillydally around with their cameras zooming in and out, trying to focus the lens on the travertine stone. All of them are doing the same thing except for Maria; she takes out a sketch pad from within her bag, and hurriedly draws what's before her. And just like that, I see an artisan's creation, a portrait penciled in charcoal, captured as if taken with the camera hanging about her neck.

Leaning over Maria's shoulder and gawking at her talent, my eyes follow her pencil. "Have you always been an artist?" I ask her, observing her hand as it slides across the paper.

Another American, Cally, bumped into me without apologizing and excitedly shared, "Stephanie, now I understand it all, how fabled children's storybooks were imagined and written here in a land with visual abundance bursting for the imagination. Where is Little Red Riding Hood with her basket of goodies? And what was the village we just passed on the hilltop? Was it Montalcino? I can truly visualize the swirl of a magical wand, the fairy godmother bringing this area into existence, and the fairy dust sprinkled from above the clouds, landing on every little tree, flower, and vine."

"Look to your right and see more of this dream," I tell Cally, as I observe six nuns strolling toward the back entrance, all of them speaking Italian and chattering a chorus of anticipating the preparation of tonight's dinner. I watch their large crucifixes dangle about their necks, oscillating as though a gentle breeze is blowing against them. And below the hem of their long, black garments, the leather-strapped sandals awaken the dirt, creating powdery dust clouds as though a fog is rising from within the earth. Mass will begin shortly, I quickly realize, seeing the sisters flock to the back of the abbey.

Close by, I notice Dr. Raybay fidgeting with two different cameras, one dangling about his neck and the other held in his hand. He's an octopus, maneuvering both of them. He holds one in the air, never looking into its viewfinder but repeatedly clicking the button. Afterward, he looks through the lens, pressing his eye against the tiny opening. Obviously, the photos aren't good enough, and an urgent retake happens.

I observe his comical behavior, watching him lift the camera again, stretching the connected apparatus of some sort, perhaps a bungee cord, to its maximum length. Seconds later, he becomes a juggler, manipulating both of them, clicking buttons as if on a timer. He finally releases one and aggressively grabs the other. The camera plunges downward on its elastic string, bouncing back and forth until it finally exhausts itself.

The performance of a juggler is captivating, quite impressive for a man with only two arms. He's a never-ending show, continually working back and forth with the two, all in an attempt to capture the magnificence of the twelfth-century abbey as though it will vanish.

"*Andiamo*, let's go," I say, feeling dizzy from the performance of cameras. "We'd better get inside, or we'll miss the monks."

"Not me. I'm with you, Stephanie," Dr. Raybay hurriedly tosses his camera within his backpack, leaving the Canon dangling about his neck.

The Americans shuffle around, some taking photos as they track behind my heels like curious sheep following their shepherd, trailing along to the back entrance of the abbey.

Karen, in her early forties, is tall and somewhat thin, shaped like a bottle of vanilla flavoring from my mother's kitchen cabinet; her golden-brown coloring accentuates the quarter-sized diamond strapped about her elongated neck. Her expensive, tight red polyester skirt does her no favors with the gawking eyes of the local nuns. Her blonde hair is shiny and thick, balancing haphazardly above thick eyebrows. When I watch her step ahead of me, I look upwards and see a perfect Hollywood hairstyle.

Arriving at the back of the abbey where the gigantic wooden doors are the only public entrance, the excitement builds when seeing them ajar, leading into a world so unbelievably foreign to American eyes. Karen goes first, stepping into one of the most beautiful architectural treasures from the Roman era, the Abbey of Sant'Antimo, a monastery that's been occupied by a brotherhood of monks since the eighth century—save a few years of desertion.

Dr. Raybay nudges forward; his chocolate-scented breath commingles with the smoky frankincense drifting through the air.

"Stephanie, I can't believe what I'm seeing. This takes me back to the biblical days not long after God spoke the words into existence, "'Let there be light,'" Dr. Raybay tells me as he pushes in closer, forcing me to scoot forward and bump into Karen's back. She takes one step forward and stops again. Her feet are refusing to budge, causing a major pile-up behind me, the Americans bumping into each other like a bad collision on Interstate 20.

"Let's sit down for a moment, up there," I direct, pointing toward the front row of timeworn pews inside the Abbey of Sant'Antimo, trying to move her onward, but it doesn't work. My face presses into her back.

"Where are the artistic hands of my favorite Italian sculptor, painter, architect, and poet of the great Renaissance era, Michelangelo? Where is the painted ceiling in all of its majestic glory?" Karen makes the sign of the cross upon her chest before genuflecting.

Her question echoes throughout the massive space before us, as more of the Americans walk in, surely wondering what's ahead. She was expecting the grandiose effects of Bernini and Leonardo, a few bronze statutes towering high with many Carrara marble statues sculptured into giant angels fluttering here and there with wings extended.

"There are no frescoes inside here," I explain in a whisper, my neck stretching upwards to the back of her ear. Karen continues to stand in front of me, blocking everyone from going further. Her hand clutches a huge purse with the Prada label visible for all to see.

"It's a shame you brought us all the way out here to see nothing of the great artists," Karen declares with a twirl of her hand, nonchalantly swinging white leather over her shoulder and creating a wave of aromatic therapy all around. The scent of costly perfume wafts up my nostrils.

"My church is beautiful. It drips with Catholic charm," she tells me, finally stepping down to the last step, looking up and down, scanning her surroundings with the eyes of a detective.

"Where's the Madonna?" Karen asks, twisting her neck to the left as she steps forward once again, nearly allowing Dr. Raybay to zoom around, but he doesn't. He stands in quicksand as well, his eyes refusing to move from the ceiling.

"Look to your right. The Madonna is over there," I tell her, pointing to the ancient statue encased in glass protection with blazing candles illuminating the face of Mary, the mother of Jesus.

"Two months ago, I started going to the Catholic church with a friend. My mother, being a Protestant, highly objected. Mom said she sees no need for so many rituals. It doesn't matter, though. I'm not going back," Karen announces to the entire population of Tuscany, her voice ping-ponging as though a microphone was lodged within her throat.

"It's all brand new to me. You know, being Catholic. I've visited the beautiful church, Sacred Heart, twice. And I had my photo taken with the crushed velvet thrones—the ornate chairs. The colors are fabulous: dark cranberry with shards of antique gold shimmering through the expensive threads. I'd say the interior decor is from Europe, probably right here in Italy," Karen tells me, still blocking everyone from going forward.

"Ah, I love the beauty within the Catholic churches and the godly reverence when entering, you know, the holiness and respect for our Lord and Savior, Jesus Christ, and the Madonna, the mother of Jesus, not to mention all of the saints, and—" I try to continue, but Karen cuts me off before the last word rolls from my tongue.

"Did you know that my degree is in interior design? And I'm starting up my business again, hoping to get the contract for the renovations and the new addition being erected as we speak at Sacred Heart."

"I had no idea you were a decorator," I whisper, seeing no need to have this conversation at the moment.

"Oh, yes. It was just days before we departed that I tossed in my credentials to Alice, my new Catholic friend. We met at the art benefit gala. She was donating her latest creations, bright splashes of paint slapped on tiny square canvases. She's not a professional artist, but says she finally found her passion in life, recreating the view from her patio chair: a backyard full of foliage, mostly oak trees with a few squirrels peeking out from within leafy branches. She even paints turtles, their eyes big and wide, abstracted with other creatures lurking about her yard. Well, that's what I see when looking at her art. There are no distinct objects of a tree or animal."

"There are no abstract paintings within here," I tell Karen, my head suddenly feeling lightheaded and dizzy. It's mental exhaustion taking over from swimming within her long explanation of art. "You do understand that this abbey is hundreds of years old?"

"Yes, of course, I do, but..."

"Ah, I understand. You're an interior designer and lover of ornateness, loving the visual décor of the Catholic churches," I whisper, rubbing my forehead while trying to step forward.

Karen doesn't budge. She stands in the same spot, her heels parked on the ageless stones. I peek around her back, focusing on the vacant bench up toward the front right side.

"I like the rules of being Catholic. It's much easier than a Protestant. I do what I want with no guilt looming over my head. However, it doesn't stop my mother's voice coming through my ears nor her endless phone calls. Nonetheless, it's so easy now—do as you please and then go to confession. It's that simple. You get to start all over with a clean slate. It's the only way to go; no capitulation of guilt, no surrender of terms, no more falling from grace to damnation."

"No, that's not how it works," I tell her with the other Americans hovering over my shoulder.

We're at a standstill, inches from the front entrance door. "You've missed the whole understanding of the Catholic faith, the Bible, the —" My words are cut off again.

"Yes, that's how it works for me now and Maria, I mean Dr. Ganzaloon. She goes to the Sacred Heart church too. She's the one who told me about the beautiful, ornate chairs. Of course, I had to see it for myself: the red velvet décor, the golden candlesticks, the marble, the bronze, the encased relics from afar, and the smoky plumes creating a scene straight out of a mythical movie. I loved it all." Karen steps forward, finally allowing me to take the lead.

"We'll talk later, Karen. You're misunderstanding the Catholic doctrine and the Bible. This is alarming to think you can do anything you want and simply confess to a man, and it wipes the slate clean, then afterward, you do it again, just like that!" I objected, Bible scriptures bombarding my mind, knowing she has no idea about the Catholic faith.

"Follow me," I motion my hand in the air, waving them on to hurriedly get to the front bench. "We'll stay long enough to hear the monks chant the Gregorian praise, or however long you want," I whisper to the Americans who are inches from my heels, gawking up and down with dilating eyes, anticipating the monks to appear in their long, white-hooded robes at any second.

Stretching my neck in all directions, I see the local faithful sprinkled around. They're settled in the old wooden benches, seated in holy reverence with eyes protruding toward us. It's not unusual for them to gawk at me with the innocent Americans by my side every year. Who could blame them for their lingering memories of that haunting episode I created here several years ago? It was quite the show, all because of the round wafer extended to me during Mass.

How was I to know the sacramental bread (the host, the Eucharist, whichever word one prefers to call it) goes into my hands with both palms joined together? I recall the whole ordeal vividly. I was eagerly extending my tongue out as far as it would go, waiting for the monk to place the sacrament onto it. The last time I took the Lord's Supper in Italy, the priest placed the round waver within my mouth.

I replay the embarrassing episode within my mind as I turn my head to the left, flashing a slight smile to the local congregation while pretending to be someone else, not Stephanie Chance, the tour guide that disrupted the Holy Mass service several years ago, right here in this monastery nestled in the rolling hills of Tuscany.

Strolling toward the front of the ancient monastery, the loud echoes of slapping shoes resonate throughout the timeworn flagstones, prompting me to tip-toe as though I were a ballerina. On each side of the pews are round travertine and onyx pillars with lions and patriarch saints chiseled within the stone. *Surely, angels are flying above us*, I think to myself, looking up at the endless sky-of-a-ceiling while imaging Samson, the strong Israelite in the Bible, pulling down two huge pillars that supported King Solomon's temple.

From our seats, brilliant shimmers of Toscana sunlight peek through the old wooden doors as they creak open. From the corner of my eye, I see Dr. Raybay lean forward, squeezing his hands together and bouncing his feet up and down. Reaching over, I whisper, "It's the monks."

"My insides are shaking; I'm going to faint," Dr. Raybay mumbles, gripping his pencil-thin legs, holding them down from the Macarena dance they're now performing.

"Take a deep breath. Stay calm, Doc," I reassure him. The monks would come inside any second.

Suddenly, the silence is broken with a loud commotion coming from the side door. We watch as six white-hooded monks walk inside in a single file, moving in a slow, somber pace as their white robes brush the timeworn floors. I feel my heart beating as I watch the monks bow their heads in perfect choreography as their shrouded legs bend in a swift curtsy, while simultaneously crossing themselves in front of the huge cross dangling up above. It's a holy moment, and it's just beginning as they proceed to the old wooden rostrums, one on each side of the aisle, and face each other.

Seated on the ancient bench's edge, I watch one of the monks standing behind the centuries-old wooden rostrum, nonchalantly reach inside the dark opening and grab a songbook. The silence is broken again as his leather-strapped sandals shuffle side to side as he nervously ruffles the pages in the timeworn book. Within seconds, the monks start the soft chanting that echoes throughout the ancient stone abbey. Spellbound, I feel as though I've been transported back to the biblical days. A rush of angels' wings brushes over my soul, taking me back to the days of long ago. My pulse detonates around the two hundred and fifty mark—if that's possible—when the tall, slim, white-hooded robed monk swings two brass pots of frankincense back and forth, filling the church with smoky plumes.

I'm lost within the angelic atmosphere, thinking of the many adversities this monastery has endured, and the countless times I've been on this bench.

It all quickly fades as Louise burps out a loud choking sound that ricochets throughout the echoing interior. The abrupt jolt collides with the mystical hymns floating around and quickly drowns out any chance of hearing the Gregorian chants. And just when I think its ending is near, I soon find out it's not. Her persistent cough intensifies, sounding as though a wrestling match is within her throat. I quickly jerk my head, stretching my body across Barbara, who is a first-time traveler with us. She stares helplessly with eyes bulging.

"She's strangling on fifty pounds of chicken bones?" Barbara whispers, drawing both hands over her ears to muffle the resonating effects of Louise's coughs, which reverberate through the wooden rafters and ricocheting back down into our eardrums.

The annoying disruption brings the local congregation to military alertness. It's a domino effect; others seated behind us join in with harmonizing echoes of coughing and sneezing. They twist and turn, shifting their bodies in the old, rickety benches. I attempt to distract the squeezing within my chest, the tickling sensation playing inside my throat, by leaning forward and concentrating on the monks. With little space between the rows, my nose edges on the back shoulder of a local *signora* who is seated inches in front of me. I strain to hear the chants through the hacking coughs and parade of trumpets blowing.

Do not cough, I tell myself, which backfires, causing the rippling urge to do so. And just like that, panic hits me, and I join the others in the procession of an embarrassing spectacle.

This can't be happening, I think, urgently searching for a solution to stop this compulsion. Is there a throat lozenge in my bag? But no, there are none. I tilt my head upwards and stare above, imagining feathery angels flying around in their heavenly bodies. The vision only lasts for seconds as the rippling urge of combustion races from my chest up, forcing its way through my throat. I shift around on the bench, sweat making its way to my face. I try to concentrate on the fading chants from the monks, but it's useless. I urgently cough, sputter, and rumble, trying my best to stop the tickling feathers lodged within my throat, which are torturing me to near explosion.

"Cough drop?" Rosie offers, leaning forward and stretching her freckled arm across the laps of Janie and Mary, trying to reach me on the other end. Her face is smeared with irritation as she silently expresses, "I'm not missing out on this once-in-a-lifetime experience. Please, allow me to hear the monks."

Within five minutes, her loud voice amplifies down the row, slapping me hard in the face, declaring, "For the love of God, take another lozenge, please!" She tosses a carton of lemony capsules toward me. Luckily, my left hand stretches out in a quick reflex, catching the little box before it flies through the musky plumes of frankincense.

No sooner than plopping the little round drop into my mouth, Rosie twists her large hips around from the left edge of the narrow prayer bench, allowing her weight to release from her end for a split-second. The bench becomes a see-saw gone wild; we bounce off, plummeting forward, smacking into the backs of the local congregation like flying arrows.

It all happens quickly as the long prayer bench slaps the stone floor hard. Struggling to get back up because my knees are jammed between the narrow boards below, my eyes remain downward, never looking up toward the monks for fear they will recognize me, which they do—surely, they do. My legs are jelly, refusing to cooperate. One of them had fallen asleep minutes ago and still refuses to awaken. Rubbing and kicking them both, I look about to my left and then to the right. The Americans have seen a ghost. Their faces are pasty white like cotton balls, and their eyes protrude outward, peering through the thick smoke of frankincense plumes.

My eyes strain as the atmosphere begins to thicken with the musty scents of frankincense. My nose tickles with the infused air streaming up my nostrils. Most of the Americans have never experienced a medieval abbey such as this, except for those who have returned with me. And now, without a doubt, they'll never forget this experience or this day.

The chanting abruptly stops. The monks return their songbooks to the wooden rostrum and robotically step down from the two facing platforms. Knowing they will be walking within feet from us to depart through the nearby door, I melt downward and pretend to search for something, which prompts Barbara to do the same as her southern etiquette kicks in. After milling around with our face to the stones, we rise up with empty hands and see the monks before us.

"What did you lose?" Barbara whispers, her mouth to my ear.

"Nothing," I say, seeing the monks before me, their eyes shooting darts. Again, I pretend to be veiled as Casper the Friendly Ghost, dropping my head downward. This is the awkward moment where I wish to be a tiny ant crawling around on the cold stones, but the sharp punch from Barbara's elbow quickly reminds me I'm not.

"Why are they staring at us, Stephanie?" Barbara's voice resonates within my ear. The heat of her breath intensifies the embarrassment that's hovering all around. My eyes become motion detectors, zigzagging, and scanning everything in sight—nervous energy.

"Why are they gawking?" Barbara tries again, asking the same question as before. My eyes land on the monks' toes, which protrude underneath their long robes.

"They know me," I whisper, still pretending to be invisible while my eyeballs move like pinballs in a slot machine.

"I think we've disrupted their ceremony. I mean, well, you know, not a ceremony, but their..." Barbara can't find the words. She's tongue-tied, discombobulated.

The musical tap dance of feet creates an echoing effect as the monks' leather-strapped sandals slap the ancient stones. We watch as they stroll out before us, and the ageless ritual proceeds. They bow their heads, curtsy under the cross, and hurriedly exit through the medieval side door. And just like that, the curtain is closed, the show is over, and the holiness of peace has returned with a cloud of heavenly hosts floating above.

My eyes flash upward, gazing toward the wooden rafters that are miles away. The abbey is still thick with smoky plumes suspended high above. Looking up, almost in a daze, I see enough airspace to accommodate hot air balloons. My eyes gaze to the ceiling, all the way up to the wooden rafters.

Seconds later, looking downward and then around through the haze of thick fog, I see the local congregation with heads bowed. The fluttering of angels' wings is all around, and suddenly I visualize heaven's gates opening up and see our loved ones in the clouds of glory awaiting our return. But the heavenly thoughts abruptly stop as Rosie shifts her oversized hips on the old bench again.

I felt an invisible slap upon my face as panic hits me hard. Without thought, I stretch forward, grabbing the back shoulder of a local faithful who is seated in front of me. We're going to plunge off as we did before—another see-saw ride gone wild. I hold tightly to the pink dress fitted snuggly around the *signora*'s tugboat body. I try to balance my buttocks on the narrow bench, and my fingers grip the fabric around the back neck of the *signora*. Unknowingly, with the weight of my body springing backward, I pull hard on the thin material, causing a makeshift choke collar. The screech is loud as the *signora*'s hands fly over her head. One would surely think she had a pull string on her back as her legs stretch out and then drop downward, repeating the same gymnastics, over and over. And without warning, another quick pull of the invisible string causes both legs to fly higher in the air, kicking wildly.

Seconds later, I realize the bench is still grounded and release my fists full of fabric. Slowly, I ease back into the old rickety bench, my spine straight as a new pencil. A sigh of relief gushes over me as I look around and see the other Americans seated next to me with eyes protruding outward.

"Pull yourself together," I whisper to the Americans, knowing it's time to go. Once again, I think of myself as invisible, tuning out the surrounding audience of glaring eyes.

I lean over, looking toward Dr. Raybay. His expression shows a wave of claustrophobia, or perhaps, a severe case of muscle distress. His face is sweating profusely, covering his upper lip as his pulse visibly pounds in his neck.

"It's time to go," I tell him, his eyes fixated to the right, suctioned to the last monk going out the side door.

Janice places her hand on Dr. Raybay's leg, squeezing it tightly, forgetting he's not her husband. "Can you believe we've experienced an ancient ritual of chants?" Janice asks as the door slams shut.

Now that the monks have disappeared out the door, Dr. Raybay puts etiquette aside and bursts into tears. Janice grabs her purse and pulls out a wad of tissues.

"Are you serious? Get ahold of yourself," Lizzy thunders, her voice ping-ponging throughout the abbey.

"I'm sorry, honey," Dr. Raybay whispers a heartfelt apology to his wife in between snorts and sporadic breaths.

"What will happen next?" Janice wonders.

"I don't know." Dr. Raybay sniffles out with a slight smile as he blows his nose. He attempts to say more.

"What did you say?" Lizzy interjects. Her face flashes red as her husband grows louder for some unknown reason, sobbing in a hiccupping kind of way with tears trickling down his chin. "This is supposed to be the happiest time in your life, seeing the monks." Lizzy takes his hand, caressing it.

"This is the happiest time of my life, but my emotions have swallowed me." He dries his tears with the wet tissue now crumpled into a tiny ball within his hand and leans in to kiss Lizzy's cheek.

Lizzy's eyes widen as her husband's lips go from her cheek to her neck, then leans his head on her shoulder like a cooked noodle, desiring to be caressed.

"I'm sure the local flock of faithful will appreciate our leaving the abbey in peace as it was before we entered," I lean over, telling everyone on the bench, suggesting we get up and go before creating a bigger scene than before.

Dr. Raybay's body is now experiencing gentle shakes of emotions.

With my suggestion of leaving the bench, wide-eyed and seeming to be scared to move out of fear that we'll see-saw off again, Janice starts, "I don't know how we'll manage to get up together without another flip off the bench routine."

She nervously laughs out loud, tapping her shoes on the stone floor, pretending to rev up her feet for a take-off.

Shuffling my shoes on the travertine stone, too, I breathe in hundreds of years of medieval history, the blood-shed during the countless wars, the crusaders march here long ago, the years of abandonment, through feast and famine, and now, days of worship with us, the Americans, absorbing this storybook setting. Turning my neck around to follow the leader of the faithful, I wait for the first American to rise from the bench, taking precaution to balance the weight as we attempt to ease up together.

To our surprise, two of the monks come back into the abbey, strolling toward the left side of the cross dangling from the ceiling. We watch as they take white papers from the wooden lectern and slowly turn around.

Softly, drawing the crucifix across their chest while moving their lips in a soft prayer, they shuffle out again. Our emotions intensify, causing many to sigh in medieval holiness.

Afterward, we slowly walk out, trailing behind the congregation. Most of my group stop and look back one last time before stepping up on the oversized step. I gaze upward again, my eyes landing on the second gigantic column on the right side depicting Daniel in the lion's den. How many times have I've studied this scene carved within the stone? My eyes glance to the next one and then to the others. Here I go again, studying the capitals atop the huge pillars, the sculpting of stone, alabaster, and travertine, symbolizing much from the Bible. And from its history, we know that one of the capitals was placed in a certain position to receive brilliant illumination of the sunlight peeking through during springtime, to showcase its artistry.

We push the gigantic, antiquated wood-carved doors and burst out into the afternoon sunlight that shimmers like a fine-cut diamond. I am drenched with emotions when one of the monks, Fra Domentico, strolls toward me, extending his hand with a small cross clasped within.

"*Mamma Mia, Stefania.* It's you again. I knew you'd be back with the *Americani*, disrupting our peace and awaking the spirits within these walls. What is it when you're stepping on these stones? You arrive with such chaotic play. *Mamma Mia, Stefania,* you started here many years ago. We remember you well. There is only one time you bring us harmony. No, never mind. I remember you stumbled and knocked over the candles, almost crashing into Sister Maria Anna Rosa. God bless her soul."

"I regret my timing, disrupting the chants and—" I look down to the ground, shuffling my shoes around on the grass. "I mean—" The words leave me again. My mind races as I try to remember which eruptions were the worst. There were many.

"You must take this crucifix and keep it near you, always. We have prayed for God's mercy upon your soul and the friends you bring to us. You are not lucky with the spirits herein. Ah, I want to say more, you must understand, *Stefania.* What is this urgency you possess within your soul? I see your heart. You bring to us nice people, desiring to ignite their souls to the heavenly realm. But, *Stefania,* you are rambunctious. You awaken paradise. You are a storm before the calm."

"I don't mean to cause such disruptions. It's freak accidents; I can't explain why. The bench flipping up in the air, plunging us forward, I had no idea it would cause such chaos. It's never happened before."

I chatter on, rambling down rabbit holes, wishing there was one to jump into, and knowing he doesn't understand me fully.

"*Mamma Mia,* you need the Madonna with you every day, and certainly the protecting angels upon your head. Why must you pursue with speed, accelerated, a torrential rainstorm? I see within you, your love for the church. But you are soaked with abundance, enough to last throughout eternity. Your guardian angel must tire, exhausted from his daily duty, catching the aftershocks of your feet and your hands, adventuring here and there with the *Americani.*"

I listen, trying to understand his words of wisdom as he dissects my soul. My face loses all color. He places a tiny crucifix into my hand, folding my fingers over it. Then he walks away, his head down as if looking for a lost item. Suddenly, he spins around and scrutinizes me again as his lips move in prayer while drawing the sign of the cross upon his chest.

The cameras start again as we inhale the fresh fragrance of Toscana air in huge swallows, replenishing our lungs with the circulation of grape marmalade evaporating from the bursting vines a few feet away. And with the turn of my nose, I smell the mesmerizing aroma of sweet jasmine, oleanders, wisteria, roses, and the showiest of all, bougainvillea, all in one gigantic bundle. As the wind gently blows, filling the atmosphere with tantalizing scents, we relish the view some more, feeling and smelling the real Tuscany, a medieval storybook from long ago.

"How old are the trees?" Paul, from New Mexico, inquires, his eye glued to the lens of his camera.

"The olive trees are twisted into hundreds of years of history. They're old; older than old," I tell him, remembering the historian priest saying these exact words in Italian.

The only thing separating us from the monks' residence is the abbey and a wired fence. Standing here looking out over this man-made separation, I feel the urge to climb over and get closer to their world of separation, but I don't.

Close by, the purply lavender flanking the abbey causes me to inhale the air more deeply. I recall that one of the monks is from France, and he planted the lavender to remind himself of his homeland. The backdrop to this fairy-tale setting is the hilltop village of Montalcino, home to the famous Brunello di Montalcino wine and its baby brother, Rosso di Montalcino.

Minutes later, we stroll down the long dirt path that leads to our coach, where Tony and Nino wait patiently for us. The walk from the backdoor of the monastery to the coach is breathtaking. It's magnificently created by the hands of man, save the rolling hills made by the Creator. It was just an hour ago that we walked this path while taking too many photos of the vibrant land rolling up and down like luscious green carpet. It's truly a masterpiece painting, except there are no paint strokes touching the canvas, only the hands of the local farmers.

We make our way back to the coach with a few lingering behind and walking at their own speed. I pass Dr. Raybay.

"Just a few more photos," Dr. Raybay hollers as he starts the juggling act once again.

"Take your time. There's no hurry and enjoy yourself," I answer, continuing onwards to the coach.

"Oh, Stephanie, I'd like to tell you something."

"Sure!"

Dr. Raybay puts his arm around my shoulder and allows his camera to dangle about his neck. "Thank you for this experience, Stephanie. I'm so grateful to you. Just minutes ago, I wanted to take a risk with my life. I wanted to change everything, even my medical practice."

"What's wrong with your life?" I had to hear his version since I'd already heard Lizzy's side.

"Everything, so I thought. But something happened to me inside the monastery. God spoke to me. I had an epiphany."

"God works in mysterious ways. He speaks to us when we least expect it. I've shared my life with you before on previous occasions— me taking risks while holding on tightly to God's promises and His hand. Who leaves a life career as a paralegal for something completely opposite as I did? What is wrong with taking a risk?" I encourage him further.

"It happened to me as I turned to walk away from the bench. I was following you, but before I walked out, I looked back to see the huge cross hanging in the air. My eyes caught the smoky plumes floating in the air, and for some strange reason, I was unable to escape the trance of bright lights streaming through the window as they flashed and sparkled. I just stood there, not walking out with Lizzy or any of you. I tried to snap out of it and walk closer to the door. I did take a few steps, but then I stopped and turned back again and stared at the cross and the cloud of smoke from the frankincense that refused to dissipate into the air. I felt a divine presence —the Holy Spirit tugging at my heart. Without a doubt, it was supernatural. There was no audible voice. I think most of the congregation trailed out with you, so it didn't come from any of them."

"Wow! What happened next?" I watch Dr. Raybay's eyes swell and fill with tears.

"I heard the whisper of God. I heard Him say to my spirit to keep doing what He'd called me to do. To stay diligent with the people He's given me. To never look to the left or the right but to keep going forward with those He sends through my doors. Stephanie, I missed the calling upon my life until just now, only minutes ago. The voice I just heard within my soul was the Holy Spirit. God, Himself. He has never left me. I am the one who left Him long ago, trying to do my own thing within my head with my obsession with monks and thinking I needed to be locked away to do the will of God. But I've been doing His will all of this time. I just didn't realize it until now."

"Thank you, Lord! Hallelujah!" I clap my hands together and give Dr. Raybay a huge hug.

Chapter 10

MAMMA MIA, WHERE'S THE TOILET?

*T*ony's voice pulls me back toward the coach. "*Stefania*, where are the other Americans? Are they still in the monastery?" he asks, scanning the long trail-of-a-road leading to the back of the abbey.

"They were going to the toilet," Louise blurts out, snapping her camera repeatedly.

"Stephanie, where are the restrooms? I never saw any signs. I should have gone with them," Mary roars out in her Tennessee drawl. She has the stature of a porcelain model, identical to the beautiful Dolly Parton, save the blonde wig. Mary's hair is strawberry red with a few highlights of blonde.

"I could have gone to the toilet too but didn't think about it until now," Lizzy swigged her water from the plastic bottle clutched in her hand.

"The toilets are behind the monastery, but you have to stroll down the long path of olive trees," I tell her, reaching into the cooler, bringing out a bottle of water and then remembering months ago they were thinking of moving the restrooms down the road by the shop that sells olive oil and local marmalades.

"Do you ever see any tourist here? It's hidden away from the world. How did you find this place?" Lizzy opens her second oatmeal protein bar of the day.

"Who lives here?" Ann chimes in. I forget Lizzy's questions.

"The monks live here," I tell her, seeing moving objects in the far distance like heads on a stick, bobbing up and down in the vineyards. I remove my sunglasses to get a better view. Seconds later, I see folks running toward us.

"Look at the people in the vineyards. They're running! Who are they? It was just the locals and us in the abbey," I ask aloud, not to anyone in particular, knowing it can't be our people because they will be coming from the back of the abbey.

"It's probably the locals coming from the village of Montalcino," I continue. "You know, up there on top of the hilltop. Do you remember me explaining the vines in this area? I went into great detail about Tony's favorite *vino*, the prestigious big brother, Brunello. It is one of the treasured highlights of the Val d'Orcia," I tell them again, knowing they probably forgot the details.

As the minutes pass, I see Susan dipping up and down like a jack-in-the-box as she runs through rows of purply grapes and silvery olive trees, her arm clutching a camera. Just behind her are more of the Americans coming toward us like a herd of bouncing balls and bobbing heads within the valley of hills.

"*Mamma Mia, Stefania!* What is this running through the vines? Is this our people?" Tony shouts, now stepping out of the coach to get a better look at the cluster of heads bouncing up and down in the thick patch of green leaves. My mouth drops, finding no words to say.

Susan, along with the other Americans, gallops toward the coach as though fiery darts are at her heels. All of them arrive simultaneously with the dinging of bells from the monastery. It's probably my imagination, but I can almost hear hearts beating while witnessing their lungs play like an accordion, squeezing open and shut, concurrently with the musical notes of snorting and grunting as the Toscana air zips in and out of their flapping nostrils. And Joe's hair is springing out from underneath his crooked Pittsburg Steelers cap, so thick and curly, deeply rooted as though stitched of red yarn, his face sprinkled with sweat. He tries to speak, but nothing comes out, only skidding vowels. They are a frazzled sight.

"*Mamma Mia!* What's the matter with you? Have you seen the not-so-friendly ghost?" Tony asked, reaching for a single olive leaf attached to a long twisted branch extending from Susan's highlighted hair.

"What in the world is going on?" I join in, pulling two leaves from Susan's high-rise neckline hair-do of thick brownish strands, exploding with colorful shades of deep burgundy brown, whisky gold, and a hint of cherry-chocolate liqueur, all shooting out from within her head, reminding me of hot volcanic ash erupting from Mount Etna as the sun pierces downward, showcasing its salon made beauty.

Bent over and gasping for air, her nostrils flaring like a squeezed accordion, Susan blurts out discombobulated sentences that have something to do with the monks running behind their heels, hollering and screaming in an unknown tongue. Gaining her composure, Janice interrupts Susan, blurting in skipping words, "We climbed over the wire fence in search of the toilets. We were in desperate need of the bathroom, having to cross our legs and practically perform the ballerina dance all the way to the door of the abbey. Too many espressos this morning—then the water," Janice rattles on, one hand over her chest, the other one squeezing the empty plastic bottle of Italian aqua.

"Susan led the way, encouraging us, leading us within a world of mystery and simplicity inside the monks' house. She said the toilets are inside. They must be—where else would they be?" Janice's eyes widen as Nino takes the empty water bottle from her hand, tossing it into the little trash bag.

"After going inside from room to room, we found the bathroom, but where was the toilet paper? We rummaged around, searching, looking, opening doors, but where could it be? We were mesmerized by the medieval surroundings. The stone floors, the crucifix, and the old Madonna, all welcoming us inside, and the aroma of freshly-baked bread drifted throughout—an invitation to come and eat. But, of course, we didn't," Janice is a news reporter, telling us important details.

Standing next to Janice, Susan pushes dark-shaded glasses upward on her long nose, reminding me of a penguin.

"Oh, Stephanie, you won't believe what happened to us!" Susan can't contain herself any longer, spilling out sentences that overtake Janice's low voice. We ease inward, waiting for the vault of cringe-worthy information to open.

"We lifted the sheets on the minuscule beds to see what the mattresses were made of, wondering if they were the same as the beds stuffed with straw as they are in Certosa Monastery. Ah, Stephanie, do you remember taking us to the Certosa on the hilltop in the south of Florence?"

"Yes, yes! We've been there countless times, but please, tell us what happened to you."

Tony throws up his hands and starts, "*Mamma Mia,* what happened? Can you tell us what happened? You say you look for straw in the mattress? This is too much for me, *Stefania.* Where do you find these people you bring to me? And Susan and Janice—they come with us many times!"

Surprisingly, out of nowhere, a gentle breeze floated through the Toscana stillness, ending Tony's sentence with an exclamation point. He covered his neck with his hands, blocking off the *colpo d'aria,* or the blow of the air that will surely put in him the hospital—another Sicilian superstition.

"Give me a minute," Susan tells Tony, her face stretched to a surprised expression. "Do you remember when you lifted the sheets in the monk's bedroom and showed us the hay for the mattress last year? I will never forget the tiny rooms, the little cells they slept in. I wanted to see if these monks' beds are the same. Just being curious."

"I panicked," Janice blurts, cutting in.

"Good grief, Janice! When you screamed, it scared all of us. What else could we do but run?" exclaims Susan.

"Yes, but what about the beds you just inspected?" I try to get her back on track.

"Oh my, out of nowhere, while we were rummaging the beds and cabinets, the monks walked in! Just like that. We got caught in the act."

Susan drops to the ground, bending her legs in a fast squat as she continues to talk. We watch her toss away the disposable camera inside the shoulder bag as her other hand pokes and prods within the lemony-yellow leather.

"Looking for something?" I ask, bending over her shoulder to hear the rest of the story, while swinging my head back and forth, trying to see if the monks are in hot pursuit. I see nothing of them, only the vineyards.

"The postcards of the monks are inside; I don't want them creased. I grabbed a few of them inside the abbey. They were free, just a little metal box beside them for donations," she tells us, sweat slowly trickling from her face.

Underneath her flat-bottom shoes, loose gravel shuffles as she fretfully pulls at the thin strap across her sandal. We watch her draw a plastic bottle from her shoulder bag, twisting the lid off the top. The cool flow of water drains down her throat. And just like that, Susan awkwardly springs back up—a jack-in-the-box and Chatty Cathy, all in one.

"We screamed, all of us. The monks did too. I think they hollered louder than we did, pontificating and swearing. God only knows what they were saying, but it was loud. Oh yes, really loud. And out of fright, I tossed the toilet paper into the air. You see, she found the toilet paper in a cabinet and preceded back to the bathroom when all of a sudden, the monks engulfed us with panicky voices. Frantically, we scared each other, scattering and running throughout their house. And Harriett sprang from the mattress, which she was testing out how comfortable the straw was."

"*Mamma Mia!* We are finished here, *Stefania. Si, si,* yes, *finito,*" Tony's eyes are electronic, malfunctioning, dilating in and out faster than I can blink my eyes.

"Their mattresses were stuffed with straw, too!" Susan shouts with excitement. Well, I can't say for sure it was straw. I didn't get a good look, but it felt like it. I didn't have time to pull the covers up."

Susan finally exhales, sweat trickling from her contorted face, a locomotive, chugging along, steam puffing and snorting from its engine.

Looking to my left, I see Becky clutching a large bouquet of wild Toscana flowers, choking the life from them.

"When did you have time to pick flowers?" I asked, admiring the beauty of the colorful bunch dangling upside down within her hand.

Becky clapped her hands together, dropping the bundle of flowers as though hot potatoes had landed within. Her face froze like a Halloween cat, electrified into high voltage.

"Oh, no! I'm going straight to hell. I stole the flowers. I didn't mean to take them. They were resting on the bed at the end corner of the mattress. I guess they were a surprise for whoever sleeps there, or else they were going to place them in water. Oh, this is terrible. I picked them up to look underneath the covers, and that's when the monks arrived and scared us to death. I darted straight past them, never looking back."

"*Mamma Mia, Madonna!*" Tony looks at Nino. Their eyes convey the thoughts flashing within their heads.

"I guess you'd say she's a full-service florist delivery," David jokes with a wink in his strong Texas accent, hurriedly bending down and gathering the flowers like lost coins on the street.

"I really didn't mean to take the flowers and their—"

"*Mamma Mia*, what else did you take?" Tony asks, throwing his hands in the air and spinning around.

"You could've thrown them on the floor, on your way out," David interjects again, a smile stretched across his face. "Gosh dang, this is truly an adventure with no itinerary at all." He taps his shoe on the pavement, antagonizing Becky more. He appears to be enjoying the show.

"Yes, you're right, but I didn't." Becky puts her hands around her head as though a headache were happening. Seconds later, she unsnaps her beige leather purse and fishes out a little wooden cross.

"Don't say anything. I grabbed this too. It was in the church, not the house. But, I think the little cross was free for the taking. It was near the books and memorabilia. It's just a souvenir, something to remember this special place."

"That's not true, Becky," Janice grabs the cross and inspects it with magnifying eyes. "I didn't see anything free in the monastery," Janice tells her, looking at the intricate filigree around its edge. "I'm not saying you're going to hell for stealing the cross, I mean the flowers. The monks don't care about you taking those dang wildflowers," Janice tells Becky as she glances toward the bundle of floral beauty. "Good golly, there are thousands of rose petals everywhere you look on these rolling hills. One can take their pick. The Italians love growing anything that will grow in a pot or land. Can you see one bare spot of land where there's not something sprouting up?" Janice rests her case, making her final decision of innocence, justifying the theft in question.

"It is true! Who takes flowers and a cross from the sacred monks? I should go to hell." Becky grabs the cross back from Janice's hand and drops it into her leather purse, snapping it shut.

"I'll give it to my church. Bishop Mark will appreciate its antiquity and pocket size. That should even the scale of my debaucheries."

Tony looks to David while rubbing his hand across his brow. "What can I say? *Fatto*, it's done. *Mamma Mia*, it's done," Tony repeats with melancholy, his head lowered to the ground.

"*Stefania*. You know what this means for you? The monks will no longer take you inside the monastery, not without, well, let me see. Never mind, never mind. Don't worry. I'll take care of everything. *Mamma Mia*, the things you get me into are unbelievable, just unbelievable." Tony shuffles his feet around on the few rocks and starts speaking in Italian with Nino, explaining the situation.

"My friends warned me about these trips and that there is always a situation causing one's hair to rise. Surely, this one wins the prize!" Amy from Orlando, Florida, declares as she snaps her camera at us. She feels the need to freeze the moment into her digital camera as we stand huddled together beside the coach.

"You can't make this stuff up, not in a million years," Amy laughs, staring at the theater performers before her. "You should go back to the monks. Tell them you've made a big mistake. Cry, plead, and beg their forgiveness. Give the little cross back if it wasn't free for the taking. You can offer them something to settle the difference: maybe your necklace, your arm, or your finger, all as a penance, an apology. But, surely, it was allowed to take with a donation from your heart. However, the flowers...well, that's a different story. How could you not realize your hand was clasping a bundle of floral beauties such as those?"

"I promise you, I didn't mean to take the flowers!" Becky's head looks like a tree. Her hair is flocked with greenery that got caught during her frantic escape. She continues to proclaim her innocence. "Have you ever been scared out of your mind to the point of not realizing you've done something terribly wrong?"

"Yes, absolutely!" Amy said, smiling wider than before.

"How were we to know they would come inside? I thought monks stay in the abbey and do church work," Janice tells her as she pulls more olive leaves from Becky's hair.

"Seriously? That's what you think? They live here, and we all just watched them stroll out the side door of the abbey. Did you see them return inside? No, of course not," Amy laughs, loving the entertainment, while Tony and Nino continue to talk with flying hands.

"I deposited a sizeable donation in the little box inside the abbey," I speak up to justify the theft.

"*Mamma Mia, Stefania*. It will take more than a few coins to *make right* this situation." Tony pulls out his phone. It's his cousin on the other end.

My heart sank. The thought of never returning to the abbey plays within my mind, causing my stomach to crawl to the back of my throat. How will they ever permit me to come again with the Americans? I feel melancholy, too, worrying about the invasion, the flowers, the cross, and God only knows what else.

"I see the monks coming!" Janice shouts, racing inside the coach.

"You're in trouble, Janice," Amy warns, loving the excitement.

My eyes flash ahead, seeing the monks topping the hill.

"*Andiamo*! Let's go!" Nino shouts in heart-racing speed, grabbing Tony's hand and pulling him inside the bus for a fast getaway.

With everyone back on the bus, I stare in disbelief, glaring through the windshield as a train speeds through my chest. Nino accelerates the engine and peels out as fast as the lumbering bus could manage. The Mercedes-Benz lugs and pulls as smoky black plumes float upward. Underneath its gigantic black tires, the gravel pops and crackles, filling our nose with a rubbery aroma of burning oil, a horrible smell refusing to escape our nostrils.

An eternity seems to pass before Nino maneuvers the coach and has it rolling on payment, going just faster than a turtle's crawl. Down below our windows, we watch as the monks reach the hilltop, waving toward us, two of them bent over, probably gasping for air. *Mamma Mia*, will we ever return to this fairy-tale storybook again? The thought zooms throughout my mind, knowing it is possible, if, and only if—Tony waves his magic wand once again.

Chapter 11

MAMMA MIA, WE'RE IN METEORA, GREECE!

*T*he gigantic vessel that awaited us in Bari, Italy, surprised some of the Americans aboard our bus. They assumed we'd depart the Mercedes-Benz coach, leave it on land, and board the ship so we could hop from island to island on the big floating city-of-a-boat. But, no, we take our bus wherever we go. With it, we can conveniently see many hidden gems throughout Greece that are tucked away from the other tourists.

Today begins our second week in Europe with a new group of Americans. We started in Southern Italy for seven days, and overnight we adventured to the beautiful east side of the Ionian Sea, while our modern-day chariot rested peacefully in the ship's lower cargo area along with cars and big trucks.

We awoke to the wonders of Greece with an itinerary fit for an adventurous king and queen. Nino drives us out of the belly of the ship onto the mainland of another world, a Greek world where the alphabet is so foreign to our eyes it's merely a jumble of strange signs and symbols.

Today, our destination is the mountainous UNESCO World Heritage Site of Meteora, Greece. The Holy Meteora, the most inaccessible monasteries in the world. The mysterious Eastern Orthodox dwellings of the monks living in the sky, a mind-blowing World Wonder that modern man can't comprehend.

The Greek word Metéora means suspended, hanging, dangling, or floating in the air. Even after bringing Americans here for more than twenty years, I still stand in awe with my heart beating fast, acknowledging God's creation of beauty beyond my comprehension.

The monasteries rise like missiles ejecting from the earth. They perch on mountainous rocks that soar through the clouds. I stare at the cloisters in awe. They are hundreds of meters high, too far for any human to conceive how such unreachable dwellings in the air could have been created, much less how anyone or anything could possibly reach its height in a tow sack.

In my wildest imagination, I still can't comprehend how they built those picturesque monasteries on the tops of cliffs. And the implausible wild adventure of monks getting into sacks tied with a rope, being hoisted up to the sky, solely relying on their brotherly monks to winch them by hand with a medieval pulley. It's mind-blowing to witness such bravery. The cliffs seem to go straight up for miles beyond my eyes' capability to see. Many of the cloisters atop nestle like eagle's nests, all built one twig at a time. Visiting The Holy Meteora is truly breathtaking, like entering a fairy-tale that is almost inaccessible.

The rocks ascending into the clouds form an impressive sight and trigger speculations of an alien invasion from outer space. The thoughts swarm—is it possible extraterrestrials from Mars or some unknown planet settled here, flying their contraption-of-a-spaceship up and around the mind-blowing cliffs, nuzzling into the mysterious caves, spiraling so far that one needs binoculars to see clearly? I'm being facetious, but only about the space creatures and spaceships. Not about how mind-boggling Meteora is.

The first time I visited the monasteries, I stood beside a nunnery and observed a little bird resting atop the ceramic shingles of this beautiful cloister. Since I'm a huge animal lover who feels compelled to feed every feathery creature, I tried to figure out how it soared high enough to arrive on the clifftop. Did it continuously flap its wings as it ascended into the clouds? Perhaps it was captured by a man with a wire cage. My thoughts wandered. Could it be that the little-feathered creature lands amidst the rocks every so often to meditate in peace?

I can't fathom how any of this beauty was created, except by God's own hands. And when I remember how I looked more closely at the bird, its mouth, its teeny-tiny feet, its glittering feathers, and its small wings tucked closely downward, I smile. God's creation is, indeed, marvelous.

Chapter 12

MAMMA MIA, WE'RE IN GREECE! (GOING TO SKOPELOS)

*A*fter saying goodbye to Meteora, Greece, we traipse from one island to another, giving the Americans the idea that it can't get any better or more adventurous, but it does. Among this fun group of Americans is the famous Kathy L. Murphy, author of *The Pulpwood Queen's Tiara-Wearing, Book-Sharing Guide to Life* and creator of the largest meeting and discussing book club in the world, tagged the *Pulpwood Queens' Book Club*s.

Before hopping aboard our tour, Kathy had promised her dedicated book club members that she would wave her colorful scarf in the wind and reenact Meryl Streep's scene by dancing up the soaring mountain in Skopelos, Greece. To top it off, she would sing ABBA's song *"The Winner Takes It All."*

Many of the Americans on board came to fulfill something on their bucket list by seeing and experiencing Italy and Greece in the personal kind of way that we do on these tours. Three couples came specifically to commemorate their anniversary, hoping for two weeks of honeymoon bliss. Two Americans came to celebrate their birthdays and one to enlighten her eighteen-year-old granddaughter about the wonders of the world. The others are faithful travelers who join me regularly in the rolling hills of Italy and other adjacent European countries.

I sit in the front passenger seat of the coach this morning and anticipate the day. A hint of sun explodes through creamy meringue clouds, so I slide on a pair of Italian tortoiseshell shades that are the size of two large pancakes. Pushing them upward and crushing my black flocked lashes against the lens, I feel a wave of excitement because I know what the day will bring. It's neither touristy nor expected from a typical Greek itinerary. Not at all. It's just the opposite.

Behind me, twenty-two Americans sing along to the words of the *Mamma Mia!* song, which blasts through the stereo speakers. Nino carefully guides us around the narrow hairpin turns here in the back roads of Skopelos.

With the breathtaking panorama of the *Mamma Mia!* movie scene ahead, I feel the urge to jump, holler, and fly through the air, barreling down the narrow aisle of the coach—acrobatic style—back-flipping and bouncing from floor to ceiling. The excitement is more than my body can contain. On impulse, I grab the microphone and stretch the curled black cable to its maximum length as I step beyond Tony's seat.

"Can you hear me?" I ask, knowing the spotlight is on me.

Tony ducks and dodges the potential catastrophe of getting popped by the springy cord. Both of his hands fly into the air to shield his head.

"*Mamma Mia, Stefania!* Why you must stretch the cord? Can you not sit and talk at the same time?" He checks his straight, silver hair that is skirted around his head.

"Tony, watch out!" Across the aisle, Jan shouts as she attempts to stop the swinging microphone cable from hitting Tony's head on its second swing.

"Very nice, Jan. You know *Stefania* well. She thinks it's funny, hitting my head like a ping-pong ball." Tony continues to rub his forehead to intensify the drama.

"You nearly got it again." Jan laughs hard, and her crystal blue eyes sparkle with mischievousness.

"You're fine. It didn't hit you." I reinforce my innocence in a calm voice while holding the cord firmly in its socket.

"*Si, si*, very nice, *Stefania*. This time you miss." Tony starts the *Mamma Mia's* from his tongue again.

I draw the mic back to my lips.

"I'd like to make an announcement. I have news."

"*Mamma Mia, Stefania*, what are you saying to the people now?" Tony turns around in his seat and checks his watch.

Nino reaches for the cord, pulling me back an inch or so.

"Do you want to know where we're going today?" I try to control the huge smile that is spreading across my face. "There's a change of plans." My voice holds a serious tone.

Their happy faces freeze in midair.

"*Stefania*? What do you mean by a change of plans? There is no change in our plans," Tony interrupts, but I talk louder and cut him off like a race car rounding the inner lane.

"Yes, yes, there is a change of plans." I wink at him after taking my sunglasses off.

"*Mamma Mia, Stefania*. What's the matter with your eyes?" Tony must have missed my non-verbal communication.

"Nothing is wrong with my eyes." I look directly at the Americans, who are sitting on the edge of their seats, awaiting the news.

"I'm happy to announce that we are heading to..." I leave them hanging for two seconds, knowing they're ready for the big day on the island. I pretend to change the plans.

"Let's detour and go to the local market. It's just around the corner." I attempt another scheme. My mind walks through my favorite shop. I visualize myself loaded down with beautiful Greek icons.

"No way!" interjects Kathy Ray, who comes alive with enthusiasm. "I don't think so. You're joking, Stephanie."

She turns around in her seat, ready to debunk my suggestion. "We have to go to the chapel today."

"*Stefania*, the people are getting upset. What's the matter with you?" Tony spins around and smiles at Kathy. He dramatically blinks both eyes, sending beams of sunshine her way to assure her that there will be no diversion of plans.

"Tony, don't let Stephanie detour us from the *Mamma Mia!* chapel! You know she will." Kathy sashays from her seat and gives his arm a hard squeeze.

"Why not?" Tony antagonizes her with pleasure. "*Stefania* can give you a guided tour of the shops."

"No shopping today! We have the wedding." Kathy knows he's a joker and a giant teddy bear.

"Whatever you want, my dear." Tony pinches Kathy's cheeks and then takes her hand in his and holds it for a lingering second. "*Che bella che sei.* How beautiful you are!"

He dramatizes the situation more with an Italian gesture, knowing he's on the stage. Theatrically, he draws his fingers to his lips, all five of them squeezed together in the shape of a closed bird's beak. He kisses the tips with a loud smooch.

"Thank you, Tony!" Kathy throws her head back and giggles like a cute little schoolgirl. She has the face of innocence, not one whose hand is caught in a cookie jar or wrapped around a forbidden choco-late candy bar. She laughs hard while leaping back into her seat behind Tony.

"You see, I make things nice," Tony brags. "*Mamma Mia*, I am *fortunato*! A very lucky man to have so many Kathy's with me. Tell me, how do I say your names without all three of you looking up? We have Kathy Ray, Kathy Murphy, and Kathy Willis!"

"It's easy with your Italian pronunciation. I love the way you say Kathy: Kat-eee Mef-oree." Kathy Ray laughs more.

"Did I hear my name?" Kathy Murphy rises from her seat.

"They are talking about us," Kathy Willis informs her with a laugh.

Kathy Murphy strolls up the aisle of the coach as though her name has been announced through the speakers. She's now on the runway as she approaches the stage with Tony. My eyes are glued to the rhythmic sway of her long silky dress as it brushes the sides of the seats in gentle waves. She is a work of art; her style is bohemian with a body sculpted of expensive Carrara marble. Her face is fine silk; she's a natural beauty with a personality to ignite all of us in flames.

"Tell me, Kathy, what is this *Mamma Mia!* to you? What do you understand of its mystery?" Tony is now talking to Kathy Murphy, the queen of books and the most sought after lady in the publishing world. If an author is lucky enough to have their manuscript land in her hands and obtain the most prestigious endorsement of all (the Pulpwood Queens' seal of approval), then the author is well on their way to having a bestseller.

My eyes widen as I watch her gracefully making her way to the front. She is swaddled in colorful layers of fabrics, and her signature turban is wrapped around her head, tied with a pretty bow.

"Ah, Tony, the small Greek Orthodox church was used in the famous movie, *Mamma Mia!* In the pivotal scene, Sophia rode a little donkey up the mountain to get married. Meryl Streep danced up the steps with her scarf whipping in the wind," Kathy explains to Tony. He already knows all of this information since we've been coming to the island ever since the movie was made, but he loves to hear the Americans' view of its mystery.

"What's the rush? There is always tomorrow," I push back, waiting for another response from someone else.

"Where'd you get that idea? Missing the chapel today would be awful." Jan's sister, Bonnie, chimes in. Then she picks up her previous conversation where she left off.

"The door is always open for impromptu opportunities." I keep the lie going, while awakening more of the Americans from behind their cameras.

"Why not? I've changed my mind. I'm game for anything today." Kathy Murphy bounces in the mix again. Her deep blue eyes twinkle with mischievousness.

"I thought you'd like a detour, perhaps..." I try again and bat my eyes to enhance the suggestion.

"*Stefania*, we go to the chapel, yes? What's the matter with you?

Do you think there's something else we see on this road?" Tony never stops. He thinks I'm serious.

"I'm joking," I finally tell Tony. "Okay, *va bene*. Are you ready to see the *Mamma Mia!* church?" I'm obviously not going to be able to pull a prank on them today.

Not waiting for a response, I turn and press the stereo button, blasting the song "Mamma Mia" through the speakers. Immediately, everyone goes into motion as a chorus of trumpets, tambourines, drums, and the distinct sound of a fueled-up piano roar throughout the coach. Whether they can sing or not, it doesn't matter. I stand up to watch them inflate their lungs with air as they belt out the lyrics with ABBA.

The flip of a switch, or in our case, the stereo button, instantly creates joy. The Americans are now singing marionettes with swirling arms. Many pretend to play musical instruments and bang their feet hard against the seat in front of them. I watch Jan dance in her seat as she belts out the lyrics of "Mamma Mia." Minutes later, I jerk around, pressing the radio off.

"Get your cameras ready; we're nearly there!" I jump up and down as Nino extends his right arm out and reaches out to steady the cord.

"*Mamma Mia, Stefania*. Sit down," Tony instructs, as Nino pulls me downward. I collapse into my seat with a thud like a heavy bag of sugar.

"Keep looking to the left; the little chapel is perched in the water, right on top of the mountain of rock." Then I press the stereo button, and the lyrics blast out again.

"*Mamma Mia, Madonna, Stefania*. The people are fed up with this music." Tony swivels around in his seat, throwing his hands in the air. "Are you fed up with this 'Mamma Mia' song?" He asks Kathy Murphy, reaching for her right cheek and giving it a gentle pinch with a slight twist.

"I love the music," Kathy hollers back in between the lyrics. She leans over and reciprocates the cheek pinch as Tony flashes an awkward smile.

Time for the big announcement. "Get ready!" I look left, anticipating the little chapel's grand appearance beside the liquid blue sea. The Americans roar with excitement, dancing in their seats. I deliberately stoke the fire.

"There it is! There's the *Mamma Mia!* church." Jan shouts from her window seat. Everyone on the right side of the bus leaps into the aisle, looking for the chapel.

"I don't see it. Where is it?" Scott peers over Kathy's shoulder from a distance, but from his angle, he can only glimpse the foamy turquoise blue sea.

"Scott, that's not it," his wife, Jeana, tells him while her gaze searches the scenery outside the window. Seconds later, she turns to him as though they are new lovers. She kisses his cheek, then his lips. The love between them radiates heat even though they've been married for many years. They're a perfect match, both kind and sweet, both complementing each other with respect. They are high voltage electromagnets, both possessing a magnetic pull with old familiarity but as powerful as two lovers who are discovering each other for the first time. They have the relationship every romantic wants: hearts deeply touched where no other has ever been before.

"How much longer before the chapel appears?" Kathy Murphy folds her arms over her chest like the royal bohemian goddess of great importance that she truly is. "The scenery is beyond words, more than a postcard."

She points to her watch, silently asking Tony when it's *Mamma Mia!* time.

"I'd say another hour or so." Tony lies easily. His eyes twinkle with comic naughtiness.

"Pinocchio," Kathy shoots back. It's clear she's figured out Tony is joking.

There's a collective sigh. Cameras click as they strive to capture the beauty of paradise. All eyes look for the prize: the chapel of *Mamma Mia!*

"Ah, we're nearly there, my dear," Tony tells the truth and eases back in his seat as the Americans chatter behind him.

"Get ready to take some photos," I shout out, hyping them up more.

"How many times are you going to tell us this?" Jan laughs, and her eyes widen again. Then she mimics Tony's favorite English words, "I don't like."

We all follow suit, repeating the same phrase and mimicking Tony's Sicilian accent with an English flair.

"Oh, Stephanie, this is the most exciting day for me. I've seen the movie seven times," Jeana tells us. She's dressed in a pretty short-sleeve summer dress, which is her wedding attire for today's event.

It's not Jeana and Scott's wedding day, nor the other two couples, Amy and Sonny, and Alicia and Dr. Clark, who are also dressed in casual, Greek-style wedding attire. No, it's a day to renew vows in the teeny-tiny, whitewashed chapel perched atop two hundred rigorous steps on a winding path here in Skopelos, Greece. This magnificent rocky mountain juts into the dazzling sea with unparalleled splendor.

With every sharp turn, Jeana taps her sandal-strapped feet hard on the coach's floorboard while she peers out to the mesmerizing sea of stillness. It's a bed of aquamarine and turquoise-blue swelling with beauty. The ocean swirls as if an artist intentionally ran a brush through its creamy palette, creating a spellbinding attraction for human eyes.

The anticipation of seeing her favorite movie scene is radiating from Jeana's face. I watch her eyes bulge as Nino guides the coach around another narrow curve. The bus skirts the edge of the road, seemingly only a few inches from a plunging drop-off.

Her husband, Scott, is seated next to her. He made this tour possible by surprising Jeana at Christmas with my colorful brochure tucked into their Christmas tree proclaiming a huge surprise: "Southern Italy and *Mamma Mia!* Greece, here we come!"

As we bump along, with the music reverberating from side to side within the coach, the excitement builds as though it's a countdown to a new year. The three brides, Jeana, Amy, and Alicia, have huge smiles on their faces. Their anticipation of renewing their wedding vows in the little chapel is growing stronger as we watch for the wonderment to emerge from the sea.

Kathy Murphy's eyes widen as she catches a glimpse of an island within the crystal-clear sea.

"We're here! We're here!" Her voice is loud enough to alert the villagers for miles.

"The sea looks like jelly. Such stillness, no movement, and a kaleidoscope of colors with hues of blue and turquoise swirling through as though a painter's brush has created a masterpiece of art." Kathy rambles on, talking to no one in particular. "It appears to be one of my alcohol art creations. In fact, I created one similar to these effects. The marbled surprise that an artist never knows will be its outcome. Art takes on its own personality as the master guides the brush onto canvas."

Kathy shares her professional art techniques with everyone on the coach. She holds the torch high, leading and encouraging all to chase their dreams, regardless of age. She proudly obtained a prestigious degree in art at the age of sixty.

I hear every word. I know she's a talented artist and a graduate of the University of Texas. She's a proud alumna chosen for many awards by her professors for her unique creations in special exhibits.

"No, that's not the mountain. You'll recognize it immediately when you see it. We have a few more twists and turns before we'll be there." The excitement level escalates, and I ready my camera for the famous photo op.

"With all the love vibes floating around within this coach, we need to get married too." Eddie Ray from Memphis, Tennessee, leans over my shoulder and whispers in my ear, causing me to jump. He abruptly squats down beside my seat in the aisle. His pin-striped, seersucker pants bunch outward around his waist with an abundance of pleated fabric in soft greens and baby blues, complementing his shirt of the same material.

"I am a married woman. I can't help you with that one." I laugh lightly. I remember telling him that we could make all of his dreams come true when he signed up for this tour.

"We're in Europe. Doesn't that count?"

Eddie's hot breath warms my ear, and I rub it. "You've read too many books. Where do you find such rules?"

"*Mamma Mia, Stefania.*" Tony comes alert. He glares at Eddie.

"Do you have an emergency, Eddie? A number two is hitting you?" Tony always assumes the worst.

"No, I'm fine, just putting in my request before we arrive at this fairy-tale chapel that Stephanie keeps talking about. I'm not sure what to expect other than Meryl Streep dancing up a mountain and heading to a tiny white church. Oh, and singing the *Mamma Mia!* song. I think Stephanie has covered all of our visual expectations." Eddie turns back around and puts his mouth inches from my ear again.

"We can go to confession, afterward." His thick brown hair brushes against my left eye.

Now my eye twitches. I blink a couple of times. "What are we going to confess? I have a clear conscience, other than eating too much baklava last night."

"We'd have to confess the second marriage. That is, if we tie the knot upon this magical mountaintop that you keep talking about. I believe that's called…Oh, I can't remember the legal term for being married to more than one man, but you get my drift?"

"It's called bigamy. And no, thank you."

"We're in Europe. Everything goes here. Just repent afterward." Eddie laughs, turns around, and slaps Nino's knee underneath the steering wheel.

Nino jumps. He's been too busy driving to have paid attention to all the chatter beside him.

I shake my head. "I'm not Catholic. It won't work. You must confess to sin, and I don't plan on intentionally committing any, especially another marriage. One's enough for me."

"Yes, you are. You know a lot about the Catholic faith. Tony said so. He says you know more about Catholicism than the pope. And we've already heard enough of its history to convert an atheist. Heck, I'm a born and bred Baptist, and I've learned many truths in this last week. I anticipate the Greek studies will quickly convert me to Greek Orthodoxy since we're in Greece now." Eddie is a jokester. He's a fast talker and a happy soul who is always laughing and saying silly things, true or not.

"That's stretching it. I love biblical history, the Holy Scriptures, and the word of God. I love the reverence and holiness of the Catholic Church, the ceremonial procedures, the lighting of candles, the respect and devotion of the saints, the admiration and care of the building. The beauty within each church that reflects a sacred dwelling for the Holy Spirit, even though the Holy Spirit dwells within us. I love the devotion of its people, the feeling of God's presence when entering inside, the—"

Eddie cuts me off. "See, I told you. You're Catholic," He does a high five but misses my hand and hits nothing but air. "I never knew so many of the apostles are buried in Italy. That's a surprise to me. I never gave it any thought, just assumed they're all scattered around Israel. And I sure didn't know the facts about the Sistine Chapel."

He rests his arm on my leg while he nibbles on a chocolate chip cookie that he'd brought from the States. They are his mother's homemade batch of gooey softness.

His stomach grumbles as he munches away. "Nothing makes a man hungrier than his mama's homemade cookies."

He tosses the last bite into his mouth and leaves an aroma that makes me want one too. Like a magician, he pulls a cellophane bag from his pocket, fishes out another cookie, and hands it to me with a smile.

"Ah, thank you." I bite into the softness of my favorite cookie and savor the chocolate chips as they slowly melt within my mouth. When the cookie is gone, I want more, at least a dozen or so.

"Now back to my proposal," Eddie reminds me, winking his left eye while brushing his thick, brown hair with his long, slender fingers. He attempts to act cool and stylish with his latest Italian glasses resting on his long nose, which reminds me of a dachshund puppy dog.

"You know I'm kidding, Stephanie. It's only James Early I want, but that's another story. We'll talk later." Eddie rises and gives Nino a pat on his shoulders and Tony a big smile. He works his way back down the aisle with his mouth full of cookie.

Back in his seat, he is welcomed by his boyfriend, James Early, a fifty-two-year-old lawyer who has been his partner and loving companion for over twenty-one years. They started traveling with me in 2006. At that time, they wanted to find an antique blackamoor statue for their new home, so we scouted around the local village markets throughout Italy. Eddie gave James their first Italy tour many years ago as a birthday gift, saying it would do them both good to relax and see the Italian Riviera, and, of course, sip the local *vino*. Months later, they won a big, notable case and felt Italy would be the perfect country to reward their efforts of years of exhausting litigation. Now, after all of these years, they still hop aboard with us.

Chapter 13

MAMMA MIA, WE'RE IN GREECE! (GREEK BOWLING BOWLS!)

*B*umping along the curves of this sliver-of-a-road, Nino continues to guide the coach along the edge of grass and wildflowers. The music still resonates inside the coach as ABBA radiates from the speakers.

"Stephanie," Barbara from Dallas, Texas, suddenly whispers into my ear.

I jump.

"Oh, excuse me. I didn't mean to startle you, but something is still bothering me."

"What did you say?" I reach for the dial on the CD player to turn the volume down.

"If you can make it happen, I'd like to get lots of flowers for the brides. You know, decorate the little church for them." Barbara hands me a wrinkled piece of paper that's a sketch of her ideas jotted down in pencil.

Slipping on my glasses, I see hundreds of flowers flocked around the tiny chapel, leaving enough space for one skinny bride.

"Are you kidding?" I look into her eyes, and I search for a hint of a jest, expecting her to laugh.

She doesn't. "No. I think we can create something special for them, just like the movie. We need candlelight flickering up the steps and flowers cascading upwards in a waterfall effect as we descend downward after the ceremony. Let me draw you the idea." Barbara squats beside my seat, clutching a long yellow pencil with a point as sharp as a bird's beak.

"We're nearly there, Barbara, just a few more twists and turns." I still hope she's joking.

Barbara looks as if she's been punched in the face; her eyes are wide as apples. "Stephanie, I can decorate it all. Just give me the flowers."

I stare at her. "Barbara, there will be plenty of flowers along the way. You are welcome to pick as many as you want."

"No, I want to decorate with more professional flowers." She is stern and insistent. "You can help me."

My mind imagines the steps to the chapel. I picture myself loaded down with flowers like the little donkeys.

What can I say? "As you wish," I respond.

"Stephanie, I'm teasing you. I knew you'd say *va bene,* okay, as you do to every request, then make it happen. You are our genie in a bottle, right?"

"No. Not me. It's Tony who possesses the magical powers when he waves his Sicilian hands through the air."

"Oh, no. I've seen your work. You wave your hands too." Barbara turns around and goes into motion, dancing and singing down the aisle as she casually slaps the shoulder of everyone within arm's reach.

I twist around and watch her laugh all the way to the end of the coach. She shares all sorts of surprises from her pockets with the other passengers.

"We're nearly there," I shout to alert everyone again.

"No, not yet." Nino flashes a quick wink in my direction.

"It won't be long now, just a few more moments," I reply to Nino as I reach for the mic that's resting on the carpeted floorboard.

I bring it up to my red-painted lips, turn up the volume again, and sing loudly with my fellow passengers. The Americans whoop and holler as their excitement grows, knowing they're nearly to our final destination.

As we tower high above the sea, gently twisting around the road with many potholes, all of the excitement abruptly stops when we see an unforeseen challenge on the only route to the chapel.

"What is this?" I lean my face closer to the windshield, trying to see more clearly.

"*Mamma Mia, Madonna,*" Nino's voice echoes my dismay as his foot slips off the accelerator.

Just ahead, the road is blocked by a large, round crater. It fills the middle of the road and leaves no room for Nino to go left or right without either crashing into a wall of stone or soaring off into the sea. A tiny backhoe sits on a small pile of dirt.

I can't even figure out how the machine arrived there. Maybe it was dropped off by a helicopter and placed directly atop the pile of dirt that rests inches from the enormous hole. How can this be?

On my left, I look down and see the drastic drop-off with the sea far below that's moving in mesmerizing waves. To my right, I see nothing but a wall of rock towering upward.

"*Mamma Mia, Madonna!* Nino, what is this ahead of us?" Tony hysterically blurts out. His hands swirl and his eyes bulge as he leans forward to get a better look.

Inches beside him, I glimpse a group of bobbing heads, although I still can't see any legs or arms as they're hidden from view in the crater.

"What in the world?" Mumbled words spill from my mouth as I refuse to accept our predicament—a land-locked dilemma with no passing or entering. I reach for my glasses as Nino inches the bus closer.

I glance to my left, hoping to see a magic wand in Tony's hand waving in the air to make the hole in the road disappear, but I see nothing from Tony—no movement, no hocus pocus, no parting waters.

He looks as if I'd punched him in the gut. His gaze remains riveted on the view on the other side of the windshield. I lean closer to him and feel my heart pound as I look again at the obstruction.

Nino's foot jams the brake as he shifts the gears into neutral. The coach kicks and jumps as we come to an abrupt stop.

The only way to get to the chapel is blocked.

"*Madonna Mia.*" Nino shifts the gears again and kills the engine. The side door opens, and he and I stumble out to inspect the situation. Tony follows.

"This can't be happening. Not here. How will we get to the chapel, the very thing we came to see on this island?" I can't help but babble as my heart drops to the ground. "The wedding! We've got to get there for the ceremony."

"*Mamma Mia.*" Tony's mantra is like a broken record. "Let me see the *problema.*"

He shoots me a sideways glance that's full of uncertainty.

We race to the dilemma before us and find five Greek men scurrying around in the hole working busily. The workers look up for a moment, then continue their task as though we're invisible.

"*Mamma Mia*, this can't be happening." The three of us are like a choir hitting the same chorus as we speak in unison.

I have the disquieting thought that we are the Griswolds going to Wally World only to find a closed door that's bolted shut.

"How do we get to the little church?" I ask Tony, who's walking toward the hole. Nino speeds in the opposite direction, heading to the back of the coach to assess our emergency predicament and see if there is any space to turn the bus around.

Side by side, Tony and I look down into the massive pit. Five Greek workers covered in mud have water pipes running here and there underneath their boots.

"*Signor*, please, we must pass through," I tell them in my southern drawl, pointing to the few feet of space between the hole and the rocks.

"We're on our way to the chapel, and we must get there soon," I continue to ramble, trying to explain our emergency. "We have traipsed from one island to the next, coming to Skopelos, Greece, to experience the wonderment of the little church and the highly anticipated renewing of vows. But now our way to get there is blocked."

"*Mamma Mia, Stefania*. They are Greek. They understand nothing you say." Tony rubs his head and pushes his sunglasses so they balance perfectly on his forehead.

I disregard Tony's news alert. "*Signor*, I bring the Americans here, to this island, Skopelos, every year. Well, nearly every year. Sometimes, we skip a year and toss in a different country to give the Americans the pleasure of seeing something different."

"*Stefania*, the Greeks understand nothing of your language, especially the long, southern twang of East Texas."

The workers stare at us and mumble something Greek. Then they grow silent, focusing their eyes toward the long coach. I turn around and look.

Some of our people are huddled together and peer through the windshield while others hang from the door.

"Don't worry, *Stefania*, we will think of something. Everything will be okay." Tony reassures me as he walks back toward the coach and looks for Nino.

I glance down at my hand where the heavy Canon camera usually rests, wanting to capture a photo of the men rushing around in the hole with their bowling-ball-like hard-hats, but it's in the coach, resting on the dashboard.

"Stephanie, how are we getting to the *Mamma Mia!* chapel?" One of the Americans hollers from the coach's open door. The others gather around me and chime in like a chorus of backup singers echoing the same question.

"Can any of you fly?" I joke, looking back at the hole and then at the narrow road with its huge pile of dirt. I turn my gaze to the Greeks. They seem oblivious to our dire situation and the calamity facing us of missing the most important site on the island, not to mention the ceremonies.

Suddenly, the Greeks start up talking again amongst themselves and point toward the big bus on the narrow road. Their facial expressions begin to reveal their thoughts about our dilemma, including some unabashed humor about our predicament. I understand nothing of their language, only that the number one priority for them is the water leaking underneath their black rubber boots.

I motion for the remaining Americans to get off the coach and see our situation for themselves. Then I try again to plead with the Greeks to fill up the hole.

"Can't you use your machine to replace the dirt and allow us to drive through?" I point to the crater. The five Greeks stop their shoveling and glare at me. I see the answer as clearly as if it is written above their hard hats.

"*Stefania*, there is no way to bypass the pit. Absolutely none." Tony shakes his head back and forth with melancholy and defeat written on his face. "And even if they refilled the hole, which is impossible for them to do with broken pipes and water still leaking, the machinery is in the way. Where would they put the equipment? There is no way to turn the bus around. *Mamma Mia, Stefania*, you are asking for the impossible. They must work hard to repair it before the sun goes down. And what do you expect them to do after they replace the earth?"

Tony points to the pile of dirt, already taller than the miniature backhoe that has a power lift attached to its bumper.

"And, *Stefania*, the *escavatore,* the backhoe, what do they do with it? And even if the machinery remains, once they fill in the disaster with a mountain of dirt, must they cling to the side of the rock to allow us a passage? *Mamma Mia*, it's another day's work to get this back to normal. This is beyond any quick repair." Tony continues to defend the Greeks' situation.

"I hope I'm not interrupting, but speaking of reverse, it looks as though Nino will be doing a lot of backing up today to get the bus out of here," Dr. Clark says as he snaps another photo of the dilemma of the coach wedged between a sharp curve and a deep crater.

I see the wheels turning within his mind. Perhaps a genius can solve this mathematical equation? But no, it's impossible to get the coach out of this situation.

"We can walk to the chapel. Can't we, Stephanie?" Kathy Murphy offers a cheerful suggestion. "A few minutes ago you said, 'We're almost there. It's just around the corner.'"

The Americans applaud and cheer in agreement as they huddle around Kathy and peer down into the hole full of Greeks.

"Yes! Yes! We will walk." I jump up and down, excited that our predicament has been resolved. How had I not thought of that myself? "It's not far, just around the corner."

"*Mamma Mia, Stefania.*" Tony shuffles around Nino and looks at me. Now the wheels are turning in his head.

"*Va bene.* Okay. You know the way, *Stefania.*" He walks toward the bus once again, shaking his head back and forth. It's clear he doesn't believe the long motor coach can make it in reverse for miles backtracking on the zigzagging curves.

While Tony and Nino confer about the bus's dilemma, including getting the long Mercedes Benz off the road before anyone else arrives behind us to cause bigger problems, I summon excitement and let my face stretch into a wide smile.

"Come on, everyone." I clap my hands and swirl around in a spin. "Let's get our cameras and purses off the coach and anything else you want to take to the chapel."

I head to the motorcoach with determination. As far as I'm concerned, the problem is solved.

"No, wait! I don't want to leave Tony and Nino with this situation of moving the bus out of here." Dr. Clark's eyes widen as he looks at the long coach jammed between the sea and the cliff. He taps his foot on the road with his nervous energy consuming him.

"Driving in reverse with this long coach is just about impossible, even with Nino driving slowly while Tony guides the maneuver." Dr. Clark can't stop talking.

I pause and let the other Americans go ahead of me to retrieve their belongings.

Dr. Clark reiterates the problem. His voice grows louder as he paces nervously. "There's no way for Nino to hear Tony's directions, not with him at the driver's seat and Tony outside the back of the bus."

I try to reassure Dr. Clark. "Oh, Nino can do it. Nino is the best driver in the world. Remember, he lives in Napoli. Nino has backed the bus down a mountain in reverse before. When we stay in Lucca on top of a soaring hilltop, there's only one way up and one way back down. There's absolutely no room to turn the coach around up there either, not unless you're a flea."

I reminisce for a second about that group with their eyes glued to the windows, while a few cringed on the floorboard, sure they were about to meet their demise in a crash-landing miles below.

"But Stephanie, Tony will have to get on and off the bus and direct Nino to make the sharp curves beforehand. Anything could happen, and they'd go plunging off into the sea." Dr. Clark takes off his hat and brushes his hand through his thick, silver hair.

"If I stay with them, I can help direct and at least be the go-between, transferring messages from Tony to Nino."

"There's no need to assist. Nino is the best driver. The Mercedes-Benz has all the latest mechanisms for backing up, including a digital camera by the driver's seat. Trust me. It's no problem for Nino. They'll be back in the village before we get to the chapel. They'll get the smaller vehicles and be back with us shortly." I give my rebuttal.

I lie. I have no idea how long it will take them to go in reverse, but I know it's no big deal. Nino is the best driver in the world. Dr. Clark is accustomed to our smaller coach, the one that holds twenty-five passengers, even though we've never put more than fourteen inside its doors. Today is not the case; it's the fifty-two passenger bus that's going in reverse, even though we've never put more than twenty-nine Americans inside its doors.

Reluctantly, Dr. Clark begins to agree as he remembers the most important thing. "Well, it is my wedding day. I wouldn't want to disappoint the lucky bride today."

He shuffles his shoes on the pavement. The poor guy obviously has a bad case of pre-wedding jitters.

I glance at the coach and see Nino flash an awkward smile from behind the huge windshield. He's already in the driver's seat, and the motor is humming.

I glance at Tony, who's standing outside the coach, ready to navigate the winding road.

"Wait, I forgot something!" I jump back on the bus and grab a bottle of water and my camera. Then I'm back with the Americans and watching Tony instruct Nino.

"Okay, everyone. We should get going." I loop my arm around Margie's hand and give her a tight squeeze of encouragement. She resembles an elegant goddess straight out of a fashion magazine for the rich and famous elite.

"I've always wanted to take a risk with my life on a secluded road that's a million miles away from home," Margie announces to us with dramatic southern Louisiana charm. "I mean, really, Stephanie? Who wouldn't want to be kidnapped in a foreign country where the language is literally Greek, and the only place to run is into the sea! My mother warned me about going off with strangers."

"Puhleeze, Margie! Bless your little Louisiana bayou heart," Kathy Murphy interrupts and grabs her hand, pulling Margie forward with a laugh. "I don't see anyone putting a gun to your head. You could've gone with Tony and Nino and helped back the bus up."

Kathy rolls her eyes and chuckles again. They've been best friends for many years and complement each other with their southern lingo and playful charm.

"I'm getting older by the day, and I've yet to see a *Mamma Mia!* chapel or Meryl Streep, or a donkey!" Margie shoots back. Her eyes are camouflaged behind black sunglasses.

I break up the banter. "Say *arrivederci*, goodbye, to Tony, Nino, and the bus. They'll come back for us with a smaller coach when the hole is covered, or they'll bring tiny cars. With a smaller vehicle, there'll be enough room to squeeze between the rock wall and the crater."

Chapter 14

MAMMA MIA, WE'RE IN GREECE! (GATHERING FLOWERS)

"This is exciting, walking the *Mamma Mia!* road and getting the real experience of the island. Look at the view and the flowers! This is what I call fun!" Jan takes three steps toward the edge where the magnificent sea of blue and turquoise laps gently below, and floral colors are sprinkled everywhere.

"We need these flowers for the wedding." Jan reaches over and pulls wildflowers from a bush that's abundant with mesmerizing purple blooms at the side of the road. Just past the workers who are still in the pit, more flowers are growing on the path.

Looking back, I can still see Nino at the wheel of the bus and hear Tony's voice as he bellows in Italian. Tony must be standing behind the long coach, so he can instruct Nino when to turn the wheel.

I holler to them as we walk further away, "*Tutto a posto,* everything going okay?" I know he can't hear me inside the coach, but I did it anyway for some reason. I should have known better.

"I still can't imagine Nino backing up for miles on those hairpin turns." Dr. Clark is back on that subject again, as he points his camera toward the coach. "He doesn't look worried, though. But all of those sharp curves and driving backward in a maze of turns. Seems crazy."

"He can do it," Jan shrugs as she eyes more flowers to pick. "I've been on thirty or more tours with Stephanie, and Nino can drive a bus on a tightrope with only three tires. I've witnessed his maneuvers at least a hundred times. That's his job. Do you think he'd be driving Tony all over Europe if he wasn't the absolute best?"

"Yes! Jan is correct. Nino is the best driver in the world. He lives in Napoli." I'm a broken record, repeating the same words. "He can back a bus in reverse on a clothesline."

I sound like I'm bragging, but it's the truth, even though I've never witnessed him drive a coach on three tires.

"Yes. I agree, Stephanie. He's driven us all over Italy, and now Greece. Nino is the best." Dr. Clark holds his camera to his eye again.

I throw my arm around Dr. Clark and say, "Let's go get you married. Are you ready? Where's your bride?"

I intersperse commands with questions. My words tumble over and into each other. "Don't worry about the bus. Nino is a professional. You know his talents at the wheel."

"Well, you know the mind can play tricks. From here, it looks impossible. The tires, I never noticed them before. They're taller than the statue of Zeus at Olympia. But never mind, I'm ready to renew my vows. I'm a very lucky man." Dr. Clark stands straight, but his eyes are still laser-focused on Nino at the wheel. His lips quiver for a brief second before he manages a shaky smile.

"*Andiamo!* Let's go." I am insistent. I grab Dr. Clark's belt loop and pull him away. He's like putty as I stretch him in the opposite direction from the bus.

"This is the place to get married." Kathy Ray emerges from behind a bush. She holds handfuls of wildflowers and wears a broad, mischievousness grin. Her accomplice in crime, Jan, also follows with bundles of abundant flowers.

"Alright. We're off to the chapel!" I shuffle my shoes in a fast tap dance.

"Yes. Let's go!" Emily kicks her legs high in the air like a cheerleader. "I'm warming up by stretching my legs. Amy and I are going to race up the mountain."

Emily is a professional barrel racer who has toured the rodeo circuit all over the United States. She's a high-energy bombshell, slim, sleek, confident, and built like a tight rope. She's a genuine natural beauty and the joy and the pride of her grandmother, Kathy Ray.

"It's a straight shot. Just follow the curves, and I'll see you at the chapel."

She runs her fingers through her shoulder-length auburn hair and with a fast twist, loops it around into a fat ball upon her head.

"I'll race you." Emily jogs in one spot, preparing for take-off.

"Go ahead. I'll be right behind you, helping them pick the wedding flowers." I feel no need to over-exert myself.

She pulls her gigantic sunglasses from her face. Her eyes are alluring with black mascara that extends her lashes to the length of a Shetland pony's tail, seemingly beyond the eyebrows. Her style is cowboy boots with tight-fitting jeans and a college-girl smile. She's the total package of a beautiful young lady.

"Ok, I'll see you up there." Emily takes off with her ball of hair bouncing up and down. She taps her grandmother on the shoulder as she passes her.

"See you there," Kathy hollers back.

"Are you alright?" Scott races to Jeana, who is bent over with her face to the ground.

Jeana had been observing the flower sprouting from the soil, but she turned as Scott touched her shoulder.

She looks up. Her eyes are the color of blue crystal, set gracefully on milky white skin. A smile stretches across her porcelain-doll face that's enhanced by a fringe of copper hair.

"Look at these. It's a perfect bridal bouquet." Jeana hands him a few twigs of wildflowers she's picked. "These must be crocus, the native Greek flower in the iris family. I read about them before our trip. Do you remember the book?"

She dreams aloud as her eyes scan the vast area of opportunity to see colorful flowers growing alongside the road. "I'd love to find wild daffodils, bougainvillea, and hyacinth."

"Oh, Stephanie, this is unbelievable. Look at this panorama—a photographer's dream. We're walking in paradise." Kathy Willis' eyes are wide with wonder as she smiles, hard-pressed not to giggle from the excitement. "This is a huge blessing from God. He is blessing us with this incredible sight, this experience of a lifetime. Just think, if the hole hadn't been in the middle of the road, we'd never be walking and picking Greek flowers."

"I feel like Alice in Wonderland; it's magical up here." Margie chimes in, and her strong dose of southern charm fills the air. Silver curls toss about her head as she snaps the last flower stem from a nearby bush. She hands Kathy Murphy her bundle of flowers.

"Where's the music?" Margie listens intently and leans toward me. "I want to hear the songs from the soundtrack."

She straightens her back then places her hands firmly on her hips. With her eyes shut, she pretends to hear the lyrics.

Kathy Murphy watches intently as I rummage through my bag, searching for the magic of music contained inside. "You didn't forget the boom box, did you?"

"Right here," I reassure her as my hand rapidly searches inside the bag. My fingers stretch out like the tentacles of an octopus, searching.

"*Eccomi qui*, here I am!" I shout in Italian when I manage to grasp the tiny box. "I found it!"

Kathy grins from ear to ear, radiating enough excitement for all of us.

With the slide of a click, the lyrics of their current favorite song blast out of the portable speaker. Suddenly, we're movie stars as we dance and skip with our arms loaded with flowers—enough for three bridal bouquets.

"Wait!" Kathy Murphy spins around, eyeing the colorful floral blooms that grow on the edge of the road. "These are the ones we need, Jeana. Surely, this is the same flower as in the photo you showed me earlier."

She attempts to pull the flowers from the earth, but her arms are too full to manage another stem.

"We have enough flowers." Kathy Willis laughs as the ABBA music plays inside my bag.

Kathy Murphy shuffles flowers and arranges them in her arms along with her bag and camera. She appears like a glow stick, all lit up like something inside her has ignited a blazing fire radiating love and excitement for the brides-to-be. Her eyes are glued to the ground, and her energy infects us all as she attempts to pull and tug another flower from the earth. "We don't have any of these."

"We want those flowers." Jeana echoes, but her hands are also too full to hold another stem. "Oh, these are the ones. Yes, the same as I saw in the photos yesterday. But are they the protected native flower?"

"I'll get them!" Kathy Ray is already moving around the flower bush.

"Do you ever follow the rules?" Jan follows Kathy Ray toward the questionable flowers. We all know she's going to pull them, regardless of the controversy under discussion.

"Sometimes, but not in these situations." Kathy crouches over and presses her breasts against Jan's back as she attempts to pull a potentially protected native Greek plant from the rocky earth.

"Wait!" Bonnie hollers at us. She drops her oversized wicker bag full of flowers on the road to help Kathy pluck more of the magnificent blossoms.

"Kathy Ray. What are you doing now?" I intentionally spin around, acting silly by pretending to shield my eyes from the impromptu seizure of more native flowers. Jan and Kathy Ray are behaving like Lucy and Ethel. These two ladies met on a tour decades ago. And ever since, they've shared a room and never missed an adventure.

"Stephanie, I can't disappoint the bride, can I?" Kathy Ray responds breathlessly to my silliness while yanking harder, pulling with force, and using Jan's back to brace herself.

"You're hilarious." Kathy Murphy jumps back with a giggle to make room for the confiscation in progress. "Good golly, make sure you include the dirt while you're at it. I mean, don't we have enough? We have the kitchen sink in every bag by now."

She laughs harder as Margie reaches down and gathers a fistful of dirt to prove her point.

"Uh-oh." Jan's knees buckle as she loses her balance from the weight of Kathy's body. She plops to the ground in a heap of flowers.

"There she goes!" I yell out, but I'm too late and too far away to help.

"I follow the rules when they're reasonable." Kathy laughs hysterically as she clutches five new stems in her hand.

Dr. Clark looks at her, serious and inquisitive. "There's no shame in going after what you want."

"That's what I say." Kathy brushes off the dirt from her two knobby knees. Their reddish color screams *ouch*. "I have no knowledge of protected flowers in Greece."

"How many more curves before we see the chapel?" asks Michelle from East Texas. She scrunches a sheet of white paper into her hand to conceal the wedding lyrics written in secret. She and Kathy Murphy intend to sing an *a cappella* rendition.

"It certainly can't be much further. Riding in the coach, it only takes minutes to get there, but on foot..." I look to my left, where the sea below gleams like a masterpiece on canvas, with a beauty indescribable in the English language.

Michelle kicks a tiny pebble across the narrow road as she softly sings the words written on the paper. They're the lyrics to "The First Time Ever I Saw Your Face."

"That's beautiful, Michelle." I compliment from my heart.

"Thank you, Stephanie. You can sing with us in the chapel."

"Have you heard me?" I try to sing the title of the song but fail miserably. "Singing is not my gift."

Michelle withdraws into her own world as she sings angelically, preparing her voice for the ceremony.

"I've already taken ten thousand photos of this view." Scott walks next to his wife, Jeana. His words float in the sky and evaporate into thin air. "Are you okay?" He reaches forward and gently pulls Jeana's sunglasses off.

Her eyes never blink.

"I'm watching for the little church where we're renewing our vows." She smiles widely.

Jan dances a few inches behind her.

"I thought it was right here, just around the corner. But..." I pause, searching for words, then gaze at the sea.

"It's hard to know where the sky ends, and the sea starts." Bonnie walks nearby. She's been talking with her sisters, Jan and Dorthia, who are all from Louisiana. They're the famous Bleu sisters. Each one is a dynamo with the total package of brains like Einstein and glowing beauty. It's Jan who can't keep her feet planted for long. She traipses all over Europe with us and dances her way through life.

"It is, except the sea is marbleized. It's an optical illusion of veins running here and there within the water, gorgeous variegated blues and turquoise all swirled together." Dorthia's eyes dance and sparkle. She's transformed as the conversation dives into her element of expertise. She's a professional interior designer, known all over the state of Louisiana.

Seconds turn into minutes with the endless views of the fairy-tale setting before us as we walk, rounding curve after curve until something familiar finally appears in the far distance. From the sea, a giant sphere soars up, but we still need to get a few steps closer. As I push my sunglasses on top of my head so I can get a better view, the image becomes clear: it's nothing more than a little island and trees.

When we look up and out into the blueness of the water, the afternoon sky glitters like diamonds upon the surface of the sea as the sun surrenders its rays. We are wide-eyed as we anticipate the thrill of what's to come—the *Mamma Mia!* chapel in the near distance. If somehow, we could have waved a magic wand and returned the dirt into the crater so we could drive the remaining distance, we'd already be at the church, ready to ascend into the sky. However, because of divine intervention, we received the blessing of walking this breathtaking road, something we'd never done before and hadn't planned.

Everything happens for a reason, good or bad, and God's wonder and his love never ceases to amaze me. Strolling along, I think, *what are the chances of five Greek men in a gigantic hole, blocking the road on the day we come to the highly anticipated site?* One could call it fate or accident, or just a moment in time when we're simply following the yellow brick road, but in our case, it is dirt and concrete. It's serendipity hitting us right in the face.

"I bet Emily and Amy have already arrived at the chapel." Margie alerts us as she leads the way several feet ahead of us with Kathy Murphy by her side. "Stephanie, how many more miles do we walk? You may have to piggyback me soon."

She stops in her tracks. She pushes her black sunglasses up just enough for her icy blue eyes to pierce through me with intensity.

Kathy Murphy laughs out loud, and her smile sends more sunlight our way.

"Margie, you're out-walking all of us." Kathy spins around like a ballerina dancer, and her colorful Greek turban never moves on her head.

Margie unsnaps her large bag and stuffs a few more flowers inside. It comes alive as plants sprout in every direction like an explosion of vegetation.

"I don't know what I'm looking for exactly, other than a church soaring up from the sea, a tiny chapel of enchantment somewhere far out there." Margie pulls her sunglasses off and points to the sea, being dramatic again. "Surely we'll recognize Meryl Streep singing as she runs up a high spindle top with her shawl whipping in the wind. Oh, let's not forget her daughter, Sophie, riding the donkey."

She makes us laugh. Her sophistication of genuine southern charm is made for the movie screen; it's so theatrical. "All I see right now is the hilltop, but how in the world are we supposed to see it from here without binoculars?" She smiles, almost giggling. Her face radiates Hollywood glamour with sprinkles of mischievousness. She might as well be transparent because anyone can see the wheels turning behind her charismatic eyes. She's on a roll.

A collective sigh goes up into the white puffy clouds. We stand loaded down with flowers and look at Margie.

"See? Everything out there is beyond words. It's magnificent."

Margie points to her left. We follow her finger and stare into the sea of fantasy that's sketched into existence. But where is the chapel?

"Margie, your curls are shining like sterling silver today," Bonnie tells her.

"Thank you, darlin'," Margie flashes a wink. "You look beautiful too," Margie compliments Bonnie. "I love your hairstyle. It fits your face well."

"Thank you, Margie. Kathy sure did pamper us last night with her make-shift beauty salon. I've never been so surprised in all of my life!" Bonnie compliments with a smile. "I had no idea we were going to her room for a make-over and the whole shebang. I thought she said it was a last-minute wedding rehearsal gathering for us girls to have drinks and laugh before the big day."

"Well, you never know with Kathy. She's always springing surprises on me. And darlin', you can only imagine how I feel when going to her little cottage in the woods. 'Murphy's Law.' That's what she calls her beautiful house in East Texas. I never know who'll be inside with her. Someone is always popping in or out. Celebrities galore. There is always someone needing her assistance in the book world, or wanting to hang onto her coattail for a free ride to the top. You know how that goes, dear. I nearly dropped my iced tea when I saw—" Margie accidentally drops her bag on the ground, but the flowers are packed so tightly that they barely moved.

"Oh, Margie! What are you telling them now?" Kathy walks toward her with both hands full of even more flowers.

Kathy Murphy had surprised all of us ladies with a beauty salon party inside her room last night after dinner. She gave each of us our very own special treatment of our choice: shampoo and set, facial, pedicure, manicure, and more. We experienced Kathy's professional expertise as we received a complimentary make-over from top to bottom. She fluffed and buffed each and every one of us with an array of fancy cosmetics, and we went from normal to extraordinary beauties within hours with the help of all of her latest enhancements. It was just unbelievable to the Americans that the world-wide, publicly acclaimed celebrity and author of *The Pulpwood Queen's Tiara-*

Wearing Book-Sharing Guide to Life was giving all of us make-overs with the same hands that shampooed and styled Joan Rivers' hair. I could hardly recognize my group today with their new hairstyles and glowing skin.

"Yes! Thank you, Kathy, for surprising us with such pampering. How in the world did you get your whole beauty salon inside your luggage? You had every color of nail polish under the rainbow, not counting all the facial and body treatments applied all the way down to our toes. Goodness gracious, I feel and look fabulous today." Franny and Mary, the twin sisters who talk in a southern drawl, run their fingers through their short hair to feel the silkiness from the professional shampoo and set last night. I look down at their toes. They are painted in neon pink with sparkling glitter.

"Oh, yes! Thank you, Kathy, for conditioning my hair. I love the silkiness." Franny can't move her arms to reach her hair because they are filled with flowers. "This is a first for us to get manicures, pedicures, and all the works on a tour—and right in your own room!"

Franny wiggles her toes that are now sparkling in glittery polish.

Many of the ladies erupt in applause. The others without flowers shout their compliments to Kathy because they also have no free arms to clap their hands.

Alicia stands like a lovely statue with her flowers in her hand. Her long, colorful Greek linen dress whips gently in the light breeze as Dr. Clark takes her photo. It creates a ricochet effect. One by one, we gather around them, shouting over each other. We are an energetic group, anticipating the reenactment of a *Mamma Mia!* wedding, but in our case, we will hold three vow renewals in the tiny church.

"Let's go, *andiamo,*" Kathy Ray says, trying to balance the array of flowers she has gathered. "Margie, there is no way to describe the mountain and the chapel. Just wait, it's coming."

She inhales deeply from her toes up, forcing all of the oxygen in Greece to fill her lungs. I watch her rib cage expand and rise above her breast, but before I can click my camera to capture the moment, she exhales with the force of a cyclone. Thankfully, the bouquet that engulfs her petite body stays intact, and not a single petal hits the ground.

"It can't be much longer. Probably around the next curve, surely." I point and click my camera for the thousandth time toward the pastel watercolors of the frothy sea that's swirled by God's own hand.

Mable Craig, from the windy city of Chicago, joins the conversation. She claps her hands and sends the bags of flowers dangling from both arms into a shaking frenzy.

"I'm a lucky woman. I came on this tour to rediscover myself, to find what life has to offer. And what did I find? Ah, so much that I want to live life again."

Lost within her own realization, she wipes tears from her face. "I want to see more of God's amazing creations. How was I to know such beauty existed outside my four walls and beyond the still photos of exotic travel magazines? And the water? Its color is so magnificent—the beauty is beyond words. I'd say it's truly paradise on earth."

Perhaps I should take her photo, tears and all, with her adorable face that resembles a regal standard poodle. With her long nose of distinct European sophistication and her extended lashes that reach her eyebrows of perfect triangles—she's such a unique creation.

"How old are you, Mable?" Margie asks out of the blue. "You look good."

Mable gazes in the air, searching for an invisible number within the clouds. I see the debate within her mind—which number will she choose?

"Fifty-nine and holding," she lies then turns the table on Margie. "How old are you?"

"Old enough to know Stephanie is leading us on a wild goose chase!" She laughs and slides her sunglasses up, revealing her beautiful blue-crystal eyes. "No, seriously, you wouldn't believe me if I told you. It's your prerogative to be any age you want."

"I prefer to be thirty-five and holding," I chime in for no particular reason. "Twenty-five was a good year, just like thirty-five and forty-five." I feel the need to chatter more. "But when you've never adventured out to unfamiliar places or escaped from the box of comfort, well, you might as well be a hundred years old and not a day younger. God created a beautiful world, but it's up to us to get out and enjoy it. And when it comes to age, I've never understood the reasoning for being so clandestine about it. Why the big secret? I want to embrace my thirty-five-year-old self." I laugh, knowing I'm a tad older.

"Not everyone is as adventurous as you are, Stephanie." Mable snaps my photo. "I never thought in my wildest dreams that I'd be in Italy with you, much less Greece on this secluded island, walking to the *Mamma Mia!* chapel. If it were up to you, Stephanie, you could truly persuade a flea to fight a giant."

"I'm excited you're with us, Mable. Everything happens for a reason; God directs our paths, and your being here at this very moment is meant to be. Aren't you glad I persuaded you to come and take the plunge into the unknown?"

"I'm not much on getting out of the box the way you are, Stephanie. I like my hometown, the security of my nest, where I was born and raised. The thought of flying across the ocean all night never occurred to me, not until I read your book. The way you described the places throughout Italy, the storybook villages, the hairpin curves on the Amalfi, and the monastery where strange happenings occur, had me immersed after the first few chapters. Well, once I got past Gladys in the body girdle. I still shake my head and laugh, thinking about the Velcro contraption on the crotch and the hidden euros."

Mable slows her pace as she looks down, searching through a purse full of flowers. "Where is it?" Finally, she pulls out a pink journal with a purple pen attached.

"Take me back to the beginning of the story, you know, day one of this adventure. I want to relive every single minute when I go back home." She grins as she hurriedly jots down a few sentences, then drops her captured thoughts into the bag that dangles from her arm.

Jan marches ahead, toting an oversize bag of flowers on her right shoulder and a sack full of local treats looped over her left.

"I see more!" She gains speed and moves toward a lonely flower that sprouts from the ground.

"Stephanie, can you pull the red flower over there?" She points while balancing the flowering cargo attached to her body as though she's a traveling floral shop.

"By all means, we can't leave one petal on the road." My comment is facetious, but I bend down and yank the plant from the earth with the roots and dirt still dangling.

"I'm really getting older by the minute, and I've yet to see anything that remotely resembles a chapel, or a 'Jack and the Beanstalk,' or Meryl Streep." Margie interrupts the excavation of flowers to stop in her tracks and evaluate the situation again. She theatrically inhales the air.

I see nothing but a sea of turquoise-blue. Are we walking the wrong road?

Chapter 15

MAMMA MIA, WE'RE IN GREECE! (RIDE TO CHAPEL)

a faint, distant roar grows louder as though a remote-controlled plane is coming in for landing.

"What is that noise?" We practically speak in unison, straining our ears. Soon the sound amplifies, and we realize a wand has been waved. A genie has arrived on a four-wheeled magic carpet.

Not one, but two tiny cars approach from behind us. Without hesitation, we wave and jump up and down in the middle of the road.

"Stop, stop!" we shout. Some of us dance in the middle of the road with arms in the air and bags of blossoms on the ground, while a few others stand wide-eyed, holding their bundles of freshly picked flowers.

The first car, a four-door model, has no choice but to stop and join in the parade of Americans.

"*Ciao*! Hello!"

We realize it's our lucky break; we're catching a ride, one way or the other.

The approaching car holds only the man sitting in the driver's seat.

"We're going to the Agios Ioannis Kastri chapel. The *Mamma Mia!*

chapel. Our bus was too big to go around the hole in the road. How did you squeeze by?"

We bombard the man with our questions before he has even stopped. I shuffle my feet and hold my arms out on the chorus of "Mamma Mia!" Yes, here we go again.

"Can we please have a ride?" We shout loudly enough to wake the island.

The car skids to a sudden halt as the driver waves his arm out the window and yells a short sentence in Greek. His happy face needs no translation; it's telling us to "hop inside." He flashes a huge smile and jumps out of his car, speaking in broken English. We understand the words "*Mamma Mia!* chapel."

That's all the encouragement needed, and six of the Americans race to the doors and pile inside. Before the last door shuts in my face, they yell, "See you at the chapel! Have fun walking."

The little car peels away, sending off dusty smoke from the pavement.

Less than a minute later, the second vehicle approaches us. The driver's arm extends out the window and waves heroically. We start the same welcoming dance in the middle of the road as the tiny vehicle abruptly stops.

"Hello!" We giggle and jump up and down like giddy teenagers.

A tall, robust man in the driver's seat throws the door open, causing us to hop back. Launched from the passenger's side, a lady with long, straight, brown hair and a body like a slim Tootsie Roll flies around the front of the vehicle.

"Howdy, mates! The big hole got you walking? Jump in, mates! We have room for some of you."

He's a fast talker, never pausing as his sentences run together. I immediately think of Crocodile Dundee. This guy is Australian, but with his flock of dark curls, he also resembles a young Tom Jones.

He smiles, showing tobacco-stained teeth, and goes straight for a tight, welcoming hug of long-lost friends and English-speaking comrades.

"Wow! You are British. Are you from England?" Dr. Clark's Texas dialect comes out as he rams Jeana and Scott Rabe into the back seat. He squeezes behind them as if he's afraid the car might leave without him.

"No, mate, we're from Australia. We were here yesterday at the chapel and came back today to experience it all again. We're going to take more photos." They open the back doors wider and gesture for more to hop inside.

"We're going to the little chapel, too." Kathy Murphy stands outside the car and scans the interior. "We have three couples renewing their wedding vows. Two of them are already in your back seat. We're going to reenact the whole thing, just like Meryl Streep did as she danced up the mountain. You know, where Sophia rode the donkey in the movie. Are you going up with us?"

There is no room for us. The other Americans are crammed in and packed on top of each other like sardines in a can but with arms and heads hanging out of the windows.

"Hop aboard," Scott's voice echoes from the back seat, and he laughs. His wife is on his lap, smiling radiantly. I suddenly wonder where her bridal bouquet is—smashed with the Americans in the tiny car, perhaps?

Only Kathy and I are left outside the Jeep-like vehicle with our arms full. Some of the others jogged ahead of us minutes ago. We are beasts of burden readying ourselves for the mountainous journey and trudging on foot to the chapel.

"Sorry, mates. It looks like you two will have to walk. No worries, though, it's only a few miles around the next five curves." Tom Jones, or rather Richard, the Australian heartthrob, jumps in the driver's seat. His fingers brush through his black curly hair that sprouts mere inches from his brow like a lawn of grass. As he drums his thumb against the steering wheel and waves his other arm through the window, we panic with the realization of what he said.

Only a "few miles"? Kathy and I simultaneously rush to the back of the vehicle, which holds a giant pile of stuff. No time to think. We pull and tug and manage to hoist ourselves up to perch on top of a tire. We grab the sidebars. My camera and large bag dangle, but I don't care.

"Hold on!" I yell to Kathy as the Australian beau steps on the gas. The toy-sized Jeep peels out with a small jerk. We hold on tightly. Part of my buttocks are suspended over the edge of the metal, and I'm sure the same is true for Kathy. The two of us are flying free in the back with nothing but air beneath our shoes.

"Look at the view!" The wind whips Kathy's voice through the air as she laughs. "This is beyond description."

"You haven't seen anything yet. Just wait until you see the view with the steep stairway coiling around the mysterious rock from the sea. And we're nearly there!" I bellow back with my voice stretched to the frequency of a high soprano operetta singer.

Elevated high above the turquoise water, we sway through the sharp curves on the road with our arms wrapped around the metal sidebars, screaming with excitement and the thrill of the moment.

"We're here! Look to the sea. It's the chapel." Unexplainable exhilaration strikes like lightning and races throughout my body, causing my arms to fly and my heart to explode. It's the movie screen coming to life. My legs kick higher in the wind that rushes past the back of the Jeep. I get to see the *Mamma Mia!* chapel once again and be overwhelmed by its beauty.

"There it is! Oh, it's *Mamma Mia!*" Kathy Murphy shrieks in delight. Her legs churn the air with nothing but pavement far below. Her eyes widen as she sees the magnificence and grandeur of the storybook setting and the impressive sphere that rises two hundred steps from the sea to the top.

"Can you believe this sight? It's better than the photographs. Better than the movie." Kathy's words tumble from her lips.

Hearing the oohs and aahs from inside the Jeep escalates my level of excitement as we slow to a snail's crawl around the sharp hairpin loop. The last twisting turn takes me into hysterical excitement with adrenaline rushing from my head to toe.

"We're here! We're here!" The words continue to fly from my mouth as the Jeep comes to a sudden stop, bringing us face-to-face with the magnificent sphere, and the rocky mountain that upholds the chapel.

We jump off, and our shoes slap the pavement just as the four vehicle doors blast open. The passengers pop out like the contents of a pressurized can.

We are enthralled as we stand in a babbling frenzy, seeing a genuine fairy-tale before us. The little chapel is erected upon a giant rock like a wedding topper perched proudly on the tallest cake ever.

My gaze starts at the top. I see the magnificence of the tiny church with its whiteness shining in the spotlight of the glistening Greek sunlight, manifesting its likeness to the Statute of Liberty and Michelangelo's David—a true sight to behold. The Americans dissolve into animated happiness.

Below its rising grace and beauty, beneath the platform that supports its creation from the sea, is the fabric of marbleized blues all swirled together as if an artist arrived ahead of us and swept a water-color paintbrush across the crystal clear waves.

"This is an alcohol ink painting before us from God's own hands. The swirl of color swimming throughout the magnificence of our God's imaginative ways." Kathy Murphy, also an artist, holds her hands in the air to allow the warm breeze to whip her colorful shawl in the wind.

After many hugs and kisses to our knights in shining motorized armor, we bid them farewell. Looking back over my shoulder, I snap a quick photo of the dashing Australian hugging Jeana and wishing her many blessings for her matrimony bliss.

Standing patiently nearby are the two dynamos, Kathy Ray and Jan, with huge smiles on their faces.

"Thank you for the ride," they say in unison. They reach up with open arms and stretch on tiptoes to smack a kiss on each side of his sun-bronzed cheeks. The Aussie bends down, happily embracing the attention of two beautiful American ladies. Jan leans her head on his shoulder, batting her blueberry eyes at him. It's a spontaneous moment of fun for both of them. Kathy and Jan are two peas in a pod, like Lucy and Ethel.

"Looks like the Aussie beau is staying with us." Dorthia grins with her hands still full of flowers. Her other sister, Bonnie, snaps a quick photo of the final embrace of the Australian who is bewitched by her little sister's magnetic charm.

Simultaneously, Kathy and Jan release their arms held stretched around his back.

"We better let you go so we can catch up with the others," Jan and Kathy practically speak in unison, both of them talking over each other.

"The three couples over there are renewing their wedding vows as soon as we climb the rock." Jan dazzles him with another ray of sunshine from her sparkling eyes.

"Yes, we've got to go." Kathy pulls again from the Aussie.

Both women laugh like they always do. Jan slips a few euros into his hand to thank him for his kindness and refuses to accept it back even though he tries to decline.

"Take your beautiful wife for a cocktail. Just a little token of our appreciation." Jan backs away and turns toward Kathy Ray, who has already joined Kathy Murphy and the others on the rocky steps.

"Come on, Jan," Bonnie hollers at her little sister as she waits by the edge of the water with their other sibling, Dorthia. Her feet are firmly planted on the rocks.

"I'm on my way." Jan grabs the Aussie's wife and kisses her cheek with full southern charm.

"Where else would we experience such an adventure?" Amy, one of the brides from Texas, catches Jan's attention, and they walk toward the others who are huddled together, ready for another photo.

"This is a movie unreeling before us—history in the making. We are movie stars with no script to memorize, just raw reality television. Unbelievable." Amy accelerates to a gentle jog and leaves us all behind.

Chapter 16

MAMMA MIA, WE'RE IN GREECE! (GOING TO GET MARRIED)

"Are we ready to go up?" Michelle asks. The white paper with the wedding lyrics is still crumpled in her hand. It won't be long before she and Kathy Murphy sing together.

"*Andiamo*, let's go!" Kathy Ray hollers ahead of us. She and Jan are already stepping onto the rocks within the water.

"Are you ready to go up?" I clap my hands in jubilation. I'm practically dancing already.

I feel an arm around my shoulder. It is Kathy Murphy urging me to start the music. So, with the turn of a dial, our theme song begins yet again. "*Mamma Mia, here we go again*" blasts from my little lime-green speaker.

Not far ahead, already assembled in a line, the brides-to-be have started the climb. They sing and dance, stop and pose for photos, and then climb again. The rest of us are launching ourselves up the mountain. The scarfs wrapped around our arms flutter in the breeze.

"Follow the leader!" I shout over the music. Kathy Murphy leads the way. She treks up the carved rocks one careful step at a time while her large shawl whips in the wind.

"Go ahead. I'm stopping to get a few photos." I lean against the rock and scan the area. Down below, Mary Earl from California looks out over the sea. She's far enough away that I can only see a small dot, but I recognize the vivid color against the turquoise-blue.

"Come on up," I shout. "You can do this." My voice echoes in the wind.

I see a slight movement of neon green. Mary Earl's scarf wafts in the breeze. I push a button on the little square CD player in my bag and mute the music, but I still don't hear her voice. I try again with words and gestures. "Mary Earl, come on!"

"You're wasting your breath trying to get her up this mountain," Kathy Murphy tells me. "She's scared of heights. Said she'd be staying below, taking in the beauty with her feet on the ground."

I'm only a few inches behind Kathy's heels. She's standing but bracing herself against the rocky side. She inhales then lets her large flower-stuffed bag drop to the ground.

"Are you okay?"

"Yes, I'm going to capture this view. That is if I can find my phone. It's in here somewhere." Kathy reaches with her left hand and rummages within her bag. I can hear the vinyl crackle and crunch.

A brief, lingering silence begins as if even the wind is waiting, holding its breath for the moment. Kathy holds the phone up and presses the button that quickly captures the unexplainable beauty around us.

I press pause again, and the music returns.

Kathy's turquoise scarf waves rhythmically as she steps ahead, one rock at a time. I drink in the sight of her colorful attire just ahead of me. It swishes and flows in long tiers of beauty. A sheer overlay of Greek drapery cascades down her legs, spotlighting a beautiful goddess with golden highlighted hair. She holds her arms high above her head as she grips yards of silky fabric. The translucent outer layer of her long, pink dress whips in the breeze as if choreographed to the music. I stop and snap my camera as I watch the reenactment of Meryl Streep's upward trek.

"*Mamma Mia!* Here we go again!" I shout, although I think no one but myself is listening as I tiptoe up the tightrope. There's a final, curving ascent before we reach the little chapel with the ancient olive tree behind its majestic Greek glory.

"Yes, indeed." Kathy Murphy shouts, echoing my voice. She turns around with arms stretched to the sky, and her mouth set wide in a smile.

"Look at the colors below." Kathy pauses again, breathing in eighty-two steps of unexplainable exhilaration.

"It's magnificent," I whisper from my chest up, trying to force more oxygen into my lungs. My eyes remain glued to the rock steps, for I refuse to look downward at the steep drop-off.

"If only you were a donkey." I joke but then have second thoughts. "Never mind. I'd never ride a furry friend up this mountain. That's too cruel; however, I would hop up on your back or throw a rope to Scott, who's already at the top and let him hoist me up."

I'm too exhausted to continue the rambling conversation aloud, although my mind keeps going.

The turquoise shawl is still clenched in her fingers, whipping in the air like a makeshift canopy hovering above her head. I glance up more often than before, watching the fabric as it flaps in the wind. I wonder if Kathy will levitate as the shawl grows larger.

"You'll be parasailing in minutes." I raise my voice with my latest prediction to compensate for the music still playing from my bag.

"I'll be what?" Kathy is having so much fun as she sings along that she doesn't pay much attention to my silly sense of humor.

"You're going up with the next gust of wind," I practically shout over the ABBA song.

"Boy, wouldn't that be a ride, flying over this enchantment." Kathy never pauses, stepping from one stone to the next while breathing in the air of Greece. "If I could be Mary Poppins, holding my umbrella..."

Kathy looks up at the sky. She pauses for a few seconds and takes a deep breath. I imagine she sees herself floating upward and landing in front of the little chapel. The thought of her magically flying causes me to smile broader than I already am.

It is so much fun to be with Kathy Murphy, the queen of books and creator of the largest book club in the world. And because I know the whimsical, fun, and creative self she truly is, I think that nothing is impossible, not even for her to rise and float to the top of this mountain mystery with a colorful shawl in place of her Mary Poppins umbrella. I speed up my pace, getting closer to her heels, making sure I am within arm's reach, just in case she starts to rise.

"Can you take our photo?" Jan stops and holds up the line. She and Kathy Ray kick their legs up in the air in such a precarious pose that I panic.

"Hold on to the railing!" I attempt to snap their photo while I balance myself on the narrow footpath. I hug the meager protection offered by the side of the rocks.

Dr. Clark breezes by without warning. Startled, I kiss the wall again.

"I've got to catch up with my bride. I'm a lucky man to be renewing my vows after all of these years to my best friend and my wife." His voice tapers off as he puts distance between us.

He seeks to overtake everyone in the path, even those who are already a mile ahead of us. He had been walking beside his wife Alicia but realized he forgot his camera twenty steps back, so he rushed back down. He is tall and lean at six-feet-five inches and gifted with the legs of a giraffe, so he takes two steps to our one.

"She's way ahead of us, probably at the top." I look down, keeping my feet balanced on the rocky ground. I watch Kathy's feet shuffling the stones as she continues to dance her way up the cliff. Her dress barely dusts the steps with its silky hem; it swishes away from her ankles and leather-strapped sandals. Her toes appear briefly, just long enough to reveal a pedicure of pink glitter.

"What's taking you so long?" Emily's voice echoes from above. I look to the top and see her leaning over the edge.

"We're coming!" I hear Scott's voice reverberating ahead.

Margie intentionally stops in front of Kathy. A glimpse of her legs flashes into view as her dress gets swept up by a gust of wind.

"If the creek don't rise, we'll be there!" Margie hollers in true southern dialect.

Carol Lynn is behind me, clicking her camera. "I got you, Mrs. Margie." Carol's voice is loud enough to damage my eardrum.

I turn around to look. Her beauty queen face is glowing as she beams with joy at the sight of the others cheering us on. I wouldn't be surprised if she floats straight to the top where most of the Americans are right now.

She claps her hands and lets the camera dangle around her neck again. I'm sure she's satisfied that she's captured a great photo of Margie.

"We're nearly there!" She announces forcefully. She wedges herself in front of me in an attempt to go past. Her voluptuous breasts swipe across my face, barely missing my eyes. I try to talk, but my lips press into her chest, while my back is crammed against the wall. My arms are forced down. I can't move. Even my sunglasses are locked upon her chest.

"Slow down!" I attempt to caution her, but she's doesn't hear me. The Americans chant louder, cheering her on from above, and she succeeds in climbing beyond me.

As I near the top of the mountain, I pause and look below once more. Such beauty! Paradise has been spoken into existence, and swirls of turquoise-green swim through the liquid blue sea. All of the Americans are ahead of me. Most of them are already at the top and celebrating their triumphant arrival.

Minutes later, when I step up, I hear the crunch of pebbles underneath my leather-strapped sandals. The Americans cheer in celebration in their customary loudness, as they prepare for the festivities of three Greek weddings.

"Stephanie!" Jan calls from above. "Do you need help getting up?" Laughter cascades.

I pause at the final curve, waiting for the drum roll of my heart to slow. I look down and see a sculpted bowl of turquoise pastels, shimmering like crystal and swirling below.

"No, thanks. I'm getting a few more shots of the view."

"Forget the view down there. The best photos are up here." Dr. Clark leans over the edge to snap my photograph from above. His smile radiates like sunshine with teeth whiter than pearls; it's a perk of being a metropolitan dentist.

Close to the top, I stop and look down again, captivated by the swirls of sunlight that reflect off the emerald-and-blue hues of the sea. My instinct is to take another photo, but I turn my attention back to the Americans who are ahead of me, chattering like playful children.

"I'm coming!" I call up to them but continue to stand on the last incline. The steep rocky step leads straight up. I wrap my fingers around the iron rod attached to the side of the mountain.

Here I am, exhilarated yet weak as though I've run a marathon and won the race, or as though I stand on top of the entire world and look down at the wondrous creation of God. As if in a trance, I stare. Time evaporates.

I slide my left hand inside my bag and fish for a remedy. I need an Italian concoction of satisfaction, a cure for this rapid energy depletion I've experienced. I trace the shape of a familiar red box with one hand, then peel the wrapper off like a pro. An instant miracle ensues as I put the little chocolate block into my mouth, and pure liquid espresso explodes. It's a pocket coffee of heavenly delight. I linger a few minutes longer as I devour the delicacy and allow its creamy blend of sugar and coffee to trigger an increase of serotonin and energy. Suddenly, I'm boosted and ready for take-off.

I slip my hand into my bag again and turn the volume all the way up on the little music box. Now, I'm finally ready to finish the last stretch and commence the renewing of vows for our three couples.

As I take the last step up to the top, I see my group dancing to their favorite theme song with their hands flying, legs kicking, and voices ringing. My own Americans are reenacting the sensational movie.

"Stephanie, did you bring the flowers?" Amy holds a colorful bundle of wild blooms in her hand.

"Yes, they're in my bag," I try to catch my breath as my heart beats faster than Liberace on the piano.

"*Stefania*, what do you think?" My Sicilian friend, Antonio, calls my attention to the ancient olive tree. He has tied some colorful ribbons on the swaying branches as part of an old Greek custom.

"I love it! Good job."

He never looks away. He has stretched his arms as far as he can to decorate the tree with the long, dangling ribbons. As he works, he never stops chattering to anyone nearby about Greek wedding traditions.

On my left, Kathy Ray and Jan are arranging the wildflowers they have picked on our way. To the right, Michelle and Kathy Murphy rehearse the perfect love song.

The twisted olive tree is directly in front of me. Its low hanging branches swish and sway, and its silvery leaves whoosh and dance, while the colorful ribbons twirl in the gentle breeze.

"*Andiamo!* Let's go." Antonio chaps his hands and opens the door to wave us all inside. "*Stefania*, I will be the priest. I'm authorized, as you know."

He flashes a warm smile as though he's a shepherd gathering his flock. Antonio's jet-black hair is thick and slicked back with an abundance of lacquer. His Sicilian genes are unmistakable as he beams with pride; his face and his character are both so beautiful.

Everyone scrambles to get into the tiny chapel. We fill it completely. Kathy Murphy and Michelle start to sing beautifully without the aid of a piano or organ, of which there are neither.

A huge container with hundreds of tall, flickering candles blazes in the center. Surrounding us are several silver and gold icons. My gaze locks onto each of them, and I savor the beauty. The wall behind us has one door; it leads into the Holy of Holies, where all except the priest are forbidden to enter.

Three couples stand before us: Alicia and Dr. Clark, Jeana and Scott, and Amy and Earl. All of them appear nervous. Some wipe away sprinkles of sweat which dot their upper lips, and others shuffle their feet as if they are virgins on their honeymoon night again. I watch through the tight zoom of the camera lens. I see the couples scrunch and fidget with wrinkled pieces of paper that contain their handwritten vows to express the depth of their love for each other.

Antonio takes his position in front of the blazing candles. "How many years have you been together?"

They all speak at once, rolling out thirteen, sixteen, and forty-plus years, and that they would love each other in sickness and health; for better, for worse; for richer, for poorer; to love and to cherish; till death do them part.

"*Mamma Mia*, the traditional wedding vows." Antonio ponders as he rubs his forehead.

"You must be more than ready to say your guarantees before God." Although he talks to the Americans, he switches back and forth between several languages. Italian, then English, then Greek, back to Italian again. The resulting mishmash only shows how discombobulated he must feel. He doesn't know they are only renewing their vows. "I've never met anyone waiting this long for the matrimony, the oaths, the wedding. I am privileged to marry you in the sight of our God."

He pauses. Everyone waits.

"Then, shall we start this ceremony?"

Kathy Murphy and Michelle start the wedding song. I begin clicking my camera, taking shot after precious shot.

"Dearly beloved." My mind supplies the words, but we wait a bit longer as Antonio prepares himself for the ceremony. He clears his voice, blinks his eyes, and fidgets with his one square piece of paper.

I lower my camera and observe this holy sight of all of us gathered as one in the little chapel on this towering mountaintop surrounded by the mesmerizing sea. My gaze locks on the three brides and the splendor of flowers that was gathered from the side of the road.

"*Va bene*. Okay," Antonio plants his feet, preparing for seriousness. He motions with both hands, urging the three couples to step forward, and they accept his invitation.

They are tightly congregated, these smiling brides and grooms. The curtain is drawn, and the stage is set. The *a cappella* music is the overture. They are the stars waiting for their cues.

In these last moments, I catch them fiddling with their hair, shuffling their feet, and sweating profusely. Even though the flowers are bundled together beautifully in their hands, the brides nervously rearrange, pull and fondle them. They are, indeed, giddy virgins once again.

After the ceremony, everyone erupts in applause and hardy, congratulatory embraces with each other.

"I have a surprise for everyone," Jan speaks louder to get everyone's attention. Two dozen little Greek pastries tied with pretty blue bows suddenly appear from her big tote bag. Jan hurriedly passes out the tasty tartlets.

"Where are the tropical drinks?" Margie asks, pulling the blue ribbon from the clear bag to reach the treat inside.

"I'm sure Jan has them cold and ready in the bottom of her bag." Kathy Murphy takes a bite of the pastry-like cake. "This is delicious, Jan. Thank you for being so thoughtful. Shall I help you serve the drinks?"

Margie laughs. She glances at Jan's large black tote resting on the rock floor. It seems large enough to be hoisted down the mountain with a crane.

"Sorry, Margie. I wasn't thinking clearly. I left the drinks down below. We'll make up for it when we get down from this rock," Jan tells her as she continues to pass out the tasty treats.

Margie places her napkin, another thoughtful gesture from Jan, over her dress. She plops a little piece of the pastry into her mouth, munching and savoring the intense flavors of the local honey and nuts.

"How is it?" Jan asks. She reaches over and flicks a large crumb off Margie's chin.

"Ah, delicious," Margie compliments with a smile. "There better be more of these little devils in that travel trailer."

"You want another one?" Jan asks. She promptly places another treat in Margie's hand.

"Don't mind if I do, darling."

"I've already had my two," Jan looks at Margie as she bites off the corner edge.

"Can I have your attention, please?" Dr. Clark holds up both hands in the air. "We're going to eat and drink and celebrate more with Tony and Nino tonight in the villa. I would like to invite you to join us."

"Look at him. He looks like his head is going to float away like a balloon." Scott slaps Dr. Clark on the back, giving him a thumbs-up about the party invitation.

Without fanfare, the ladies scurry around the little chapel, gathering up this and that and tossing the empty wrappers and trash inside Jan's container.

The three brides gather their flowers and grab their newly re-wedded husbands, as they had when they arrived an hour ago. They stroll to the entrance, ready to take the lead down the steep rocks.

"*Andiamo*, let's go!" I jump in front of them with my camera dangling in the air. "I'll take the photos as you stroll down."

I smile broadly, satisfied with another successful event and life-long memories of two weeks in Italy and Greece with the Americans.

Chapter 17

HOT AFFAIR ON THE ISLE
OF CAPRI

*H*ere on the Isle of Capri, in front of the colorful turquoise door at number 690, in the passageway of local residents, Louise Crumbatal and Charles from Cincinnati, passionately kiss. They recklessly radiate heat behind a purple bougainvillea acting as though they're invisible—oblivious of gawking eyes.

Peering ahead at the unavoidable situation, there are ten thousand questions racing through my mind faster than I can ponder them. How did this happen? Was this an innocent stroll through the winding streets of fairy-tale bliss when love collided as a serendipitous encounter between our people, two Americans on foreign soil?

There they are, two American strangers from different states who hopped aboard my Italy tour, now wound together as one. Or is this a case of mistaken identity? I question myself as I push my glasses upward, taking a closer look. It can't be my people—they only met a day or so ago. My mind spins, thinking of the infamous introduction at the Dallas airport. It was me who brought them together.

"Hey, Cincinnati, meet Texas," I had said to them before I walked off and bounced from one new passenger to another while making polite introductions before boarding our plane for Italy.

Things aren't always as they seem, are they? I conference with my thoughts as I peer deeper into the passageway, finally realizing these are...maybe...perhaps—my people.

"It's got to be a mistake," I struggle to keep to a whisper. My voice refuses to cooperate as we hide behind a bush.

"No, they are unmistakable. Unless they are identical twin look-alikes to our fellow Americans," Jacque whispers louder. I notice her shoe is on top of mine.

The lemony-hued moonlight shining down on the turquoise door was a spotlight enhancing the sultry entanglement of two lovers wound as one. We watch as his left hand slowly combs through her long black hair, while the other hand explores the mountainous breasts struggling to stay inside the purple linen fabric. Forbidden love is a scandalous situation, especially when doused with the ambiance of Italy, the seductive island of the rich and famous.

"How are we getting to our rooms without them seeing us?" Jacque whispers again. Her heart beats against my shoulder.

"We're not. We'll have to wait. It will ruin their trip if they know we've seen them like this."

"We're going to be here for a while, probably all night." Jacque leans in more, nearly pushing me over.

"Too bad we forgot the popcorn," I joke.

Looking at them hiding behind the trellis of purple bougainvillea and flamboyant orange roses is almost comical. In fact, it would be if it weren't for the fact that Louise is married to a financial advisor who is friends with several of the passengers aboard our trip.

The encasement of the narrow street-like sidewalk with a bed of green grass showcases them like a highlighted shrine in a reliquary—except for the clothes puddling below. Their lips lock as they push hard against the creamy-tangerine stucco wall. Pulsating heartbeats keep pace with the heavy, passionate breathing as shrieks of ecstasy explode through the thick air. It's a night of passion—shocking illicit sex—right before our eyes.

"I don't think they'll notice us walking past them with this much racket," Jacque tells me as she places both hands over her ears. She's pretending to be dramatic.

"I'm not moving. They'll see us. Thank God the music is muffling some of the noise. Can you imagine if there was complete silence with their carryings-on?" I tell Jacque.

"Come to my bed," Charles croons, sounding as though he hit a high note in the school choir when he yelps out the word *bed*. Louise struggles to gulp the thick air as Charles twists his lizard-like tongue around her ear, slurping and licking as though it were his last taste of passion. His hands are constantly grabbing, yanking, searching, and finally landing tightly around her small waist. The jerking and pulling reels on until finally they helplessly fall below the floral beauty with a loud thump, hitting the nearby green turf as though it were a soft mattress.

Nerves are surely swimming rampantly as Louise stammers, "No, I didn't mean—Charles, I'm not young anymore. I shouldn't be here with you. Charles, you need to know—you must know—I am—"

Zippers part, fabric rips, and voices groan. A full explosion of ecstasy fills the air like a powerful detonation of serotonin erupting within, breaking the sound barrier and blasting forth from its normal levels inside the brain.

"Oh, Charles, I've never—well, yes, yes, I mean, no—"

His fingers touch the strings of her dress and toss it aside. She leisurely shifts her thin body against him and tangles her legs around his. Her hands are jelly. They drop onto his thigh and lay there quietly, lifeless, then agreeably move recklessly, upward, nearer to his groin.

"Good gosh! I'd put my sunglasses on if I had some," Jacque tells me. We fidget around, going nowhere while feeling the moist air drift through the walkway and hearing the gentle surf of the Mediterranean below.

"I don't think they'll notice us if we walk around them." I lie with wishful thinking. Our room is just around the corner, and this is the only way to get there—a human roadblock is before us.

"You might as well get comfortable on the grass. It looks as though we'll be here a while," I tell Jacque as I shift around on the turf beside her, crossing my legs and watching the show before us.

Jacque taps five fingers against the leather strap on her left shoe, not knowing what else to do. Her lips are slightly parted, and her crystal-blue eyes are fixated as the other hand twists one loop of hair around her fingers. I glance at the couple, then back to Jacque.

"I think we should get away from here—if we can," I whisper, pulling her sleeve as a suggestion to follow me. We're dead weight on the ground. Our posture perks up as we peek at them, but then slumps down. Jacque's eyes narrow in doubt. It's going to be a long night.

Seconds turn into minutes, then suddenly they abruptly break. Did lightning flash? Surely it did, as they bolt back together—like twisted pretzels, finding new secrets to explore. Untamed arms and legs spread as the ornamental trees creak, and the flowers bend to kiss the ground where tattered fabric hugs the earth.

Just when we thought the show was ending, it would start again. Jacque and I struggle to stand, shuffling and stretching our legs, awaking them from slumber. How will we get to our room that's around the corner from number 690, not far from this passionate movie reel before us?

Louise threw her arms around him and kissed him again, this time dramatically with the force of a hammer.

"Good grief, this is going to last all night," Jacque repeats as she analyzes the steamy situation that is a roadblock to our room.

How will we escape? I think to myself with heart-skipping emotions. I pull across my mind an old, red damask curtain to see the heartbreak hidden behind. It's Louise's husband, Mr. Crumbatal, who waits across the pond in Texas with their many curly-headed children. It was he who gifted this beautiful two-week tour to her. Said he wanted to make her dream of seeing the Isle of Capri, the island of the rich and famous, come true. It was a bucket-list wish for her fifty-eighth birthday. He paid in-full months ago, requesting me to type a note to tell her she's going to Italy with his blessings. Such a dream come true to have a two-week adventure through indescribable places without him and the six kids.

I think about the intense emotions she showed when she passionately hugged and kissed her husband in front of Decorate Ornate, right before leaving to the airport as she stretched her arms tightly around his shoulders and whispered sweet nothings in his ear. Promising lewd, hair-raising advances when she returned—a rain check, so to speak—all of it causing embarrassing shades of red to dance across my face. I stood nearby and waited for everyone to load up into my truck. Afterward, she bent down and hugged and kissed the children as she told them how much she would miss them while in Italy.

"It was daddy's birthday gift to me—a much needed get-away for a little rest and relaxation. Mommy will be back in fourteen days." She gushed with happiness and dramatic tears.

I remember the theatrical performance well. I wiped my own eyes, saying mommy would be home soon, better than ever, with life-long memories of fairy-tale bliss and bringing them surprises. My thoughts run rampant while I stare again at their unbridled passion gone wild.

Charles takes her by the arms and lifts her up on her toes before she realizes her skirt and blouse are nothing more than tattered shreds. He kisses her again, hard and long, and then lets her go. Her legs wilt like week-old flowers folding to the earth.

I think this must be the moment when we could try to walk past them or twitch our noses and become invisible, or better yet, levitate over them. If only it were so easy to avoid this scandalous situation blocking us. But for now, with no trees to lean against, no marble benches, or iron chairs, we sit among the flowers with our legs criss-crossed.

"My legs ache. They've fallen asleep," I complain to Jacque.

"Mine too," Jacque stretches her left arm upwards to touch the petals of pink blooming hydrangeas that grow like an umbrella shading the moon. We turn and continue to watch the latest episode in the shimmers of light with the Mediterranean Sea splashing below.

Exactly forty-six minutes later, I lie down with fifty chapters written within my mind: Louise and Charles, their outward indulgence, their transgressions. I don't remember when the replay stopped so I could sleep, but it finally did. The curtain closed until the morning sun peeked into my room.

I couldn't prevent the frown from crossing my face as I rose from bed the next day. Was it a dream, or did it happen? Last night's rendezvous was such a scandalous affair, especially with Louise's husband being the financial advisor for several of the Americans onboard. Can there be a simple solution to this romantic dilemma without hearts breaking? I think not, but I pray anyway for God's intervention. I pray for Louise to snap out of it, for the fog of lust that has consumed her mind to dissipate before she throws away her marriage and family.

I don't know how two American strangers, one single and one married, can unite so quickly. I think back to their initial meeting at the airport. It was unusual and so magnetic. And, last night's sexual explosions right in front of my face, I can't forget. They devoured each other.

Putting my thoughts aside, I hang from the balcony window as though I'm a see-saw. My stomach balances my body on the ledge while I anticipate the day's events. Looking to the left and right, hoping to see some of the Americans doing the same, I spontaneously shout, "*Buongiorno.* Good morning," at the top of my lungs, only to hear just my voice echo.

Many of our rooms are on the same floor and have timeworn balconies made of intricate iron that drips with floral beauty, one after another. A stone's throw away is the Mediterranean Sea, a turquoise-blue artwork painted by God's own hands, a gentle beauty where the rich and famous float on luxury yachts, a playground for movie stars mixed with locals.

The Isle of Capri is like a two-tiered wedding cake rising from the sea, and the topper of this enticing beauty is Anacapri, one of two villages towering high in the air. A few years ago, the fortress of Roman emperor Tiberius was for sale for a mere forty-four million euros.

It was just days ago that we sat, elbow to elbow, with a rock star.

Yes, right around the corner, three of us Americans sat sipping towering fruit drinks with mountainous swirls of whipped cream on top with Mick Jagger only a few feet away.

Below my balcony is a veritable amusement park. It's a chaotic festival of locals going about their daily lives atop this mountainous splendor. The clanging and clashing of pots and pans draw my eyes down to where a local *signora* waters red geraniums in front of her shop full of colorful ceramics. Several feet over is another *signora* who is busily sweeping the cobblestones with a straw broom that reminds me of the fabled storybooks from my childhood. Directly in front of them is a lively two-story building that pumps out musical notes of Italian laughter. I imagine the children within and the momma preparing another day's activities.

Breaking my attention away from the rhythm of life below is a tiny car zooming by on a street no wider than a regular-sized side-walk with the local trash truck hot on its heels. My eyes are all over the place, then back on the *signora* busy with her floral beauty and scurrying about her morning's chores. It's such a colorful parade with everyone marching to their own beat. Their culture is so different from ours.

My eyes refuse to leave the *signora* with the witch's broom as I continue to balance my stomach across the marble windowsill as though I'm a professional tight rope performer. I feel as though the pages are swiftly turning as the chaotic parade marches on in the procession of daily life. Such theater, so much drama. The acoustics upon this mountain amplify the voices, even the little dogs' barking.

I'm captivated, but my attention is still on the older *signora,* who is so tiny and cute. Her hair is immaculate with a silver bun atop her head and thick ankles stuffed into white orthopedic shoes. Her dress is casual linen with purple flowers on soft pink. She continuously sweeps the same area, polishing the ancient stones in front of her shop while shouting *"Buongiorno"* to friends. It's the quintessential Italian village, a conglomerate of happy faces.

My eyes take in a real-life Romeo. He's a local shopkeeper leaning against his yellow storefront wall, just feet from the *signora* with the witch's broom. He's more Italian marble than man—so chiseled and perfect. His head is a deep sea of thick wavy blackness, sprouting a million strands. He looks up and shows off his golden bronze complexion, oozing seductive masculinity.

From where I dangle high above him, his face still captivates me —those eyes of black coal. He's a Romeo with a flirtatious, sultry suggestion in his smile. The Italians' confidence is the blessed assurance of self-worth that trickles down from the bosom of the momma. They love and worship women; it's embedded within their DNA.

Nonetheless, it's the American ladies who revert to giddy schoolgirls when they step on Italian soil. Regardless of age, when they spy the manly bronzed hunks, something happens inside them that ignites a flame of hunger in their libido and surges their hormones at the speed of light. All it takes is a simple gaze of the eyes or a quick whiff of intoxicating cologne. The mixture is a powerful concoction that permeates their senses. I've repeatedly witnessed the lethal results of the enticing entanglement of foreign seduction.

Regardless of marital status, many of the American women go crazy in Italy and lose their recollection of matrimonial bliss. It's the Romeo's smile, the dark eyes that offer a rendezvous, the entrapment in a fantasy, the desire for a romantic adventure, or perhaps the yearning for unknown pleasures. Entertainingly, they morph into Juliet Capulet and long for a mysterious lover to quench the burning desire of unleashed hunger. It's a dangerous game once you've tasted the forbidden foreign fruit and the guaranteed after-effects of the explosive eruption of emotions.

In the coming days, it will be impossible for me to forget about Louise and Charles, how they rendezvoused in front of the colorful turquoise door at number 690. How many times will I witness the metamorphosis of two human beings when lust collides? I try to direct my mind back to the happenings below my balcony.

Right beside the shopkeeper sits a little dog with a tail as long as its body. It joins in the parade of fascinating entertainment and stylist fashion with its shimmering black fur. The two of them look like an advertisement in an Italian fashion magazine with Romeo's sugar-white linen pants and red scarf.

A few feet to the right, I hear the loud clinking of porcelain cups and saucers. It's music to my ears. I watch as the locals order their morning espressos underneath large umbrellas shading the little square tables. Arms wave in the air with shouts of friendliness.

"*Caffé, per favore.* Coffee, please!"

My attention follows a chic *signora* with a hearty sweet tooth. She hollers in her mother tongue for another *dolce*—the sweet home-made croissant equal in size to half an American loaf of bread. She must be craving an adrenaline rush before the village bells ring out nine o'clock. Their consumption of such sugary indulgences has already added an imaginary six inches around my waist as I continue to dangle above with my head hovering over the commotion of sounds and colors.

My eyes land on the one who sips a foamy, milky espresso with one hand and holds a cigarette as long as a twelve-inch ruler in the other. She's gorgeous in Dolce & Gabbana, my favorite designers, with her long black hair and alluring wide eyes.

Stealing the show is another *signora* who walks from a shop holding a gift-wrapped box in shimmering gold. It's the mailman who receives the welcome as she passes the package to him for delivery.

Seconds later, a young *signorina* waves both arms in protest against another croissant and shouts, "No, no!" at the baker. He speedily trots in the morning's procession while pushing a two-wheeled cart that is loaded with delectable treats.

The large, colorful bougainvillea that twists up the iron balcony below my nose suddenly fills my nostrils with the pollen of a thousand stamens. Interrupting the busy street scene is me. I couldn't help myself from sneezing. I make a loud racket, which causes my discreet observance to be noticed.

Still leaning over the iron balcony high above, I manage to say, "*Buongiorno, signora.*"

In return, a sweet voice echoes back the same sentiments with a smile flashing with glossy red lips. A triangle of little boys with black curls atop their heads—none of them look older than four—skip and hop their way down the street as they giggle while reaching for this and that. Their mommas doing their morning shopping are just behind them, and their voices echo in Italian, while one grabs the cheeks of a little *bambina* and gives them a hard squeeze with a quick twist.

Out of nowhere, a little three-wheeled *ape* rattles up the cobbled stones and abruptly stops in front of the restaurant. Behind the wheel of this toy-like truck is a canvas-covered bed filled with fresh seafood from the Mediterranean. He yells out from the window as he shuts off the engine.

"*Buongiorno!*" he shouts as he springs from the cab.

His feet hit the stones before slamming the door. I watch as he races toward the back and energetically rolls up the blue and white striped canvas to display a colorful array of sea urchins, octopus, cod, silver-colored fish, prawns, and other strange creatures never seen before other than in my imagination—such European delicacies. Surely, all that the deep sea has to offer can be found on the back of his truck, beautifully displayed on ice. I watch intensely while he prepares his make-shift market as the locals gather around.

Afterward, my thoughts briefly go back to Emperor Tiberius, who retired to this island of Capri. I think how well he feasted and lived a life of luxury from his terrace above the sea that overlooks the private islands afar. The mysterious magnetic pull of this mountainous rock remains Italy's most beautiful get-away. Although, it's the cemetery that I love most. There is abundant floral beauty everywhere there with towering marble statues. If I had to choose another favorite destination here, it would be the Via Krupp, a zigzagging coastal path below the Augustus Gardens. Or perhaps I love most the many caves along the rocky coastline, especially the famous Blue Grotto.

The village folk begin to gather as the bells chime. That's a reminder to stop the show and get ready. Slowly, I slide backward and push my feet to the floor.

Right now, I'm doing my best to forget about last night, trying to distract myself from the replay that's probably forever frozen in my mind. I'm not one to dwell in the past, but it's hard to dismiss the fireworks that I witnessed or the force of their connection. The two of them acted as though they were in love, behaving like a hormone-crazy teenage couple.

I sit on the bed's edge and allow the thoughts from last night's rendezvous to play. Did they already know one another from somewhere previously? How? They're from different states. So, no. The questions bombard my mind because the speediness of their love connection is perplexing.

I have plenty to think about, and my mind races in too many directions. I've never had a sizzling rendezvous in Italy, other than with my husband.

"Stephanie, I'm out of the shower if you need the bathroom," Jacque startles me. I forgot she was here. I'm not used to having someone share my room with me on the tours.

"Have you recovered from the movie last night," I asked Jacque, hoping it was just an erotic dream and she knows nothing.

"Talk about X-rated. Wow, I've never witnessed the real thing right before my eyes with two strangers. I mean, I've only known them less than twenty-four hours."

Jacque checked her watch and hurriedly slipped on a lemon-yellow blouse with Mediterranean blue tiles highlighting its diaphanous linen. She purchased it yesterday as we were strolling through the many shops. But less than two seconds after pulling it on, the cheery outfit was stripped off and tossed back on the bed with the other colorful assortments.

"Steph, I'm not the one to ask about uninhibited emotions when it comes to men, but last night was truly a shock, seeing them behaving like wild college kids. I'm exhausted from it all. It's such untamed behavior. I'll never get those images out of my mind. Will you?"

"Never. Do you have an extra pair of jeans I can wear?" I joke as I look at the mountainous pile of apparel next to my little mattress. Jacque had her entire closet, every article of chic pants and tops, laid out on the bed.

"I couldn't decide which ones to bring, so I tossed in all my favorites. Maybe it's a good thing I brought a few extras. I think Louise may need to borrow a top since Charles, more or less, ripped it off. Heck, if they keep going the way they were last night, well, her wardrobe will be dwindled down to nothing by the time we go back to the States." Jacque laughs and hurriedly gathers up every article on the bed.

"I don't know what to say, other than I'm sorry. I've never had any of my people connect from the first introduction. Do you remember how they locked together when I introduced them at the Dallas airport? They seemed to have known each other, perhaps, in a past relationship."

"Maybe that's why Louise was so exuberant with her husband—making that display of missing him in front of us. I don't know, but..." Jacque reaches down for her size-seven white leather sandals and leaves the other seven pairs scattered on the floor.

A knock at the front door startled us. Hearing the helpless female voice ricochet off the blue stucco walls in the hallway alarmed us both.

"Stephanie, are you in? I need to talk to you. It's an emergency," Louise declares. We can hear her shifting about nervously on the doorstep. "It's an emergency, please help me. I was with Charles last night, walking, having a good time, when my purse disappeared."

Louise speaks louder as if knowing her voice is slightly muffled through the door. "I need to talk to you. I'm sorry to disturb you."

Louise taps the door in a rhythmic pattern, growing louder, one after another. "Stephanie, are you inside?"

Still zipping and struggling with my long-legged pants and stumbling over my shoes, I shout, "I'm here! I'm coming."

I race to the door while Jacque continues stiffening her hair with hairspray in the bathroom. By now, it sounds as though Louise is performing a tap dance on the doorstep.

When I open the door, my mouth drops. Obviously, she didn't have time to smooth her ruffled feathers. Her long black hair resembles a bird's nest with grass and twigs jetting out, and her heavy make-up is smeared. She's a mess.

"*Mamma Mia!* What's happened to you? Are you okay?" I pull Louise inside. She bolts past me and sits on the bed, cross-legged, looking haggard. Jacque walks out of the bathroom in a cloud of hairspray.

"Louise, are you okay? Your clothes, your—" Jacque inhaled all the oxygen from the room.

Louise sat there in tattered clothes with her makeup smeared and her hair a disaster. Her eyes, though a bit sunken with dark circles beneath black smudge, are dilated. She has the face of a scared raccoon. In a dramatic response, she swings both legs outward and starts recounting the events.

"I'm going to regret this, but I've got to tell you. I was out with Charles last night, and early this morning, something happened, and it's not good. Ugh," Louise lost her words. Stammering and looking for them on the floor, her eyes examine the tiles. Afterward, she makes an innocent face and presses her lips together as though a fresh swipe of her favorite bright red lipstick was applied.

"Charles and I are just friends—," Louise stops in mid-sentence as if an invisible hand slapped her face.

"Come on, continue the story," I stand with my hands on my hips, ready to hear the replay of last night's performance.

"I didn't mean to do what I did. We were just having fun, enjoying the view of the early sunrise," Louise attempts to keep the story PG-rated and within the boundary of innocence. Jacque and I wait for the confession of her rendezvous.

"What happened to you? You are a mess. Your hair, your face," I reach for her head and pat down that one stray strand of hair that has a leaf sticking out of it.

"Thank you," Louise says when I pull the leaf out.

Louise sprang from the bed and began to pace as if the soles of her size ten shoes were on fire. "I was out last night with Charles, exploring the sites of the island," Louise repeats.

"Yes, we heard you the first time. What happened?" My eyes dart back and forth from her to Jacque.

"I wanted to take a risk, have a little fun. I wanted to do something never done before, or at least not for me," Louise confesses.

"I thought coming to Italy was your 'something you've never done before adventure.' That's what you told me weeks ago in my shop. Isn't this enough, without taking more?"

"That was a scare, at first, the take-off in the plane from Texas. But, yes. I mean, no," Louise stops, struggling for words. "I wanted to feel the rush of adrenaline, the excitement. And I did. Wow, I did."

Louise shows a guilty smile with her medically enlarged lips pressed together, and lipstick smeared all about her cheeks.

"There are more ways to achieve an adrenaline rush than—"

Louise interrupts me as I recall last night's romp by the door. "It was magnificent, so thrilling. I've never been so high. It was a little hard for me to stop, but I did. Yes, I hopped off just in time."

"What! Spare us the details," I object by holding my left hand up like a stop sign. I feel my face burning red. Jacque has both hands over her mouth. She's speechless. We're the three monkeys: see no evil, speak no evil, and hear no evil—save one, and that would be Louise.

"What are you talking about? It was so much fun." Louise looks confused.

"I don't know what to say, Louise. Do you really think it was worth it?" I question as I pace around going nowhere.

"Yes, I want to do it again, but I have no money." Louise gets emotional, and melancholy covers her face.

"Louise, you're married. Do you remember? It's only been a day or so since you hugged and cried, telling your husband how much you loved him, and the children. Do you remember you have little ones?" I stand dumbfounded. Has her memory failed so suddenly? Is she not aware of the destruction and the coming aftermath?

"What are you talking about, Stephanie?" Louise shifts gears, now defensive. Her eyes widen like a bug in a jar. We look through the glass, waiting for her next move.

"The same thing you're talking about, Louise, you know the romp you had last night with—"

Louise cuts me off again and turns the tables. "What? Charles and I got in the lifts yesterday, taking us up the mountain. We went up to Anacapri. It was you who suggested the chairlifts, was it not?"

"What? I'm confused, Louise. I thought you were talking about Charles—you and him last night. You know?" I try to turn the table back around. "You and Charles were on the lifts last night? What can you see in the dark beside the lights reflecting from the sea?"

"Yes, we were on the chairlifts before dinner, and it wasn't dark. What are you talking about? Last night?" Louise breathes hard. Her back is as straight as a brand-new pencil, and her eyes are wide with questions...and maybe a little guilt. "I felt safe with him, and he is adventurous and well-experienced."

"Yep, we already know that." I look at Jacque, and she nods her head in agreement. Louise doesn't seem to hear. Instead, she starts her defense.

"Stephanie, as a little girl, I would swing all day in the summer sun, as long as my mom would allow. When my older sister had moved onto swimming in the pool, I was content and happy on the swing, dreaming of flying in the air. And with every downward plunge, I tried harder, attempted to go higher and higher, just like we did yesterday evening. I reverted to that same little girl last night, the exhilaration of my feet dangling in the air. It was the best thirteen minutes of fun, ascending over vineyards, gardens, chickens, and the Mediterranean off to the side. I saw the Faraglioni rocks and Marina Grande from atop Monte Solaro. Do you remember? You told us about it all. We even saw Augustus." Louise is on a roll, a different one than we obviously took.

"Louise, we saw you last night. Jacque and I were on our way to our room, past the little nook you were in, the dead-end area to our suite," I tell her, reaching for words down in the rabbit hole.

"What nook? What?" Louise changes faces. Her eyes balloon outward. "Stephanie, don't judge me. I didn't plan this—I had no idea. I've never been unfaithful to Tom," Louise starts to break.

She's got to tell the truth, or she will explode. We see it on her face as it contorts up and down in an agonizing kind of way. In front of me, Jacque chews a pink fingernail in an attempt to reduce the tension in the room, while Louise nervously wads the end of her blouse within her hand, crunching and pulling on it.

"Oh, I can't believe my marriage is over," Louise bursts out crying, stumbling for words and telling it all while nervously plowing her fingers through her matted black hair. What a mess; she's flushed and drained.

"Don't get mad, but did you fall out of bed and hit your head or just swing through the bushes, romping with Tarzan all night?" I joke, but not really, trying to lighten things up.

She's now hysterical—babbling, rambling, and going all over the place. I can see the maze of perplexity upon her face. She jumps up and begins to pace as if the answer to her dilemma was across the room.

"My mother has always warned me about other men, about letting down my guard." Louise starts to blame herself.

"So it was him? Did he hypnotize you?" I had to ask.

"I did what I wanted to do and have no regrets," Louise sits down on the bed for one second, then jumps up and paces more.

"I don't know what came over me, but it's not what you think," Louise tells us as she sits on the edge of the lemon-colored chair. She slumps over and nervously shuffles her leather-strapped sandals as though a wad of bubble gum is pulling them to the ceramic tiles. She flashes her small black eyes and nervously twists and pulls that one strand of wiry hair away from her matted eyelashes.

"Charles and I are friends, just friends," Louise starts her rebuttal, then drops her head in her hands while slowly rubbing her fingers over her eyelids as though a headache is coming on.

"You're smearing your make-up, what's left of it," I tell her.

"Who cares?" Louise threw her hands up in a helpless attempt to talk and then stood up and walked back to the bed's edge and dropped down. She rubs her eyes more and then her face. "Give me a second. I'm exhausted."

It was just two days ago on our way to the airport that she shared her life—a happy life, so we thought. She bragged of being married to a wonderful man and giving birth to six children, one set of twins, the loves of their lives. She even emotionally articulated the difficulty of leaving him for two weeks, but it was his gift to her.

It should be enough. And she thought it was. She'd thought they were happily married and living the good life in West Texas, with the big house and nice cars, an Olympic-sized pool, and anything money could buy. Clearly, she didn't want to give me the bad news, but she had no choice. She fiddled with her pink-painted nails, clicking them together, and rearranged her silver watch, spinning it around her small wrist until the words finally spewed out all over us.

"Stephanie, please don't be mad at me. I didn't mean to cause an inconvenience. I know you're already thinking unkindly of me, but I didn't mean for this to happen."

"Things happen, and I'm not your judge. Nonetheless, you need to snap out of this imaginary fling and remember your husband, your children, and your life in Texas. This is not worth losing your family over. There is no romp in the sex pool worth tossing in the towel for your loved ones," I tell her, breathing hard. My heart beats fast, knowing the huge mistake she made last night could ruin her life and destroy her family. Thank God Charles is not married. But he saw an easy prey—a woman burning with lust.

"Stephanie, I lost my passport and six thousand euros last night!" Louise blurts out as she collapses back onto the mattress.

"What? You lost your passport?" My heart drops to the floor, hitting the ceramic tiles hard, knowing it's a big deal and now requires a trip to the American Embassy in Napoli.

"How did you—" I ask, but she cuts me off again.

"I think my purse rolled off into the Mediterranean. I mean, well, I'm not sure, but Charles helped me look all night. I mean this morning. I'm not sure how it landed in the sea, but I think it did," Louise admits sheepishly.

"Wait a minute. You think the passport is in the sea?" I squat on the tiles, feeling faint.

"What are you going to do, Stephanie? Can you get someone to go look for it? Can you get a boat and search? I need to call my husband this morning; I need more money. What other options do I have? Tell me where to have him send the money. Are we leaving the Isle of Capri tomorrow? Charles said he'd give me money, whatever I need. He offered three thousand euros, but...Oh, Stephanie, how will I get a new passport?" Louise can't stop talking now. She runs and bumps every word into one big fragmented sentence. I understand nothing.

"Oh, Stephanie, I'm so scared!"

"You should be."

"This is the worse day of my life! What will I do without my passport?"

"You will remain in Italy. It takes time to get another passport, all the red tape you must go through." I keep a straight face.

"What do you mean I stay in Italy? I must go home to my husband and children!"

"Why? I thought you are with Charles now. Are you not?" I antagonize her, trying to rouse her conscience, hoping she realizes a romp with an American playboy tycoon is only that, a fling, nothing more. I'm sure Charles has no intention of marrying or carrying on this rendezvous past the two weeks in Italy. He's here for the good times, seeing and experiencing exquisite places as the rich and famous do and more.

"No! I'm not with Charles! I love my husband!" Louise falls on her knees as if a bolt of lightning struck across her chest. Her hand grips her breasts. I suddenly think she's encountering a heart attack, or is it theater? Before my thoughts flash across my mind, she sucks in air like a vacuum cleaner.

"What was that?" I say in shock.

"She's having a panic attack!" Jacquie runs for water. "Give her space. Move away from her protective bubble! My sister-in-law has them."

"No! I'm okay." Louise perks up like a wilted flower before Jacque splashes her.

"Gosh dang, you scared us to death!" Jacque stands over her with a bottle of water.

"Really? You were going to pour water on her head?" I sit down and think like Tony. I can almost hear his words in my ear, his continuous mantra, the lingering question that dangles in the air upon my arrival to Italian soil—"*Mamma Mia, Stefania!* Where do you find these people you bring to me?" I'm beginning to wonder myself.

Louise starts again, this time displaying a ripple of claustrophobia, so strong she starts to hyperventilate with her eyes ballooning to small cantaloupes.

"Take a deep breath and calm down," I tell her. "Think back where you were and what you were doing last night when you lost the passport. It's okay. We'll find it or get you another one."

I reach for her hand and squeeze it. She's never been out of the United States, and now she resembles a glow stick. Her face is blinking red.

"Yes, you have to slow down. Go back and reenact the evening. Surely, it will come back to you. Hopefully, the purse will show up, probably where you left it." Jacque doesn't realize what she just asked Louise to do—reenact the evening.

Louise sits up, tears streaming down her face. The slow drizzle washes the remains of last night's make-up off, dissolves it into black drops that are now dripping onto the bed.

"I'm worried about my passport." Louise nervously swings her arm and sends her Rolex watch flying over my opened luggage on the floor. It hits the wall with a loud bang.

Adding to the commotion is a voice that calls out Louise's name. Charles sticks his head through the door with black binoculars dangling in his hand. He appears like a wide-eyed deer caught in the headlights of last night's adventures.

"Charles, I was just telling Stephanie and Jacque about my purse falling into the Mediterranean, and how we've looked for it all night after we watched the moon set, you remember, after we drank the *vino*," Louise rambles on, fidgeting and sweating. Her quivering lips make it hard to breathe. She's an informant, taking the lead for Charles to follow.

"I told Stephanie and Jacque about the chairlift and what we did last evening," Louise sets the scene, hoping Charles will follow.

Charles leans awkwardly against the wall as if he has no strength to stand. He's a lifeless rag doll, slumped and drained from exhaustion. Feeling awkward, I'm sure, he shifts his shoes on the tiles and adjusts his shirt, restlessly pulling the ends down while thrusting out his chest.

Later that morning, while the Americans enjoy the Mediterranean breakfast, I confer with Tony, telling him about the lost passport and the steamy love connection between Louise and Charles. Tony sat at the little round table in the corner of the hotel, shoving a plate of scrambled eggs aside while reaching for a glass of blood-red Sicilian orange juice with the other hand.

"*Mamma Mia, Stefania*, we must go straight to the American Embassy in Napoli. We must go immediately to get the new passport." Tony starts in again with his hands twirling in the air. I prepare myself to listen and watch the various emotions across his face.

Tony gestures wildly and continues without stopping his thoughts. "*Mamma Mia, Stefania*, why must they rendezvous when they arrive in Italy? Thank God the Italian was innocent this time. It's always the *Americano* chasing the men here. What do they think, we're all Casanovas?"

"No, it's the other way around!" I defend the American ladies, and Tony smiles. He knows I'm correct.

"In all our twenty years of bringing the Americans to Europe, this has happened twice. Well, maybe three at the most, but never two Americans making out with each other, not that I'm aware of," I continue, not ready to rest my case. I want the last word. "It's always the Italians, the Casanovas' fault."

"*Mamma Mia*, you must be joking!" Tony nearly chokes on his mouthful. "What about..."

"Take a drink," I tell him, pushing his juice toward him.

"It's the truth. It doesn't take much to fan the fires. They're always ready to comingle with the Americans. It's the Italian DNA. What else can it be? And age doesn't matter!" I joke, trying to hype Tony up more, but in reality, I know it's true.

"Perhaps it's your language that cranks the motor of the Americans, the musical purr of linguistic chaos seducing their ears? Or, could it be the olive-kissed face with the fiery eyes balancing majestically on sun-kissed cheekbones? Smoldering black coals ready to ignite into burning flames of passion." I refuse to stop the playful jest just to watch Tony's reaction.

He wipes his mouth, removing the peach marmalade smeared across his upper lip. I see the twinkle in his eyes. He's ready to start his deliberations about his long consideration of the Americans.

"You know, *Stefania*, every tour we do with the Americans, there is always one. One who does something so unbelievable? How do we escape the escapades they bring to us? The men try to be good, to be faithful to the wife, but with the people you bring to Italy—*Mamma Mia*, regardless of age, they seek the pleasure of a Casanova."

Tony rests his case for a brief moment and hangs his head low as though looking for something on the floor.

"And you are Pinocchio. I see your nose growing before my eyes." I laugh, satisfied with my closing statement.

Tony wants the last word. And he gets it.

"*Stefania*, we must go to Napoli, to the American Embassy for the document. *Mamma Mia, Madonna!* How many times do we return for the *passaporto*?"

Chapter 18

TOO MUCH EXCITEMENT IN THE MEDITERRANEAN - MAN OVERBOARD!

If she hasn't been in an accident lately, she's probably caused one, I think to myself, watching Linda leap into the blue and white boat as it bobs in the turquoise-blue waters of the Mediterranean Sea. Her long, string-bean of a leg acrobatically kicks backward in the air and crashes into a tall blue and yellow ceramic vase that was resting peacefully on the concrete walkway.

Minutes ago, the captain of our boat left the beautiful masterpiece in plain view of everyone so he could help one of the Americans into the boat. And now, seeing how clumsily Linda jumped in, I'd say she deserves the name "Agnes Moorehead." Growing up watching Agnes Moorehead play Endora on the hit series *Bewitched,* I can see the resemblance. Linda is not only clumsy but has the charm and adventurous behavior of Endora too.

With the fast pace of technology and the advancement of space travel becoming clearer, who knows, perhaps someday Mars will be added to my itinerary for those seeking adventurous excursions that are "out of this world." And if so, Agnes, I mean, Linda, would be the first to sign up. She's been traveling around Italy with me for a few years, never asking a single question of where we're going, just tossing a check my way as she laughs like an exotic parrot and exclaims, "Stephanie, make sure you get me an aisle seat next to a good-looking man."

The reason for her eager participation to travel with me, besides being adventurous and a talented artist, is that she loves the bronzed Romeos. I'd say she's been to the moon and back, at least a hundred times—if you know what I mean. Just like Endora, except for the twitch of her nose. I'm joking about the sexual innuendos, but she does enjoy scouting out handsome men for her sister's modeling agency in Los Angeles.

It's mid-May, and we arrived in Napoli, Italy, two days ago with adventurous Linda and twelve other lively Americans who are hyped up from the magnificence of the famous Amalfi Coast. After breakfast this morning, we started the drive with Nino at the wheel and me with the microphone lodged at my throat. The zigzagging road is more exciting than the tallest roller coaster going upward and then plunging downward at a thousand miles per hour. Yesterday, I prepared the Americans' minds for the heart-palpating ride and the adrenaline rush of experiencing and seeing world wonders.

"Don't forget your cameras and your heart medication, my friends. For tomorrow will be an experience you'll never forget." I hyped them up, but my carrying-on didn't come close to describing the actual experience. There are no words in the English language that can describe the hair-raising and out-of-your-mind thrills of the Amalfi Coast drive. None.

It's absolutely electrifying being inside the coach, looking to the Mediterranean Sea, and then seeing rainbow colors of terra-cotta tiled terraces exploding with flowers as if the gardens were on steroids. The villas hover over the cliffs, clinging to the side of the mountains with wrought-iron balconies and candy-striped canopies. Vineyards cascade down the mountainside, using up every square inch of land.

"How do they harvest the grapes without falling into the sea?" The questions started, one after another, and I answered proudly. They oohed and aahed at the floral-laced pathways hanging in mid-air with gigantic lemons and oranges swishing in the breeze.

And just when I thought the Americans would knock the windows out of the coach as they banged their cameras against the glass trying to capture the perfect photo, they broke the sound barrier with the shrieking of their voices when a little donkey came into view. The excitement ricocheted throughout the bus. It is always the same, regardless of which group of Americans have come with me.

The Amalfi Coast drive is a thirty-six-mile wonderland of twists and turns stretching from Sorrento to Salerno. In 1997, it was listed as one of the most spectacular drives in the world and declared a UNESCO World Heritage Site.

Just yesterday, we had spent hours in the tiny village of Amalfi with everyone milling around, going here and there, some venturing to the beach and swimming in the Mediterranean, while others followed me inside the walls to be star-struck by the Amalfi Cathedral.

"Follow me," I told the Americans less than twenty-four hours ago, as we trotted across the narrow streets with cars zooming past.

"Look to your left, don't look to the right," I instructed as we played "follow the leader" into the wonderment of Amalfi.

It was Ann who asked the question, "Why must we look to the left and not the right?"

"Because you must look to the left or you'll have bad luck," I joked with Ann.

As we made our way past many people and shops, I hollered, "Stop! Everyone, look to your right!"

The majestic Cathedral of St. Andrew brought oohs and aahs as they looked upon the sixty-two steps leading upward, the colorful inlaid gold tiles, and the majolica tiles. Its massive architecture resting ornately in the tiny piazza was enough to make me dance with excitement too.

"Inside is the crypt with the remains of St. Andrew. Do you remember which of Jesus' disciples he was?" Not able to wait for an answer, I blurted, "Andrew! He was Jesus' first disciple, and he was crucified in Patras. Go inside and see for yourself, or rejuvenate with an espresso, or cappuccino, or a towering cup of gelato. I'm heading to my favorite place for pizza. If you're hungry, follow me."

I remember glancing around at the Americans and seeing their faces filled with wonder at the biblical history before them and the reality of St. Andrew resting inside this majestic beauty-of-a-church. The words rushed into my mind of what Jesus said to Andrew: "Come, follow me."

Andrew left everything—his nets, fishing boat, and his life—and followed Jesus. That's what the Americans have done. They've left their nets, their boats, and their normal way of life, and followed me to another world to wander around in mystery and excitement as they discover and learn.

"I'll meet you back here tomorrow, in front of the cathedral, at 2:30 p.m. for those of you who want to go out in the boat to see and experience Amalfi from the Mediterranean. We'll go by private boat and experience the beauty with the ocean mist on our faces. I want you to have both experiences: land in the morning and water in the afternoon. It's beyond words to see the coastline and the enchanting villages dotting the shore. And for those who want to stay, the beach welcomes you with umbrella loungers and Romeos galore," I told them.

Now, as we finally launched with most of the Americans on board, we float along as waves of turquoise-blue lap against the boat. The water is crystal clear blue.

Seated across from me is a couple from Georgia: Sarah and Dale. They signed up for this tour after reading my book *Mamma Mia, Americans "Invade" Italy*.

Sarah, a forty-three-year-old blonde-haired beauty with thick, highlighted strands of hair squeezed tightly in a sophisticated pony-tail, spontaneously grabs her husband's camera. Yanking the camera strap hard in a theatrical attempt to capture the picturesque photo of a villa resembling a real-life sandcastle on the shore, she accidentally propels his body into the sea.

Panic should be slapping Sarah in the face right now as her pencil-thin husband flies overboard like a bottle rocket, but the only thing she does is burst into laughter as she drops to the floor of the boat and roars uncontrollably. As fast as she went down, she springs back up with the confidence of being a certified life-guard. She had bragged about working on the beach as a professional twenty-one years ago.

Sarah blew a hair-raising whistle and shouted, "Man overboard!" causing Ernie, a retired Navy Seal, to rocket off the boat and dive deep into the Mediterranean in hopes of rescuing Dale.

I'm seated inside the cabin with the microphone in hand, where I had been narrating the view. The captain of the boat sits nearby with his hands tight on the wheel.

We watch the scene unfold in disbelief. Nearly giving us all whip-lash, the captain pulls the throttle and stops the boat, while the deck-hand rushes to the back of the boat to grab the red and white floata-tion device and tosses it to Dale.

"*Mamma Mia, Stefania*, what's the matter with this *signor*? Why must he swim? Did you tell the *Americana* they can swim before we stop the boat?" Tony pulls on the rope that's now tightly secured around Dale's goose-like neck. He's pulling him in as though Dale is nothing more than a small fish, flipping and flopping in the water.

"Everyone, stay in the boat!" I shout, not believing that we have not one but two men overboard. "This is a first for us to have someone tossed into the sea."

"Good golly, I hope to God it's the first. Why in the world would Dale jump in the water? Couldn't he wait until we stopped the boat or at least go ashore over there?" Linda "Moorehead" points to the sandcastle.

Ernie is splashing and swimming around Dale—a shark circling its prey as Tony pulls harder. Dale bursts into laughter as he slips the life preserver from his neck.

"I'm okay, Tony. No need to pull." Dale tossed the device away and intentionally did a somersault, then splashed about hysterically pretending to be drowning and intending to enhance Tony's alarm.

"*Mamma Mia*, I don't believe this behavior." Tony wiped the sweat off his forehead and away from his sunglasses. He knows it's trickery now and that Dale is playing with his emotions—or least I hope he knows?

"Are you okay?" I holler to Dale, who is intentionally bobbing up and down like a cork. I see he's entertaining us and enhancing his ten minutes of fame as another nearby boat drifts closer. Tony hangs from the boat, looking irritated, and shakes his head while trying to regain his composure. His hand is over his heart, and sweat continues to drip from his brow.

"It's okay, Tony. He's joking with you. He is playing around," I say to soften the blow, knowing by now Tony probably needs a change of underwear. Dale intentionally yanks the floatation device back to his body and slips it back under his shoulders as Tony looks down, trying to breathe.

"I want to tell you something." Tony is too winded to speak any louder than a flea without a tongue. I read his body language. He's become Rodney Dangerfield again with bulging eyes and his brows lost somewhere in his hairline. I know what he's thinking and wanting to say—it's written on his face: "This is no joking matter, *Stefania*. What's the matter with this American jumping into the sea like some kind of crazy! *Mamma Mia, Madonna!* I can't do this anymore. You're killing me with the people you bring to me."

Down below in the water, Ernie joins the fun and whacks his wet hand across Dale's frail back. "Man, it's a good thing you've got witnesses. I saw your wife slap you right off the boat."

Ernie flips over on his back, attempting to impress all who are hanging over the boat's edge. Two seconds later, he performs acrobatic flips, spinning himself around in the sea, then hurling up and down—a dolphin at Sea World, and we are his audience. Most of us are now laughing uncontrollably, save for a few who are still holding their breath.

"This is a first for us," I repeat, not believing the last few minutes of events. "We've never had anyone go overboard."

"Stephanie, this is another chapter for your next book," Ann from Tennessee, reminds me. "Didn't you have someone who flipped a little rowboat over here?"

"Oh, yes, I did, indeed. I'll never forget that incident."

"How did it happen? I'm curious. It must have been a tiny boat to rock over," Ann asks.

"Yes, it was an American who insisted on visiting the Blue Grotto years ago. She didn't jump overboard. She capsized while trying to hoist herself into the little rowboat with her friend inside, which caused the tiny two-seater boat to flip sideways. It was such an unforgettable spectacle that is forever etched within my mind."

"Keep going, Stephanie. I want to hear all about it. I never thought the stories in your first book could be true. But, I'm here to testify, they are indeed." Ann smiles big with her vocal reaffirmation of events. "You've got to share this adventure with the world. Tell them about Dale. Oh my, I can't wait to get back and relay the whole story."

"Don't get too excited. We're only on day two of the tour. We've got twelve more days to go, and trust me, this is only the beginning of the stories."

Ann laughed. Her eyes sparkled up at me, waiting for more.

"What's so funny?"

"Stephanie, all of this is normal to you, right?" She inches closer to me.

"Of course. Well, no. It's just life happening with hair-raising situations. Italy does strange things to people, especially us Americans. We morph into—well, different people. One never knows what will happen next. I hope you will come again and again with us. Every tour is different. There is always something happening, but some things I can't share or tell in a book. I've brought Americans from all over the United States over here, even a tap-dancing princess from Mexico City. I could never divulge that ordeal of the ballerina royalty married to the multi-millionaire, or the secret lifestyle they live."

"*Stefania*, where are you?" It is Tony forcing my thoughts back to the present as the boat gently sways as it sits in place. The water softly kisses its side, giving me the urge to jump in, but I don't.

Seeing that Dale is in no danger of drowning, Ernie swims underneath him and shoots up like a torpedo tossing him back into the boat—like a wet fish flopping on the deck, then pulls himself back in.

"*Mamma Mia!*" Tony bellows. His eyes are bulging so much that it makes me think they will surely pop out onto the floor. Tony releases the rope from his grip. A loud thump echoes as the braided threads hit the floor of the boat. Tony looks ready to shout, sweat covering his face, but there are no words, at least for two seconds.

"*Mamma Mia!* This is unbelievable, *Stefania*. This is too much." Tony pulls a white napkin from his pocket to wipe away the dripping sweat and exhales with enough force to blow us off the deck.

Looking ahead, I see the sun shimmering off the white celebrity yachts hovering nearby. I drag my red-painted nails over my flushed cheeks while shaking my head with a slight smile. Dale pretends to be an Olympic winner, beating his chest and bouncing on his toes while bragging, "What about that backflip?"

The Americans join in on the fun and pump his confidence. Like a flying dart, Dale leaps up onto the gunwale.

"*Mamma Mia, Madonna!*" Tony jumps to his feet again, clutching the rope in his hand and hollering, "*Basta*! Enough! What's the matter with you?"

"He's joking," I interrupt Tony, flashing him a calming smile.

"He's not jumping back in," I reassure Tony. It's hard not to laugh at his seriousness.

"*Mamma Mia*, we'll see," Tony mumbles, knowing the jury is still out for deliberation. Taking a deep breath, he pushes his sunglasses upwards on his Sicilian nose, then ceremoniously tightens the colorful scarf wrapped about his neck. He scans the group with a suspicious mind.

The Americans begin oohing and ahhing at the canvas of beauty before them again. I motion for the captain to continue.

"*Andiamo*, let's go," I shout. I feel my own adrenaline rush. A burst of energy explodes throughout my body, urging me to spring back-flips through the salty air or at least do a classy high kick to express the excitement zipping throughout my body.

Suddenly, we're surrounded by white multimillion-dollar yachts, the ones you see in movies with the rich and famous lounging on deck—a few wave to us with raised glasses in their hands.

"Who are they? I bet they're celebrities," Lynn from Galveston, Texas hollers as she waves both arms as though she's a castaway, ship-wrecked and being discovered.

"Yep, it's probably rock stars looking to party with us," Dale answers. He skirts closer to the boat's edge and waves his left hand while twirling the other one as though performing for the Super Bowl crowd. "Surely they are. I mean, look at that yacht...the swimming pool on top. It's probably..." Dale squeezes out every famous person's name from his voice box in a matter of seconds. He's star struck and now hyperventilating as imaginary celebrities materialize in his mind.

I'm sure the Americans can smell the wealth of the Mediterranean, the lifestyle of the rich and famous, with the backdrop a UNESCO World Heritage Site. Being here again for the hundredth time and experiencing this amazing beauty with the Americans is a privilege. I never take it for granted. And I wonder if others appreciate what we're all experiencing right now and the beauty of God's handiwork.

The Americans are laughing and taking photos, except for one, and that would be Dale, who is still teetering on the boat's edge and making Tony nervous about his debatable gymnastic abilities.

Tony spins around and flops down hard on a seat with both arms dancing and twirling over his head. "*Mamma Mia, Stefania*. What else can possibly happen with these people? I do not understand why this *Americana* propelled into the water. What's the matter with him? And look at him. I believe he'll jump again."

Hours later, the afternoon's mishaps are nothing but faded memories. We've arrived at the shore of Positano, and before our boat completely stops, the legs and arms of the Americans begin to dance and squirm as though they're infested with fleas. I've never seen such fidgeting as they look upon the landscape of pastel-hued villas stacked one on top of the other, all clinging to the soaring mountains. The mesmerizing view starts at the foot of the turquoise-blue sea and gracefully ascends into the white, puffy clouds. But the view depends upon where one's eyes start looking. When seen from the sky, the homes cascade like a beautiful waterfall, spilling dramatically toward the blue depths below.

My eyes always attach to the large majolica-tiled dome of the Church of Santa Maria Assunta. I've looked upon it a hundred times or more and stood in front of it with cameras flashing. The church is cradled like a newborn, enveloped by villas stacked one on top of the other.

"This is the place," Linda whispers in my ear. It startles me.

"The place for what?" I ask, rubbing my ear.

"I don't want to have a love affair in Amalfi. I want it here." Linda twitches her nose, pretending to will it to happen. But nothing does. I see no Romeo appearing yet. She is such a jokester, always laughing.

"Of course you do. But what's the location have to do with it?" I joke.

Linda blinked as though something hit her eyes and then dramatically says, "Everything. When it comes to lovers, I want the ambiance to be equally as beautiful as me. I want the table set with flickering candlelight, the atmosphere alluring with red roses, the stage accentuating a dramatic mood for fireworks. I want to open my eyes and see beauty all around. Don't give me a plain vanilla love affair or a wall of whiteness with no fabulous accessories."

"I see. I've heard they're great fun and quite acrobatically enhancing to one's physique." I try to rouse her up more, knowing this is her favorite topic. It's all fairytales within her mind. Her husband of forty-nine years died a year ago in her arms. Perhaps she entertains the lingering memories of ghosts in the past.

"My body doesn't require an excessive workout where acrobats are required. Remember, with the twitch of my nose, I can ascend to another planet," Linda elaborates with a smile while batting her distinctly long lashes, which confirm my sentiments of her similarity to Endora. She knows I often joke about her name, the resemblance, the eyes, and the same hair-do, not to mention the flowing, floor-length attire that is identical to the iconic star of long ago.

"I suppose you've got me on that one, levitating upwards into another world. However, I don't need to twitch my nose for that." I laugh, intentionally leading her on and trying to pull more from her spirited mind.

"This is Positano, another playground for the rich and famous," I shout as I jump off the boat ramp and run through the dark sand, squashing its granulated brown sugar between my toes. I throw my arms in the air, presenting Spiaggia Grande, the large beach and the heart of this village.

"Linda, here it is, just for you. Positano is pure magic and guaranteed to put a spell of enchantment on you."

"We can only hope, Stephanie," Linda says while scanning up and down and all around. She sees the raspberry-colored explosions of bougainvillea plummeting from the balconies with assorted rainbow shades of coral, lemony yellow, and creamy white villas clinging to the soaring cliffs.

"Are you going swimming? If so, take your pick of a place to lounge," I tell her, pointing to the neatly lined up rows of gigantic umbrellas and lounge chairs all around.

"The clock is ticking, and I'll see you later." Linda throws a blue bag over her bare shoulder and marches forward, her shoes digging into the rocky sand.

"Go up the steps and to the left. The shops are everywhere," I hollered, knowing she usually prefers to explore on her own when shopping and scouting for potential models for her sister's modeling agency.

The rest of the group stands with cameras glued to their eyes, spellbound by the beauty. I look at the little wooden boats bobbing up and down behind us and imagine the local fishermen working for the catch of the day. Sprinkled around them are beautiful luxury yachts. It's a postcard of an exotic getaway.

I make my way up the stairs navigating around the narrow walkway to Via Pasitea, home to the elegant boutiques that drip with eye-popping tropical linens and art. It's there along the way that Linda excitedly grabs my shoulder, stretching the fabric of my blouse and pulling me to a skidding halt. She's spotted the boutique with exotic decor.

"Come inside with me." Linda pulls my arm, forcing me into the colorful apparel boutique. The walls are covered in oil paintings with ornate, gold frames showcasing the paint strokes of local artisans. I see nothing of interest, but Linda does. Thirty minutes later, she walks out with a pretty gold and blue bag tied with a yellow bow. Inside is a thread-of-a-swim-suit and an expensive bottle of perfume; I walk out with nothing.

"Stephanie," Linda motions for me to come closer. "Ever since I watched the movie *Under the Tuscan Sun* and saw her and her boyfriend here in Positano, well, I've dreamed of being here, plunging my toes into the sand, and the Mediterranean, and..." Linda looks over her shoulder, making sure no one is within ear's reach, then turns her face closer to mine.

"Stephanie, find me an Italian, just like the one in the movie. I don't mean identical, but someone in that vicinity. I mean, surely you can. You know so many locals around here. Everywhere we go, someone is hollering your name. They all know you. Will you introduce me to one, just one?" Linda is serious. I stand speechless for the first time, waiting for her to break out in laughter and tell me she's joking as we like to do.

"What about that gorgeous hunk over there?" Linda points to a tall, tan Romeo-of-a-man who is swirling his lizard-like tongue around a heaping cone full of chocolate gelato. I watch her eyes glaze as Romeo walks closer.

"Looks as though you don't need my help. I'll be on my way. I have lots of shopping to do." I speed away, as Linda nudges closer to him, enveloped in her newest Italian perfume that is radiating like a sprung leak of exotic air freshener.

Being curious, I turn around and slip behind a rack of colorful linens to observe what happens. I watch as Linda goes into action. I hear her nervous laughter. Within seconds, the unthinkable spills out from her mouth: the unintelligible, the jumbled lyrics of one of my favorite songs.

"When the moon seems to fly like a big pizza fly, that's *amore*; when the squirrel seems to climb like it's had too much wine, that's *amore*."

"*Mamma Mia!*" I cover my mouth to catch my laughter. She's lost her mind completely. Is it love or just her trying to snag a potential model for her sister's agency? Whichever it is, I escape to things of more importance, such as finding another passenger, Sandra, the perfect oil painting.

"Stephanie, you go find me a nice painting of Positano, you know, the art we saw last year," Sandra had said an hour ago when she stuffed my hand with euros and took a seat beside Tony under the gigantic umbrella, both licking *gelato*.

Making my way through the maze of colorful shops, I finally find Sandra the perfect painting—brilliant oil strokes on canvas of Positano that flaunts the turquoise-blue sea with a pale, yellow moon casting its shadow over the Mediterranean.

"*Perfecto*," I say, tossing two hundred euros on the counter while smiling at the *signora* who's insisting the masterpiece be rolled in paper and wrapped with a bow. Initially, I protest, but the *signora* pulls harder and wins. Twenty minutes later, after digging through mountainous stacks of floral paper for the perfect color of her choice, she labors with minute detail to fold and crease the paper as though she's competing in a gift-wrapping contest. I stand on bouncing feet, anticipating the grand finale. Thirty minutes after the first delay, I finally make my get-away with the bubble-wrapped masterpiece in tow—complete with a massive pink bow.

Three shops down, I'm stopped by a *signora* who pulls me aside and states, "A spectacular choice, *Stefania*."

She peels an edge of the paper and snips the pink bow with her tiny scissors.

"*Stefania*, Maria has nice art in her shop, but let me show you something much nicer," Delfina says, turning her nose up as she pulls down a large painting of Positano—bright orange and pink hues catch my immediate attention.

"*Grazie mille*. Thank you very much, Delfina, but one is all I need.

This is not for me, but for a friend that travels with me. I'll tell the Americans of your treasures and recommend your shop," I spill out words all the way to the exit. Delfina continues to insist her art is much better and that I need more.

Hours later, I look at my watch and feel the urgency of time ticking away. I remember the promise made to Ann as we arrived, agreeing to meet her on the beach underneath the blue and white canopy shading the local artisan.

"I want to find the perfect painting of Positano for my bedroom, and I need you to help me negotiate the purchase. Will you assist me after we shop?" Ann's words echo in my mind.

Retracing my steps to the beach, my adrenaline starts to rise when seeing a sea of white coming my way. It's a huge wedding parade whooping and hollering and blocking my way. Without thought, I dart through another pathway, and within seconds, a medieval dressed band with loud horns and drums are at my heels, marching in a fast trot. They are so close to my shoes that the Italian lyrics hit straight into my eardrums. A burst of energy makes me jet away with lightning speed, bypassing locals with arms and shoulders loaded down like me. I'm a packed donkey, my body strapped with Sandra's painting and bags of local treasures.

The race is on as I side-swipe too many people with my excessive load while whisking through the narrow alleyway. Trotting fast, I feel the magnetic pull from the parade of lemon-scented shops and fine leather sandals. Every color of linen is hung with such splendor, reaching out for me as it flaps in the gentle breeze. And the locals, the handsome, bronzed Romeos, are so immaculately groomed in vivid pastel shades with cashmere sweaters draped over their shoulders in the warm air.

You don't come to Positano to see historical sights, except for the church. You come to shop for the finest linen, the handmade leather-strapped sandals, to see the staggering villas, the majolica-domed cathedral in the background, the breathtaking Mediterranean colliding with the rainbow colors of Positano's beauty, and to watch the passing parade of gorgeous locals. Whether young or old, they are all beautiful.

Arriving with my heart pounding from my foot race, I catch a glimpse of some of the Americans licking towering Italian *gelato* cones.

"Stephanie, look what we purchased," they hollered, holding up flamboyant cashmeres and linens in all colors. We are in a shopper's paradise, whether it be for the local artisans' paint strokes, the handmade leather sandals, the colorful ceramics, the creamy limoncello, the exotic jewelry, or the explosion of spicy Italian gastronomy, whatever you choose, it's all fabulous.

Chapter 19

LIVING LA DOLCE VITA - THE GOOD LIFE

*W*e stripped Positano clean in four hours. Most of us tote colorful bags of this and that as we head to the boat. Nino carries a four-foot canvas, rolled up and secured with bubble-wrap, along with a hundred more items in assorted bags. The roll of art is the painting I purchased for Sandra, but only God knows what the other things are strapped about his back and dangling from his arms.

Among the happy array of Americans trekking through the sand is Kathy Murphy, the legendary Pulpwood Queen. She walks beside her best friend, Margie Dilday, from the alligator state of Louisiana. They look like two dancing bobblehead dolls.

They wear bright scarves that tower high above their blonde and silver curls. Kathy had taught me how to swath the colorful wrap and tie it with a gigantic bow atop my head to create the perfect exotic Mediterranean look.

Observing them is comical, with their camouflaged bodies wrapped in Italian fashion with at least twenty sacks of assorted rainbow pigments dangling from their shoulders to the ends of their fingers. What did they purchase, I wonder?

Slowly, my group makes their way toward the boat. Linda "Moorehead" strolls as though floating on water. Her designer sunglasses hide her face as she blows kisses to an exceptionally dark, exotic man who walks forlornly beside her. I imagine he's longing to return to America with her, where in his mind, the oil wells pump black gold, and we all drive cars the length of trains.

"I'm coming!" Linda hollers, hoisting her gigantic bag in midair like a heavy dumbbell. She looks back to her Romeo and stops to wave her one free hand to him and blow another kiss in mid-air before she trudges through the sand again. Suddenly, her shoes bog down in the quicksand that begs her to stay.

By the time she reaches the ramp, Linda is breathless. I don't know if it was from the long haul of a heavy load, or the sultry farewell to her Romeo with a head full of curly, midnight-black hair.

There is so much happening at once with the Americans as they make their way toward the boat. Many hold up this and that, trying to show me something from afar and others take last minute photos. I look at everyone, making sure each passenger is accounted for as they scurry about and pass me with laughter and too much cargo.

When the church bells ring quarter to six, the colorful shutters swing open from the balconies, and the locals appear. My eyes glance up toward them, and I wave my arms high in the air as they continue with their lives as though the daily happenings below are invisible.

"Stephanie, do you think happiness is a choice?" Ann asks from behind my ear. She startles me with her sudden appearance and interrupts my amusement with the locals.

"Well, hello, my dear! Where did you come from?"

"I walked past you five minutes ago, but you were looking up there." Ann points to the rocky mountainside with the villas dangling high above the Mediterranean.

"To answer your question, yes, indeed. Happiness is a choice when you are an adult. It's up to each one of us to get out of the box and make things happen. Don't you agree?"

"Yes, I do. This place is beautiful, and I'm thanking God right now for choosing you and Italy. I will relive these memories forever. I had gelato with an Italian lady and her little dog. Then I made my way into the church with a thousand candles burning around the Madonna. And real flowers were everywhere. Real roses! I saw dozens of them exploding out of every corner. Surely a wedding is planned for today with all those flowers," Ann talks and talks. She's overwhelmed by the magnificence of Positano.

"Yes, I saw the bride and groom earlier and a marching band. Did you enjoy yourself and find lots of treasures?"

"Yes, and I found too much. Look at the leather shoes I purchased from the shoemaker." Ann pulls and tugs from one bag to another, searching for her purchase.

"Nice!" I examine the sandals, running my long fingers across the soft leather-bottom sole.

"I'm giving them to my mom. She asked for a pair of Italian-made slip-on sandals. She'll love them."

"Yes. They're *magnifico*!" I glance at my watch. "It's time to go. We have more surprises!"

With everyone back on the boat, we playfully float along the lapping waves and flirt with the Mediterranean coastline. The canvas before us is the same as before: a postcard of colorful villas dangling from the rocky cliffs with bountiful grapes clinging to the vines of a thousand vineyards tumbling down from the sky.

The Americans, our paparazzi, go wild clicking their cameras as they did when we arrived. It's been a fun day with lots of adventures in Positano.

I love to show the Americans the Amalfi Coast from below. When we travel above it on the narrow sliver of road engulfed by eye-popping surroundings, we see and experience the Amalfi Coast in a different way. Being on top of the cliff, swinging around the endless fish-hooks of the corkscrew road, high above the most famous area of all, the rainbows of life mesmerize us with the immense beauty. Even the brightly colored laundry whipping in the Mediterranean breeze is happy. Everywhere we look, there are explosions of flowers, vegetables, ceramics, and lively painted villas, all clinging to the green and purple vineyards covering the staggering cliffs.

Sailing back the same way we came earlier is double the pleasure, especially for those seated on the opposite side of the boat from departure to Positano. It's a different view to see the storybook setting of rainbow beauty up close.

I pick up my bottled water and drink it slowly while moving closer to the captain's wheelhouse, which is nothing more than a tiny square enclosed with two seats—one for him behind the wheel and one for me with the mic.

"I've got to tell the Americans about the area we're approaching," I tell Tony, who leisurely sinks back on a padded cushion outside the door of the little square. He is talking to Kathy Murphy.

"*Mamma Mia, Stefania.* Is it impossible for you to stay calm, to give the people rest?" Tony asks, then turns back to Kathy as though he's completed a commercial.

"Ah, I can smell the fragrant fruit groves from here and almost taste the limoncello," Dee tells Tony, as she joins him and produces a biscuit wrapped in yellow cellophane. It's lemon with the distinct smell of strong liqueur. Tony takes it with appreciation, slowly unwrapping its protective covering, then he extends the same piece to Kathy's lips, insisting she takes the first bite.

"*Grazie.* Thank you very much." Tony smiles at Dee as he chews and savors the lemony liqueur and creamy chocolate. Tony points toward the stunning groves. "Look to the left. It's the *Limone Costa d'Amalfi*; the trees that grow along the Amalfi Coast."

"A lemon is a lemon," Dee tells Tony, plunking another biscuit into her mouth and offering more to Tony and Kathy. She savors the taste and nonchalantly unwraps another one.

"Depends on its region," Kathy says. "The size and shape of them in this area are enormous —large baseballs and volleyballs. Good golly, they're big!"

Tony takes charge of the lesson. "Ah, to an American, a lemon is just that—a lemon. But not in Italy. No. You must see the difference. One can easily identify the *limone* or Sfusato *Amalfitano* by its elongated and pointed shape. Do you remember seeing in Sorrento, the *Limone di Sorrento*, which is much rounder than the ones here in Amalfi? No, you don't remember. Things such as this are not important to the American ladies. I know you prefer to observe the dress, the bag, and the shoes. *Si*, yes, I know very well how the mind of a woman works."

While they're carrying on outside the little enclosure about the importance of the size, shape, feel and taste of lemons, I feel the need to give a surprise shout-out to an iconic movie star's home as we gently bounce with the waves.

As we approach the anticipated area, the boat's motor hums in lazy calmness as we putter closer.

Looking through the tiny windshield with the captain by my side, I grab the microphone and stare at the view.

"Here we are!" My voice blasts through the microphone as we sail by the front of the celebrity's villa.

"Do you know who lives here?" I ask, watching them flash photo after photo without answering me.

"This is Sophia Loren's villa," I announced. I, too, grab my camera and snap the photo as though it's my first time seeing her residence nestled in the mountainous cliff, and then continue with the elaborations.

"Sophia is from Napoli, home of the pizza," I tell them with excitement as I stretch the cord of the mic to its maximum.

We spend the next hour gawking from the boat, seeing more than before. It's a parade of villas, churches, castles, and convents, all dangling from the soaring cliffs with tumbling vineyards rolling toward the Mediterranean. We approach another celebrity villa, and I grab the microphone again.

"Look at the white villa nestled above. That was Michael Jackson's home," I tell them, springing to my feet. "The locals say he purchased the cliff-hanging beauty and paid millions of dollars only to keep the shutters slammed shut, totally avoiding the sunlight and the Mediterranean's vast blue expanse. They say the shutters swung open only on cloudy days."

I place the microphone on the dash in front of the little window and race outside into the sunshine with the Americans. Are they expecting Michael Jackson to appear from the window? My mind grows animated as memories rush in, triggering thoughts and creating excitement as everyone whoops and hollers and sings out snippets of Michael Jackson's songs. That's enough encouragement for me to perform the moon-walk across the deck's floor.

"Stephanie, where is Sean Connery's villa?" Zander from Minnesota hollers. "Is that a real sandcastle over there, the same one as before? How did they build a house to be identical to sand?"

He points with his left hand. His brown cap is parked on his head, struggling to stay balanced in the sea breeze. I resist the urge to pull it forward. I start to answer, but Zander shifts to another question, cutting me off like a piece of salami. Before he gets the last word out, he starts coughing from his toes up. Maybe he's a heavy smoker, three to four packs a day? Although, there is no evidence confirming my verdict, so I put the thought from my mind.

Another surprise waits ahead. Within minutes, the boat slows to a snail's crawl, inching closer to the rocky shore. Knowing we're nearly there, I glance back to Tony and Nino, who are shrouded with colorful scarves wrapped tightly about their necks. Their eyes are squeezed shut as though a sudden windstorm has landed in front of their face. They appear to be one, scrunched together with shoulders hunched, trying to avoid the *colpo d'aria,* or dangerous gust of wind. It's rumored to be the reason for catching ill at any moment in Italy, causing a myriad of health issues, such as a stiff neck, pounding headaches, and even the deadly influenza.

"You must protect your neck and face from the dangerous airflow, *Stefania. Mamma Mia,* when the wind hits your face, the body will become ill. You never listen to me," Tony's voice replays throughout my mind like a roaring train, never slowing down, pleading with me for years to bring along the bloody shawl. "Always have the *sciarpa,* the scarf in your purse," Tony's voice repeats within my subconscious, the perpetual memory chip that refuses to be deleted. "And *Stefania,* regardless of a warm summer day, the *colpo d'aria,* the hit of wind, will get you."

"I am *Americana*, Tony, regardless of bloodline." I always remind him a thousand times. "My body loves the breeze, the wind, the air. It's an American thing. We must have air, or we'll be sick!"

Looking at them, I laugh knowing it's not just the *colpo d'aria* that will get you, it's a long laundry list of things in Italy including the deadly air-conditioner of artificial air which is much more "dangerous" than the natural air. And drinking a cappuccino after dinner is detrimental to one's digestive system. One should drink only an espresso if you don't want to experience the horrible bloating effects during the midnight hours. Thou shalt not drink any sort of substance from a cow such as a cappuccino, caffe latte, latte macchiato, or any milky substance in coffee after breakfast. If the urge hits for this wonderful concoction, then you must consume it before the clock strikes noon.

In contrast, I look at the Americans who are basking in the warm sun with their arms free of fabric, enjoying the Mediterranean breeze and stocking up their Vitamin D.

I see Linda with her huge tortoiseshell sunglasses and her legs dangling over the boat's edge. She has shared her philosophy of life with me many times. "There's something soothing about the Mediterranean. I can retreat into my own world and recall chapters from long ago within its blue seductiveness. The mind is a playground if one will allow oneself to reminisce. But in order to do so, one must have lived a life of fulfillment, chock full of love and romance. Age has no borders; therefore, one must make things happen."

I think of my own philosophy of life: always keep something fun and exciting before you—a highlighted adventure marked in your calendar, and never let go of God's words.

Isn't it funny, the way we know when someone's watching, observing, or taking in the thoughts of another? But this time, Linda doesn't sense my observation. Her golden hair is bobbed and teased, and she is wearing her signature overlay of long, flowing fabrics, the kind of pantsuit outfit of movie star icons. Her diamond-studded fingers tap her forehead. From the grin of satisfaction and her outward ivory glow, her face is genuine, not artificial, and her breasts are large torpedoes peaked beneath a five-carat diamond on a long gold chain.

She looks like an expensive bottle of champagne, but not Prosecco. There is a difference. The Prosecco grows stale with time, but not Linda. I wonder what she experienced in Positano with her Romeo, if anything at all. Seeing her deep in thought, I imagine she had a rendezvous. She is radiating contentment, and is the epitome of outward feminine beauty, like a literal work of art who is, no doubt, living *La Dolce Vita*.

Chapter 20

DANCING IN THE CAVE - THE AFRICANA

*F*our days ago, I arrived in Italy with a new group of Americans for our September southern Italy tour. Among this group is Gloria from Houston, Texas. Thirteen more hail from other parts of the United States. This is Gloria's tenth trip with us, but it will be her first experience for the big surprise I've planned for today along the Mediterranean coastline.

Gloria claps her hands as though her favorite football team had just made the winning touchdown as our boat slow dances in the Mediterranean Sea. "Are we stopping? Please, tell me we're stopping!"

Her plea comes at the perfect time, just seconds before the boat engine's rumble changes to a loud roar. The captain pushes the royal beauty's throttle in short bursts and carefully accelerates the motor to bring us closer to the rocky shore.

Just thirty-five minutes ago, we boarded our very own yacht for today's big surprise. The only tidbit of information I gave the Americans this morning was for them to bring their cameras.

We adventure along the Amalfi coastline today, experiencing it from the water instead of the land. Yesterday, Nino drove us on the hair-raising UNESCO World Heritage road that zigzagged for miles and filled the Americans with lifelong memories.

Gloria inches toward the boat's edge with her camera pointed toward the staggering cliffs and colorful villas that nestle within them that rise above the turquoise sea. The view is different from her last excursion along the Amalfi Coast. We didn't venture closely to observe the structure with steps leading up to a villa inside the mountains. Or, is it a grotto with an elaborate terrace for one's own private entertainment? Is it another celebrity's home?

We are on the route of the rich and famous. It's the coastline where money buys the heart's desires, and anything imaginable is easily obtainable. The local residents might as well be genies in giant bottles because, with a blink of their eyes, they seem to possess anything.

Exquisite yachts with swimming pools on top are anchored by the seaside. Many of the clustered villas along the rocky cliffs show off beautiful iron railings around their fenced yards—the adornment of Italian class. Medieval lighthouses and look-out towers dot the way. There is even a fortress, one I repeatedly describe to the Americans. From the boat, it appears to be a life-sized sandcastle built along the shore. We sailed past it minutes ago, and now we've arrived at something just as magnificent.

But what is this place chiseled within the rocky cliffs that suspend over the sea? The carved stone steps cut into the steep hillside lead the way up to...where?

I solve the mystery when I bring the microphone to my red-painted lips.

"Look up, my friends. We have arrived at Praiano, one of the picturesque villages on the coast of the Mediterranean. Can you see inside the cave?" My voice blares through the boat's speaker inside the tiny square where I sit beside the captain who is at the wheel. "Can you guess what's above us, inside the grotto?"

I hear the Americans exclaiming excitedly and a chorus of cameras clicking. Their heads tilt as they gaze at the mysterious beauty.

Tom, from Oklahoma, claps his hands and attempts to announce,

"This is the villa of..." Everyone holds their breath. But he can't remember the last name. "Wait, it will come to me."

Gloria, a petite fifty-four-year-old firecracker, amplifies her voice loud enough to reach the shores of North Carolina. "Okay. Stephanie, tell us more!"

She's everyone's favorite on this tour. Partly because she's an amazing dancer, especially when it comes to salsa and the fox-trot. When the music is right, Gloria's little feet will smoke the dance floor.

Just last night, we witnessed a full dance show complete with disco, boogie-woogie, and her signature salsa. I'm still exhausted from the two-hour presentation that was our very own recital for just the locals and us.

Tony got in on the fun too. Gloria swung him around like a yo-yo for a few minutes; he was near ecstasy and a heart-attack at the same time. I don't think he's recovered yet. Today he's showing signs of fatigue, and at the breakfast table, he said his knee was hurting. I had rubbed the bottom of my feet in sympathy.

"Whose villa is this?" Gloria sits down on the boat's edge. Her voice is so loud it echoes.

"I think it must be presidential royalty," Jim, from Florida, tells Gloria as he clicks his camera for the hundredth time.

Gloria swings her legs off the narrow edge of the boat and then looks back with her eyes begging for an answer to the mystery.

I tap the microphone three times, intentionally delaying the answer. Standing close to the windshield, I bat my eyes dramatically. To add to the show, both hands fly up as I shrug, insinuating that I don't know anything about our whereabouts.

"We're slowing here to get some amazing photos. Go ahead and prepare yourself for when the boat stops." I smile bigger and press my nose to the glass.

The Americans entertain themselves and continue playing the guessing game as the boat gently bobs up and down in front of the soaring mountains. I love watching adults act like awestruck *bambinos* on Christmas morning. I'm gloating as I anticipate their reactions to the unusual surprise that awaits them.

At the front of the boat, Jim stands straight as a ruler, tall and lean with tight black jeans revealing his long, giraffe-like legs. "I've never seen anything so dramatic as those steps leading up. And how do you even get up there? It's so steep!"

His left hand clenches tightly to his chest as his mouth gapes wide enough to drop an apple inside. "This is the perfect honeymoon suite. A hideaway."

His hands squeeze over his heart; he clutches the silky fabric of his shirt and knots it into a shield with his fingers as if he feels vulnerable in the face of beauty he can't comprehend.

Three steps behind Jim is his companion, Harry, who gawks through binoculars, which have little silver sequins sprinkled all over them. Harry drops the binoculars and lets them swing from his neck as he gropes for his camera. After snapping many photos, he clasps his cheeks with both hands. His face is round and furry and sprinkled with prickly salt-and-pepper whiskers. He peeks through his fingers as if the splendor is also too much for him to contain.

"Tell me, Stephanie, is this the place we're going to? Is this the surprise for today?" Jim taps his brown leather shoe on the wooden floor of the boat, then abruptly drops to his knees. Such a theatrical gesture. With a wink at Gloria, he begs for details. They both look hopeful and glance up to the hanging cliffs of jagged rocks where umbrellas and tables perch dangerously near the drop-off.

Inches away from him, I smile with anticipation. My heart flutters, and I bounce on my toes. "What surprise are you talking about?" I slip my dark Italian sunglasses over my eyes to hide the glee.

The boat floats as close to the rocky cliff as it can without bumping. The motor idles down to nothing and eventually shuts off.

"We're going up there?" Jill, from Galveston, Texas, throws her pink straw hat up in the air as excitement propels her from her seat like a launched rocket. I know she's saved for this tour of Italy for years. She worked even when she was sick, and while the kids were out for the summer, even spending weekends at a second job at the local bakery so she could fill her vacation jar with every spare coin.

Her efforts finally made it possible for her to be here in Italy with us. And now, Italy is more magical than she ever imagined.

Walking closer, Jill throws both arms around my waist as if trying to lift me from the boat's floor. Happy tears stream down her face that reminds me of a cute porcupine. Her pointy nose flares and snorts as bottled-up emotions break free. She quivers, babbles, and breaks out running around and around, circling but going nowhere.

My pulse is pounding loudly, and I'm about to explode with excitement. The Americans have no idea of our whereabouts, except that we're in a boat out on the Mediterranean Sea. They have no idea that Aladdin's cave is hidden inside the towering mountain. And they have no idea that it's Nino's old playground where he often accompanied friends inside to go disco dancing, long before he married Susy. They don't know we're about to hobnob where the elite of this area dance and socialize.

"Okay, my friends. Along this coast are eight hundred square meters of grottoes, which are natural caves, tunnels, and hidden coves that pirates used to use, all glowing in aquamarine and turquoise.

"Up above, inside the rocks is Praiano's Africana Famous Club. Unfortunately, the Africana is closed today—it's only open on Friday and Saturday nights. I'm so sorry, but we wanted to stop and present its beauty to you and show you where the movie stars and locals come to party, dance, drink, and socialize."

I'm deliberately adding to the tension and excitement with my speech. Can you imagine the millionaire yachts bobbing beside us now with the socialites elbowing each other on the dance floor? Oh, yes! This is the place where it all happens.

"And if you don't have a boat, preferably a double-decker cruiser with its own swimming pool on top, you can enter from Amalfi Coast Drive. That is, if you know the right person. You've got to have the right connection."

Tony hollers, "*Mamma Mia, Stefania!* What's the matter with you? Why do you tell the Americans such things? *Stefania.* Why must you joke too much? *Andiamo*, let's go!" Tony swirls his hands over his head, motioning for everyone to come along with him.

The surprise has been sprung.

"Okay, yes, we're going up. Tony had the owners open just for us, for our own private party with treats, music, and dancing." I jump up and down, as dramatic thrills of excitement overflow.

"Follow me!" I skip forward to the front entrance of the boat as my passengers shriek with enthusiasm and bump each other to try to be first behind me.

Two men magically appear out of nowhere to let a ramp down that swings across the water to the boat.

"Hold on to the rope, and let's go see what's inside the cave above us." I float across the ramp, leading the Americans like a marching band.

"You're kidding, right?" Jim says, looking up to the cliffs surrounded by brightly colored umbrellas that are perched precariously on the edge. He pushes Harry across the ramp, his excitement growing with every step.

"I can't believe we're climbing this mountain and going into a real grotto!" Jim can't stop gawking.

I turn my gaze backward, appreciating the surprise on everyone's faces. Many of the Americans stop on the steps and take more photos.

As we make our way from the boat to the cave, I wave to Giuseppe to start the music. He is an employee of the Africana as well as a friend who accommodates us today with a huge buffet as well as our very own live band.

Once at the top of the cave, we bypass an iron veranda which skirts a huge, elaborate bar festooned with mountains of food and wine. A chef in a tall white hat greets us and offers exquisite glasses of *vino* harvested from the local red and white grapes of this region. Tables and chairs are neatly arranged with views of the dance floor and the sea in the background.

We are kids in a candy store or, in our case, Aladdin's cave. The music bounces off the enclosed cave ceiling with perfect acoustics. Purple strobe lights flash brilliantly.

Over the music, I hear Gloria clink her flute of champagne with its tiny bubbles swimming to the top against Giuseppe's ice bucket. "Come on and have a dance with me." She grabs his black leather belt and yanks. He drops the bucket of ice on top of the see-through acrylic bar.

"Ah, *Signorina*." Giuseppe doesn't even glance back at the disarray of ice cubes scattered on the bar, even though some have come to rest on top of the food. He slides across the stone floor as the lyrics of an Italian song pulse from huge speakers.

Gloria runs her fingers through her hair and grabs her wide rubber band to stretch it out until her tiny ponytail is free and a thousand strands cascade below her neck.

I watch the preparation for the coming show. Ten of us take our seats, ready for another performance. We've seen Gloria dance before. Just last evening, we saw the way she slowly ignites, tapping her shoes, then moving her legs as electricity runs all the way up to her arms. It's a gift to see a professional level of talent with the right moves choreographed as though televised on *Dancing with the Stars*. My heart starts pounding, my feet tap with the music, and my fingers drum with the beat.

Before I can swallow my iced limoncello, Gloria fastens both hands to the front of Giuseppe's pants and forcefully nudges her left leg in between both of his. He trembles. I couldn't look away if I wanted to. As the cool lemon concoction slides down my throat, I watch Gloria grip Giuseppe's belt, sliding her whole body between his legs to magically pop up on the other side of him.

Tony cheers and shouts without reservation. My legs kick the side of the stone as I try to keep in time with the music.

"*Mamma Mia*, this is unbelievable," Tony exclaims in Italian. His legs stretch out in front of the little table and dance in place.

Fireworks spark and crackle on the dance floor, and Gloria is steaming up the room. She reaches for Giuseppe's shoulders, first pushing him away, then grabbing his shirt with an iron fist and pulling him hard against her breasts. The sizable gold crucifix he wears around his neck thrusts back and forth against his olive chest.

We see hunger within her eyes and can almost feel the heat radiating from his pants. They flash through the air, kicking and singing, flexing up and down faster than lightning. They are magnificent, the best we've ever seen.

Mamma Mia, watching them dance together, is electrifying! Only a few feet from them, I feel the sparks of passion percolating their bodies. Giuseppe spins and twirls Gloria around, zipping her in and out like a ragdoll.

The energy is too much; I jump to my feet to dance too. Tony flies up, grabbing my arm. We spin around, and the rest of our group follows. We are out of control, twirling each other back and forth like hot potatoes.

Not long after, I realized my heart is beating too fast and my legs are putty. Twenty minutes of non-stop dancing is enough for me. I head back to my seat and watch Gloria and Giuseppe whiplash each other at record speed on the dance floor. It is captivating.

The music suddenly switches to another fast song, and before I reach for my lemon-flavored concoction, Gloria backs up at full speed like a car jammed in reverse, then shifts gears in a flash. She accelerates across the stone floor, jumps high in the air, and lands in Giuseppe's arms. Surely, the force is too much. I hold my breath.

Though she's like a tsunami wave crashing ashore, Giuseppe miraculously catches her, and both her legs wrap around his tiny waist and her arms envelope his neck.

"*Mamma Mia, Madonna!*" Tony's voice ricochets across the cave as we watch Giuseppe's legs pedal backward like a tornado spinning out of control. The one-hundred-and-thirty-five pounds plastered around his Tootsie Roll of a body is too much, and they make a crash landing. They hit hard against the stage and wipe out everything in sight. Salvatore and Antonia, the two singers, topple over along with their amps and guitars. The drummer and horn player barely escape the brutal blow.

Lying helplessly on the stone floor, Gloria appears more like a turtle shell sprawling on top of Giuseppe. The rest of us freeze, suspended in time as the curtain closes on this day's adventures.

Chapter 21

JANICE GETS RUN OVER IN AMALFI

*T*he sky above the church is a kaleidoscope, exploding with a thousand shimmers of color over the gold majolica of the ancient Byzantine Duomo di Sant'Andrea. The Amalfi Cathedral is a magnificent creation. It's a medieval Roman Catholic Church dedicated to the Apostle Andrew, one of Jesus' twelve disciples.

Every time I walk inside its doors, I think of Saint Andrew, who was martyred upon an x-shaped cross and buried in Patras, Greece. Later, his remains were retrieved by the crusaders and brought here to the Duomo di' Sant'Andrea or "the Church of Saint Andrew." Inside these walls are remnants of that cross. It's just to the left of the main sanctuary, and his skull is displayed inside a reliquary to the right.

"Go see Saint Andrew's remains beneath the main altar in the crypt," I've said to the Americans ten thousand times, but many never do. They're too awestruck by the procession of ordinary local Italians going about their daily lives.

"You do know that the Apostle Andrew is the brother of the Apostle Peter, don't you? As in Saint Peter, whose tomb is underneath the high altar in the Vatican? It's housed in Saint Peter's Basilica in the smallest country in the world, the Vatican City, which is situated in Rome and surrounded by a towering wall." I try to entice them by dangling historical facts before them in the hope that they'll show a spark of interest.

There are so many steps to the entrance of the Duomo di' Sant'Andrea that it's not an exaggeration to say there are "countless" stairs. I always stand with my head tilted to admire the twelve Moorish-influenced arches, the small niches that house statues of the apostles, and the overall magnificent craftsmanship. I'm always amazed at how they built such grandeur, and I'm thrilled to see the Americans stand in awe of its enormous beauty before they scatter to explore the village. They race to the pizza and gelato shops or grab tall, slender bottles of the locally-made limoncello.

When I lift my gaze high to the portico, I see splashes of gold, blue, and white in the countless number of mosaics depicting Jesus Christ and his worshipers kneeling around him. This magnificent church is nestled into the mountains on a street no wider than a ribbon that streams down the middle of the Amalfi village.

The town is so small that as soon as you leave the last step of the church, you are on the street among a parade of little cars. People are everywhere, strolling as though time is only a suggestion. The miniature local delivery trucks bounce steadily along, while the townsfolk walk with their dogs, which dart in and out as though the vehicles are invisible. As the tiny delivery trucks make their way past the church, the street becomes even smaller, so narrow that one must glue oneself to the walls of the shops or dart inside their doors.

"Watch out for the vehicles if you want to keep your toes," I tell the Americans over and over again out of concern for their safety.

Tony often asks, "*Stefania*, do you ever tire of coming here so often? What is it with this Amalfi village you love so much?" He's never satisfied with my answer because of its vagueness.

This year marks twenty years of bringing Americans to this village. Year after year, I've come to this seaside that was discovered around 596 A.D. When we arrive with the Americans, we usually hop aboard our private boat first and view the Amalfi Coast from the sea. Later, we disembark and walk across the street, dodging the tiny cars that zip along bumper to bumper on the narrow road until we squeeze through the crowded archway beside a large painted map on the wall of the entrance into the village.

Not long ago, we were floating along in the Mediterranean and flirting with the Amalfi coastline, gazing at the wealthy villas while seeing places most people only read about in magazines. We floated for miles taking thousands of photos.

Now on dry land, I motion for everyone to follow me. The Americans march obediently as they eagerly anticipate the surprises and adventures waiting behind the walls of this famous Amalfi village.

"Get ready to see the most beautiful church," Margie hollers out. She zooms to the left like a jet, but she's heading the wrong direction.

"Margie, where are you going?"

"I thought we go this way, past the shop over there where we purchased all of those adorable blouses last year. Do you remember, Stephanie?"

"No, that shop was inside the village of Taormina," I smile. For that shopping trip, we were hours away from the mainland of Italy and across the Mediterranean on the island of Sicily.

"Oh, Stephanie has everything recorded within her mind. I have no idea how she remembers one little alleyway in one region of Italy from the next one, but she does. Everything pertaining to this country is neatly filed away. And, trust me, her future came with an adventurous recipe. She walks through life as if she knows where every turn is even in a maze of ten thousand turns. I guess living this dream is a plus," Margie tells anyone who cares to listen.

"This way, Margie," I wave my arm, motioning for her to follow the path around the statue of an anchor.

She spins around and joins the others who are marching behind me like characters in *Snow White and the Seven Dwarfs*. The seasoned Americans who've been here with me before take off like a wild tiger is behind their heels, either anticipating the local pizza or the colorful apparel on display along the narrow street that stretches from here to the end of the one-way road.

"Stephanie, when was Saint Andrew brought to Amalfi?" David, from Las Vegas, asks as he pulls a pen and paper from his shirt pocket to jot down the facts. He must have forgotten the history lesson from my newsletter that I mailed out months ago.

"On May 18, 1208, Saint Andrew's remains were brought to the cathedral from Constantinople after the Fourth Crusade. His remains were kept in Saint Peter's Basilica in Rome, technically in the Vatican. I recall it was the year 1964 when the Apostle Andrew's skull was finally returned here to Amalfi and placed inside the church. They like to dismember the body and share a bone here and there with the many Catholic churches. But I believe everything is back here now." I talk as we continue to make our way through the crowded alleyway.

"St. Andrew's relics are entombed below the crypt where they discovered a strange liquid secreting from his bones. It was deemed miraculous, and they decided to name it after another miraculous item: manna. As with other saints' manna, it's collected carefully and used to bless visitors and the church. They collect it at least four times throughout the year, in January, June, November, and December. The November collection always happens the night before St. Andrew's Day—his official feast holiday on the 30th. Sometimes the collection of manna is extremely bountiful, and other times it isn't. Part of the great miracle mystery, I suppose."

"How could we get to experience this miracle?" David edges closer to my heels.

I feel his breath warm my ears.

"The Catholic Church doesn't recognize the manna as a miracle, or that's what a priest told me. Nonetheless, it's a miracle to me. Wouldn't you say so, David?"

"How can it not be? The church doesn't celebrate the manna at all? Surely they do something on Saint Andrew's Feast Day." David is a Baptist, and this is a new concept for him.

"Yes, it's observed, and the locals ask to be blessed by being anointed with this manna every year, and many miracles have been known to occur."

He seems extremely interested, so I keep talking. "When we have time, I'll tell you about the skull that sweats. I've seen it with my own eyes, as have some of the other Americans with me. It's in Napoli down in the caves. Tony took us there. We actually had lunch delivered to us at the entrance. Can you believe having pizza delivered there with hundreds of skulls nearby? That's another story, an unbelievable one, but true."

I make sure I have everyone's attention. "Come on, we're nearly there. I want you to see something of importance and the history before your eyes. You could read a hundred books, but what you see for yourself, you'll remember forever."

"Don't look to the right side," I remind them again as I lead them through an open archway. I insist they look at the left side while they dodge the many local shoppers. We pop out from the shrouded arch in a fraction of a second and blindly swim past the sea of colorful shops and outdoor restaurants. The temptation to stop is great since we're surrounded by energetic vitality on both sides while trying to keep from walking into people in front of us.

"Keep going, but look to the left," I repeat, which, of course, causes some to crane their necks to view the theatrical excitement on the right side.

"No! Don't look!" I blurt again and jump to the side in an attempt to block their gazes. My arms unfurl like giant wings stretched straight as a tight-rope.

Just inside the village, the allure is great. Mesmerizing flavors dance on the breeze full of the aroma of garlic and onions caramelizing in oil. Trying to avoid a little girl careening across my feet, I glance to the right and see flames leaping from the baker's oven as he retrieves a round of pizza with a large wooden paddle. The local red wine flows like soft rain, filling glasses atop every little red-and-white-swathed table.

Laughter and happy faces abound, and the Italian dialect drowns out our own language. It's as loud as a theme park with bottles being uncorked, popping here and there with deafening effects, not to mention the loud chorus of a hundred glasses clinking on the little round tables. It's a pageantry of chaos. Savory aromas ignite our taste buds and fuel our appetites. I can't help but watch as a margherita pizza is scooped into the mouth of an Italian man who is lost in ecstasy while gooey mozzarella, tomatoes, and basil gush from the edges of the large slice. Meanwhile, the *signora* nestled beside him dashes sea salt on a honey-smothered slice of bread. I fight the sudden urge to grab it from her.

"Get ready to look to the right," I shout, but my voice collides with loud drums that thunder through the air in amped-up reverberations. We inch forward a few more feet and see an energetic dancing quartet of passionate Italians. One heroically squeezes a red accordion at record speed while three others belt out Italian lyrics and exercise their vocal cords at the highest possible volume.

"Get ready, but don't look to the right. Not yet," I shout again and jump with excitement as my fingers tense against the camera that's strapped about my shoulder.

Ten more steps finally bring us into the open-air square, the Piazza del Duomo. I maneuver around the beautiful baroque water fountain that was erected in 1760, and the Americans tag along as though they're little children being led to Disney World. My heart beats rapidly; it's almost time for the grand announcement.

After taking two more big steps, I pause and spin around with the force of a cyclone. When I face them, they look shocked as though they've been caught with their hands in the cookie jar.

"Stop! Cover your eyes and get ready to see the most spectacular sight of the Amalfi village," I shout, using all the air in my lungs. "Okay...get ready...now look to the right!"

I stretch my arms and point to the magnificent cathedral where the apostle Andrew rests.

The piercing surprise of my voice shocks the nearby locals, who are seated at food covered tables sheltered by giant umbrellas. Before our arrival, they were peacefully sipping the local wines, devouring mountainous heaps of pasta sprinkled with the famous Parmigiano-Reggiano cheese, and listening to the rambunctious quartet of musical instruments.

But now the silence is broken as my voice reverberates. Not only do I disrupt the peaceful setting, but so do the cheering Americans.

The beauty before them has uncorked their bottled-up jubilation. It's an explosion that blasts those around us who were eating, drinking, and leisurely basking in the shade of peacefulness.

"*Mamma Mia, Madonna!*" shouts a tall, sun-kissed Romeo with black curls sprouting generously on his head. He springs up like a jack-in-the-box and knocks his chair backward.

I jump away.

He rolls out raw Italian profanity and complains that his marriage proposal was just ruined by the blast through his ears. He pushes his hands on the rim of his plate in an attempt to shove it backward but upends the little table and sends his lover's wine glass crashing onto the cobblestones. The red *vino* escapes and splatters all around, including on my legs.

"*Scusami*, excuse me!" I automatically jump and look left and right to see a hundred eyes glaring back at me—and, of course, the Americans. The musical quartet has drifted away off into the sunlight.

In spite of the slight malfunction of my plan and the resulting disruption, most of the Americans are fixated on the Duomo. Those who are seeing for the first time react in the same way as those who've been here several times already: stunned and amazed. They stand with jaws open and chins practically dropped onto the cobblestones. Their eyes protrude with pupils dilated like cartoon characters as they gaze up and gawk at the beautiful masterpiece with its long stairway and sparkling mosaics. They are speechless; their tongues are tied tightly but only for two seconds. Then the oohs and ahhs spill out, and the cameras start clicking. We are the American paparazzi once again.

The excitement ignites; it spreads through the Americans like a wildfire blazing behind their heels.

Lynn and Mike, a cute couple from upstate New York, shout out in unison, "We're going to the church. See you later!"

Pam and Mary, from Dallas, Texas, dart in front of the little cars and disappear inside the lemon shop that sells hundreds of bottles of the famous limoncello as well as a creamy chocolate liqueur.

"We're going swimming in the Mediterranean. Don't forget us when you leave the village!" Roger yells in excitement as he dodges the toy-like trucks.

While I'm in Amalfi, I intend to surprise my dear friend, Maria, who has a tiny shop down the street. My heart beats rapidly with anticipation as I eagerly head in her direction.

Before I arrive at her shop, I bump into Austin Jones, a New York City attorney who signed up for this Italy tour specifically to celebrate his change in marital status—newly divorced and finalized only three days prior to our departure. Happiness radiates from his face that resembles a basketball—perfectly round with coarse black sprigs of hair waving in the soft breeze.

I seize the opportunity to bring him joy. "Come along with me to Maria's shop. It's just down the street, and she has a beautiful cousin. I'm sure she'd love to show you around."

I grab Austin's hand and jerk him forward, not waiting for his response.

Hours later, I stroll back toward the square down the narrow street, often plastering my body to the sides of the buildings as cars bump along the cobblestones while I hold my breath and hope the wheels avoid the top of my shoes. I left Austin with Maria's cousin, an Italian beauty dripping with sex appeal. As I witness two lovers kissing at a nearby table, I can't help but wonder if Austin and Maria's cousin will make a connection.

Making my way closer to the church, I spontaneously dart inside a clothing shop with hundreds of colorful scarves that stream down the front door. Back in the corner, I glimpse Lucy from Phoenix, Arizona, one of the Americans on this tour. She's engrossed by the local apparel. She gasps as the shopkeeper tightly binds a lacy pink corset around her ample waist, and the oxygen is squeezed out of her lungs. She watches herself in the long, narrow mirror, squinting a little as if to get a better view. Her bleach blonde hair spills over her bare shoulders in jagged layers, held back by a leopard-striped hairpin covered in rhinestones that keeps her bangs out of her pale face. Her green eyes are impossible to miss, especially with brushstrokes of royal blue eyeshadow surrounding them and long curled lashes stretched by midnight blue mascara.

The shopkeeper hands her a beautiful dress that's the color of my lips: bright red with huge pink swirls embroidered all over it.

"This fabric is beautiful." Lucy slips it over her thick mane of hair. The translucent material hugs her breast, so the shopkeeper pulls and tugs to stretch it out over her hips. Uncertainty flickers across her face as she wonders if it will fit her body. She squeezes her eyes shut until the shopkeeper stops fussing then slowly peeks to see herself in the mirror.

I watch her astonished expression in the mirror, for she is obviously surprised that it went on. Then I wonder how in the world she will ever get it off!

The dress is skintight, stretching every fiber of the thin fabric and rolling up from the bottom like a slow draw of window shades. She smiles and lifts her chin up as if to show she now feels like she is an Italian *signorina*.

"It's perfect. Yes, I will take it," she blurts her decision with the dress still molded to her body.

"*Va bene*, okay," the shop owner says. Her cheeks are the color of roses and glowing on her bronzed face. With her hands crossed over her chest, she nods and beams.

I back up and leave the store like a car easing out in reverse, not wanting her to see my bewilderment. I continue my stroll to Saint Andrew's Basilica.

As I approach the church, I see a crowd of people gathered around a tiny car, waving their hands to signal others to walk around them. When I'm a little bit closer, I recognize six of the Americans who begin to wave their hands and holler at me.

"Stephanie, hurry! Janice got run over. The car rolled over her feet!" A chorus of voices speaking English drowns out the locals.

When I hear the words "ran over her feet," it hits me like a hard slap in the face. My feet seem to have a mind of their own; they begin to run before I even think about it. I push through the street, dodging towering cones of gelato clutched in people's hands and making my way to my people.

I arrive with heart-pounding speed. Everyone tries to talk at once with a chorus of alibis testifying about the run-over.

"Oh, Stephanie, you're finally here." Karen's voice quivers like a bad connection to the microphone. "Janice was stepping off the last step of the church, looking up and talking about the beauty within Saint Andrew's, and low and behold…"

Her voice breaks into pieces, then she tries again. "When the tires rolled over the top of her feet, Janice screamed. She was beating on the car with her hand, then the driver jammed the car into reverse and drove backward, rolling over them again. He rolled over her twice!"

Gary takes over and tells his version as he wraps his arms around his wife of over twenty years.

"We were all walking down the steps, and none of us were looking to the left. We were not aware of the little cars bouncing by. We didn't know we had to stop for them. Janice stepped off the last step looking to her right, laughing, and talking and saying she wanted a gelato. That's when she stepped forward farther into the road. The car rolled over her feet, both of them," he's talking and gripping his wife's blouse as if he doesn't know what else to do.

Behind me stands Tony's wife, Pat, who has gathered the whole story from the driver. He's an elderly Italian man the height and size of a tall can of biscuits, along with his shorter wife.

"Janice!" I holler as I run to her. I feel my heart hit the road.

"Stephanie, I am okay. I don't think my foot is broken." Janice awkwardly smiles. "The car is so tiny. I barely felt the wheel as it ran over my foot twice."

"Oh, my gosh!" I can't stop repeating myself. "Twice?"

"Yes, twice," Janice replies, showing no panic or hysteria. "I'll be okay. I can wiggle my toes."

"No! You must let a doctor make sure there are no broken bones!" I can't calm down.

With Pat's help, it's clear that they are more than willing to help, so we help lift Janice into their backseat and the driver and his wife jump in.

"Wait, where are you going with her?" I ask the driver. He and his wife both answer at once. Their Italian dialect and their habit of finishing each other's sentences are too confusing to follow. They are too hysterical for me to understand all the words shooting from their mouths.

"She must go to the hospital!" I tell the driver, who is revving up the motor. "I need to get inside the car, but there is no room."

"Stephanie, I'll go with Janice, and you stay here. I will translate to the doctor," Pat keeps talking. "The hospital is not far from here, just a few curves around the Mediterranean."

"What! I need to go with you, but where do I fit?" The car is barely big enough for three people, let alone four or five.

"*Madonna Mio*," Pat exhales the words, cutting into the flood of Italian like a sharp knife slicing a cake as she crawls into the back seat with Janice and shuts the door. "Stephanie, the driver insists they take her to the hospital to get her feet x-rayed to make sure they're not broken. They feel bad. Giuseppe—that's his name—said he didn't mean to drive over the *Americana's* feet. I'll call you as soon as we hear from the doctor."

She extends her hand in the air out the window and waves good-bye as Giuseppe presses his foot hard on the gas pedal, which causes the front two donut wheels to squeal and spin.

The cobblestones burn hot, and the aroma of burnt rubber fills the Mediterranean air. The driver and his wife leap forward, leaving us in their dust. But no sooner than they speed off, Giuseppe hits the brake and backs up.

"*Mamma Mia!* Don't worry, Stephanie, I will call you immediately when the doctor sees her." Pat's head is still hanging from the window as Giuseppe hits the gas once again.

I jump back and watch the toy-like car lunge forward—a space-rocket firing up for take-off. Poofs of black plumes smolder from its undercarriage. He probably just forgot to take his foot off the brake for a moment, but I have the impression that the little car rears up like a black stallion, and then plunges forward at the speed of light.

Within milliseconds, there is nothing in front of the church except us and the locals shaking our heads awkwardly and picking our proverbial dropped jaws up off the smoky cobblestones.

In all of my twenty years of bringing Americans to Europe, we've never had anyone get run over twice. Thoughts race through my mind, but I can't capture any of them.

I turn around slowly. Six of our group huddle around me. The thick fumes and clouds are dissipating and fanning out toward the Fountain of Breasts, the beautiful baroque fountain made of white marble featuring water that pours from the perky breasts of the statues.

I stare at the Americans, not sure what to say.

"*Mamma Mia*, can you believe this just happened?" Jack's chocolate *gelato* drips down his fingertips, reminding him to keep eating it.

"I pray her feet are okay and not broken. She seemed fine, no tears, just limping as though walking on hot, fiery coals." Collene wipes strawberry *gelato* from her pale pink lips and continues to speculate. Her pea-sized brown eyes water from the burnt rubber smell still lingering in the air. "I hope she's able to walk for the rest of the tour. Oh, what about tonight—the dancing? She can't miss out on all the fun tonight."

Collene's chatter makes my head spin. I wish I had answers to her questions.

"I'm going to look around. I'll see you all later on." Collene walks away, slinging her new lemon-colored tote bag over her slim shoulder and disappearing into the chaotic crowd of townspeople.

"I'm heading to the hospital!" I holler back as I make haste to Maria's shop up the street. She's been a dear friend of mine for over twenty years, and I know she'll take me, or one of the family members will with pleasure.

Less than two hours after the emergency rush to the hospital, I'm surprised when the pint-sized car reappears in front of the basilica. It was just minutes ago when I returned to Amalfi. I had hopped on the back of Maria's scooter. She took me to the hospital, which is only five minutes from the church when flying at full speed. There was no way I could wait for the results from the x-ray. I had to be with Janice, even though Pat was by her side, interpreting the language and making sure she was okay.

When Maria and I left the hospital, Janice was laughing and insisting her toes were moving just fine. Nonetheless, I told the doctor to check her out from head to toe and make sure nothing was broken.

"Good gracious, Stephanie. It was only my foot, not my entire body! There's no need to x-ray everything." Janice laughed more.

I joined six of our group seated around the outside table with a gigantic umbrella towering over them, licking gelato and sipping the local wine. When the little car shows up, it's *déjà vu* before our eyes. We watch the vehicle roll in as fast as it launched off. It stops in the same place where it drove over Janice's feet, in front of the church.

"It's them; it's Janice and Pat! They're back," I shout.

Magically, Pat and Janice pop out from the backseat while the driver and his wife emerge from the front doors. Those who are indulging in the array of treats on the little table toss down their drinks, grab their *gelato,* and rush across the cobblestones as though the Red Sea had just parted.

"*Stefania*, the news is good, very good," Pat announces, catching her breath.

"My feet are okay. They're not broken!" Janice beams. Her smile stretches from east to west, and she exhales as though the world was lifted from her shoulders. "I'm okay, it's a miracle. No broken bones at all. I told you I was okay."

Hours later, we sit around an oblong table, laughing and singing with the Napoli music and sipping the rich red wine. It flows like Niagara Falls—from the bottle to the glass, from the glass to the lips. All of us are singing, and some are dancing. I'm the only one who prefers to sip the strong espresso with cream on top.

Just a few feet away, in the little work area with the pizza oven, Lorenzo's arms plow up and down as he pounds and punches a huge ball of dough as though it's fighting back and refusing to submit. The skilled pizza maker is a one-man magic show as he stretches the pizza dough wide like an accordion, then slams it back into the heaping pile of flour, creating little white puffs of flour-smoke. He smashes it flat, then tosses it high in the air where it spins inches from the ceiling.

I take another swallow of espresso, wondering if it really might have hit the ceiling. Surely if it did, it would have stuck to the top before peeling away and plopping back down hard onto the counter and sending cumulus clouds of flour exploding into the air.

Every so often, in between shoving antipasti into my mouth, I holler, "Look at the pizza dough! It's flying."

I jab Minnie from Baton Rouge, Louisiana, in the arm, alerting her so she can watch the dough spin through the air.

"Lorenzo went to pizza school in Napoli to learn the skill of perfect dough creation," I tell her.

She nods with tipsy enthusiasm and fills her glass with the wine once again.

On my right, a few tables over, Janice drains another shot of limoncello, the Italian lemon liqueur made right here in Sorrento, Italy.

The Americans behind me laugh and pound the table. Some whoop and holler. It's a party gone wild.

"*Mamma Mia*, what's the matter with them?" Tony springs from his chair. The music continues because the two singers with the microphones must not have noticed the commotion from the back table.

"What do you mean?" I answer Tony. "They're having fun, as usual."

I swivel my neck, straining to see the excitement. Laughter rocks the nearby table. Standing up to see better, I gasp. My breath is caught. What is going on?

Janice's face is resting in her plate of pasta.

This is Janice's tenth tour with us in Italy. I know how she likes to play around. What in the world is she doing? She loves to joke. Is her face really in her plate? The thoughts chase through my mind swiftly like race cars zooming around the track. Which one is it: joking or not?

Nino flies across the room. "*Mamma Mia, Madonna!* Tony, come!" he hollers.

I jump up and leap over chairs as my breath catches in my chest. I don't think she's playing now, but everyone besides her continues to laugh.

"*Mamma Mia, Stefania.* Does she play with us?" Tony rushes toward Janice, who is squashed into the plate of pasta. "What's the matter with her, *Stefania*? Does she ruin the pasta and the sauce with her jokes?"

The laughter continues at their table. Her daughter and husband sing louder. No one seems concerned except me, Tony, and Nino.

"Is Janice okay?" I holler over the music.

"Yes, yes." Her daughter waves her napkin through the air.

"Look at Janice! Your mom! Why is her head in the pasta?" I squeeze through the crowd.

Janice raises her head up, then down again.

"*Mamma Mia*, she needs air!" Tony is like a mother hen. "Nino! Janice needs help!"

Before I get close to Janice, Nino and our waiter Romero have her stretched out on the floor like a slab of meat. Her limbs appear like limp spaghetti. It's all happening too fast. My head spins with adrenaline pumping at record speed.

The entrance to our favorite ristorante is buzzing with locals all dressed in their sleek Italian fashions. The tables are close to each other and filled with the young and old and everything in between. The music is blasting out lyrics as the waiter's cart presents trays with the local cuisine. Around our emergency, it's normal life in an Italian restaurant: eating, drinking, dancing, kissing, laughing, gesturing, and talking loudly.

The locals never notice the stretched-out *Americana* who's whisked through the air as though she's riding Aladdin's magic carpet as it glides through the air. The music never stops; many are dancing and never notice the drama going on among them.

When I step out in the open air, I see a little black car already revved up with both backseat doors wide open. Before I have time to wipe away the sweat accumulated on my forehead, Nino and Romero have carefully placed Janice inside. As soon as her dead weight hits the black leather seat, the teeny-tiny Fiat screeches away as the few pebbles underneath its spinning rubber tires pop and crackle.

"*Mamma Mia*, it never ends with you, *Stefania*." Tony pulls a large white napkin from his front pocket, swings it through the air, and dabs his face where glossy sweat slowly trickles down his cheeks.

"Wait!" I holler, but it's too late. The car is nothing but faded taillights.

"*Stefania*, go with Alessandro to the hospital. He waits for you on the scooter." Tony tells me.

Back in the *ristorante*, the music pumps higher, and the Americans sing, waving their hands in the cool air to the beat of "Y.M.C.A." There is rhythm even in the food. The waiters dance and leap as if they've been zapped with electricity. They are dancing ballerinas as they cover the tables with platters of local cuisine.

Lucia, a friendly local, stops to say hello to Tony.

"It's been twenty years of entertainment with *Stefania*. *Mamma Mia*, you have no idea about the Americans she brings to us. There is always one in every group. They do the most unbelievable things. Always something with the *Americana*." He sits at the table with his gigantic white napkin tucked underneath his collar that has droplets of spaghetti sauce clinging to it.

The phone rings inside Tony's pocket. He grabs it and swipes the button. "*Pronto*, hello."

There is gibberish through the phone. It's Nino reporting Janice's condition in his loud Neapolitan dialect.

"It's Nino at the hospital; she is okay," Tony waves the phone quickly as he gets up and walks away to hear more clearly.

"It's no heart attack or stroke, thank God," Nino tells Tony as I stand next to him at the hospital. "We will return her to the villa instead of the *ristorante*."

As soon as Tony returns to the room, the Americans huddle around to hear the diagnosis.

"She's okay," Tony tells them. "*Mamma Mia*, she's going to be okay!" He is too exhausted to relay any further information, but it was enough.

The Americans clink their glasses together and shout, "*Brava, brava,* Janice is okay."

Tony takes a seat next to them. Everything is a blur. Twice in one day, we had to rush one of our Americans to the hospital; now, here we sit, celebrating life.

Tony clinks his glass to everyone at the table, mumbling, "Cheers."

Hours later, Nino, Romero, and I arrive back to the *ristorante*, wearing wide grins on our faces. We are exhausted, but happy with the good news.

"*Mamma Mia*, Nino, this is unbelievable. Janice goes to the hospital twice today! Do you remember the *Americano Stefania* brought when we were—" For a split second, Tony tries to remember. Then he shrugs. "Well, it was far south, many miles from Sorrento. The same thing happened to that *signora*. The bloody *vino*—the wine. The *vino* is too strong for the *Americana*. They are not used to strong drink as we have in Italy. In America, they drink the tea, the iced tea and *Mamma Mia*, we must warn the *Americana* to be careful with the *vino*."

He turns to Pat, swirling his hands in the air. "This is unbelievable, Pat. Janice was drunk. The *dottore,* the doctor, said she is healthy, a strong *signora,* nothing wrong with her, just too much *vino*. I told Nino and Romero to take her home, to take her to the villa for a good night's sleep. She will not remember a thing of tonight's adventure."

Tony tosses down a glass of *aqua,* a glass of water.

Thirty minutes later, we call it a night and head to the villa.

This morning after a short night's sleep, I hear light taps on my bedroom door. Through the thick wooden door, Maria tells me,

"*Stefania*, Tony wants to see you in the breakfast room when you are ready."

"*Si*, okay," I tell Maria, "*Grazie mille!*"

I grab my bag and camera and head downstairs. Around the corner of the villa, past the round ceramic table with huge lemons painted on it, I hustle down another set of stairs beside the enormous green demijohns, following the aroma of the freshly baked bread and cakes that wafts through the Mediterranean air.

To my surprise, when I step inside, the first person I see is Janice. She is sitting at the little table. Her friends are fanned around her with their plates loaded with a towering breakfast feast. To my left are Tony and Nino, who are sharing some bread smeared with peach marmalade.

"*Stefania!*" Tony greets me. "The *signora* is okay this morning. She doesn't remember anything, not a thing that happened last night. In fact, she came to me this morning and thanked me for another wonderful and fun evening. *Mamma Mia, Stefania.* I do not understand."

Tony crunches the big block of bread, smears more of the peach marmalade on it, and then drenches it by pouring olive oil on top.

Mamma Mia, what a day in Italy. After two runs to the hospital, but no cost to *Americano* lives, all is well within our souls as we adventure on to the fairy-tale village of Ravello. I advise everyone to keep their toes away from the little donut-tires and limit their intake of the *vino* that flows so freely in Italy.

Chapter 22

SICILY, MIDNIGHT SWIM, & HOOKERS - COLPO D'ARIA

*A*s Nino guides our coach closer to the stately old palace that's now converted into a beautiful hotel that faces the Mediterranean Sea, twelve Americans seated behind me sing at the top of their lungs. The array of words bounces from their mouths in colorful confusion. The lyrics from the CD are in Italian, and not one American on board can pronounce the tongue-tying words in their entirety.

The effects from our Sicilian feast around the white-laced tables adorned with fresh flowers and flickering candles are still visibly clear even though the last morsel of food was consumed over an hour ago. Everyone is filled to the brim, and many are swimming from a hefty consumption of the strong *vino*.

Continuous laughter and singing bounces from one side of the coach to the other as the music flows throughout the speakers. This late September evening has been spent making memories with Sicilian friends and family. For the last twenty years, we've gathered around Giusy and Mimmo's table with the Americans creating so much laughter that it surely echoed all the way back to the mainland of Italy. The hours quickly flew by as we sang and danced inside the medieval farmhouse and celebrated the last harvest of the grapes in

Zafferana Etnea, Italy, which is minutes from Mount Etna: the largest active volcano in Europe.

Just hours ago, we observed tractors rolling in and out of the double-wide iron gates and pulling wagons behind them up the long dirt path. Each was loaded down with baskets of luscious bunches of grapes piled high. We watched the workers dump freshly picked purple-grapes into towering piles on the concrete floor to prepare them for the sorting machine.

We walked up steel steps and looked down into huge vats filled to the top. Gazing down into the gigantic containers, my eyes locked on the plump fruit swimming around in a sea of reddish thickness like Jell-O.

Next, we followed behind Mimmo, who is Tony's life-long friend and caretaker of the vineyard. We watched him demonstrate the process of winemaking. Before us were huge wooden barrels filled with succulent, fermenting grapes. I visualized the dance going on inside the barrels like a slow waltz wherein fermentation changes grape juice into wine. What an experience we shared tonight with food, wine, family, and friends!

The parade of every imaginable Sicilian cuisine was served with gusto. Giusy and Mimmo had cooked for days to prepare a feast for us. When we sat at the table, so much happened at once: parading of food, their cousin pumping the accordion, the uncorking of bottles, Giusy trying to show us her enormous pan of eggplant caponata, and Mimmo bringing out pans of linked sausages and holding them up in the air as they dangled. Eyes rolled like pinballs as the continuous displays of food arrived. That was just the first introduction, a tease of what was still to come.

It was a spectacle of beautifully prepared Sicilian foods, a procession that lasted for the first hour or more. The apples, the cherries, the tomatoes, and the clusters of grapes were all displayed throughout the house. I saw the purple beauties dangling from above my head, hanging on the arms of a chandelier. The big clusters were in colorful ceramic bowls on every table and towered as high as

Mount Etna. Everything inside the house was shrouded with a fruit or vegetable.

Within arm's reach, a gigantic wheel of Parmigiano cheese sat proudly as though flaunted inside a glass reliquary. It seemed like it was a royal shrine for all to pay homage to. I watched as Giusy placed another candle beside its golden-aged skin to highlight its exquisite beauty. I quickly deliberated if we should all stand and genuflect ourselves in prayerful gratitude before the flaming splendor.

Giusy twirled about from counter, to oven, to tables, to Tony with bowls of this and that, presenting it all for his approval. And just when we thought we'd get to eat—absolutely not. They came back with spoonfuls of one thing or another, still only offering a taste of the coming deliciousness.

"More bread is coming," Mimmo shouted in Italian as he refilled the wine glasses from an old demijohn. "Let's start the meal!"

The *vino* was toted from the cellars to the tables in marvelous abundance and uncorked before our eyes. And just when we thought it was impossible to consume another bite or for them to present another dish, their son Fredericka popped in the front door with freshly baked chocolate and vanilla cannoli.

This is the normal lifestyle in Sicily. It's our annual tour to celebrate the last harvest of grapes in late September. Many of our regular travelers would never miss this opportunity to be with their extended family, their loved ones who are bridged together across the pond by our tours.

"Someone in the backseat had too much of the *vino*," I tell Tony, who is pumping everyone up more than they already are with his braying donkey routine that ricochets through the coach.

It's a chaotic whirlwind, and adding to the madness, Ralph from Albuquerque, New Mexico, stands up and shoots out a drunken solo with the voice of an inebriated cartoon chipmunk. He sings along with the Italian lyrics and raises his voice as though a microphone is lodged in his throat. He performs and then decides to pump us up more with a few cartwheels down the narrow aisle of the bus. It's the potent effects of the Sicilian *vino*. He's a professional choreographer and dancer and can bend his body in nearly every direction. Ralph had tossed back countless glasses of the famous Marsala while saying he only drinks white wine, but after the punchy acidity tantalized his taste buds, he welcomed the red.

"They didn't listen to your warning about the potency of the wine." Lana, a real estate tycoon from East Texas, comes alive on the coach tonight as Nino drives us back to our beautiful villa. "You told us through the microphone minutes before we arrived at the farmhouse. Just like you always do. I have your words memorized."

"You should have my words memorized. How many times have you been to Sicily with us now?" I turn around in my seat to find Lana in the darkness of the coach.

"Oh, gosh, I think twenty or more. Heck, it could be thirty by now! But I do remember you telling them to be careful with the *vino* tonight."

I tap the microphone and blow into it, preparing to recite the warning again, even though we're now on our way back to the villa for a good night's sleep.

"Be careful with the drink tonight. Do you remember my words? I told you on the bus as we drove through the iron gates of the vineyard. I also said that Mimmo and Giusy would be serving their prized harvest this evening and bring out many bottles. The Sicilian spirits are potent. If there's anything more intoxicating than the view you had today atop Mount Etna, it's the *vino* here in Sicily."

"Yes, that's exactly what you said," Lana affirmed.

"The grapes that are harvested from the soil of the active volcano are nothing less than dynamite balls of flavor," I explain with the mic to my lips. "All around are black mounds of ash. The microclimate impacts the vines to create a powerful punch within the fermentation barrels, and the sugars are converted to invigorated ethyl alcohol. It's a liquid atomic bomb."

The conversation gets interrupted by Mary Lou, from Louisiana, squealing out the sound of a trapped pig while simultaneously slapping her hands on Tony's head as though he's a drum. I quickly joined in with my hands zipping across the dashboard, playing my imaginary piano.

"*Mamma Mia*, I can't anymore," Tony breathlessly spills out, holding his heart as it performs the tango while his body shakes with hysterical laughter.

I wonder if he'll bounce out of his seat as he veers on the edge of a catastrophe. His buttocks are now barely hanging from the edge of his seat. Seconds ago, Nino flipped a switch and illuminated the coach. The Mercedes-Benz has all the latest gadgets with tiny LED lights in assorted colors running down the aisle and overhead. We are now in high-def. I can see everyone.

I turn to observe Nino at the wheel of the coach. He jerks his head back and forth with the music as though someone is pulling a string as he tries to fit in with hoopla of excitement behind him.

"*Mamma Mia!*" Nino blurts, looking at me as his eyebrows shoot to his forehead. His black licorice eyes quickly return to the narrow road.

Along the Mediterranean Sea, our coach crawls as the walls expand in and out with the pumped-up music that's blasting within. Tony is hyped up more than ever, slapping his legs, squealing out hair-raising howls, and emulating a chimpanzee swinging from limb to limb.

"Stephanie, let's go swimming in the Mediterranean tonight. Some of us want to jump in as soon as we change into our swimming suits," Roxy, from Dallas, Texas, informs me. Her lips as thin as guitar strings nearly touch my left earlobe as her fingers snatch the lifeless microphone from my lap.

The wine has loosened her inhibitions, and she blows into the mic and blasts the coach with an inhuman sound to get everyone's attention. I imagine her lungs vacuuming up oxygen, starting from her red-painted toes to her throat. Then she forcefully ejects the words: "Stephanie said we could go swimming tonight. Who's going with us?"

"*Mamma Mia!*" shouts Tony with hands waving in alarm above his head. "What you mean you go swimming tonight? It's midnight! Total darkness! You must be joking. You go to bed! You can't be out in the night's air."

Tony turns toward me. "*Stefania*, what's the matter with these people? Do they not understand the *colpo d'aria,* the dreaded zap of air that causes the cold—or God forbid—the flu?"

"No. They do not understand," I mumble the words in a low voice.

"*Mamma Mia, Madonna*. I forget you are Americans. You know nothing that is good for you. You drink the sugary colas, you eat the butter, and you blast your homes with the bloody air-conditioner, the artificial air slapping you in the face. You are the worse one, *Stefania*. You should be an example to the people. What do you mean the *Americana* can go swimming tonight in the dark? The pneumonia will get them. Where do you see the water? There is nothing but blackness before us. Absolutely not, tell the people you are joking. They will be sick tomorrow," Tony explains as his words tumble together. He is clearly alarmed at such talk of swimming in the midnight air of the Mediterranean Sea.

"What? Swimming! Tony, they are joking. I'm going to bed. There is no way I'm jumping into anything but my little mattress." I flash my eyes innocently.

"Stephanie, at our age, we have nothing to lose." Roxy laughs. She doesn't care what Tony says; she's going swimming. "And what else do you plan to do tonight? We're on the Mediterranean, for crying out loud!"

"Are you serious? It's midnight, and there's nothing to see but the stars and the moon." I thought Roxy was joking before. I turn to see our beautiful villa coming up, then swing back and see the street that's sandwiched between us and the Mediterranean, which is somewhere in the blackness of night.

"I'll need to get my swimsuit out of my luggage." I hear one of the Americans say.

"I'll be ready in ten minutes. Just give me enough time to run upstairs to grab a towel and bathing suit," shouts another one from the backseat.

"They're joking, Tony. Don't worry," I reassure him again.

Less than fifteen minutes after Tony's meltdown over the deadly midnight air, most of us have already laughed our way through the front entrance of our villa while a few of the others lag behind, whispering.

"Stephanie, meet us back down here in ten minutes with your swimsuit on," hollers Blinky Louise, from New York City. Her whip-poorwill voice echoes in the far distance, urging me to run faster.

"Yes, meet us by the front entrance!" another one chimes in.

"I'm going to bed," I holler back as I jet to my room as though the Red Sea is parting, and the waters are rolling in to devour me.

At the stroke of midnight, my brain shuts off, and my eyes close, ready for the night's sleep. There is no way I'm going to the Mediterranean tonight. My toes will not touch the mushy sand.

The thought of going out tonight never enters my mind as I kick my left shoe across the room. It hits the wall with a loud thump before landing on the white marble floor. My eyes glance at my watch as I unstrap it from my wrist. It's already half past midnight. I feel the warm, breezy airflow through the opened door of my balcony, and the taste of the Mediterranean Sea races across my nose. It's not salty but smells of freshly baked bread and exotic flavors. The old world spices dance in the air twenty-four hours a day in Sicily. The night is still young for the Italians; in fact, it's just beginning.

I fluff my pillow underneath my head and stretch my legs as the lethargy of sleep settles in as if the curtain is drawn, and the day's adventures are nothing but sweet memories.

Minutes later, while dozing into a good night's sleep, I hear roaring laughter ricochet into the air as though thunder and lightning are flashing across the Sicilian sky. The loud commotion startles me awake as though a bucket of cold water was dumped on my face.

"What the heck?" I whimper out in shock. Is it morning already?

One would think my bed was on fire as I leap up and run to the opened balcony. I lean over the third-floor iron railing and glare down at the cars bumping along the cobblestone street. There is no view of the Mediterranean, for it is hidden within the darkness—total blackness behind the line of vehicles. The only thing separating our villa from the sea is the narrow sliver of road sandwiched between us.

Was I dreaming? The thought races through my mind. I see nothing but a stream of headlights, bumper to bumper, all lined up below. But where was the laughter and chatter coming from? I sleepily return to bed.

"Stephanie! Where are you? We're waiting for you!" I hear voices shrieking through the air the moment my head hits my pillow.

"Hurry up! Come join the party!" I hear again, louder than before.

I'm sure the whole island of Sicily is wide awake by now, or at least the local geriatric residents who prefer to go to bed before one o'clock in the morning.

"Are you coming?" Their voices are choreographed together and soar over my balcony. They might as well be announcing their whereabouts through a loud PA system.

"Shhh! Lord, have mercy!" I launch out of bed again and run to the balcony and stretch my eyes into the darkness. Do I see naked women standing in front of the concrete ledge that separates the narrow road from our villa with the Mediterranean feet behind them? I rub my eyes again.

"Stephanie, we see you!" they holler again.

My heart beats through my pajamas. I look below and see even more cars with idling motors. Suddenly, I see clearly. It's them. My group of ladies. What are they wearing, swimsuits, some bikinis, and what else?

Like a robot programmed to respond, words blurted from my mouth, "I'm coming! I'm coming!"

"*Mamma Mia, Stefania!* What do I hear from you? Is there a problem?" Tony bellows out.

An immediate rush of panic erupts. I lean over my balcony and look up. I see Tony and Nino above in their white underwear. They stand like toy soldiers looking out, but not below.

"Stephanie, come on. What are you waiting on?" they holler louder. All of them are seated on the concrete ledge in front of the cars lined up in front of them.

"*Mamma Mia, Stefania!* Is that you below us?" Tony and Nino are now hanging over their balcony with their eyes ballooning at me.

"*Si, si!* Yes, it's me. I'm okay. The ladies are staying out a little longer. They are okay. They are Americans. They love the cool air. Go back to bed. They will be fine. *Va bene*, okay!"

"*Stefania*, you must go with them. What's the matter with you? Do you go to bed while they stand alone in the bloody air? I do not understand where you find these *Americani*. They have gone mad, being out in the midnight air. Tomorrow, they will be sick, and the day will be ruined. The *colpo d'aria*, the dreaded zap of air, will surely bring them a cold," Tony mumbles loudly, turning back to his bed. I assume Nino does the same.

My legs sprint through my long rectangular room, and my arms reach for a towel as the cool Mediterranean breeze marches through the window. The centuries-old villa swooshes and rustles as the jet-stream of air creates a turbulent vacuum—the repercussion echoes across the room as the door slams at my heels.

My feet propel me through the hallway, rounding the corners and out onto the narrow street. The Americans are now standing on top of the concrete ledge whooping and hollering, anticipating the run into the Mediterranean with me. But wait...who are these men in the line of cars? Why do they have roses?

"Oh, my," the words roll from my mouth. I watch the tiny cars all honking and waving in unison at the Americans. It's like a drive-through parade or a take-your-pick of women. The bathing beauties stand before the drivers' eyes. The only thing missing is a sign advertising their services.

I stop and face the driver's side of the vehicles just before crossing the street. On the other side of the cars are the ladies parading themselves as though in a swimsuit exhibition.

"Stephanie," I hear some of them calling me with their voices bellowing across the cars. "Come join us!"

I sashay in front of headlights, nudging around cars and squeezing between men with roses dangling in their hands. By the time I get to my Americans, they're sitting on the concrete ledge with their legs crossed, kicking them out in unison as if on the stage of a cabaret show.

"Where are all of these men going?" Carol asks, accepting two long-stemmed roses from an Italian who is old enough to be her grandfather. He stands below her, and his smile stretches seemingly to both sides of the island.

"I think they're going to an event." Ann accepts three roses: one pink and two red.

I joined them on the ledge with my towel wrapped around my pajamas. We sit shoulder to shoulder on the ledge with our legs swinging back and forth, laughing together and wondering at the Romeos springing from their cars with bundles of flowers.

"This is an amazing country!" Beth blurts as she accepts a velvety rose as the man reaches for her hand. She bends down, slowly sliding her feet to the ground.

"Oh, my, what is he saying, Stephanie?" Beth breathlessly asks, hurriedly returning his flirtatious gestures.

"Take a guess! Italian men love females, especially nude ones."

I think nothing of the men's behavior and their politeness while oblivious to the long line of cars that have stopped with the motors still idling.

"This is amazing. My goodness, these roses must cost a fortune, and they're giving them to us and offering us a ride." Ann sits close to me in a pink bikini with thin slivers of fabric barely covering her white marble shoulders with her legs swinging back and forth. "But where do they want to take us?"

We all sit in a perfect line, holding at least one rose or more. The cars keep coming and honking at us with their drivers waving enthusiastically. They park on the other side of the already parked cars and leave the motors running. The laughter continues as we whoop and holler at them, waving our hands as though we're on a Christmas float.

More men shoot out from their cars, racing to us with hands stretched wide, insisting we go with them. They are overly excited like elderly schoolboys. We giggle and laugh like teenagers flirting with silly passion.

"Oh, *signor*, I can't go with you," Joyce teases. She smiles flirtatiously as she kicks her legs higher in the air and bats her eyes.

He understands nothing, except she's flirtatious and an American, and it's an unusual encounter wherein she refuses to get up and go with him.

"*Mamma Mia!* Come with me," he says in fast Italian, pulling her arm and stretching it towards his little car.

Joyce giggles more. She pulls his shirt toward her and yanks his scarf about his neck. "Oh, Romeo, sing me a song."

Another lady joins in the fun and plays along with them, teasing and flirting and batting her long lashes of a little pony's tail. The Sicilians are old but eager to participate. The anticipation mounts more.

Lights beam brighter and cars zoom closer. The sun-kissed men swarm around us like bees to honey. Everything about this evening is bewildering, but the thought of where they came from or where they're going never enters our minds until the moment is shattered by a familiar voice.

"*Mamma Mia, Madonna!*" Tony shouts. His voice thunders through the array of swarming bees. Nino is glued to Tony's side, and they're both wrapped in huge white towels with more clutched in their hands.

"*Basta!* Enough," Tony shouts hysterically, telling the Romeos to leave. "What's the matter with you, *Stefania*? *Madonna Mia!*"

We are deer in bright headlights, caught by Mother Superior, or in our case, the head monk.

"We're going into the sea for a swim! Just to get our feet wet." One of the women hollers. Her voice drowns me out.

"This is unbelievable!" Tony can't stop mumbling. His eyes inflate. "What would Allen think of you down here in the air, the sickness that will attack you tomorrow? *Mamma Mia*, I have never seen you behave this way."

Tony leans against the concrete wall, grabbing the end of his towel to wipe large droplets of perspiration from his distorted face. I watch his chest expand in and out. I can almost hear the beating drum within. The lights from the villa barely highlight his face.

"It's warm out here!" I protest. "And I couldn't leave them alone. Remember, you said so!"

"*Madonna Mia!*" Tony continues his mantra as he robotically shrouds the women with the extra towels that he and Nino brought to save them from the dreaded *colpo d'aria*. "You are risking your lives in the night's air!"

If this is not enough disturbance to wake the dead, it is when one of the ladies shrieks in fun and grabs Nino's hand and yanks him hard, forcing him to gallop through the sand towards the alluring black abyss of the Mediterranean beyond us. The other Americans take off after them screeching and singing. They run madly toward an invisible sea.

"*Stefania!* Look what you've done! They are *pazzo*, crazy! What kind of people go to the sea in darkness?"

"Americans!" I say, smiling, but soon we see nothing but twinkling stars before us as Nino and the ladies vanish into the night.

Tony's feet struggle to move. His toes pinch downward, sinking hard into the sand and alerting him the water is near.

"Nino! Nino!" Tony calls out in desperation. "*Mamma Mia, Madonna.* Where is Nino?"

Tony mixes his words with Italian obscenities. "*Stefania*, we must get the Americans inside."

But we are ghosts in the darkness. There is no one around. They are all in the sea, splashing and frolicking.

"I can't see anything in front of me." I look ahead, but it's blacker than black like the bottom of the sea.

I could be blindfolded inside a lion's den and not know the difference. I can only go off the sound of the Americans playing in the sea.

"Nino!" Tony continues to shout.

An earthshaking splash bursts through the Mediterranean. The Americans spring high in the depths of the water like dolphins. I can only imagine their playful movements.

"*Mamma Mia!*" Tony can't stop repeating himself as he desperately tries to call his children back. It's useless. They hear nothing.

I change the subject. "Tony, why were the elderly men handing out beautiful roses to us as they lined their cars up beside the concrete ledge? Was there a special occasion? A party tonight?"

"*Mamma Mia, Stefania!* You know what the *signori* want. *Buona fortuna.* Good luck to them! The *Americana* likes to play with the mind. The woman enjoys herself very much, playing flirty with the man. They pull strings and then shut the curtain without delivery. You know what I mean, *Stefania*?"

"Italian men are too passionate. They take everything to the next level, like dynamite. The men were old enough to be my ancient ancestors and..." Tony cuts me off.

"*Mamma Mia, Stefania!* What do you mean too passionate? What kind of woman displays herself like that in front of Italians? You are the worst as the one who gets the Americans into these situations. I forget you have the mind of the *Americana* even though Italian blood runs through your veins; your brain cannot understand how the Italiano thinks."

"Yes, I understand! They are old Casanovas, senior seducers. They are hot pepperoncini—Viagra on a stick with two legs. They must be ninety years of age. They were just playing around, having a little fun. They are harmless, sweet souls. Good golly, they're old enough for the nursery." I joke more, saying anything that pops into my mind with an attempt to calm Tony. But he hears nothing.

"*Mamma Mia, Stefania.* After a hundred years of us being together, you understand nothing. How many times do I tell you? There is no stop sign or age limit with man's libido, that is, if Italian blood runs through the veins. Perhaps the *Americana* is different. I don't know. How would I?"

"It was all theater! They are in their swimsuits!" I try to defend.

"They are naked. Thank God you have clothes on. *Mamma Mia!* What would Allen think of you tonight? *Madonna*, he would be very angry. Yes, Allen would..."

"Oh, my gosh! Tony. You know the Americans are different. We don't care about the bloody air. We give it no thought other than welcoming its coolness."

"*Mamma Mia, Stefania!* How quickly you change the subject. We are not talking about the bloody air right now!"

"Tony, the Americans had no idea..." I try to find words that he will understand. I can't think of an Italian translation. I try again. "The Americans thought the men were lined up for an event, a party tonight. There was no harm in playing along."

"*Madonna, Stefania!* The men think you all to be *puttana*! *Prostituta*! Do you understand my Italian, my English? Tony continues in raw dialect that I struggle to understand. My ears burn, but my eyes see nothing. The darkness shrouds my eyes from the theatrics of a Sicilian.

Bells ring the early morning hour, and Nino and the ladies splash out of the Mediterranean as if on cue.

"*Mamma Mia, Nino!* What's the matter with you? You must drive the bus tomorrow." Tony rushes to them and automatically covers their heads and bodies to shroud them like Italian mummies on a cool Arabian night.

Will they all be sick tomorrow with the blast of the bloody air?

Chapter 23

MAMMA MIA, I HAVE SINNED!

"*S*he's a metropolitan whirlwind on steroids, a showstopper of elegance with the wardrobe of a celebrity fashionista, and a long-time customer of my shop, Decorate Ornate. She never meets a stranger and will out-talk any human being on Planet Earth. Her pedigree and street address stretches out to the posh neighborhood of Chelsea, London. She's a rich lady, international interior designer, and contributor to a famous magazine known throughout the world," I tell Tony through the phone line that stretches from Texas to the Italian Riviera.

"*Mamma Mia!* Where does the list stop?" Tony asks.

"It doesn't. She's a loudmouth comedian with big blue eyes that give a piercing, darting look. A woman fed with a silver spoon who is always proclaiming, through that brassy, ear-piercing, shrieking voice of hers, her connections to royalty. She's captivating, a one-woman show who always takes things a step further than expected. And, are you listening, Tony? She's coming to Italy with me."

A brief silence lingers on the line. I think Tony must have fainted, or, perhaps he's pondering my words, mulling over the *Americana* who will be on our next adventure in Italy. A *signora* joining the stage, giving him a little competition.

Weeks later, it's my first day in the Umbria region of Italy with a new group of Americans. Among our fun group is Kim, the colorful, fashionista princess, and, oh, I forgot to mention to Tony, along with her many accolades, she's an oil tycoon heiress! She brings along her costly array of perfumes that fumigate everything within a fifty-foot radius. I wonder how the next thirteen days will go as she rooms with her best friend, Shelly Ann.

In this particular villa, my room is adjacent to Kim and Shelly Ann's with connecting balconies and a huge window-like passageway allowing us to talk with each other and go from one room to the other if we choose to do so. The unusual entrance must be at least eight feet tall, large enough for me to see just about all of their furnishings when standing in an awkward corner of my room. It's a strange layout, but when renovating the old palace for guests, they preserved the medieval beauty.

As I make my way into my room, I toss my purse onto the bed and swing open the glass doors that lead to my balcony. The moment I twirl around, it starts. Kim's voice ricochets through the opened windows like a tidal wave slapping me in the face. I hear and witness it all.

"Set the luggage inside the door," Kim tells the porter. She tosses the key on the nearby wooden table and extracts her most prized possession from within her designer bag: a bottle of perfume.

"Hmm." Kim folds her arms and looks around the room as she leans against the royal blue damask bedspread.

"I'm putting my toiletries right here," Kim says aloud to herself as she picks up the bottle of perfume again and gives it a long hard squeeze into the air, drenching the medieval furniture with an abundance of scents. Within seconds, the room fills with her favorite aroma of jasmine and rosewood made from expensive extracts. The pure oils are so strong that they could wake the dead.

"Give it a rest," Shelly Ann thunders as she tosses her small backpack onto the twin-size mattress that's just inches away from Kim's bed.

"I can't breathe," she blurts. She grabs a towel from the adjacent bathroom to hurriedly cover her nose as the potent fragrance swims to her nostrils.

"What?" Kim calmly asks as she squeezes the spongy ball on the bottle again, releasing a wide spray into the little room.

"It is too much," Shelly Ann mumbles while pressing the white towel to her nose and rushing to the other side of the room to push the green shutters open. Her irritated eyes crave the fresh air and perhaps the brilliant view of the Toscana hills.

"Good grief, Kim! Why do you feel as though you need to squirt that awful stuff every few minutes? It's too much! Look at my eyes. The overwhelming fumes are choking the life from the Sacred Heart of Jesus on the wall!" Shelly Ann coughs and snorts and reaches for her little pocket fan. She snaps the folds into a full-blown peacock span and swishes it back and forth, creating a whirlwind of air as though the room is billowing with smoke.

After a few hard swings, Shelly Ann slowly opens her eyes. Her short brown lashes are matted together and stick to her eyelids as though glued. The heavy blast of chemicals has created a full-blown fog in their beautifully decorated room, causing her eyes to burn. Tears race down her cheeks and drip from her chin.

"You're not accustomed to the finer things in life," Kim says, running her manicured fingers through her Farah Fawcett hairdo as she bends over. Her hands plow through her hair and give it a hard shake for the grand finale. It's a peculiar habit of hers, a constant bend-over with her head to the floor while raking through the golden locks.

"You're causing my eyes to swell and my head to hurt. I can't breathe in this room with that much perfume." Shelly Ann stands firm with her arms folded over her chest, totally disgusted.

"I use genuine perfume, and the weak drops you use are, well, nothing but colored water," Kim snaps. Her crystal-blue eyes pierce through her friend.

"You smell like lilacs mixed with nun flowers. Like a funeral."

"What the hell are nun flowers?" Kim lifts her chin higher in the air to sniff the fragrance. "You don't know how to articulate its natural aroma. The ingredients are from France and are the finest blends of exotic flowers."

"I know what I smell, and it's pine trees saturated with lilac or maybe lavender. Yes, it's lavender with—"

"When did you become a professional perfumer? Scent is exclusively learned. It's a cultural upbringing."

"I've worn one perfume all of my life. I've never known anyone else who rhapsodizes about their fragrances. Gosh dang, give it a break. Please!" Shelly Ann is insistent. "Smell is the strongest of our five senses! You're killing me with your excessive use."

Kim opens another bottle and inhales the scent. She grins, remembering when she purchased it in Dallas at her favorite store, Neiman Marcus.

"I can't stay inside this room if you're going to continue spraying that stuff!" Shelly Ann fans herself.

"Give yourself time and enjoy the finery of French perfumeries. Close your eyes and smell the difference." Kim sprays again.

"I'm accustomed to the finer things in life too, such as the natural flowers that God gave us, not the concoctions you buy with fancy designer names branded across the front. Having a designer label on your perfume bottle doesn't make it any better than my lotions that are all made from natural herbs," Shelly Ann defends.

She steps to the bathroom and blots her face with cold water then tosses her sandals across the marble floor while reaching for her tennis shoes. She plans to go for a quick run on the medieval streets of Assisi, thinking the fresh air will relieve her swelling eyes.

Both of them signed up for our *Tuscany Surprise* tour months ago. Kim invited her "best friend since third grade'" to be her roommate by promising her two weeks of bonding and reminiscing about old times. I clearly remember Kim arriving in my store, Decorate Ornate, and excitedly proclaiming, "Oh, Stephanie, I'm so excited to bring Shelly Ann to Italy with me. We haven't been together on an overnight excursion since we were little girls."

"We haven't seen each other in years, not since we ran into each other in Las Vegas at the slot machines. You must know, Shelly Ann is different. She's not like me at all. No, she's interested in those dreadful sports, continuously running as though her pants are on fire. You know the type: always worried about the extra pounds at her waist. She's a tomboy and doesn't like to decorate at all." Kim whipped out a photo of them together in Las Vegas. Both of them are the same height, one blonde and one brunette, and both barely tipping the scale at 120 pounds.

"Put us together in the same room. We want to reconnect our friendship and experience Italy together," Kim requested, flashing her teeth.

I stared at her voluptuous lips that were painted glossy pink and plumped by the latest cosmetic surgeon in Dallas, Texas. I watched her unconsciously whip out a large mirror studded with Swarovski crystals from her latest Prada bag. She stared into her reflection and admired her magnificence.

She puckered her big lips, somehow making them grow larger, then nonchalantly smeared more gloss across them and smacked them together. With a loud clank, she dropped the mirror back into her purse.

"Stephanie, I know you will, but make sure you give us a splendid room with the best view. I'm accustomed to the best. Make it happen. Wave your magic wand. And, oh, I'd like to have my own personal porter. I mean, how in the world could I enjoy my trip if I'm loaded down with luggage?

"But don't worry about Shelly Ann. She's such a tomboy since she was raised in New Mexico and always wore those cowboy boots and blue jeans. Don't be alarmed if she shows up with a cap pulled down over her head, mashing her ears out like Dumbo.

"Of course, I've never had a pair of those horrible blue jeans on my body. Goodness no. My mother would never permit." Kim rattled on in her braggadocious way and interrupted herself only to swing her head down again, almost dusting the floor with her blonde curls, while running her fingers through her layered mane.

How different the two women are is an understatement. Kim is a queen accustomed to all things being tailor-made. She's spoiled and born with a silver spoon.

On the other side of the coin, Shelly Ann is independent, hardworking, a master gardener, and athletic. She's born to exercise and always stretches her legs by running several miles a day. She sees no need for the finer things in life except the best running shoes. Shelly Ann married money, but her husband holds the purse strings tightly to protect his empire.

Staying inside the medieval walls of the fairy-tale village of Assisi, home to Saint Francis, is beyond magical. Every morning after breakfast, we do what we've done for over twenty years: take the Americans to hidden jewels throughout Italy and beyond.

After a week in Assisi, we're now in the village of Orvieto, another hilltop village that's one of my favorites. We're spending the next few nights on top of this rock, right next to the towering, majestic black and white-striped cathedral that would dwarf the Jolly Green Giant.

After an energetic day of eating the local pastas, sipping the table wine, and perusing through the many ceramic shops, we stroll around the narrow medieval alleyways and find ourselves face-to-face with the soaring facade of the cathedral.

Lorenzo Maitani started this masterpiece in the year 1300, and it took more than one hundred years to complete. It's hard to fathom one hundred years to build a church, but it's not just a church. It's a creation that leaves you standing in awe and wondering how it came to be. It was so majestically designed with inlaid gold and marble and adorned with countless tiny mosaics. And the gigantic bronze doors. How do you describe such beauty? It leaves one wondering if an enchantress assisted in the creation of such majesty. After gazing upon its beauty, one must think that perhaps God himself breathed it into existence.

Standing in awe outside this indescribable beauty, we are mere specs of sand compared to its endless height. "It takes an elevator to reach the top of the door," I joke to the Americans who stand beside me. They're all clicking their cameras as though they're the paparazzi.

"Tomorrow morning, they will hold Mass. If you want to go, I'll be inside the doors at eleven a.m. It will be an amazing experience for all of you, and the music is heavenly," I explain as I walk to the right side of the church and head down the stairs to our hidden villa we're staying at for the next few nights.

This morning, Orvieto has been awakened by church bells resonating throughout the medieval village. It's a glorious wake-up call that clangs every half-hour. I stand on my balcony and gaze at the beauty before me. I stare at the cathedral towering high in the sky and inhale the mesmerizing aroma of freshly baked pastries wafting through the air. I look around but see no sign of the baker.

Down below is a little *Piaggio Ape*: a toy-sized truck filled with loaves of bread wrapped in brown paper and tied with a pretty bow. Before the bells finish their chime, the bustle begins. Shutters swing open, and the musical starts. Doors below me pop wide and out walks a *signora* with hips swaying in her long blue cotton dress, shoulders arched, and breasts thrust up as though ready for a salute. I watch from above as she takes three loaves of bread and tosses her euros to the delivery man. I lean out over my balcony, drumming my fingers on the black iron and taking in the chaotic play of everyday life in this Tuscan hilltop village. We're in a true-life enchantment. Even the brooms are like those in my childhood fairytales.

Shelly Ann was up and out the door forty-five minutes ago in her running clothes and white tennis shoes, eagerly escaping Kim's fumigation and morning dressing ritual. She runs up and down the steep, red volcanic cliff. Thirty minutes later, Kim crawls out of her little twin bed, never noticing that her roommate is gone.

"I slept like a *bambino* last night," Kim's voice echoes from the balcony after a loud slam of her shutters. "Leave the doors closed. You know I hate the pollen, the clatter, and those dang church bells. I was sleeping delightfully until—oh, I need the bathroom. Are you nearly finished?"

Kim scurries to her toiletries and squeezes out the last few droplets of her beloved perfume. The air is filled with the sweet aroma of a lavender field and roses—or perhaps a funeral home—

along with huge splashes of sweet jasmine. Excitement builds as she sings while fluffing her blonde curls, preparing for the day's events in the medieval village of Orvieto.

"I can't wait to see the local ceramics that Stephanie told us about. Are you planning on shipping any back? Oh, never mind, if it's not the Texas décor of horses, cows, and oil wells, you're not interested. Silly me. I know that's your taste and mine, too, but I need more than that." Kim rolls her deep blue eyes balancing high on distinguished cheekbones as she swipes mascara on her extended lashes, never realizing Shelly Ann left the room a while ago.

She's dramatic in every way as she ceremoniously sings while primping in front of a little mirror she brought from home. Kim reaches for the perfume again, but the decanter is empty. Not giving it a second thought, her right hand reaches for another bottle of her prized bouquet of oils stockpiled in her carry-on bag. In less than two minutes, the obsession starts again, and soon the stench has drifted from her balcony down into my room.

Hours later, standing at the enormous bronze door of the basilica, many of the Americans eagerly wait to go inside. Most of the Americans with me on this tour are Protestant, not Catholic. They have no idea what to expect during Mass. Last night, I told them about the Eucharistic Miracle kept inside the reliquary. Shelly Ann, a devout Catholic, had requested to participate in Mass. I remember her words from last night as we sipped some wine.

"Stephanie, please take us inside tomorrow. I have envisioned this moment of participating in an Italian Mass. I've read about the doubting priest and the miracle cloth. This is going to be one of the highlights of this tour."

Shelly Ann turned to Kim and continued, "Don't worry, I'll be in and out in no time, and then we can go to that little porcelain doll shop you keep rattling on about."

Under the moonlight last night, I had explained the miracle inside that particular cathedral.

"It was in the year 1263 that a Bohemian priest went on a pilgrimage to Rome to strengthen his faith. On his return, he stopped in Bolsena, Italy, to celebrate Mass. He was tormented by doubt, asking himself and God whether the consecrated host was indeed Christ's body and blood. The priest was going through trials and experiencing heartache and troubling times. During Mass, disbelief and uncertainty swept into his mind, causing turmoil within his heart to doubt that the body and blood of Christ were represented by the Eucharist. The priest questioned the teaching of his faith. Did the bread and wine really represent Jesus's body and blood? The thoughts swept in, and he questioned God over and over as he went through the motions during Mass.

"As the bread was broken, blood began to drip and run from the host. History tells us that this miracle happened after the prayer of consecration, or the blessing. It was a miracle right before his eyes, one the priest couldn't deny.

"Afterward, he came to Orvieto, where Pope Urban IV resided, to relate the unusual events. You can imagine the whirlwind investigation that his comments spurred. Afterward, the Pope decreed that the miraculous host and the stained, linen altar cloth be moved to the Orvieto cathedral for display."

Now, as we stand inside the cathedral in awe at the beauty before us, our feet are locked in place. Our eyes are drawn to the architecture of the ceiling. This is one of the most spectacular Romanesque basilicas in Italy. I'm in love with its beauty.

"I could fly my airplane around in here." David, from Texas, never looks down. His eyes are enraptured by the craftsmanship of the hundreds of wooden rafters that supports the marble and travertine.

"The beautiful frescoes are inside the two chapels: Cappella del Corporale and Cappella di San Brizio. That's where we're going next. They contain priceless art of world-wide importance. Do you remember last night when I explained the miracle of the bread? It's inside the corporal chapel. The chapel was built to house the relic of the stained cloth known as the corporal," I explain a little more.

"How do you get to the ceiling to change lightbulbs?" Jan changes the subject. Her husband is an electrician in New Mexico, where ceilings are typically not two hundred feet high.

"You'd need my airplane," David answers for Jan.

"That would work." Jan laughs while snapping a photo of its massiveness.

"I want to take you inside for Mass. Follow me," I tell them, making my way to the front. The chapel is filled with smoke from the incense.

I look over my shoulder at them. "We'll sit on the bench ahead." The Americans are on my heels, following their leader into a world they do not know.

We make our way through thick plumes of frankincense as the local residents file out from their pews, one row at a time, and move toward the front to stand in line.

"What do we do, Stephanie?" Mary asks.

"Take communion if you feel lead to participate. However, make sure you have a clean heart without sin. You understand the scriptures in I Corinthians 11:29?"

"Tell everyone to watch Shelly Ann. She's Catholic," someone speaks up.

"You can't participate if you're not Catholic," Shelly Ann speaks out.

"How would they know if we're not Catholic? Do you guys carry around an identification card from the pope?" David takes a seat on the bench.

When it comes time to file out from our pew, Shelly Ann eagerly takes the first step and moves to join the locals.

I watch Kim as her hands tighten around the back of the bench in front of her. Suddenly, she stands and follows her friend. In the aisle, she turns and waves her right hand, motioning for us to come along while verbalizing her intent.

"Come on! Let's join Shelly Ann. We can't let her go by herself." Kim's voice cuts like a knife, slicing through the thick smoky plumes of frankincense.

In an instant, we are suddenly exposed as a long line of Americans standing together, shoulder to shoulder. Without thought, several follow Kim to join the locals who are standing in line to see the priest.

We spoke in muted whispers, and our feet dragged heavily across the medieval tiles.

"Stephanie, we are not Catholic. What are we doing in line?" Margie asks. Her eyes scan everything, taking in the heavenly surroundings.

"It's okay. We're partaking in the Lord's Supper," I respond in a hushed whisper, respecting the sanctity of the Holy Spirit that hovers all around. "You can't have any sin in your life. You know the scripture, right?"

"I will ask for forgiveness before I participate." Margie follows along.

I look to my left. We have become a long train as we slowly make our way to the front. The light shining down upon the pews and the shimmering of the golden candlesticks is mesmerizing. Magnificent floral arrangements explode in a rainbow of beauty, and the frescoes above appear as though we're in a miniature Sistine Chapel.

Shelly Ann now stands before the priest in his long white robe. His hands stretch toward her face, and he places the host in her hands before she reverently steps aside. She genuflects to the crucifix, crosses herself, and walks to the left.

Kim is next and steps in front of the priest. She flashes a smile as though she's been reunited with her long-lost friend. The joy of the "reunion" is one-sided. The priest has no idea what's in store for him.

After batting her eyes and grinning broadly, Kim begins spilling atrocious confessions to everyone inside the soaring cathedral, "Father, I have sinned a lot according to the good book, or at least that's what I'm told. I have wished death upon many. I have lusted after another. I have hated my brother, my neighbor, and my daughter-in-law."

The harmonious melody of chanting stops, and the small congregation stands in disbelief at the unabashed noise of a foreign language ricocheting within God's Holy of Holies. The priest blushes deeply.

"*Signora*, no," he whispers in shock. He awkwardly nudges closer to the other priest who clumsily drops the censer with the frankincense inside as though it's burning his hand.

Kim keeps confessing, almost unaware of the shiny brass container crashing onto the floor.

"Oh, yes, I have sinned big time! And that's not all I've done," Kim rambles louder without shame. "I wished for Sally, my horrible neighbor, to drop dead. Oh, yes, it's true. I hate her. And her pencil-thin husband, who is a loud-mouth idiot who refuses to move his golf cart to the back of their house. We live in a gated community in Dallas, Texas, among professionals with manicured yards. You know what I mean?" Kim covers her mouth, now trying to whisper. "I wished the husband's death too. Do you blame me?"

"*Signora*, please, you must go." The priest motions for the other priest to help him, but he's on his knees nervously gathering up the brass censer and frankincense from the floor.

"*Signora*, this is not confession. This is..." He crosses himself in horrified confusion. With the wave of his hands and words spoken in Italian, everyone else goes down on their knees as if a human wave was choreographed. I look at the congregation, then back to Kim, who is still babbling. I look to the priest in the white robe who stammers over his words in Italian.

No one was prepared for this outburst of so many awful truths. It's a sacred moment that Shelly Ann will never forget or forgive.

I clutch my hands together, looking around for a side door and a fast getaway. The others behind me stand frozen, their legs refuse to move. I look up and see the second priest back on his feet with sweat dancing across his forehead. Kim hasn't stopped gushing sins.

"Excuse me, I'm sorry," I try to speak to the priest as I lean toward Kim. "She's not Catholic."

Kim keeps rambling despite my efforts. What am I supposed to do? I look for an escape, a hidden departure of some sort. Should I make a run for the door?

Now looking directly at me, the other priest stands before me with deep melancholy creased into his face. His eyebrows are like a black cat's bushy tail. His eyes pierce into my soul, and I look down, pretending to have lost something of importance.

It's déjà vu all over again. I quickly remember the monks at the Abbey of Sant'Antimo and the flying bench ordeal a few years back. My heart races, and I feel faint. I think he recognizes me from my many visits throughout the years, but I keep my face lowered and pray he doesn't.

The heat from my embarrassment glosses over my face, and without thought, I race to the entrance, never looking back. As if on cue, the others follow immediately, but Kim stays to confess her entire life to the priests and the Italian congregation.

The next morning, Kim and Shelly Ann sit apart from one another at the breakfast table. Kim's voice is loudly declaring that yesterday was her first Catholic confession.

"I've decided to be Catholic. I love the beautifully festooned chapels. Did you see the little dollhouse temple and flowers cascading all around the gold?" Kim takes a sip of espresso from the usual tiny cup.

There is a dreadful pause of shock. I almost choke on my double espresso. I've heard these same words from too many Americans who say things in complete ignorance. The memories rush in like a bad case of measles.

"What religion were you before?" Mary Lee asks while I'm still coughing.

"Nothing, really. I see no reason to hang a sign over my door, if you know what I mean."

Kim bites into a *cornetto*, a delicious Italian roll like a flaky croissant. It's a taste of heavenly delight made with eggs, butter, sugar, vanilla, fresh orange, and lemon zest.

"My husband is a devout Baptist. But me, not so much." Kim drinks her coffee like an American, slowly and leisurely, savoring every sip.

More memories echo inside my head. Just a few tours back, there was an American who wanted to switch her faith. She had also thought that all of the Catholic churches back in the states would be dripping with marble, bronze, and mosaics, and have angels of gold the size of giants floating from the ceilings. Now, here I am with another one.

"Wow! You converted just like that?" Mary Lee keeps the conversation going.

"Yes. I think so." Kim leans over to Mary Lee, brushing blonde curls behind her ears as she loudly whispers. "You have peach marmalade smeared on your upper lip and across your face.

"Being Catholic will be quite the adventure. Don't you agree?" Kim leans back over her *cornetto,* heaping scoops of scrambled eggs into her mouth.

Mary Lee, a shy, devout Catholic from New York City, grabs her napkin and rubs her mouth repeatedly, while her face flushes red. Is the embarrassment from the jam smeared across her face? Or could it be the newsflash of Kim's new claim to Catholicism? Whichever it is, Mary Lee is a saint. She politely smiles and nods her head as Kim continues her vain proclamations.

"I was born to be a Catholic. I love the way the ceremony went. We were there minutes, not hours, and no long sermon. All we had to do was walk in a line, and bam! Tell the priest all of our sins, and then we were free to go and start back over again," Kim brags. She has failed to realize we didn't go to confession or to understand the true spiritual meaning of taking communion.

What is this huge misconception of being Catholic the Americans have? My heart hurts for those who have no sound doctrine or real experience and relationship with our Lord and Savior, Jesus Christ. I want to conference with Kim and explain the truth, but now is not the time or the place.

Kim digs in her purse, bringing out a large Swarovski-studded mirror. She does a quick inventory of her face and then slams it shut.

"Well, girls, I'm out of here. I've got to get my luggage ready for the porter to pick up. I did most of it last evening, but, of course, all of my toiletries had to wait until now." Kim tosses back the last swig of espresso and wipes her lips with a large white-linen napkin before squealing out her usual spine-tingling good-byes.

"I'll be back in a second," Kim tells us. Her voice thunders across the room, ending on an unexpected pitch that causes everyone to laugh hard.

"Oh, my heavens," Claire laughs uncontrollably, spewing juice across the table and barely missing David. "I'm sorry."

"I'm out of here too. It's time to get going. I'll see you on the bus." Claire takes one last sip of orange juice before grabbing a peach from the ceramic bowl.

Kim makes a heart-wrenching discovery when she returns to her room: her beloved perfume bottles are gone. She frantically searches the room, turning her handbag upside down across her bed, then hurriedly searching through the large over-packed suitcase and dumping it out onto the floor, then hysterically pulling drawers out, crawling underneath the bed, and slinging clothes into the air.

"Where are my perfume bottles? They have to be here!" Kim shrieks, yanking the bed sheets back and tossing pillows onto the polished tiles. "I just had them last night!"

"Tony, *Stefania*, help! The maid stole my perfumes! Oh, my heavens. Yes, the maid stole my perfumes!" Her voice ricochets like bullets soaring across the mountains, hitting every target along its way.

"Help, someone! Help me!" Kim continues to scream.

Not waiting for anyone to rescue her, Kim darts out the door and races through the hallways. "I've been robbed! The maid stole my priceless perfumes! Shelly Ann, where are you? Help me! I've been robbed."

Her voice rises and cuts through every sharp corner, piercing in and out of windows. Even the donkeys in the meadow must be alerted. The only person her voice didn't reach was her roommate, who had escaped their room hours ago to jog up and down the cobblestone streets.

Tony and I had been sipping our morning espresso with the rest of our group, reminiscing about the last thirteen days of being in Italy.

When the hair-raising shrieks reach us, Tony spills his cup of espresso on his white cotton shirt. The thunderous voice tells us something horrible has happened.

"*Mamma Mia, Madonna!*" Tony springs from his chair, and the ceramic cup slams to the floor, breaking into a million pieces. I jump up too. All of us stand as Kim shoots into the room, hysterically wailing as though she's lost her dearest loved one.

"Oh, my gosh! What's happened to you?" We rush to her.

She repeats, "The maid stole my perfume bottles!"

"*Mamma Mia*, what do you mean the maid stole your perfume bottles?" Tony asks. "The housekeepers do not steal or take anything. You must be joking. They would never take perfume bottles or anything else. You must understand how it works here in Italy. They are very thankful for their jobs. They are family here. Do you understand?"

Drawn by the alarmed voice, the staff arrives and stands around us, asking what is the matter. Before Tony opens his mouth, Kim starts accusing the housekeepers, shaking her fingers in their faces. I watch as their heads drop, alarmed and saddened.

"*Basta, basta!* Enough!" Tony intervenes with a roar that finally silences Kim. He doesn't believe her. Surely, she's misplaced the sacred bottles. "Kim, are you sure the housekeeper took your perfumes? Did you see her take them?"

"Yes, the housekeeper took my perfumes! Without a doubt, she took my expensive bottles!" Kim throws back; her words get louder.

"*Mamma Mia*, which one of these people took your perfumes? If you're so certain, you must have seen which one." Tony points to all of them.

The staff stands with tears flowing down their cheeks. They don't understand all of the English flying in every direction. Tony pontificates in Italian, throwing words in the air with his hands.

"I don't know which one of them took my perfumes, but they did." Kim stands straight as a tin soldier.

During the commotion, Shelly Ann walks in, listens to Kim's accusatory words, and shakes her head in disbelief. She turns and walks away, saying she must pack and will be back in thirty minutes.

"Wait!" Kim hollers to Shelly Ann. "Did you see the maids in our room last evening or this morning? While I was asleep? Before your run?"

"No. I haven't seen anyone in our room. No one but you," Shelly Ann replies. "Nevertheless, I'm sure if you sniff around, the aroma will lead you to the guilty culprit. Everything you own has flowers on it. God only knows what else you soak your body in." Shelly Ann swings her ponytail in a dramatic attempt to prove her point, then turns the corner to her room.

A while later, Tony and I hug and kiss our beloved inn-keepers goodbye, saying we're sorry for the confusion and the mental break-down of the American. We claim that she probably forgot to take her medication.

"Surely the perfume will appear somewhere within her luggage," I had told them in an effort to console them.

It wasn't until we were on the plane returning to the states that Shelly Ann taps my shoulder.

"Stephanie, can I talk with you?

"Is everything okay up there?" I ask while bringing my seat up to talk.

"Kim was seated next to me, but I switched seats. I took the empty chair up there." Shelly Ann points. "I just couldn't stand to be with her one more second. That horrible perfume; her refusal to open the windows for air; the list rolls on with her selfishness. She's always been pampered and spoiled, but I never dreamed she'd be so self-centered and childish. I'm disgusted with her, and I never want to see her again."

"Oh, no! I hope you two can work things out. You should tell her how you feel."

"Trust me, I did, but she's a one-way street." Shelly Ann paused for a moment. "I have terrible anxiety, and my stomach hurts from spending two weeks with Kim, my used-to-be best friend. Yes, I just said it. She WAS my best friend. I had no idea she was so difficult and spoiled."

"Had you two ever spent the night together or gone on a trip?" I ask, trying to understand.

"Not since we were eight years old, and that was at my home with ten other girls. But Kim's led a pampered life. She's not used to anyone saying no to her. And the perfumes, well..." Shelly Ann drops her head.

"What do you think happened to them?"

Shelly Ann paused for a moment. "Do you really want to know?"

"Yes! Do you know what happened to them?" I sit up straight with widening eyes.

"I'm sorry to say, but yes, I do." Shelly Ann cleared her throat. "I tossed them in the dumpster when I left to go jogging this morning. I couldn't take the constant spraying anymore. I never knew she was like that, so self-absorbed. I'm sorry I didn't speak up when Kim was accusing the maids, but I just couldn't.

Shelly Ann crouches next to me like a wilted flower. "Stephanie, I will never tell Kim about this. Never. Please, can you keep this between us? Our husbands do business together. Their paths will cross, and this would ruin it all."

"*Mamma Mia!*" I am speechless.

Chapter 24

MIDNIGHT RUN TO PERUGIA

*W*e arrived in Assisi, Italy, four nights ago with fourteen Americans from all over the United States. Many onboard this tour have been with us three or four times already, except for Mary Jane from Texas, who brags that this is her tenth time. She boasts that she doesn't really care where we go as long as she's on board with us. Her Minnie Mouse voice tumbles around the large banquet room tonight, and her laughter ignites us like wildfire. Seated around the large, oval dining table is David, who has Tony and Nino saying, repeatedly, "*Mamma Mia, Madonna*" as though they're stuck in a broken mantra, knowing no other words.

This is our second night in Assisi, and we're staying at our favorite place: an old palace perched above the flowing hilltop inside the village walls. It's a fairytale here, so enchanting and spiritual. We awoke to the church bells ringing across the valley and watched the nuns and the monks in their long brown robes stroll along the cobblestone streets and sing praises to our Heavenly Father.

This evening, we sit in the dining area of the medieval palace, all gathered around four large circular tables just eating, drinking, and laughing. The orchestrated dance of food started over an hour ago, beginning with a taste of the *vino*. Then Tony had requested an abundance of the local cheese, salami, and our favorite bruschetta as the antipasto, or the traditional warm-up before the meal. The delightful banquet continues with the primo or the first course, which includes a variety of soup, polenta, and mountainous heaps of pasta with locally made mozzarella sprinkled heavily on top.

The carts of food roll in every direction. Maria pulls the cart up to our table and heaps large spatulas of the main course, *il secondo*. It is my favorite: eggplant parmigiana or the *melanzane alla parmigiana*.

Earlier today, I peeped into the kitchen through an entrance made of pinkish-white rocks from the local Assisi stones. It's a beautiful archway that would surely take my head off if I forgot to duck. I hid behind its rough exterior, watching them work as they toted baskets of the long, purple beauties to the washbasin. They got a quick bath underneath running water, then were unceremoniously heaped onto the cold slab of marble to start getting sliced and trimmed. The thought raced across my mind: will they soak the slices in salted water? To the left, I saw bowls filled with flour and sea salt and remembered the salt is not to rid the eggplant of its bitterness but to collapse the tiny air holes in the eggplant. My mother prepared eggplant parmigiana every week and taught me these valuable secrets.

"Don't forget to soak the round slices in the salt to draw out some of the moisture, so it's not soggy when cooked," she'd reminded me as though it was my first time preparing them.

Nino, Tony, and I sit around a table with several other Americans. David Leo from California sits close by. He works for the government as a special agent. When he telephoned me at Decorate Ornate, he rambled for several minutes about his hectic lifestyle and a need for some relaxation in Italy. He said it's his favorite country.

When asked how he heard about our tours, he replied, "At home, in California. I was purchasing a new pair of shoes from a saleslady, and she bragged about your Italy tours. Her aunt started traveling with you over twelve years ago. She said something about you and a comical Sicilian man taking Americans all over Europe. And, oh yea, she said your driver was your bambino—something like that."

I jump back to the present when Tony leans over and whispers in my ear.

"*Stefania*, do you know what the *Americano*, David, just asked Nino? *Mamma Mia, Madonna!* This is unbelievable to me. He asked Nino to take him to see a *signora*, as it had been many months since he's seen a woman. What does this have to do with Nino? I mean, if you want Nino to take him to a woman, then *no problema*. Nino can drive him to Perugia. You know the village with the Baci chocolates and the university. Oh, yes, there are many girls there, *no problema*," Tony stretches his neck around and stares at David, studying his face, then turns back around, leans into Nino and whispers, "*Madonna*, this is another one *Stefania* brings to us with a *problema*. It is already nine o'clock, and by the time we finish with our food, the wine, the grappa, the dolce, and—*Mamma Mia*—then you must fetch the bus, get it out of the *autorimessa*, the garage."

Tony rambles on, forgetting Nino already knows all of this news, since we are on top of the medieval hilltop with the monks, nuns, and Saint Francis, and our coach is parked miles away for safe-keeping.

"What does *Stefania* say about this? Does she approve of his request? I mean, *no problema* for me to take him tonight, but it will be after midnight before we get to Perugia. But after he takes the woman, *Mamma Mia*, only God knows how long that will take," Nino explains to Tony, as though he's the *bambino*.

Before I swallow a juicy red tomato, David is back in Nino's ear. "Do we go get a woman tonight, my friend?" David asks on bouncy feet. His eyes are wide, and his mouth is watering.

"*Si, si*, yes, yes. *No problema*. Carry on with your food and wine. You will need all of your energy," Nino says. Then he turns to Tony to repeat the message, and Tony turns to me and recites the same.

"What's going on?" Marilyn from Texas leans over and asks me.

"Oh, nothing at all, my dear. David is really enjoying the food and wine tonight." I smile, holding up the nearby bottle while pretending it's all about the wine.

When the dinner was over, Nino and David discreetly set out on their mission, which Nino told us about the next morning over breakfast.

"*Mamma Mia, Nino,* I tell *Stefania* everything in English. I already know what happened. How many times did you tell me the story when you arrived back to our room?" Tony tosses down an espresso and starts again. "By the time you translate this word and that word, the morning will be gone."

"Hurry up, Tony. Start at the beginning. I want to know everything that happened last night!" I take the empty cup and push it aside. "Don't leave out one word."

Tony starts, but Nino remembers more. Both of their words crash into each other. "*Mamma Mia, Nino.* I talk to *Stefania* in English. She will understand everything much faster."

I might as well have been a fly on the wall as my mind absorbed every word from Tony and Nino. Even though Tony was not with them, he translated everything Nino had told him. I felt like I was in the club with Nino and David as I heard the details from Tony.

By 12:20 am, Nino and David stood below a stage in the front row of a go-go club in Perugia, Italy, staring at ten topless women dancing around. Nino and David watched for fifteen minutes—not a second longer—and with arms crossed over his chest, David leaned into Nino's ear and said, "Okay, I'm ready to go. I've seen enough."

"*Che cosa?* What? *Che ne dici?* What do you say?" Nino asked him, thinking he was fed up with watching the show and wanted to get a woman.

"I'm ready to go back to Assisi," David replied and turned to walk out.

"You wanted a *signora* tonight. You don't like?" Nino asked in broken English, not understanding David's request to leave.

"I did. Yes, thank you very much for bringing me here. They are nice." David smiled with satisfaction.

"*Scusami,* excuse me, David. Sorry, but I do not understand. My English is no good." Nino leaned in closer to his ear. "You said to me we go, *Andiamo?*"

"Yes! Let's go! I'm getting sleepy, aren't you?"

"*Mamma Mia*, David. I do not understand. You want woman or not." Nino tried again to understand.

"No. I'm finished. Thank you. The ladies were nice. I enjoyed myself," David repeated.

"No woman for you tonight?" Nino asked slowly again, trying hard to pronounce each word.

"No, I saw several, the ones I liked. I really appreciate all of your help with that, Nino."

"*Scusami.* Excuse me, David, but no woman for you tonight?" Nino refused to move until he understood.

This was a bizarre situation. Nino driving all the way to Perugia with David, only to stand for fifteen minutes with his arms crossed.

Nino tried one last time. "David, you want...woman? No pleasure tonight?"

"Oh, no, thank you! My process doesn't require that I touch a woman. After all, that would be extremely inappropriate, don't you think?" David looked shocked that Nino would suggest such a thing.

"*Mamma Mia!* I understand nothing!" Nino was frustrated. "How do you get—you know—satisfied? I mean, without the touch?" Nino looked behind him and around, sheepishly embarrassed and not believing he was actually having this conversation with a grown man.

"It's simple, Nino. I remember every curve. I take a mental shot of her image, and then I go back and replay it all over in my head. I sketch it out on paper."

"*Che cosa?* What do you say? *Schizzo*, sketch? I don't understand, but never mind. *Andiamo*, let's go!" Nino was ready to drive back to Assisi to discuss this alarming situation with Tony. Perhaps he didn't understand the English correctly.

My mind springs back to the present as Tony says, "*Stefania*, this is unbelievable. What does the word 'sketch' mean? David told Nino he must sketch the woman." Tony turns to Nino, both shaking their heads.

"Oh, look, here comes David, you can ask him about this sketch," I tell Tony, knowing he can't wait to hear his story.

"*Mamma Mia*, David. Please sit with us. Tell me about last night.

Did you enjoy yourself?" Tony's eyes dance because he's thinking Nino didn't understand David last night.

"*Buongiorno!* Good morning," David says, plopping down in front of Tony and Nino. I pretend to check my messages on my phone. I don't want David to feel uncomfortable with me knowing the whole story.

"David, was something wrong last night—with the women? Were they not nice?" Tony asks.

"Ah, we had a great evening, thanks to Nino." David grins, slapping his hand on Nino's back, which makes Nino spring forward.

"Thank you for asking. You should have gone with us last night. The ladies were nice," David downs his teeny-tiny cup of espresso with one gulp then smiles at Tony, leaving the question still dangling in the air.

"*Scusami*, David, but I do not understand. Why did you not take woman? You requested Nino to drive you to Perugia, many miles from here, and you didn't *partecipare* with woman. I'm sorry, but I do not understand," Tony shakes his head and stares into his empty espresso cup as though looking for something inside.

"That's all I wanted, Tony. I just wanted to look at a woman—an Italian woman. I needed to see if she is different from the American women, compare the body.

"*Mamma Mia, Madonna!*" Tony gasps in confusion and blurts out a nervous laugh. This is a peculiar situation, and it makes no sense. He wipes the sweat that's now beading across his upper lip. David is confused, and his eyebrows reach his blonde, spiked hair that sprouts thinly from his receding hairline.

"What? What's so funny?" David asks, running his fingers through his freshly mowed spikes.

"*Mamma Mia*...nothing, nothing at all," Tony sighs, too exhausted to press for any more information.

"No, really. What's so funny, Tony?"

"David. I do not understand this compulsion to see the woman. *Mamma Mia*, Nino drove you many miles, but nothing happened. You didn't take her. No kiss, no hug, no..." Tony stops as though he bumped into a stop sign.

"Aw, Tony. That's all I wanted, just to see the beautiful ladies. Like I said, that would be inappropriate to touch a woman. I am satisfied. You, Nino, and Stephanie are a dream team, truly remarkable, making all my dreams come true. Thank you. I will be back again on the next tour, if possible."

Tony pushes his espresso aside and shakes his head up and down, agreeing in motion to be polite.

In Italian, Tony starts with swirling hands over his head. "I will never understand the Americans," Tony says to Nino and motions for another espresso but thinks perhaps a bottle of *vino* would be much better.

Inches from David's espresso, his sketch pad rests on the table. But Tony and Nino make no connection to its rectangular thickness or the new yellow pencil attached to its side pocket.

Chapter 25

NAPOLI - RED LIPS MEET CHANEL

*T*he sun shining over southern Italy looks like a million diamonds dazzling through the white puffs of clouds as we disembark from our coach in the heart of Napoli. It's late September when I arrive in this incredible city with fourteen Americans from all over the United States. Many of them return with me year after year.

It seems like yesterday that Tony and Nino picked us up at the airport. Now, two weeks later, we've made enough memories to write another book and fill up a hundred photo albums. Every morning after breakfast, we've surprised the Americans with wonderful sights, not to mention all of the surprises hidden throughout Italy.

Since starting the European tours in May of 2000 and bringing two to three groups of Americans to Italy every year, I wonder if there's anything left that can possibly shock me or outdo the last adventure. And when looking at the Americans on our coach, I think it's strange that nothing abnormal has happened on this trip yet. No shocking, hair-raising situation that would prompt me to write a chapter in the next book. Nothing. Everyone seems to be perfectly normal.

"Tony, can you believe the Americans did nothing to cause alarm on this tour? Not one single person did anything," I remind him again for the hundredth time in the last two days, knowing that's strange and unprecedented.

"*Mamma Mia, Stefania.* The tour is not over. We have today, tonight, and then on the way to the airport tomorrow. Don't count your chickens before they fly!" Tony tells me.

"What? Chickens before they fly! That's a new one." I laugh. "You're correct. There are a few hours left on the clock before boarding the plane. And this makes me nervous, knowing there is always someone who breaks the mold and raises the bar higher than the one before. Can you believe there are no outrageous escapades they've gotten themselves into yet?"

I look at our group, wondering who might do something shocking in the next few hours.

Stepping off the coach, my black, leather shoes hurriedly kiss the warm, cobbled stones in the heart of Napoli. Before I motion for the Americans to follow behind me, a pink *Vespa* transporting five people zooms inches in front of me.

"*Mamma Mia!*" I shout, observing the entire family on the little scooter. Their bodies are piled on top of each other, dangling in all directions.

"Stephanie, what did you say about Naples, the population?" Roger asks, his mouth to my ear.

"Napoli is the third-largest city in Italy with about one million people. It's one of the most chaotic, charming, and colorful places in Europe. I've never been to another place like it. You will either love it or hate it. Watch out for the scooters darting in and out," I tell him, motioning for everyone to follow me.

"Look at all the fish for sale!" Ann hollers behind me. "This is unbelievable. Oh, there are street musicians playing, and there must be hundreds of sea creatures over there on the table." Ann gives a news report of the area as we make our way through the narrow streets clogged with people, scooters, and colorful houses clustered together, one on top of the other.

We zigzag from street to street, seeing more liveliness than a Cirque du Soleil show. Clothes-lines crisscross above our heads, and the air from the oven-baked pizzas wafting through the narrow alley-ways jazzes me up more than usual, causing me to yell to my group.

"Come on, my friends! I'll show you where we're going." I point ahead, barely taking a breath. "Take a look at this first," I tell them, pointing to a little wicker basket tied to a rope that's dangling four stories up. Their heads fly upwards as we watch a local *signora* hanging over her iron balcony, slowly lowering the empty basket down to the local delivery man.

"This is exactly what I imagined Italy to be." Roger snaps a photo. He's from Miami, Florida, where his wife died six months ago, leaving him behind with no children or family, only friends from the local church who pushed him into hopping aboard this Italy tour.

"What is she doing with the basket?" Cathy from North Carolina asks.

"She's probably getting her daily supply of bread or milk, or maybe cheese?" The Americans are asking questions and shooting them toward me faster than I can answer.

"The architecture is magnificent," exclaims Roger. He stops for more photos.

He and his late wife, Susie, had built their dream house seven years ago with her insisting the ceiling be massive in the main entrance, tall enough for astronauts to fly. As an engineer, he lived to make his wife happy. He created her dream home as the largest European villa on the block with thirty feet rafters. Everyone in the coach had admired its stately beauty from the photos on his iPad. Roger was a solar eclipse of pride, presenting his happiest accomplishments as a devoted husband. Now, half a year later, here he was with this happy bunch of Americans experiencing Italy as though they were locals.

Roger was suspended in a state of euphoria without the use of any psychoactive drugs, experiencing a visual overload. He never thought he would be in Italy, especially the chaotic city of Napoli with its historic center, a UNESCO World Heritage Site. He never thought he would outlive his wife of twenty-six years, but he had. He hadn't expected a life without his best friend beside him, abandoned in a home that's nothing more than a hotel now, with too many rooms and a need for a fire truck ladder to change the light bulbs. They'd talked about traveling someday to Europe. He hadn't foreseen a time when he would be standing in Italy, with thirteen other Americans, laughing, enjoying himself, and forgetting the melancholy of loneliness.

"*Eccomi qui.* Here I am," he says with a happy face. Those were the first words of Italian that I taught him.

"Bravo! You remembered the words," I tell him with a pat on his back.

It was weeks before departing America when I told him, "You will find peace and contentment again. And you will most certainly laugh when you least expect it. Come to Italy with me, experience God's magnificence, and allow Him to restore your soul."

And now, here we are.

A milk-man stands just in front of us, tapping his fingers on the hood of his tiny green truck, a mere Tonka toy. He patiently waits to grab ahold of the basket coming toward him. We watch the scene unfold as three large bottles of milk are deposited into the little basket.

On my other side, Linda swirls her tongue over her coral-painted lips, savoring the scent of sweetened pineapple and mandarin orange as if it were ambrosia smeared underneath her nose. The aromas are mesmerizing, wafting through and crashing together from the hundreds of balconies above. Seeing the chaotic rhythm of Napoli is like being in a perpetual theme park—a Walt Disney world of medieval fun.

I have an overpowering desire to run and shout with the local Neapolitans and the large melting pot of beautiful, sun-drenched people. My head fills with endorphins, and my eyes swell, seeing the drama of everyday life here.

"This is Napoli! The city of chaos with more attractions than a carnival," I tell the group of Americans, who are clicking their cameras faster than I can count. "Let's watch the daily routine of life on this street before we go any farther."

I point upward to the activity. "Look up toward the balconies and the clotheslines displaying the family's wardrobe. Watch as the locals holler to the delivery men down below, asking for their daily cheese, milk, bread, and so forth. Look at the white corded ropes. Do you know what they are used for?" I point to the ladies hanging over the balconies, tying buckets to ropes.

"This is wild and so amazing. My head is spinning, seeing so much at one time. Look at the lady putting something in the bucket!" I hear one of the Americans telling another as we all stand unable to move.

It is me who breaks the trance of fascination when I intentionally drop my bag on the concrete curb of the bustling narrow street.

"I need a photo of this little truck." I bring my heavy Canon camera to my left eye, attempting to capture the piles of vegetables loaded on its bed.

We hear the name "Roberto" hollered across the street by a momma hanging from a balcony as another delivery man wheels his vehicle in front of us. We watch as he abruptly brakes the little two-seater car, jumps out, and circles around to the trunk, pulling out brown paper packages all tied pretty with a yellow bow.

The passion, grittiness, and loud drama of the Neapolitan people are on full display. They are like wind-up toys, or battery-operated toy soldiers, like a Christmas village of chaotic commotion. We haven't even arrived at Via San Gregorio yet, the home of the *presepe* artisan's workshops. This is the street I anticipate the most because of the creations made before our eyes, the beautiful nativity.

We are surrounded by people speaking the charming Neapolitan dialect rather than the standard Italian. There must be one hundred thousand scooters whizzing by with toy-like trucks bumping along-side them. And in the mix are glamorous mommas pushing baby strollers along the dirty, cobbled streets.

"Oh, I smell something delicious," Ann wrinkles her nose as if she were sniffing my favorite Baba au Rhum cake.

"That is the aroma of dark, strong espresso piping through the air and pastries filled with lemon ricotta," I say, also inhaling the bouquet of mesmerizing scents.

This city has postponed modernity and is immune to the influences of the outside world as they showcase their wardrobes for the world to view. The clotheslines are filled with colorful dresses of all sizes and white, clean underwear, all flapping in the cool breeze.

Nearby are two lovers leaning against a gigantic old palace made with volcanic stones that's older than Egypt's pyramids. Our eyes flash in every direction, and before we step forward, the young lovers romp toward us. On her feet are towering stilettos, and her skirt melts like warm butter over her vivaciously sexy body, just inches from revealing too much. Our eyes plunge to the ancient stones, watching the sharp points of her leather-bottomed soles pinging across the pavement—clickety-clack.

"*Andiamo*, let's go," Tony hollers, leading the way to the towering medieval palace, which will be our home for tonight. As we enter inside to go to our rooms, my eyes glance to the right as I pass the marble counter. A huge sign declares, "Chanel, Welcome to Napoli." I pay no attention to it.

Months ago, Roger requested we celebrate his birthday in the heart of Napoli. Without thought, I had agreed, "Of course! It would be my pleasure."

I had asked Tony to prepare the necessary arrangements for the party and the cake in Napoli.

Now, anticipating the beauty of this special cake, I hurriedly tossed my bag across the wood-carved bed inside my room and head to the kitchen to inspect it before it gets delivered to the table tonight. Glancing at my Timex, I realize the minutes are flying. In less than half an hour, everyone will meet in the lobby, and away we'll walk the short distance to the dining room.

Roger is going to be surprised by the cake, the party, and all of the hoopla this evening. I'm especially anticipating the fun tonight given that Roger thinks the party is tomorrow night.

Flying out my door and skidding around the corner, I look up at the endless stairs and sigh. Why does the elevator have to be out of order? Taking a deep breath, I start the long haul up the stairs, running as though the fire alarm has sounded. Reaching the sixth floor, I zigzag around the colorful hallways and come to a dead stop, sweat glossing my forehead.

"*Buongiorno!* Hello, *signora!*"

"*Ciao,*" I say to a worker who passes me while pushing a white cart towering with beautiful flowers. I watch him disappear down the long hallway as I stand before swanky, gold, double doors with two gigantic, shiny brass handles. Excitedly, I push the doors hard and create a slight rattle, but nothing happens. I try again, but they're locked.

"*Scusami.* Excuse me," I say loudly, peeking through the glass panes of the door. The man with the basket of flowers never looks my way.

"*Eccomi qui.* Here I am," I try again, thinking the glass must be soundproof, or the man is deaf. Again, no response. He walks to the next floral arrangement, placing more flowers in the vase. My eyes widen, scanning the extravagant, elegant room. Every standing piece of furniture is swathed in white linen, and on top of every table stands a towering crystal vase filled with satiny red and pink roses.

I gaze at the dazzling ceiling, a sky-painted world where jets could surely fly. The galaxy of white puffy clouds is magnificent, reminding me of creamy-whipped meringue. I gasp at the exquisite royal blue and pink swirls with triumphant saints cloaked in majestic garments who peer downwards, ready to descend upon the tables. Their wide wings ruffle the silence of wonder. I'm awestruck, and my breath is caught somewhere in the air.

I'm brought back to the reality of standing outside locked doors by the sound of shuffling feet and rattling of pans. It's a parade of chefs fluttering around in white, busily preparing for the night's birthday party in grandiose elegance.

"*Buongiorno!* Hello." I heroically push and rattle the doors again with greater force. My voice reaches high notes.

"Hello!" I try again, observing many chef hats moving closer, waltzing with baskets of bread in their hands.

"It's me, *Stefania*, the American. It's my party tonight! Please open the door." I beat the glass with my hand, pulling and rattling the doors.

"I am *Stefania*, here to inspect the cake," I explain through the thick glass, my nose pressed against the surface.

And just like that, the lock clicks and the doors open.

"*Signor*, I am *Stefania*. I'm here for the birthday party—for the cake," I tell him, but he looks mystified. "I came to see the cake. I know it's a little early, but I need to inspect the cake."

I'm a broken record, stuck on replay with the word "cake," trying to explain in English and then in broken Italian. He understands nothing from the look on his face.

"*Signor*," I expound more, backing up and taking a new approach. I repeat the English in my southern drawl sprinkled with Italian. He understands nothing until I say *torta dolce* (sweet cake) and *buon compleanno* (happy birthday).

"Ah, *si*, yes. *Un minute.* One minute," he says, taking off like a race car heading for the finish line. I run behind him, both of us scurrying around the corner through a swinging door and into the kitchen. My mouth drops when I see more white hats scurrying around in a chaotic frenzy. One man is rolling pasta out, and another is stirring a huge pot of bubbling spaghetti sauce. And to my right, another chef is tossing pizza dough.

"*Signora*, follow me," he says in Italian, taking four steps to the right side of the kitchen and then stopping abruptly. He stands straight as a brand new pencil while tapping his black leather shoes on the marble floor. We stare into each other's eyes for a mere second as he nervously drums his fingers on the counter. He appears as though he'll take the stage any moment, just waiting for the curtain to part to perform a ballerina dance. Then he excitedly points to a shrouded lump that presumably has a cake hidden underneath.

"*Mamma Mia, signora*! Are you ready to see my masterpiece, the cake?" The baker asks in Italian. He smiles widely in excitement.

"Yes!" I jump up and down, clapping my hands in unison. He yanks away the white linen cloth and presents his masterpiece.

It's a tall, gigantic pancake towering close to ten inches tall, no decorations or mention of a birthday. It's plain and naked; there's nothing pretty about it, and I hate it. My face hits the floor as melancholy slaps me in the face. Soon afterward, hysteria chimes in with the realization that there's no pretty birthday cake for the party.

The baker is a proud papa as he presents his creation as if it's the royal cake for a prince. His flour-kissed face stretches to a puppet's wide grin. He proudly blurts, "*Bellissimo.* Beautiful."

I'm speechless, tongue-tied, and dumbfounded. This is not a birthday cake. It's a pan of southern-made cornbread, nothing more and nothing less. *No, this cannot be the cake. It's not a birthday cake. Where are the decorations?* The thoughts swarm like honeybees. I specifically requested a birthday-themed cake.

"*Signor*, the cake...this can't be the cake! Where is the birthday cake you prepared? Surely you made another one?" My voice cracks. I look at my watch. It's nearly time to meet the Americans and lead them here to the surprise gathering for the royal feast.

I know the cakes in Italy are nothing compared to the fancy ones in the United States. Italians see no need for all of the sugary piles of décor. It's all about the taste with gigantic candles flickering and blazing straight up—a bottle rocket ready to launch.

Staring at the tall pancake and then the baker, seeing his face beaming with pride, I accept the fact that this is the only birthday cake.

"*Signor*, I must prepare a little more decorating on top for the *Americano*—American style. I can add to it," I explain, my eyes scanning the kitchen between the parade of shuffling feet and clanking pans.

"*Signor*, sir, do you have white powdered sugar," I ask, already pulling drawers and cabinet doors open, searching. "Ah, here it is," I say, feeling relief.

"*Si*, yes, *signora*. You want to use the sugar?" he asks in Italian as I grab a white-laced doily from underneath a ceramic vase filled with silver spatulas and various utensils.

I place the doily on top of the plain cake and tilt the bag of white powdered sugar, shaking it on top to completely cover it up. I lift the doily and take a few steps back, standing and inspecting its unique-ness. Still not satisfied with its continued simplicity, I move forward again, and shake more of the white powdery dust atop the cake.

Afterward, I remove the doily again, placing it down on the antique table that's cluttered with bottles of their most prized posses-sion: extra virgin oil. The chef stares in disbelief, mumbling, "*Mamma Mia*," with his hand crossing himself as though he's before the Madonna and asking for forgiveness for the sins before him.

I stand back and inspect the cake, thinking it needs something more, but there is nothing, not even candles. I pace the floor while the chef leans over the cake and examines the sugary dust.

One by one, the other chefs follow behind, each one leaning over the other and studying my creation with raised eyebrows and bouncing eyeballs.

The silence is broken when he finally speaks. "*Signora*, why must you do this to the beautiful Baba au Rhum cake?" Before I answer, they uncork a bottle of red *vino* and urge each other to drink, hoping to ease the pain of their ruined creation.

"*Grazie mille*! Thank you very much. It's my favorite." I tell the truth because it is, indeed, the best cake with its yeasty, leavened sweetness, soaked in limoncello and rum. Ah, the Baba au Rhum is fantastical. However, it needs a celebratory face atop its crusty brown beauty to resemble a birthday cake.

I glance down at my watch. I'm late to meet Tony and the Americans.

"*Signor*, I must go for now. I will bring the *Americani* back to eat in a few minutes. Afterward, you present the cake."

I speed out of the kitchen and through the dining room that is filled with the elegance of royalty. The beauty tempts me to break the silence in the dining room and sing with my arms stretched out like an airplane. Yet before I start, I suddenly remember what's in my pocket for the party. Reaching inside, I fish for the package of red lips.

I first started using red wax lips on my first Italy tour twenty years ago. I handed them out to each American at the farewell dinner, thinking it would be fun and silly to use them in the photos.

Little did I know that they would become a huge hit. We laughed uncontrollably with the jumbo enhancements plugged into our mouth. The Americans not only wore them on our last night together but also when we celebrated a birthday or anniversary. It seemed only appropriate to share the oversized beauties with my friends since my lips are continuously painted in my favorite color: red.

I had initially placed the lips inside my pocket with the intention of placing it on top of the cake as an added enhancement of the signature symbol of Decorate Ornate Italy Tours: jumbo, glossy, red, wax lips.

Ah, perfecto! I think as I swirl around and race toward the kitchen. I swing open the double doors, shocking them again.

"*Signor*, I must put the lips on the cake!" I shout as though they're deaf and speed to the corner where the cake is shrouded with the white towel. I swiftly remove it and press the big, red lips in the center of the cake.

"Ah, this is perfect," I remark, much more satisfied with the outcome. "*Signor*, I am in a hurry to meet the Americans downstairs. I will be back in a few minutes with everyone and the birthday boy!"

With a big smile, I make my way back through the ornately decorated dining area and race down the stairs.

As I come to the lobby, Tony and the Americans stare in disbelief.

"*Mamma Mia*, what happened to you, *Stefania*?" Tony asks.

The Americans harmonize the same words and stare at me with mouths agape. Unbeknownst to me, I'm sprinkled from head to toe with white sugar. I look like a powdered donut thanks to the after-effects of dusting the cake with a whole bag of the powdery substance.

"Tony, I went upstairs to inspect the *dolce*, you know, our dessert for tonight." I give a hard wink, not wanting the others to know about the birthday cake.

"What's the matter with you, *Stefania*?" Tony brushes me off with both hands, causing the powder to fly. "What's wrong with your eye?"

"I had to repair the cake," I whisper the dreaded details, explaining how I corrected the mistake but still need the birthday candle.

"You must be joking, right?" Tony gapes at me, discombobulated. He rearranges his feet as though he's ready to take flight.

"*Mamma Mia, Madonna, Stefania!* We don't have cake here! We don't eat here. We go outside, around the corner to my friend's *ristorante!* Do you not remember Marcello? He prepared everything. All they can eat of the Neapolitan favorites, and the cake, ah, it is ready and decorated as you like," Tony explains as he wipes droplets of sweat from his upper lip.

My face flushes ruby red then fades to white. "But—," I start to say, but no words come forth. I try again.

With each stammer, I raise my voice higher. "Tony—the dining room upstairs is decorated beautifully with towering vases of gorgeous roses and the food—it's a feast prepared just for us! And the cake, they prepared the cake! I decorated it with powdered sugar and red wax lips."

Now I ramble repeatedly, convincing myself that Tony must be the one who is mistaken.

"The ballroom is magnificently flocked with thousands of flowers. It's filled with roses, and each table is decorated as if the president was the guest of honor. And the cake I tried to fix—" I sigh. Melancholy floods my emotions as the realization that I made a huge mistake hits me.

I turn around, seeing Tony already at the desk talking with the owner. I watch Tony's face blush, change colors, and his eyes bounce. I know this look of embarrassment—and it's not funny. Tony hurriedly walks back to me, motioning toward the door. "*Andiamo,* let's go," Tony barks with his eyes focused on the exit.

Carefully I ask, "I'm confused. I thought we were eating here—upstairs in the room with the decorations, the flowers, the cake?"

"*Mamma Mia, Madonna, Stefania*. This is too much. I asked Pietro what's going on in the dining room because of the aroma floating above us and all around. I said nothing about you decorating the cake, but he already knew about the confusion." Tony points to the telephone, insinuating he'd received the call from above.

"Pietro laughed when telling me about a foreigner instructing his chefs on how the Baba should look. *Mamma Mia, Stefania*. He thinks it was someone else. Thank God. But never mind. Why must you do the things you do?" Tony shakes his head back and forth. His mouth becomes a runaway train. He can't stop talking about the mishap of my involvement with such a high profile event.

"*Stefania*, Pietro said she was a French-*Americana*. You know how the French are, thinking they make the best pastries and all. Pietro said the lady was *pazzo*, crazy. She practically ruined the Baba au Rhum with all the sugary powder." Tony confides more as he glances to the right to see if Pietro has left the counter and hopefully disappeared until we depart tomorrow morning.

"Never mind, *Stefania. Andiamo*, let's go. We must get to Marcello's for the food," Tony hurriedly speeds ahead, motioning for everyone to follow.

"This is unbelievable, *Stefania*. I can't believe you dismantled their cake." Tony walks faster than normal, unaware of his adrenaline rush, which makes him rush like a race car.

"Do you know who the guest is for the royal party tonight, and who the cake is for?" Tony asks, already out of breath as we round the corner and step inside his friend's restaurant. The aroma of Neapolitan delights greets us with a kiss.

"No, I thought it was for us," I say, still thinking he's joking. Surely we'll turn around and go back upstairs to the royal banquet and eat the cake with my big red lips resting atop its lemony tastiness.

"No, *Stefania*, look at the billboard," Tony points to the huge, creamy-white sign with gigantic red lips on it and huge letters reading: "Welcome to Napoli, Chanel." We stare at the bright lights of the marquee flashing in giant letters. The only thing I see is the iconic name, Chanel.

"*Mamma Mia*, I don't believe it! You mean, as in the real Coco Chanel? And I decorated the cake?" I stand in speechless awe. Shock consumes me.

"*Si, si*. Yes, you decorated Chanel. You destroyed the cake," Tony breathlessly says.

Chapter 26

GOING TO THE CHAPEL IN GREECE (CONFESSIONS ON THE COACH)

*T*he new group erupts in applause, whooping and hollering as Nino makes a sharp turn to barely miss the little furry sheep that are following their modern-day shepherd in the fields of Greece. The fourteen of us Americans have been together for a week. We started out in southern Italy on the western side, gallivanting around the many hidden jewels in the Amalfi Coast area, then headed to the eastern side, stopping and exploring as though we were Christopher Columbus's crew. Now it seems as though we've known each other forever.

Most of the Americans on this tour have no idea what's to come in the next few days. They don't know the motives for our excursion on this adventurous trek across the Aegean Sea to Skopelos, the island of the famous *Mamma Mia!* movie? No. Not all of them. They think it's just another one of our legendary adventures in Greece where we take our coach and go to unknown places off the tourist trails.

Listening to the chatter behind me, my mind begins to wander as I stare out of the window from the front passenger seat, pondering the many details of the upcoming Greek wedding that's a surprise for the blonde beauty who's seated down the aisle from me. It was just weeks ago that I was asked a very special request.

"Stephanie, I want to remarry the love of my life in Italy or Greece and have you plan it on your next trip. However, she cannot know anything about the ceremony. It's a secret—a surprise. It was just weeks ago that we legally tied the knot again. Nonetheless, that's not enough. I want to have a beautiful ceremony, something special and magical. Will you handle the details and surprise us? There are no specific requests other than to blow her away and to somehow show her my endless love has no boundaries for how far I'll go to make her happy. I want her to know that she's everything I've ever wanted. She's my life, my inspiration, my reason for living."

The thoughts about creating the surprise roll around my mind as I think of the different personalities on our coach. The first are Ann and Mark, a happy couple who were married for twenty-five years, divorced, and then reunited by the grace of God. They are here to celebrate their love for each other; however, Ann has zero knowledge of Mark's matrimonial intentions.

Ann is anticipating a two-week holiday of fun, nothing more and nothing less, just an exciting adventure throughout Italy and Greece with her newly re-wedded husband.

Then there's Patsy, a genealogy expert who doesn't believe in love after two horrendous marriages. Both ended in divorce, and one left her barely escaping to freedom.

Then on a completely different note, there's Dinky, a real-life deputy sheriff from Texas who Nino fell madly in love with. She's a jigsaw puzzle with a thousand tiny pieces that fit perfectly together. Her talents and accomplishments are many, including her expertise in forensic science and DNA, which led her to be featured on two episodes of Forensic Files.

Another traveler is Anthe, an adorable Greek-American medical professor and wedding coordinator. There's also Kathy and Carolyn, who are long-time best friends, and Linda, who surprised us toward the end of the tour with her operatic vocal cords. And when we almost forgot a huge detail, it was our avid traveler, Lana, a real estate tycoon, who magically produced the perfect bridal bouquet as though she was a magician.

Taking the lead roles in this wedding are Danny and Gerald, a hot-blooded, passionate couple from different countries who believe in love.

The list rolls on with the other Americans seated behind me, who make up this fun group.

In the short time that we've been together, although we've learned much about each other, there is still a question of fascination left dangling in the air about the love life of one of the three men in our group, Danny, who is a first-time traveler with us.

"Do you ever think about getting married again?" Patsy asks Danny nonchalantly. She shifts her slender body around in the blue velour seat of the coach to comfortably stretch her long legs into the middle of the aisle, attempting to balance her body for an eye-to-eye focus on Danny.

"Me? Thinking of marrying again? Well, heavenly days. Of course, I do, but only when my mind has fallen into amnesia, probably after watching a romantic movie on television. You know, the yellow brick road of make-believe bliss, not the shocking reality of my past marriage to my ex-wife, who was nothing more than self-centered blackness like a dead channel on the flat screen of narcissistic behavior chipping away at my soul," Danny spills out the scandalous truths of his past life while theatrically lifting his left hand up as though it's a hammer. He slowly pretends to bang the shoulders of the scholarly man seated directly in front of him, who is Gerald, his love potion number nine, his lover and soul mate.

Gerald is a certified public accountant and his companion for over six years. He completes Danny in every way. Today he's wearing a creamy blue designer shirt with the top buttons undone to offer a slight glimpse of his Canadian manliness. At the make-believe hammering from Danny, he folds over, pretending to be jabbed with the imaginary knife and squirming in pain. His colossal white hands grip his chest through the thick forest of furry hair darkness. He slowly dies before us, dragging out the chilling performance until his head slumps over like a wilted rag doll, dangling in the aisle.

He ought to apply for a Broadway show, I think to myself as my left hand clutches my heart, feeling the pain of the knife while laughing at Danny's funny facial expressions.

Thirty minutes later, Danny hasn't stopped talking or helping Gerald's hilarious performances. They're a comedic duo, each completing the other's sentences.

"Oh yes, Patsy. For Pete's sake, I had the wicked witch of Oklahoma. She rode a broom to work and kept it beside her desk. Wait, I lied. She never worked, but with the twitch of her nose, anything could happen. She could magically transform into another person, but sometimes, depending on who's around, she'd be syrupy sweet while inside she was scalding habanero peppers. That's the benefit of having multiple personalities. The medications didn't help her mood swings, not at all. And her eyes never seemed to blink enough. They were always intense and bulging with anger like a mad dragon belching out pointy glass shards—and that was on a good day." Danny announces his graphic illustration with his whole body engaging in the story. I think for a split second that, surely, Danny has Italian blood running through his Oklahoma veins with his personality that could certainly entertain the dead.

"Heavens to Betsy, I can still visualize her corded neck with the veins popping as her blood boiled. Not to mention the flaring nostrils and the animalistic growl from her throat," Danny says. He sucks in more air, never taking his eyes off Patsy.

Suddenly, Danny crumples down in his seat with a long, pained look and droopy shoulders. He puts his fist to his mouth and begins a slow, agonizing, disbelieving head shake. The marionette has died from mental exhaustion.

"*Mamma Mia, Madonna!*" Tony is in shock and exhausted, too. He turns around to Nino to reiterate the story in Italian while adding in his own interpretation of many English words, such as the wife being a wicked witch with a broom. Nino's eyes pop wider, but never veer from the road.

"*Mamma Mia,* the wife looks like *La Befana*?" Nino asks, scrunching his face up like he'd eaten sour grapes as he visualizes the fabled good witch of Italy. In reality, she's not so pretty but rides on a broom to deliver gifts throughout Italy to the good little children on the Epiphany Eve, January fifth. Tony nods his head in agreement.

"*Si, si, Nino*. The wife is a *strega,* a witch," Tony says this matter-of-factly; his mind is already made up. He directed the final judgment and there is no need for a jury.

Nino looks at me intently with question marks dancing across his eyes.

"*Si, si*. She is a witch," I reaffirm Tony's verdict and Danny's expert opinion.

Danny is an open book. The secrets are written upon his face as they slowly spill out. We dangle in the air, suspended on his last word. And obviously, he's planning to say more because it appears as though horrid flash-backs of deep-bottomed sorrow are racing recklessly within his mind, replaying twenty-five years of a marriage gone wrong. It was like time spent in the Dead Sea, never being able to swim, just aimlessly floating along and going nowhere.

From where I sit, I see the back of the Americans' heads, all centered on Danny and leaning inwards, mesmerized by his melodramatic opening statements. And with the slight movement of Anthe's head, I see that every muscle in Danny's body is knotted with anguish and bitterness. His handsome face has turned to sadness from the memories of the harsh imprisonment of living in lockdown with Lucifer's sister. Surely, she was a fallen angel, as well. She certainly started out under the pretense of being someone else.

"I did drink the Kool-Aid, you might say, falling for her," Danny revs up, needing to say more. "I truly believe she put something in my punch at the first party we had together, a premeditated brew, a cocktail infused with lovemaking spells. I remember putting my glass down for a brief time, and it was filled to the brim with her home-made pineapple concoction, and when I came back for a sip, first swirling my tongue around the edge, it tasted peculiar, like gasoline and oil. No joke, it was thick, and the heavy chunks of lemons refused to sink."

We absorb every word, with our buttocks perched on the edges of seats. Nino struggles to understand as Tony translates with theatrical punctuation.

"I spewed it out like a broken water pipe back into the red solo cup. My throat became greasy, lubricated, and slimy. I remember her insisting I have another drink—a thick green punch with floating red cherries on top. I tried to refuse, saying I wasn't thirsty, but it was too late—the love bug had already bitten me, going straight to my brain. I had fallen for her, desiring her desperately. For Pete's sake," Danny says, disgusted by the agonizing memories and now wondering why he allowed such repulsive behavior.

Gerald sits silently, inches in front of Danny. His face is swaddled in the fog of silence that has slowly descended upon him and everyone else in the coach. The sound I hear is my heart beating. Nobody else responds, not even Patsy, until Dinky cuts through the thick silence, slicing it off like a fresh slab of sausage on the butcher's table.

"Bless his little Oklahoma heart," Dinky spills out, dramatically. A broad smile stretches her beautiful face. She sits in the back of the coach, intently listening from her preferred section—the middle row with the straight line of seats that have no space in between them. Her eyelids are stroked with hues of purple, and her blouse is lavender linen from Amalfi, where we just were a few days ago. Her hair is sandy brown and compliments her twinkling topaz eyes. Dinky is not your typical lady; in fact, she's just the opposite—a prickly pear, sharp and piercing, and nothing gets past her in the investigative field.

"Are you stating for the record that you were intentionally poisoned?" Dinky has to ask.

"Is this an interrogation, Officer Stubbs?" Danny takes the stage again. He's ready to perform, but first, he turns the case back to Dinky.

"Yep, you might say it is," Dinky replies with a serious face, never blinking her eyes.

"Danny. Do you ever think about getting married again?" Dinky pushes in with her authoritative voice, causing everyone on the coach to lean in closer. Even Nino glances in the rear-view mirror.

"Yes, Danny. It's a simple question. Answer yes or no?" Patsy cuts in, flashing her persistent smile.

Everyone watches with eager eyes, hanging on every word. Patsy has known Danny a few days, but the instant connection they have together, bouncing back and forth in conversation across the aisle, is incredibly entertaining.

Not wanting to miss a word of Danny's answer, I twist around more, forcing my torso to its maximum stretch.

Patsy shoves her wire-frame glasses upwards to the top of her nose. Her eyes are an icy pale blue, scrutinizing the evidence. And in Patsy's line of work, as a professional genealogist who guarantees family secrets are unearthed to create ancestry shockwaves, we're sure to hear the truth. Simultaneously, her hands begin to move through her hair, gliding through a sea of short, curly, brown strands. Her bangs are a straight line, chopped perfectly across her forehead. Her eyes are focused on Danny as if he were a tiny insect in a jar and ready to be dissected. Patsy, never batting an eye, leans in closer to Danny.

Danny inches closer to Patsy as well, pursing his lips, wrinkling his toes, and squeezing his butt cheeks, an accordion going in and out, anticipating the truth being told.

"Well, Patsy, surely at some point, the thought of marriage has swiftly flashed through my mind. But, honestly, I don't recollect the thought of it or its vividness. You know how the story goes when one endures traumatic treatment, the brain has a way of blocking out the painful memories. However, there are some things you can't block out. And I remember it all."

"Yep, that's the truth," Patsy laughs. Her face holds the memory of her closet with two worthless skeletons inside its dark hole.

Danny wipes away the perspiration that's forming over his upper lip, then starts right back up. "It took seven, long, agonizing years to reach a verdict and agree to an emotional division of our matrimonial assets and sorting through community possessions, splitting our lives into pieces. And the dang judge nearly died before we finally gave in, consenting to the distribution.

"Well, it was me finally, agreeing to give her more than she deserved. I finally caved in—disgusted with her devilish behavior and low-life tactics. Oh, it was a horrible experience, walking through the valley of death for so many years—not a hilltop in sight. Heavens to Betsy, I was out there with the Israelites, strolling around for forty years and forty nights with no hope of ever crossing over into the land of milk and honey," Danny explains. He testifies truths in his southern vocabulary and confesses it all to our small group of Americans and Sicilians.

We've completely forgotten we're traveling through the hidden jewel of Greece. Nevertheless, no one seems to care right now about the sights around us. No, we are caught up in the tale of a tragic romance gone wrong.

The microphone fell to the floorboard minutes ago, but I didn't notice until Nino stretched over and pulled the cord back up to place it in its holder. The spotlight is still on Danny; he's on the stage. We're mesmerized by his enormous personality, enticing us and pulling us into his world of honesty. Glancing around, I see that everyone is suspended on the tips of their seats, dangling with strained necks extended to hear more.

"Good golly, I'm the one who worked my butt off, acquiring an empire worthy of the Queen of Sheba, providing her with the finest worldly goods that money can buy, and serenading her with beautiful love songs. And still, that wasn't good enough for the little—the wicked witch of Oklahoma. And to tell you the truth, she didn't work at all, not outside the home. She refused to contribute one cent. However, I'll give my Momma credit this time. She advised me repeatedly, 'Don't mix your assets with her empty baskets.' Yep, Momma told me a thousand times, but did I listen? No. It was that dang love bug slapping me hard in the face, thirty years ago, and I didn't know the difference between love and lust. Or at least that was my excuse. Heck, who knows the difference between the two at such a young age? She could have been a teetotaler or a drunk, but would I have cared at the time? Puhleeze!"

"Reeeally! Good grief," Patsy interrupts. Like the rest of us, she's soaking in Danny's confession of a marriage gone bad. I see the wheels turning within her head.

"Yes, it was definitely lust, Patsy. A pretty face—a beautiful face—yanking my hormones all out of whack. And Momma warned me, but I wouldn't listen." Sweat glosses Danny's upper lip profusely now, and his heart rate escalates.

"*Mamma Mia, Madonna!*" Tony hangs on every word spilling forth from Danny's mouth. "This is unbelievable. I can feel his pain. Why did you keep the bloody witch so long—twenty-five years? And the momma told you to get rid of her, didn't she? I do not understand this behavior of the *signora* mistreating you so bitterly when your momma knew she was a rotten apple."

Tony spins around to translate the details to Nino, who is still taking us around the many smooth curves in Greece with the turquoise-blue water surrounding us, but we don't care.

Tony quickly explains to Nino how some American women are beautiful on the outside but crunchy bitterness on the inside. "They're *pazzo*! Crazy!" Tony tells Nino, emphasizing the mentally incompetent part. And not missing a word, Tony jumps tracks in mid-sentence and pops a question to Danny.

"Ah, do you have the oil wells?" Tony inquires. He's clearly thinking of John Wayne and the cowboys and Indians in the Wild West.

Danny doesn't hear Tony and continues his narrative, articulating his words with precise southern charm until Patsy jumps in, saying, "Lord, have mercy. Mommas usually know best. He should have listened to Momma!"

"It all worked out for the best, Patsy. I mean, I'm still here in one piece," Danny laughs and squeezes Gerald's shoulder as though it were pizza dough. Then he launches out of his seat and springs over to Patsy, whom he's only known a week. He stands beside her, ready for the next scene.

I scan the flock of Americans behind me, and my eyes land on Ann and Mark, the elegant couple from the piney woods of East Texas, husband and wife. They appear as one, leaning inward, under the spell of Danny's voice. Releasing her attention for a split second, Ann sinks back into the blue velour of her seat and turns her head toward the window to see a tropical paradise and the turquoise blue sea.

"So, marriage is not for you," Mark chimed in, needing to say much. Ann turns back around and brings both hands to her creamy, porcelain face, intensely hanging on his every word.

Seated in front of Ann and Mark is Patsy. She is determined to get her answer. And if Patsy and Dinky can't get the response, then there's no hope of us ever hearing the truth.

"Now listen to me, Danny," Patsy instructs as she leans inward, flirting with disaster. Her buttocks are two small biscuits clinging to the velour of the seat. "Twenty-five years is a long time to stay with an angry woman, especially the one you had who was crazy and all. But, thank God, you escaped, and now you can start over—if you believe in love again."

Patsy's eyes are lasers, seeing into Danny's heart, and the curtain is slowly parting for us to see more.

"Danny, I can tell you right now, I don't believe in love." Patsy delivers the direct statement as though honesty is her greatest attribute. "I was married twice and for many years, and neither one of them worked for me. After the honeymoon phase wears off, probably six months to a year, if you're lucky, you'll see the real deal, the true person," Patsy reflects with her lips pursed tightly. The memories of abuse race in which piques our interest in her life, as well.

My eyes are fixed on Patsy. I agree with her one hundred percent about her truthful analogy of love and the six months to a year time-frame in which you go crazy head-over-heels in love. My mind reflects back to my first book, *Mamma Mia, Americans Invade Italy*, where, in Chapter 28, I explain the fatal love bite where the serotonin starts pumping like a magic potion and before you realize what's happened to you—BAM—you're floating in the clouds of ecstasy, never to be the same again.

My thoughts hurriedly turn the pages of truth to my own experience of falling in love when I saw my husband, Allen, as my prince charming in shining armor with an angelic voice. *Mamma Mia!* The emotional ride was higher than any road ever before traveled, and when the fatal love potion resumed its normal level...wow! I saw Allen Chance for the man he truly is, the complete opposite of his camouflaged image.

My mind crashes back to the happenings inside the coach as Tony bellows out, *"Mamma Mia, Madonna!"*

My eyes are still on Patsy, noticing that she's doomed to a disastrous landing if she scoots forward one more inch on the blue velour padding. Her right leg stretches outward, pressing hard against the undercarriage of Gerald's seat while fighting to stay balanced. I glance back and forth between Patsy and Danny, trying to keep up with their bouncing conversation.

"I don't believe in love, because—well, love is just a word—no meaning. However, I do believe in lust, and that's exactly what I had, but only for a short time." Patsy's sincere honesty reverberates throughout the coach. Her truthfulness is one of the many assets we love about her glass-castle personality.

Patsy pauses for a quick second, hurriedly swallowing a sip of water. She starts to speak again, needing to tell more, but suddenly gets cut off by Danny, the race car speeding beside her, who takes over the lead in both lanes as though he's driving one of his many collectible cars.

"Heavens to Betsy, Patsy," Danny hammers louder with his southern sayings. "Do tell, do tell. I understand lust...no love involved."

Danny ramps up, shifting his gears in full force to reveal more.

"To answer your question about marriage and the way I feel now. Well, Patsy, yes, of course, I do think about it. Especially every time I look at Gerald with his thick silver hair and blueberry eyes, and his long firm legs. As Tony says, "*Mamma Mia!*" I get all flamed up. Those feelings slap me hard, you know, feelings of love start rolling in, kicking up my hormones and boxing my insides, slamming me around like a ragdoll. And seeing those two Italian lovers caressing each other yesterday, the cute elderly couple sunbathing in front of us on the Amalfi Coast, well, those feelings shook me hard, again. They were truly in love, enjoying each other's company. They were soulmates, best friends...understanding each other. They'll probably be together until the end of their lives, having fun and enjoying this beautiful world."

Danny squeezes Gerald's shoulder again, kneading it like mountainous piles of flour being prepared for the pizza oven. "So help me, Hannah, I want you all to know the truth. I'm upset. I'm smiling on the outside, but on the inside, it's a different story. I keep hearing Momma through the phone. She called me again last night, upset about Gerald being with me. Her breathing was so heavy that it nearly knocked me out for a few short seconds through the phone line.

Then, three hours later, in the wee hours of the night, the phone rang again. Momma doesn't acknowledge the seven-hour time difference between Europe and the States. And, did I mention there are a million years of distance between Momma and me? Her mind is set in the old standards and she doesn't know my heart and soul. But bless her heart. God loves her. Momma is a sweetheart. Her flowery pink cheeks...the face of peach cobbler in the rosy sunshine...it pulls at my heart. If you met my Momma, you'd first notice her midnight–dark eyes, often red underneath from the constant testiness of my love life or the countless sleepless nights she spent at the prayer altar, trying to alter my choice," Danny testifies.

He's become an Italian talker, full of melodrama, lifting his hands up with dramatic gestures. His words are pumped, intentionally arousing our spirits and emotions. Danny is the epitome of Italian conversation as he bellows emotion with his words and actions before us.

In all my years of touring, I've never witnessed Tony sitting on the edge of his seat as he does now, totally enthralled and captivated by Danny. We all sit waiting for more, forgetting we're in Greece. The cameras rest idly, missing the dreamy paradise surrounding the coach with the little donkeys being led with bundles of packages upon their backs. No one cares what's happening on the outside of this coach; we're captivated as we hear Danny's answer and explanations.

"My heart is heavy but happy," Danny continues. "I can't hide my feelings anymore. Momma has totally discarded them—tossed them away. I'm nothing but a bag of autumn leaves, lying dormant in the coolness of fall, and she's ready to light the match."

Danny shoots up out of his seat and bursts out into song: *"Feelings, I have so many feelings..."*

"*Mamma Mia*," Tony exclaims, keeping his eyes on Danny. He's unable to process what's happening inside the coach. "Danny's voice is very nice, but..."

He is suddenly lost for words and scrambling to find more, but only for a second.

"I do not understand anything he says. Well, some words, but when he sings, ah, it's nice. I like him very much. He's a funny man. What does he say to the people back there, more of the marriage?" Tony questions me, making sure he hears the details as he swings back and forth, conversing with Nino about the directions of which road to take.

"Tell me, *Stefania*, I am confused. What is he talking about? The momma is nice or not? And the *problema*, the problem with him, and the marriage?" Tony swirls his right hand in the air with his Sicilian gesture that's necessary to talk and communicate, if you're an Italian. But before I could reply, Danny roars louder.

"Momma is not happy about my situation. But I do have a situation, a wonderful situation," Danny gushes, batting his eyelids up and down as though his boisterous self has suddenly become bashful.

Then he smiles wide, dazzling Ann across the aisle, flashing his pearl-white teeth.

"None of you know my situation except Stephanie and Gerald, of course." Danny sets us a headline. His eyes of black diamonds sparkle with anticipation. He's on the brink of telling it all, or will he keep us suspended?

"Gerald is from Canada. He's not an American," Danny says slowly, looking to Mark with a wink. "And Momma is preaching in my ear every dang day practically driving me crazy. She says that Gerald just wants to be an American citizen, and there's absolutely no love connection between the two of us. Momma says she can see it clearly with Gerald flashing his seductive blueberry eyes toward me. Gerald wants to be a legalized citizen of America, that's all he wants, Momma says repeatedly. She is convinced Gerald is courting me only long enough to get his green card to become an American."

Danny stretches his Popeye arms forward and pats Gerald's back, a love tap. His eyes sparkle like the Fourth of July, pulling us inward with special effects. He's a seductive poodle with eyelids flashing up and down in a flamboyant, theatrical performance.

"*Mamma Mia*, this is too much," Tony detonates in exasperation. His eyebrows are boosted beyond his bronzed brow. "I do not understand you Americans. You were previously married to a woman, a *signora,* and now a man?"

Danny hears nothing of Tony's inquisitiveness and flamboyantly continues to talk about Patsy's questions and the deeper conversation he wants to reveal about marriage that's been left dangling high in the air.

"I want to know the secret—what Gerald and Stephanie know." Patsy jumps back in, demanding a new answer.

Everyone looks quickly to Patsy, then Danny, then Gerald, then back to Danny, who is nervously fidgeting. Suddenly Gerald brings both hands to his face and taps his fingers on each side of his mouth, silently chuckling.

"What the hell! Shall we tell them?" Gerald bursts uncontrollably. His hands drop, and he gives an eye roll of resignation to his audience, knowing there is a huge announcement to be made. Danny contemplates his next words carefully.

In the seconds of silence, Danny refills his lungs. His audience edges closer, yearning to hear more. Before my eyes blink, Danny's voice rumbles from his toes up and saturates us with emotions.

And before Tony understands the commotion, Danny rolls out the most beautiful words, *"Feelings, feelings of luv..."*

And if that's not the most beautiful voice we've ever heard, Carolyn rounds out the chorus and joins in with Danny. We now have a country star and an angel on board—the most angelic voice I've ever heard. I pull the microphone cord hard to bring the mic to Carolyn's lips. Danny doesn't need to be amplified; his voice ricochets like hot popcorn kernels inside a microwave. It doesn't take long for the whole coach to erupt in chorus with Danny and Carolyn.

I realize again that I've known Danny and Gerald only briefly. They both signed up for this tour of Southern Italy and Greece while shopping at Decorate Ornate, a few months ago. They had no idea they'd be flying off to Europe with me when they entered the shop. Both of them strangers to me, and now it seems we've known each other forever as I listen and watch their magical story unfold.

Danny is a corporate professional, a rare gem, a sensational success, and a magnetic force, suctioning us up with aerodynamics. His flexibility is energetic, stretching himself from Texas to Florida, jetting back and forth, weekly, juggling two empires. His southern charm ignites others, propelling upon us like a fine mystical potion, hypnotizing all within his reach, even the cute little donkeys outside the coach look up, hoping to catch a glimpse of his charismatic magnetism inside.

Danny has missed his calling as a professional comedian, not the owner of high-end assisted living conglomerates that take his residents on Cinderella excursions. It was just a few weeks ago that he lined his collection of rare vintage cars up in front of one of his many facilities, having the residents dressed in their finest before magically zooming them off to an evening of midnight dancing. Ah, such exquisite taste and eccentricity, a rare gem, cut from a different cloth, perhaps a Parisian textile.

And now, Danny's true love is a tall French Canadian, a genuine hunk of burning love, towering miles upward into the sky, just below the seven-foot mark, surely. Gerald is slim and statuesque, sculpted to perfection with baby-blue eyes highlighted by thick, black eyebrows. His distinct voice is the total opposite of Danny's southern charm, more prestigious and naturally calculated with a correctness that draws you in like a hot fudge sundae, dripping in whipped cream with a jumbo red cherry waving proudly on top.

As the chorus winds down, I shout with excitement when Nino rounds a curve on the narrow road. "Look to the left side, to the sea! Do you see the narrow jetty where the cast sang in the *Mamma Mia!* movie?"

I click my camera as though I've never been here, and the Americans follow along, capturing a storybook page and a forever memory. Our eyes are glued to the windows, peering out into the full sun to see a foreign vista of unexplainable beauty. One moment we had been on a seemingly country road in East Texas and then suddenly past a gorgeous blue seaside, then a visual tapestry woven with groves of olive trees speckled with purple plums.

Then I remember where our conversation was on the coach, and I push the microphone back toward Carolyn and encourage, "Louder! Sing louder."

"*Mamma Mia*, this is nice. I want to learn this song," Tony declares, knowing his wife will appreciate him learning a new love song.

Afterward, finally ending the song, Danny stands straight as a tin soldier in the aisle of the coach as though he's ready to say the pledge of allegiance, with his hand drawn to his heart and the other one on Gerald's shoulder.

"I'd like to make an announcement and answer Patsy's question. Miles ago, she asked me a simple question, but I took a few detours and went around the world trying to answer," Danny says, chuckling with an eye roll of mischievousness.

Tony shoots me a surprised look, then turns around to hear Danny's latest announcement.

I watch Danny hold his breath then smooth the front of his colorful designer-label shirt as he collects his thoughts. He springs back in his seat and leans firmly against the blue velour with his spine straight as a number two yellow pencil. His hair is thickly rooted—a black forest flattened to the furriness of the headrest. We watch as he slowly drops his hand onto the leather armrest and clutches it with a firm grip.

Tony robotically reaches for his knee—the one that endured the painful hit on Rome's wet cobblestones a few years ago. He rubs and massages it, never taking his eyes off Danny. And in the split-second silence, I can feel the drum roll beating within my heart. Surely, the trumpet is about to sound, surely it is.

"Heavens to Betsy, the question was, do I ever think about getting married again?" Danny fans himself with his right hand as he brings us back to the beginning.

"Hmm, well, yes, I do," Danny gives us a morsel of hope then slumps down as though that's all there is to it—a simple answer of yes with nothing more to say, leaving us highly disappointed and desiring to know more.

Silence looms over us, and the gap of quietness is alarming. We're not ready for the show to end. No, we must hear more. We continue to stare at Danny, speculating whether or not the silence will end. The pause is so long I begin to think he's fallen asleep or perhaps never talking to us again. But, no, he finally shifts his body away from us and looks out the window. And just like that, we're left dangling on the Farris wheel, wondering if we'll ever get off.

"*Mamma Mia, Stefania.* I don't know what to say anymore. I understand nothing. What's the matter with him? And who is this 'Betsy' he speaks of so often?" Tony spins around in his seat again, staring at Danny while drumming his fingers impatiently.

"'Heavens to Betsy' is a term of southern exclamation. *Esclamazione.* Similar to '*Mamma Mia,*'" I quickly explain to Tony.

Minutes ago, Danny had lit up the coach with his shining performance while he took us up a majestic mountaintop with bright rays of sunshine illuminating his life. But, in the blink of an eye, he left us on a cliff with no closure in sight.

Highly disappointed, I shift back around in my seat and stare through the huge windshield. Before me is the gorgeous exoticness of Greece. We're on the secluded island that most tourists know only from the movie *Mamma Mia!* We're long gone from the tourist paths —many miles from Athens and the popular islands of Greece. So far, we've seen no floating cities—cruise ships with thousands of foreigners flocking to the Greek islands. There's no hoopla here, nothing that attracts the gazillion vacationers and honeymooners who yearn for an exotic taste of the rich and famous lifestyle. In time, we'll go to Athens and stand on Mars' Hill, where the apostle Paul preached the gospel, but now we're content to see and experience the local life of living and existing on a secluded island, far away from any others.

Who in their right mind would venture from island to island to get to this secluded place? Me. Yes, me. Traveling on the narrow road beside the glistening sea, I see many tiny wooden boats bobbing up and down in the bright turquoise-blue water and the locals leading their little donkeys with woven baskets on their backs. I see the enchanting beauty right beside me, but I can't stop thinking: is the show really over? How can Danny leave us stranded on the edge of nothing? He took us deep into his personal life and then nothing, absolutely nothing. I continue to stare through the gigantic windshield, knowing there's more to say, more to hear. The brief silence is deafening, and just when I think Danny will never speak again, he does.

Danny jumps up from his seat and spins around like a cyclone, sucking us back in. The light pops on, the curtain draws open, and he starts, capturing our undivided attention once more.

"Gerald and I are here in Greece, on this tour with Stephanie and Tony, to do just that: get married, to say our vows and permanently attach ourselves to each other." Danny spills the beans and dazzles us with his eyes and shows off his pearly whites as though in a dentist chair.

"Danny, puhleeze! Do you really expect us to believe that?" Patsy asks in her East Texas southern drawl. She pulls a cookie from a little package and takes a bite, but her eyes never blink from Danny's face.

"Yes! Gerald and I are getting married in the little church where Sophia rode the donkey to get married in the movie *Mamma Mia!* And I'd like to extend an invitation to all of you to join us. Please, it's our pleasure to have you all attend as our new-found friends and stand with us to say our vows." He raises his hand in midair, to ward off the questions, squeezing his eyes shut to summon the rest of the story.

Clearing his voice like an amplified trombone, Danny demands the stage. We watch as he intentionally bats his eyelids, deliberately creating more suspense as he leans across the aisle, ready to make an announcement.

"Ann, may I ask you a huge favor?" Danny stretches over Mark to get to Ann. "Would you stand beside me and give me away? You know, stand in for my momma on our wedding day? Your beauty reminds me of her."

Before Ann can respond, Danny hurriedly steps back to his seat and plunges into it as though the show is over. Seconds later, he shoots back up and leans over to Mark.

"Mark, would you stand in for Gerald's daddy and be his best man? We'd both be honored. I realize we've only known each other for a few days, but it seems as though we've grown up together." Danny flickers his dreamy black diamond eyes. We gasp for air, reaching for more, but it is suspended high above us and refuses to come down. I feel the urge to shout, but I restrain from the emotional outburst.

Our eyes are now on Ann and Mark, waiting for their response. Mark covered his ears in shock. And Ann is laughing, spreading delicate hands against her breathless chest, then slapping them hard against her porcelain cheeks. Her eyes swell as her mouth drops into her lap. Before they can give the acceptance speech, we already know their response. They're suddenly proud parents, ready to step in and do their part to make Danny and Gerald's wedding a successful event.

Applause erupts and echoes inside the coach as everyone shouts in congratulatory happiness. Danny dances acrobatically down the narrow aisle of the coach, blowing kisses to everyone, which causes dire concern for Nino as he makes a hairpin curve before a sudden stop to let us out to shop in our first village on this Greek island.

Chapter 27

GOING TO THE CHAPEL IN GREECE (FINDING THE RING)

"*Andiamo!* Let's go," I announce for everyone to grab their bags and climb off the coach, and everyone hugs and congratulates Danny and Gerald as they pass by. I breathe a sigh of relief as Mark taps me on the shoulder, gives me a quick wink and thumbs up to let me know he's well pleased with the plan. Last evening Mark had asked Tony where to find a big, sparkling diamond ring for Ann to compliment her wedding ring.

"I want a show-stopper diamond, something Ann will love and be proud to wear alongside her big solitaire. A ring that will remind her of this enchanting journey we're on. A studded band that will take her breath away," Mark explained to Tony as they sipped the *vino* at the table under the colorful cabana with the peaceful sea swirling beside them.

Now, wandering through the connecting shops here in Skopelos, Mark contemplates how to get away from Ann to search for the perfect ring. I see his eyes bouncing all over the place but not in my direction. I motion for him to look my way, but he and Ann dart into a shop.

Clearly, Mark is walking a tight rope. Will he find a diamond ring this afternoon, here on Skopelos? The question dangles in the air as I wonder if there is such a ring on this island.

Cloaked in anxiety, Mark produces a wad of euros and eagerly pushes them into Ann's hand. "Get anything you want," he whispers into her ear. "And while you're looking here, I'll stroll around and meet up with you in a few minutes. I want to find a nice watch today, and I'll check out the other shops. Surely I'll find some unique time-pieces on this island."

Mark shifted his feet anxiously, bouncing from one foot to the other foot, knowing the clock is ticking. With an inability to concentrate on anything else, Mark rushes his words as though he'll never speak again. I helplessly watch as he blows out a long, endless breath, smiling at the same time that Ann flashes her magnificent eyes at him.

"Hopefully, I'll find a few antique Greek ones to add to my collection," Mark fibs again, repeating himself to make sure Ann understands the importance of the watch. "Is that okay with you?"

Mark kisses Ann's left cheek, and before she can respond, he is out the door.

Engrossed in the local textiles, Ann slowly responds to Mark, who has already disappeared.

"Yes, go ahead. I'll catch up with you in a few minutes," Ann replies, dropping the wad of euros into her shoulder bag, and reaching for a pillow behind a colorful curtain. It's a locally made pillow of creamy white. "Ah, this is the perfect color for our new lake house."

I'm busy looking at Mark trying to make an emergency get-away and a large array of colorful wares before me. Not knowing who's coming around the corner, Kathy and Carolyn barely avoid slamming into me as I reach high above a glass-filled shelf for a linen blouse. The keeper of the shop glances at me and nervously smiles, fingering the necklace of blue stones strapped about her neck. Nervously, she tosses her black fringe away from her gigantic brown eyes and peers at me while mumbling in Greek. She maneuvers toward me and reaches for the blouse. Wrinkling her brow, she politely hands me the bright yellow top while shaking her head in silent disapproval.

Waiting in fervent anticipation, thinking this will be the perfect apparel for tomorrow's arrival at the famous chapel, I excitedly take the blouse from her and bring it underneath my chin to examine in the mirror.

"No, this is not for you. The color is no good for your face," the Greek lady professes in broken English, stepping forward in my direction with both hands extended out to reclaim her inventory. I lower my head and hurriedly hand the top back to her—as if it was hot coals burning my hands.

Mark is already six shops down the seafront, jetting in and out, searching for the perfect ring with our little Greek-American, Anthe, tagging along to help Mark in the language translation department. I can't imagine Skopelos has exquisite diamonds, but come to think of it, I've never shopped for fine jewelry on this island, just beautiful Greek cloths and icons.

After hours of wandering through the colorful alleyways surrounded by explosions of tropical flowers and shopping in the local clothing shops, I run into Lana, who has been traveling with us for many years.

"Surprise! Have you eaten lunch already?" Lana shifts colorful shopping bags from one arm to the other while juggling a beautiful bridal bouquet.

I clap my hands with excitement. "Let's have baklava, soaked in local honey! Afterward, lunch." I can taste it now, the sugary sweetness dripping down my chin. I run my fingers over my bottom lip to catch the illusion of its honeybee nectar.

Lana smiles while nodding her head in agreement. "I'll first have a Greek salad, then baklava." Lana knows I'll do the same with pleasure.

"I like how you're thinking," I tell Lana. "I plan on eating as much Greek freshness as possible before we get back on the plane.

We wander along the walkway bordering the sea. We watch the everyday life of Greek locals unfold before us. In the nearest building is an older woman looking out the window, pressing her leathery face against the glass and motioning for us to come inside to eat—but we don't, not yet. Two steps past her, another elderly local with bouncy hips eagerly waves to us, talking in Greek while pointing to the local menu written on a chalkboard that has little round pompoms dangling around its outer rim. We're surrounded by tantalizing aromas wafting out all around. Yards away from our sandal-strapped feet are six little donkeys styling colorful blankets and loaded with packages and bundles of mail.

The island of Skopelos is an exotic backdrop for travel magazines with the villas and churches clustered together, one on top of another in a half-circle, stacking up into the sky. Looking out from where we stand is a picturesque vista, a kaleidoscope of tropical blues and deep emerald greens in narrow strokes and wide spirals. It's a photographer's dream, and for us Americans running here and there, searching for treasures, well, it's a magnificent lifestyle beyond our imagination.

In minutes, Lana and I have found the perfect outdoor restaurant with huge white canopies enveloping the area by the sea. No sooner do I scoot my chair up closer to the table than two white-suited men approach us, eagerly carrying baskets of freshly baked bread and bottles of olive oil. I try to resist the big round loaves, but I could no more do so than I could stop drinking Italian espresso with fresh cream on top.

"Look, I see Mark coming toward us. He's gushing with excitement, but his hands are empty," I say to Lana, who's already pulling the fluffy, white bread apart on her plate.

"And there's Ann with him. I hope he found the perfect ring," I tell Lana, who is now waving her hands and motioning for them to come join us. Behind them are more of our group: Dinky, Linda, Kathy, Caroline, Anthe, and Patsy, all clutching colorful shopping bags.

"*Ciao a tutti!* Hello, everyone!" I shout, forgetting about the large chunk of bread in my mouth.

"What did you find?" I manage to say as I quickly reach for a glass of lemon water. I look at Mark; I know he found the perfect ring from the sparkle in his eye.

"We covered a lot of ground in a short time. This village is spectacular, but I didn't find the watch I was searching for," Mark sadly confesses, lowering his head down and looking at his shoes. There's a long, melancholy pause as Mark displays empty hands, causing alarm and confusion at the same time. I thought his face was smiling seconds ago, but evidently, it wasn't.

"Oh no! I was hoping you'd found the perfect timepiece. But don't worry, we'll be on a different island in a few days, so surely, you'll find one," I reassure Mark loudly, disturbing the locals seated around us.

"No such luck today," Mark repeats the verdict but portrays a different look this time: comedy and tragedy.

"Are you sure there were no watches anywhere?" I question Mark again, knowing tomorrow is too late to keep looking for a ring—this can't be happening.

"No, not a single one. Anthe and I searched the shops, but absolutely nothing," Mark flashes a sad face but with tiny twinkles in his eyes. Not being able to interpret intentional acting, if it is, I question myself, then come to the realization there will be no ring.

I play along. "I'll ask Tony to inquire more about where to find the r—, watch," I nearly speak of the surprise. Seeing no sign of triumph on Mark's face, my heart drops again, knowing this stop was our only hope of finding a ring. It's not like we can hop aboard a boat and go to the next island within minutes. No, we're hours away, and what kind of ring would Mark find if he couldn't find one here? A locally made beaded one, or perhaps a seashell balancing atop of a wired band?

My mind rambles all over the place, desperately wanting Ann to have another beautiful diamond to complement her mountainous solitaire that Mark gave her months ago when they said their vows in America. And what will Mark do if he can't find one? I stab the huge chunk of feta cheese in my salad; my smile is temporarily upside down, staring at Mark's empty hands.

Before I swallow another chunk of feta, I notice Mark. This time his expression is different. He's put on a joyous smile with crystal blue eyes behind his polished glasses. He looks every inch the successful businessman he is, with a full head of silvery-white hair, lacquered and styled to perfection.

Mark winks quickly while giving a thumb up behind Ann's back, signaling the hidden treasure was indeed found. I can't help but question his gesture. In a short time of shopping, he found the perfect ring? I look again at Mark, my eyes asking for confirmation. His face is sunshine and satisfied with his purchase as he nods vigorously behind Ann.

Happily, I try to nonchalantly scoot the empty chair closer beside me and shove it underneath the table, trying to hide the beautiful bouquet of pink roses. It was less than an hour ago that Lana jetted off down the narrow alleyway, discovering a quaint floral shop stocked full of beautiful roses with vibrant petals.

Hours later, everyone is back on the coach except for Danny and Gerald. As we wait, Nino, Tony, and I look through the windshield and observe a flying saucer heading straight for us.

"*Mamma Mia, Madonna!*" Tony says, blasting out of his seat and gluing himself to the windshield alongside Nino, who is leaning over the steering wheel with his nose pressed to the glass, too.

"What is this coming to us, *Stefania*?" Tony presses in harder. "What is this on the head of Danny?"

"I don't know. It appears to be a hat." I forced a smile, not believing my eyes.

"*Matrimonio*? *Cappello*?" Nino tries to talk, but I can see he's taken aback by Danny's extravagance, so much so that he pulls his sunglasses off, rubs his eyes, and blinks.

"*Si*, yes. It's a matrimony hat, for his wedding." I don't have the energy to explain more.

Tony pulls a large napkin from his shirt pocket and wipes his forehead, then his eyes. "*Mamma Mia, Stefania.* Where do you find these people you bring to me? There is always one who..."

"I've arrived!" Danny makes a crash landing, his voice bellowing loudly to Tony. "I had a fabulous time shopping, darling, just fabulous!"

Tony's eyes blink like a malfunctioning brain circuit has gone haywire. His eyes are focused on the gigantic hat.

Danny excitedly squeezes through the aisle, loaded down with shopping bags and his new floppy hat "spaceship" that's balanced gracefully atop his head.

"Lord, have mercy!" Patsy can't stay quiet for long. "How in the world did I miss that big purchase on this island? You look quite wealthy, sir." Patsy examines his hat, his shirt, his pants, and finally, his toes that are dangling from the leather strapped sandals.

"*Mamma Mia!* Very nice," Tony finally speaks, his eyes widening more.

"Don't get any ideas, Tony. I'm not giving my hat to anyone."

Danny pinches Gerald's cheek and flashes his eyes dramatically. And it comes like clockwork. Everyone burst into applause as he fans the flames of theater again.

"The hat—is it for you?" Tony questions, thinking it's surely a kind gesture for the momma like a peace offering to settle the differences.

"Yes, absolutely, darlin'. Isn't it just fabulous?" Danny echoes in his charming, southern drawl, shifting some of his excessive purchases into the overhead bin, while more bags patiently wait on the floor, waiting to be stuffed somewhere. Everyone in the coach leans over into the aisle, wanting to get a better view of Danny, who's now spinning around on his catwalk to model his newly purchased headpiece.

"Where did you find the adornment?" Ann leans over Mark to ask the question. She doesn't like floppy hats on her head.

"It's mine to wear for the big day. Isn't it marvelous?" Danny gushes, batting his long eyelashes while giving Mark a high-five before plunking down into the cushiony seat across the aisle.

"*Mamma Mia, Stefania,* I do not understand anything. What do you mean Danny is getting married? To Gerald?" Tony is on the edge of his seat and looking confused and inquisitive all at once.

"*Si, si,* yes, I understand we're having a wedding in the church of Agios Ioannis Kastri on Skopelos where this bloody *Mamma Mia!* was filmed. *Si,* yes, I understand everything. The church rising up out of the sea, the one we always go to. But what I don't understand is the people, the bride and groom. I thought—never mind, I know nothing anymore. You have everything under control. And Adelfo will be the priest. He's excited to marry the two *Americani*," Tony explains, whipping out a large napkin from his front pocket again to mop the gloss of perspiration dancing across his forehead.

I see his eyes dance like the tango, racing back and forth and communicating with his thoughts. Clearing his voice for the second time, he starts again.

"*Stefania*, I do not understand," Tony tries again. He turns to Danny and Gerald then back around to me. "Never mind, we will talk about this later."

"Tony," I whisper, motioning for him to lean over. "He found the ring! Mark got the ring a few minutes ago for Ann."

"*Mamma Mia, Stefania.* Very nice. Yes, very nice, Mark finding the ring. But what does he do with another one? The wife already has a matrimony band, a *grande fede nuziale*. Why must he spend the money on another one? I do not understand this urgency? Ah, perhaps it's for the romance. *Si,* yes. It's to prepare. How do the *Americani* say—ah, I remember, to butter her up."

Tony scoots back into his seat, satisfied with his resolution. But only seconds later, he appears to have fire ants stinging underneath his white linen pants, which make him twist in his seat to look back at Ann and Mark, then Danny and Gerald. I see the uncertainty, the scattered puzzle within his brain. The ex-wife, the marriage, the momma, the ring, and Danny's face that's filled with the brightness recognized by lovers when finding true love and supposedly within hours of marrying the love of his life: Gerald.

"Tony," I try to explain again. "Mark and Ann are—" Tony hears nothing; he's already made a U-turn in his seat to talk to Nino and tell him that Danny and Gerald will be married in the *Mamma Mia!* church tomorrow.

Chapter 28

GOING TO THE CHAPEL IN GREECE (REHEARSAL DINNER)

*T*onight, once again, we sit together as one happy family. All of us gathered together and nestled underneath a huge, white, open-air canopy with delicious buffet-style cuisine mesmerizing our taste buds. The turquoise-blue sea slaps at our feet only a few steps below the elevated wooden deck, but tonight it could be an Egyptian desert, and we wouldn't care.

There's so much going on at the three long tables with many of the Americans trying to decide this and that about the upcoming event. The chaotic excitement of matrimonial bliss floats thickly through the cool air. With racing thoughts, I bounce about from Danny and Gerald to Mark and Ann, nearly exploding with the secrets about tomorrow's event.

Danny and Gerald, the happy groom and groom, sit together for the last time as two. Tomorrow is their big day, the *Mamma Mia!* wedding that will unite them together, forever padlocked and sealed as one. Among the many conversations bouncing along, we briefly reminisce about the happenings of today's impromptu excursions around the island then land back on tomorrow's wedding and the big question: what will Ann wear since she's the mother of the groom?

"I packed a long black dress to wear tomorrow when going up the *Mamma Mia!* steps," Ann tells us with dazzling blue eyes. "I had no idea I'd be attending a wedding and standing in as the groom's mother. Stephanie had suggested in her last letter to bring a flowing outfit to reenact Meryl Streep going up the stone steps to the little church. So, I threw in my favorite one, but it's jet black." Ann illustrates by pointing to her midnight dark purse as two piercing dimples appear around her rosy lips.

"Black! You can't..." Lana tries to speak, but I kick her leg.

Kathy and Carolyn both elbow me as quietly and forcefully as possible with panic dancing all over their faces.

"Oh, what do you call the dress you're wearing tomorrow, a sundress or fancy party dress?" Kathy blurts out nervously from hearing about the color black.

"It's a lovely, long, black sundress, perfect for tomorrow, except for the color, but it doesn't matter." Ann doesn't seem alarmed.

Lana's feet were off the floor; she jumps up and then flops down. Nervous energy in an emergency situation.

"Are you positive you want to wear black tomorrow to the wedding?" Dinky politely interjects. She arches her eyebrows in a detective kind of way in the direction of Danny and Gerald, knowing it probably doesn't matter to Gerald, anyway. But to Danny, that's another story.

"Oh, black is such a dreadful color for Greece! Don't you think?" Caroline is thinking out loud. Kathy kicks her leg underneath the table.

Dinky squeezed her hands together. We see the wheels turning. Did she have the problem solved? We stare at her, waiting for the next move.

"I don't know about black. I've never much liked the dark color. Have you, Ann?" Patsy asks, but doesn't wait for an answer. She claps her hands together, startling everyone for a brief second. "Let's have cake!" Patsy is trying to help the situation along, but we keep shuffling our shoes around underneath the table until Kathy uncorks another bottle of wine.

"Ah, you're going to get us all inebriated before the wedding, aren't you?" Danny flashes his seductive eyes across the table at us.

No one verbally responds to Danny. We're too worried about the black dress.

"Sorry, honey, I can't let you wear black to Danny and Gerald's wedding tomorrow," Anthe speaks up with a smile. "You aren't really wearing...?"

"Yes, is that a problem?" Ann laughs, glancing at Danny and Gerald, who hear nothing but their laughter mixed with Mark's. "The guys will never notice the color. I'll sashay up the mountain and back down before anyone ever notices it's black." Ann smiles.

Seated across the table, face-to-face with Ann, Linda seizes the spotlight as she sees we're going nowhere with the black dress.

"Ann, I have a beautiful white dress, long and flowing; you should wear it to the wedding. It will be fabulous on you. I brought several outfits for Greece, and the white one is perfect—the size and all. Besides, you can't wear black to Danny and Gerald's big day. That would be awful. What would everyone think since you're the mother of the groom, or is it the bride? Whichever one you are...you must wear white," Linda explains emphatically.

"Besides, I purchased another long sundress today, but it's a nice, lightweight, cotton fabric that's multicolored and looks like silk. I was in the same shop as Lana, Carolyn, and Kathy. You saw the dress I purchased?" Linda asks Kathy while looking for Carolyn.

"Ah, yes. I purchased several cute tops for Emily," Kathy responds, lifting her glass up in the salty ocean air as a self-congratulatory toast for finding another treasure.

"It's meant to be, Ann," Linda starts again. "The dress is perfect for you, and we're the same size, and if you come to my room tonight, I'll give it to you. Remember, it's a wedding, not a funeral. You'll sparkle tomorrow, walking the aisle with Gerald. I think it's meant to be."

Linda is on a roll, talking continuously. She's filled with persuasion, not taking no for an answer, and confused about who's the bride or the groom—Danny or Gerald?

Hesitation floats in the late evening air before the suggestion is accepted, but before Ann concedes to peer pressure, Lana remembers her own purchase hanging about her neck.

"Oh, Ann, I have the perfect accessory to go with Linda's white dress," Lana excitedly scoots her chair closer to the table, setting her glass of wine beside the platter of gigantic lobsters with their bulging eyes.

"I purchased this string of pearls in the village today; look at the little shells dangling in between the large ones. I had to have them; they'll be beautiful on you, that is, if you wear the white dress," Lana insists, hurriedly removing the string of shells from about her neck and proudly handing them to Ann with a huge smile across her face, hoping it will seal the deal.

"You're very particular, all of you, aren't you?" Ann hesitates, and her heart sinks. She sees the love of her new traveling friends. She taps her perfectly manicured nails on the tip of her wine glass, keeping us in suspense.

"We want you to be perfect tomorrow, for Danny. You know, standing in for his mamma." Lana speaks up with sincere eyes, twinkling like topaz stones.

"And the photos...Stephanie will be taking lots of them. What would people think? Remember the wedding album, seeing the mamma of the groom in black." Dinky leans over the table, she's in her detective mode, not taking no for an answer.

"And it's bad luck to wear black to a funeral. Oh, I mean a wedding." I toss in my opinion.

"You're too beautiful to be in such drab colors," Anthe speaks up.

"Oh, my, okay. I accept your offers, Linda and Lana. Thank you so much. They're perfect, and both of you are so thoughtful and kind." Ann lays the string of pearls and shells on the table beside her glass of wine and caresses its smoothness and beauty.

Our attention is suddenly turned back to our waiter, who's balancing a huge tray over his shoulder that's loaded with my favorite Turkish dessert, but made famous by the Greeks: baklava. The delicious pastry is cut in triangular-shaped pieces and placed elegantly on several plates. In Greece, baklava is usually made with thirty-three layers of phyllo dough to represent the years of Christ's life. And to me, each bite is a little piece of honey-drenched heaven. If only I would have remembered it was coming before the end of our delicious meal tonight, I would have saved room to eat the whole tray— oh, yes, and with pleasure.

"Oh, my, what is this?" Carolyn asks, eagerly stabbing her fork into its many layers, squashing honey everywhere on the ceramic plate.

"It's baklava! You know, the famous Greek dessert. I made my first batch when I was twelve years old in my mother's kitchen. I remember the fun of layering the thirty-three sheets of phyllo dough in the long glass Pyrex pan. But the Greeks and the Turks both claim its beginnings," I tell them. The honey slowly drizzles from my fork as I hold a big chunk up, proudly exhibiting its beauty.

"Opa!" I spontaneously shout with excitement, loving the sound of the Greek word and wishing I had a stack of ceramic plates to toss in the air, which seems to be the normal Greek thing to do at this joyful moment with all of us indulging in the delectable baklava. My mind zaps back to the needed ingredients to make this masterpiece: pounds of yellow, melted butter, gallons of pure, locally made honey, cups of sugary, chopped nuts, heaping sprinkles of cinnamon, lots of cloves, and a little orange zest. And for me, a small bottle of pure vanilla is a must.

"Eat!" I encourage them, indulging in the sweetness and a short intermission from the discussion of Ann's wedding attire. But the interlude is cut short when Anthe lifts the string of pearls and shells from the table and brings the necklace up to her chest.

"It's a beautiful necklace, Ann. You now have something 'borrowed' for the wedding. Wait, I think Danny should be wearing the necklace since he's the 'bride.'" Anthe stares at Danny and then Gerald. Confusion is dancing across her face.

"How lucky can a girl get, thanks to you two? I'm officially ready for the big day. Me, a mother, giving away her 'son,' one I never knew I had." Ann laughs, causing a chain reaction. "And what are you two ladies? Houdini the magician producing the necessities just like that?"

"Sit down, Tony," Kathy says, pulling a chair from behind her to our table so Tony can join us. Tony hoists the wine bottle from the table and begins to refill our glasses. "Come on, everybody, let's toast the bride and groom."

After filling the glasses with the smooth wine, Tony lifts his glass in the air and says with excitement filling his face, "Cheers, everybody, and to our friends, Danny and Gerald, happy wedding day tomorrow!"

We applaud heroically, then clank our glasses together.

Dinky whistles and Carolyn pretends to blow a horn. Tony grabs two spoons and a knife, turning both spoons side by side and placing the knife in between them. Magically, he's now drumming the knife up and down and creating a loud rhythmical sound. We have gone full-on Greek party. Even the fish swimming in the sea below us are alerted, knowing a celebration is in full swing. Our two waiters join in, reminding me there's more coming—bowls of fresh fruit from the island.

Kathy dabs her make-believe tears. "This is awesome, Stephanie. Look at Mark and Ann; they're both so happy."

Kathy grabs her iPad and snaps a photo of them nestled together. My eyes flash over to Mark. He's leaning back in a colorful cabana chair, captivated with the conversation. He's seated comfortably with the swimming pool behind him and the cool wind drifting off the sea...a perfect evening. I watch as he leisurely slips a hand underneath the back of Ann's blue cotton blouse, moving slowly up and down her spine, anticipating, remembering, and hoping the surprise of the diamond ring will be special and a day she'll never forget when the times comes for them.

Minutes later, I watch Mark ask for a refill of his wine. I can't get Mark's attention, but it's obvious that he has pre-wedding jitters with the responsibility of being the father of the groom and not to mention his own surprise wedding. Looking at Ann, who is continuously talking, she reminds me of a one-hundred-watt lightbulb that's brightly shining. The couple's backdrop is turquoise blue, and the swimming pool reflects its beautiful color onto her, like a strobe light dancing through her hair.

"This is more fun than green bananas," Patsy says with a huge smile stretching her adorable face.

Patsy leisurely wipes her lips with the oversized linen napkin gripped within her hand, nonchalantly smearing the sticky-sweet baklava across her upper lip. Patsy knows that when she intentionally verbalizes the two words "green-bananas," it throws the day's topic back into the mix and, Danny will spring back with a glass-shattering response, never disappointing his American followers.

"I don't know about that, Patsy," Danny chimed in. His mouth is stuffed with locally-made Mosaiko, a lip-smacking chocolate Greek biscuit. It's soft, creamy, and has a crunchy delight exploding within that's infused with strong cognac, vanilla, sugar, salt, dark chocolate, and tons of creamy butter.

"I'd love to have some green bananas tonight," Danny slowly confesses, shooting back to Patsy as fast as he can with a mouth full of chocolate that's drizzling from his chin, which prompts Gerald to hand him a napkin.

"You better save those green bananas for tomorrow night—your wedding night." Patsy throws the joke back into his court. The jest of green bananas started on day one when we saw the long green fruit dangling from the trees in southern Italy—prompting Danny and Patsy to make it an inside joke.

With roaring laughter and visualizing the green bananas, the subject quickly changes as Carolyn starts the song, "*Going to the Chapel*" again.

"This is exciting, being in a wedding. I love them both and feel as though we've known each other forever," Ann tells Patsy, who is sipping the *vino* of Greece, allowing it to swish and tumble within her mouth as she savors the piney flavors from the local vineyards.

Before I contemplate too much about the wine, the curtain is up and out pops Linda, singing operetta in her beautiful voice. We turn to her with amazement. We had no idea she could sing.

"*Mamma Mia*, where does this voice come from?" Tony asks, his eyes inflating to large black balloons. "I didn't know you could sing like this."

Unexpectedly, Danny thrusts his chair away from the long table and springs to his feet, trying to be serious, but we laugh.

"Can I have your attention, please?" Danny raises his voice, holding his wine glass high over the table. "I'd like to say a few words."

Danny fishes for something within his pockets, keeping us in suspense. Nino leans over Tony and asks, "*Tutto a posto?* Everything okay?"

"*Mamma Mia*, I know nothing anymore," Tony laughs, leaning in to observe the coming mystery in Danny's pocket.

"Ah, here it is," Danny mumbles, whipping out a small piece of white paper folded in a neat little square. He prepares to read a heart-felt commitment to Gerald, the love of his life, as a pre-wedding declaration of his devoted love.

"*Mamma Mia*, this is very nice," Tony pulls his chair closer to the table. Nino does the same.

"I want to take a risk with my life again. I want to marry the love of my life." Danny looks deeply at Gerald while forcing his eyelids to bat up and down as though a malfunction within his brain has happened again.

"I know Momma is upset with me. She doesn't approve of Gerald. She would much prefer him to be a Geraldine with two perky breasts saluting everyone in sight. But I'm gonna get married up on that *Mamma Mia!* chapel, so help me, Hannah!"

"*Mamma Mia, Stefania!* Who is Hannah?" Tony asks again, not understanding the southern exclamations.

"I'll explain later," I tell Tony.

"*Va bene.* Okay." Tony sighs.

Nearing the end of Danny's heartfelt devotion to Gerald, Linda leans over to Carolyn and whispers the question, "What wedding song shall we sing at the wedding?" Carolyn hears nothing, so the question is left dangling in the air as Danny concludes with hugs and kisses for everyone.

Chapter 29

GOING TO THE CHAPEL IN GREECE (THE WEDDING)

*W*here is Houdini? The question races throughout my mind this morning, thinking today will certainly require his assistance. Not that I can't handle today's wedding events. No, this is my fifth ceremony for the renewing of vows in the little chapel, but today is different. It's not like any of the others. Ah, not at all.

Bouncing along the narrow road to the little white-washed chapel of Agios Ioannis, I sit in eager anticipation, clutching the microphone as though I were about to sing. I don't need Houdini's magic tricks to get us to the top of the mountain for the wedding. No, we can trek up the narrow path of steps while singing *Mamma Mia!* lyrics or Tony's new favorite song: "Going to the Chapel." Either one will be fun and, knowing us, we'll sing both of them. However, thinking of this wedding party dancing upward with long flowing dresses and Danny's white floppy hat, well, Aladdin's magic blanket could come in handy. Last time I counted, there were close to two hundred steps, but I lost count when my heart lodged within my throat, causing me to stop for air.

"*Mamma Mia*, you look very nice today," Tony compliments as he turns around in his seat and looks at Danny. His voice zaps me back to reality.

"The hat suits you nicely. Your face, ah, it was made for a nice fedora, but today is your wedding, so this one will do," Tony says, now reaching for its floppy white brim and pushing it back upon Danny's forehead just a smidgeon.

"Thank you, darlin'," Danny says in his charming southern drawl, intentionally stretching the 'darling' out like pizza dough and batting his long, thick eyelashes of a French Poodle, which makes Tony laugh uncontrollably.

Seated directly behind me is Anthe, who is busily connecting flowers together. She's an octopus—six hands and two legs—reaching across the aisle and taking various stems from Kathy and Carolyn, who are helping her create two floral crowns for the groom and groom. Among the beautiful array of flowers are orange blossoms, puffs of pink hydrangeas, and red-pink roses.

"*Mamma Mia*, what are you doing?" Tony leans closer to examine the long floral garland.

"I'm making the ceremonial wreaths. The Greek marital crowns made of orange blossoms and linked by white satin ribbons to be placed upon their heads and switched back and forth three times," Anthe tells Tony, now bending down to pick up a beautiful rosebud that hit the floor.

"What do you mean Danny and Gerald wear the flowers? Danny has the wedding cap on his head. *Mamma Mia*, I understand nothing," Tony tells Anthe.

"Tony, you'll understand later. It will make sense today, at the ceremony," Anthe tells Tony as she threads another flower on the corded string. She continues the explanation with seriousness.

"After the crowns are switched back and forth three times, the bride and groom walk around the altar three times as prayers are repeated to seal their union by the priest. They'll be dizzy by then—three times this and three times that—representing the Father, the Son, and the Holy Ghost as the Trinity," Anthe explains. She never looks up as she continues to explain the Greek wedding traditions while Tony, still confused, listens intensely.

"What do the crowns or the wreaths upon their heads represent?" Carolyn interrupts Anthe, who refuses to lose time by making eye contact with her or anyone else.

"The wedding crowns represent glory and honor. And the two crowns are joined with a silver ribbon that symbolizes the union of the couple." Anthe shifts her legs, trying to balance the flower petals scattered across her lap and unintentionally kicks the back of my seat. I jump and shift around. Anthe never looks up, just weaves another flower onto the long string.

"Looks beautiful," I tell Anthe, Kathy, and Caroline, the three busy bees working hastily as Nino drives us to our anticipated destination.

"Is this how you want it to look—more flowers here?" Kathy asks Anthe.

"Yes, it's perfect; keep working," Anthe tells Kathy, pressing another rosebud into the corded thread.

Tony raises his hands in a silent *Mamma Mia* as Carolyn breaks out in song again. We join in, joyously singing.

Looking behind me, I see the intense love in Anthe's hands, the excitement within her voice, the explicit details of explaining the Greek ceremony, and the way she meticulously places each flower on the long string that will soon be looped around and tied pretty with ribbon. Anthe is in her element.

"The bride and groom will wear these floral crowns until the end of the marriage ceremony," Anthe explains more, thumping Gerald on the shoulder to remind him of the long laundry list of pertinent details which will be happening within an hour or so. Gerald hears nothing but Danny's voice now bellowing up the aisle.

"Heavens to Betsy, yes, I love classic vehicles," Danny tells Mark. He gives him details of his massive vintage car collection, which requires a weekly routine of revving motors up and popping more than thirty-five hoods to guarantee a smooth ride and healthy pistons.

There are many conversations going on, but Anthe never stops working and talking to her captivated audience: Kathy, Caroline, Lana, Tony, and me. And surely Gerald listens, too—at least with one ear.

"And that's not all," Anthe continues the details, reaching for more roses across the aisle from Kathy. "Please, remember to do this. As Danny and Gerald circle the altar, all of you should shower them with sugared almonds and rice, which are symbols of prosperity and good fortune."

Anthe stretches the long string of flowers over to Caroline, inspecting its length.

"Oh, no! We forgot the rice and almonds." Anthe remembers, and her face falls for a moment, but it doesn't interrupt the call of duty to make the necessary headpieces.

"No, don't worry, we've got almonds—lots of them. And, I brought Greek pastries for everyone," I tell Anthe. Her smile returns from its short collapse.

"I couldn't find the white ribbon, but there was plenty of blue satin with little white specs, which I purchased on impulse," Anthe tells us, lifting the large spool from her lap as she gives us a quick glance. "And the orange blossoms were in short supply, but, thankfully, I found a dozen or so yesterday—another last-minute purchase." Anthe grabs the end of the string of flowers from Caroline's hand, folding it into a circle, connecting it together for the perfect headpiece. Shifting her petite body on the blue velour seat, Anthe gives more instructions, never stopping her floral duty.

"Mark, since you're the best man, you must remember to hold the wedding rings over the heads of the bride and groom and bless them three times for the Holy Trinity. Do you understand? The rings must be exchanged three times to seal their promise to each other." Anthe takes the circle of flowers and plops it on top of Gerald's thick, silver hair.

"Ah, a perfect fit," Anthe yanks it off. "Oh, don't forget, after the ceremony, the bride and groom must wear their rings on the right hand, not the left. Then after the priest has declared you husband

and wife, I mean, husband and husband, you must perform the dance outside."

My eyes are on Gerald, watching his reaction to so many Greek instructions being thrown to him. He appears to be a deer in the headlights of an eighteen-wheeler truck bearing down upon him.

"*Mamma Mia*, you are good. You know the Greek matrimony well," Tony compliments Anthe, impressed with her knowledge and talents.

"*Mamma Mia, si, si*, yes, you look very nice for the matrimony," Tony continues with the compliments, examining Anthe's outfit. It's a pretty Greek-style sundress: multicolored cotton, size six petite, with a full-skirted flair that is covered with the happy array of magenta, salmon, coral, and tangerine orange with a splash of blue.

"And did you get the sandals yesterday, here in Greece?" Tony notices her feet, which are strapped in flat leather sandals and extended outwards in the aisle, balancing piles of petals.

"I did," Anthe mumbles in slow motion, nodding her head up and down in agreement.

Looking back, I see that Ann is wearing the string of Greek pearls with dangling seashells about her neck and a long, white linen dress, both borrowed from Linda and Lana. Her beautifully tanned shoulders are cloaked with a silky white scarf that's tied in the front with a knotted loop. She styled her hair with movie-star glamour—straight and bouncy, sweeping below her face and brushing against the white linen. Her eyes dazzle, performing the Macarena dance across a tropical sea of blueness. Her lips are outlined in coral-pink gloss, glimmering softly.

Mark is dressed in white linen pants and a matching shirt. In the sunlight, his hair resembles silvery-white cotton, a frothy field of thickness that is also styled to movie-star, pompadour perfection. Looking at them snuggled tightly together, they are obviously connected and coordinate stylishly. They are a perfect match, like Barbie and Ken or Romeo and Julieta. You can see their feelings in their body language; it's a magnetic love sparking from within their souls. If all goes well, there will be fireworks for tonight's celebration.

Minutes later, getting off the coach and making our way down the rocky steps to the sea, Nino stares at Ann, watching her beautiful white dress whip in the gentle breeze.

"*Ciao bello*. Hello, beautiful," Nino greets Ann.

He gives her a hug and continues, "*Mamma Mia, bello sei oggi.* Beautiful, you are today." Nino compliments her with sincerity, appreciating a natural American beauty with so much class.

"Thank you, Nino." Ann smiles, standing in awe at the magnificence before her of an indescribable rock towering forth from the gentle swirls of blue, turquoise, and lime green sea. A thousand variegated rainbows merge together, swishing and swooshing as if a fairy godmother waved her magic wand to create a magical setting.

The beautiful imagery overwhelms Ann and brings grateful tears to her eyes. She tries to speak, but she can't. Her lips quiver and purse. I think she's in shock as her eyeballs swell as if air is being pumped into them. *Will they pop out onto the ground?* The thought races through my mind. Ann tries to speak again; her mouth open. Sounds crawl upwards, from her toes to her throat, but dwindle back down. She can't speak. The emotions are too much.

"Come on, Ann!" Patsy hollers. A perfumed fragrance of honeysuckle wafts in the air as Ann wanders over to the ladies.

"Oh, darling—this is too much." Danny straightens his floppy hat that balances majestically on a flowerbed of black thickness with a little pink rose sprouting from its brim. "I'm going straight to the chapel to prepare myself for the ceremony."

Danny walks toward the sea with his right hand clutching a bridal bouquet of pink roses.

"Wait for me," Gerald hollers to Danny as he tries to escape the clicking cameras of last-minute photos before the group climbs the soaring steps to the tiny chapel.

"Tony, come with us," Dinky hollers without looking back.

"*Mamma Mia*, you must be joking. I wait here with Nino." Tony points to the ground, causing Dinky to look back. "My new shoes are on holiday. They prefer to rest, sitting right here underneath the umbrella with a nice cream. You want?"

Tony takes a towering scoop of vanilla Greek yogurt from the old lady behind the makeshift stand and leisurely plops down beside Nino, who is licking his lips from the honey-glazed baklava that's already half consumed.

"No, you enjoy," Dinky tells Tony. Instinctively, she knows Tony is much better left underneath the canopy of shade.

Danny, Gerald, and Mark start the climb appearing like three little ants crawling upward and disappearing in the far distance.

The ladies lollygag around, giggling and primping, adjusting dresses and smoothing hair. "Shall we go?" I asked the girls, snapping another photo of Ann, who is now holding her white wrap in the gentle breeze, allowing it to whip and sway in the wind.

Ann looks perfect—the hair, the dress, the shawl, the necklace, and her giddy anticipation.

"Shall we go?" I ask again, looking up and seeing a local man walking ahead of us.

"*Kalimera*. Good morning," he says to Patsy with a happy face, flashing his teeth that likely have been tarnished by too many cigarettes.

"Let's start the climb." Kathy gushes enthusiastically while looping her arm around Carolyn's bag and dragging her forward. "We need to go up so we'll have enough time to assemble ourselves inside the little church."

I intentionally wait behind as they fall into a reenactment of Meryl Streep dancing up the stone steps.

"Go ahead," I tell them as I push the button on my phone to play the *Mamma Mia!* song.

"I've got it playing on my phone, too," Caroline hollers back, but I hear a different song, "Going to the Chapel."

I watch as they shuffle in front of me with their colorful attire flapping in the gentle spring breeze. The quick clicks of shoes scurry ahead with enough excitement for Tony and Nino to feel below. I intentionally lag behind them a few feet to focus my lens and seize forever memories of this extraordinary day. My main goal is to capture Ann gracefully treading upwards, just like Sophia did but without the donkey. And with her long white dress flowing in the sun, the perfect photos are created.

"Where is our donkey?" Dinky hollers from up ahead. Before I respond, a local elderly lady flutters up in front of me, boxing me in. She's swathed in jasmine perfume and mumbling something in Greek as her bouncy arms loaded with wax candles rub against my camera. From the click-clack of her shoes pounding on the rock, I should have known she was in a hurry. I cling to the rock as I work my way up. The chiseled-out steps leave little room to walk, much less provide a passing lane with cargo. I can't climb the wall; therefore, I cleave to the side of the rock, never looking downward. Deep breath, I tell myself—perspiration bursts across my upper lip.

"I'm walking a tightrope. I've always wanted to take a risk with my life—but I don't want to plunge a hundred miles below!" I yell to Dinky, who is way ahead of me. She knows I dislike heights.

"You're always taking a risk with your life and mine too. What do you mean? You're our fearless tour leader, taking us here and there. Remember Bangladesh...as in Italy?" Dinky proves her point in her own detective kind of way.

"I need a bungee cord around my feet." My heart is pumping faster. I stop for a second breath. "Why do I bring us to these places?"

"I don't see anyone pointing a gun to your head!" Dinky proves her point again.

Seconds later, I start again, looking ahead. The Americans are a colorful ribbon of beauty, a floral garland floating higher as they inch up the soaring mountain. I'm the last one in line.

Finally, taking the last step atop of the never-ending mountain, I pop out like a cork from a perspiring champagne bottle and safely land on the rocky cement platform surrounding the little, white Agios Ioannis chapel. How can one possibly describe a site so unbelievably magical?

I see Adelfo, our Greek guide and Tony's friend. He lingers by the railing, with the alluring turquoise-blue sea swishing and swooshing miles below. He is the priest for today. *Surely, he's going to change into his black vestment,* I think for a second. I see that he is wearing a

powder blue T-shirt. His shoes, his pants, his shirt, his backpack—
they are all blue. I moan internally with a smile, missing Antonio,
who is Tony's other Sicilian friend. They grew up together in Sicily,
but he couldn't join us today.

Now, seeing his face more closely in the midafternoon sunlight, I
can't help noticing his hair is perfectly polished on top. It reminds me
of a glossy football helmet, so coarse, almost appearing as Madame
de Pompadour with a fresh new color treatment. I think I've never
seen black until now. I feel the urge to flash my camera to capture this
iconic moment with him standing beside the ancient olive tree as if
Michelangelo himself were there to paint his portrait. But I don't. I
allow my thoughts to run rampant, thinking what God deducted
from his petite stature, He blessed him in hair. He has enough to
cover the entire bald population of Greece.

I hurriedly rush to the chapel door. "Wait here, outside," I tell
Danny and Ann, who are fidgeting with the bridal bouquet. Danny
clears his throat, which alerts me to the fact he's more nervous than
he is pretending not to be.

"The ceremony will start momentarily," I tell them, already
hearing Carolyn and Linda singing, "*Ave Maria.*" Sweat suddenly
glosses Danny's forehead underneath the hat.

Everyone else has already rushed inside, hurriedly lighting
dozens of tall, wax tapers that are nestled in the center of the chapel.
Sticking my head inside the door, I see everyone smooshed together
in a half-circle with Mark and Gerald anxiously fidgeting in the
middle. I close the door to hide the view from Danny and Ann as they
continue to stand outside. With hands looped together, ready to make
their grand appearance, the last words I hear before Danny walks
with Ann down the aisle are, "Well, Momma, are you ready to do this
again?"

I speedily dash my way inside the chapel, and my eyes focus on
Mark and Gerald, who are standing against the red velvet partition
veil, shoulder to shoulder, appearing as two virgins who've never
been touched. They stand at attention, like two faithful devotees.

The white-washed walls are adorned with beautiful icons and old

Greek Orthodox ecclesiastical pieces. *There are no musical instruments and no organs to play the wedding march. No pews, chairs, or prayer alters —none, not even a confessional. Where would they fit?* I think to myself. There's not a single petal in sight, except for the bundle of pink variegated roses that Lana purchased in the village, which are now clutched in Danny's left hand, and the two floral crowns dangling from Anthe's arm.

Looking around this minuscule chapel, I know it's perfectly adorned with love coming straight from the Madonna—so the Catholics would say. The priest stands with Americans on each side of him, except for Danny and Ann, who still wait outside behind the wooden door perspiring in the warm afternoon sun.

I look up and snap another photo of the groom, Gerald, and his fictitious father, Mark. I notice the anxiety dancing across Mark's face as he nervously shifts his weight from one foot to the other. He rocks back and forth but goes nowhere, shifting both legs as though ants were crawling up his trousers.

To the right of the back door is a red velvet curtain, the veil that separates us from the Holy of Holies and the sacred wine. I was here a year ago when the sudden urge hit me to go behind the veil and see the hidden treasures. Without thinking, I allowed the voice of Satan to lure me in, entrapping me with his strong suction of evilness. Inside, I saw beautiful gold and silver icons lining the tiny wall, bottles of wine, the chalice and host, and more candles. I had taken a bite of the apple, nibbled it, and then consumed it—until Antonio's voice broke the silence of my sinful indulgence.

"*Stefania*, where are you?" He called out, knowing I was inside the chapel. Quickly, hearing his voice, I hollered back, "I'm in here, behind the veil looking at these beautiful icons." Not giving it a second thought, just leisurely admiring the icons, I poked my head out of the little room with a huge, ruby-studded icon in my hands. I'll never forget the horror burning from Antonio's face and how his feet pedaled backward in utter terror of God's wrath.

"*Mamma Mia!* You will die," Antonio tried to shout. In his mind, I had committed the unpardonable sin, a blasphemy, desecrating the holiness of God's dwelling.

"Oh, Antonio, I'm fine," I reassured him, cuddling the icon like a newborn bambino and walking toward him. His feet became quicksand, refusing to move. His hands flew to his heart, astounded that I survived the Holy of Holies—a forbidden area to the people where only the sanctified priest shall enter.

I reminisce for a brief second until I feel the nudge of Patsy's fingers tapping me on the back of my shoulder.

"Look at Mark's face. He has surely seen a ghost." My eyes flash right to see Mark's countenance speckled with perspiration and blushing with colorful red hues. He frets more than before as though a number two is surely coming.

"He's anticipating his beloved Ann coming through the door any second now," I whisper to Patsy. "Or, perhaps, he's nervous playing the part of Gerald's daddy."

Carolyn and Linda abruptly switch songs, alerting everyone it's time to begin. I suddenly envision two black-bearded Greek Orthodox priests popping out from behind the veil, swinging little brass pots of frankincense, wafting their thick aromatic plumes into the air. But the vision quickly vanishes, and my eyes magnetize to the door.

We join in together with Carolyn and Linda singing, "*Here Comes the Bride*." The excitement is palpable as the door swings open, and Ann and Danny make their grand appearance. We stare through the sea of a hundred flickering candles. A little stream of sunlight beams through the small window, highlighting them as though they were floating in on a cloud of glory.

Through the camera lens, I see Danny's white hat slowly coming through the haze; below the brim, his eyes sparkle like two ten-carat solitaires. By the smile stretching his face, he is delighted that his audience looks at no one else.

Carolyn and Linda stretch the last verse as Danny and Ann slowly stroll, making their way around the array of flickering candles and stopping in front of Adelfo with Gerald and Mark to their right. We watch with teary eyes as Danny releases Ann's hand from his while balancing the bridal bouquet. Adelfo steps back, and Gerald and Mark step forward—a changing of the guards.

Danny clears his throat as he gently takes Ann's hand in his, caressing it for a few seconds, appearing to search for words to say. We watch as he strokes her hand and gazes into her eyes, emotions drumming within.

Danny slowly reaches for Mark's hand. We gasp, waiting breathlessly for the climax to unfold. A few more moments of dramatic silence pass, then finally, Danny's lips move, and we lean in to hear.

"Ann, darlin', it's you that is getting married today, not me." Danny places her small, white, marble-like hands into Mark's that are already extended out to her.

Danny's words cause a thousand flowers to bloom. I lean over Patsy, Kathy, Dinky, Carolyn, Lana, and Linda, to stick my camera in the air, and capture the shock racing across Ann's face. She's dumbstruck, and her eyes flutter and swirl all over the place in utter confusion. Is this really happening? The mind can play tricks. I see these questions flashing all over Ann's face.

"We did it," Danny smiles, his lips quivering and barely able to speak. Gerald reaches for Danny's hand, squeezing it hard in a gesture of love, which prompts a wider smile on Danny's face.

The priest now visibly confused, shuffles his sandals against the stone floor, swaying his body back and forth as though the sea rock is shaking. He nervously squeezes a cracker-sized square of brown paper in his hand, crunching and wrinkling it. I think he's ready to read something, but he delays.

The tears are streaming now, rushing down Ann's face, dribbling from her chin. We stand huddled together, closer than before, with our breath tossed into the air. Did we hear Danny correctly? Did he just say Ann and Mark are getting married? I see the shock on everyone's face, except for the few who already knew.

Gerald kisses Ann's cheek, saying softly, "Congratulations, my dear. You are the bride today, and Mark is the groom—again."

Choreographically, they move backward, looking at each other silently with moving lips, "We did it—oh, heavens to Betsy, we did it!"

The chapel mists with whirlwind emotions and tears of joy and shock. Ann holds our eyes with emotions. Everything is happening so fast. I notice the white, floppy hat is now crushed atop of Ann's satiny hair. It was Danny who impulsively yanked the hat off, seconds ago, plopping it on top of Ann's head after joining her and Mark together. I wonder if she even notices the adornment.

A stream of sunshine bursts inside the chapel, creating mystical enchantment. Suddenly, as if a voice calls, Ann looks up at the rafters, knowing somewhere beyond the ceiling is the sky, and beyond the sky is heaven, and somewhere in the heavenly realm sits God the Father with his son Jesus seated at his right hand with the host of cherubs fluttering here and there and all around. And high above in the spirit world, where the streets are paved with gold and no more tears are shed, the angels rejoice, knowing two hearts are back as one. Ann places both hands over her chest, and the tears come again with a dimpled smile.

The shockwaves reveal the story written upon Ann's face, her cheekbones rising and falling, rapidly talking, bouncing on toes, then—for a moment, she's silent, numb from the category five hurricane, the storm exceeding 156 mph. Her creamy white skin is now highlighted in hues of red—a flashing windstorm of colors streaking frantically across her cheeks, displaying a hint of claustrophobia as we squeeze tighter together, creating a heatwave. Ann tries to speak again, but her breath is tossed somewhere above, and, like magic, sprinkles of sweat profusely dance across her face, tiny splashes of raindrops popping in to say hello.

Minutes later, after Ann's heart resuscitates and her brain receives more oxygen, the white floppy hat becomes a nuisance. With both hands gripped in Mark's and the hat balancing gracefully atop her head, Ann blurts, "Take this hat off my head! Take it off."

Putting etiquette aside, Danny rushes inward, taking two steps forward and frantically yanks the hat from Ann's head, placing it back onto his—a hot potato.

"Oh, my gosh!" Ann says frantically, struggling to inhale more air as her lungs fill with the foggy haze of flaming candles, never taking her eyes off Mark's crystal-blue ones. For a moment she seems to fall into hysteria overload

We watch Mark grip Ann's hands, tightly squeezing and whispering in her ear. They are magnetized—two hearts that have found their way back together. The love they show for each other is contagious and makes those who've lost love believe again. I stand next to Patsy, the one who doesn't believe in love, but now weeps. We are united as one, all of us, along with Ann and Mark, who've shown us what true devotion looks like.

Through teary eyes, Mark fishes in his pocket, nervously searching for the little piece of paper inked with his vows. We watch as his hand grows shorter, getting lost within the white linen pants—an enormous pocket, possibly a purse lodged inside. As we observe with our breath caught somewhere in the air, a folded wad appears clutched within his fingers. We see his intense desire to speak or recite the words, but he struggles to focus on the vows.

The brief silence is broken with the shuffling of Mark's feet. We lean in closer, watching Mark open and close the piece of paper as though it's an accordion.

Slowly the endearments flow, but after a few words, the paper falls to the floor, for there's no need to read from the paper when they're already written within his heart. The silence within the little chapel is so serene that even the tears falling from our eyes echo like a soft gentle rain when splattering onto the floor.

After the vows are spoken, neither of them can look at each other without more tears. Then Anthe takes over, stepping in to instruct the proper wedding procedures of a Greek Orthodox wedding: the ritual of looping each other with the ribbon and crowns and walking around the flaming candles three times for the Holy Trinity.

Afterward, Anthe motions for Mark to kiss his bride. Mark and Ann are frozen, unable to move.

"Go ahead, you may kiss your bride," Anthe tells Mark, trying to be professional.

"I present Ann and Mark to you, as one—husband and wife," the priest tells us, extending his hands out to them and congratulating them with two kisses.

Mark kisses Ann on the cheek as they turn around and face the door. And just like that, a ray of sunlight streams through the little side window, spotlighting them as though a million floodlights had flashed before them. It's magical. Mark takes Ann's hand and slowly leads her to the door.

The priest steps back and looks to Danny and Gerald, and then to Ann and Mark, and back to Danny and Gerald. Should he kiss them too? Congratulate them on their matrimony coming next?

Danny sticks his chest out with pride and squeezes Gerald's hand. "Momma is smiling right now," Danny whispers to Gerald.

"Why is that," Gerald whispers.

"Her son is still single."

"She got a reprieve, but only for a little while. I don't plan on going anywhere." Gerald returns the squeeze.

The sway of Ann's long dress is in rhythm with Carolyn and Linda's voices as they continue to sing. The tiny chapel is in unison as we watch Ann and Mark slowly glide across the ancient stones. With each step forward, the tunnel of light follows around them as though they're inside a circular tube of fog. I've never witnessed anything so perfectly orchestrated as the rays stream straight across the church, highlighting their hair like a halo.

Once outside into the sunlight, we gather around Ann and Mark, congratulating them, kissing them, and taking more photos.

"Toss the bouquet of roses," Carolyn and Kathy shout, gathering together and lifting their hands in the air with the other ladies.

"I'll toss it from the steps when you're below me, on the flat ground," Ann tells them. The waves of happiness and disbelief are still crashing and slapping her in the face.

"Let's eat cake!" Anthe says, clapping her hands together.

"Oh, no!" Ann shouts, realizing something is wrong. "What about you? Your wedding?"

Ann looks to Danny and Gerald with panic gripping her heart as the realization of her vow renewal occurring, not Danny and Gerald's marriage.

"I wanted you to get married, Danny. You and Gerald were supposed to be married!" Ann frantically rambles with waves of confusion hitting her hard, which causes her eyeballs to inflate rapidly.

"Oh girl, you stole the show. You yanked our wedding right out of our arms. And thanks to Mark, well, he stepped right in and booted us out the door." Danny steps on the stage, and the curtain goes up. Intermission is over.

"Momma will be happy about this outcome." Danny smiles big, flashing his long lashes of an enticing poodle. He's intentionally being dramatic and causing more alarm while grabbing his heart as though a sharp arrow is piercing straight through it. Beside him, Gerald raises his hands in defeat while rolling his eyes.

"No, seriously," Danny jokes more, not allowing the cabaret to end. "Ann, it was our privilege to reverse the marriage. I mean, really, what else can a man do when knocked out of his own wedding?"

"Seriously, though, Gerald and I have been together for years—six to be exact. We'll surely get over the hurt and disappointment, probably sometime after the gigantic holes within our hearts heal." Danny brings his palm to his chest, feeling the pretend open wound.

"And only the good Lord knows when, or if we'll ever get back to Greece, especially this secluded island. Heavenly days, we hopscotched how many islands to get here? And once we arrived, I had to start the search. You know, all the endless preparations, me seeking out the floppy hat, running all over Skopelos in search of the darn thing. Not to mention us memorizing the lengthy wedding vows, night after night, and, oh, there's more—I just remembered, the agonizing ordeal with Momma and the endless telephone calls landing in my bed every dang night."

We watch as he presses his fingers to his temples, frowning in horrible pain, then swallowing hard, making a disturbing noise within his throat.

"I forgive you and Mark, stealing our show and snatching up our wedding dream...stomping it into a million pieces. But don't worry, it really is okay. No hard feelings. Heck, I'll just contact a therapist when we get back to Texas, you know, get a high dosage of antide-pressants to pump-up my broken spirit," Danny exaggerates more, hitting Mark on the shoulder with a theatrical wink of his right eye, demanding the curtain to stay up. "Of course, I've never taken psychi-atric medication or been to a therapist, but as they say, there is always the first time for everything."

We begin to say our goodbyes to this enchanting setting, gath-ering up and proceeding down the towering steps surrounded by the captivating sea. The click-clack of shuffling shoes can be heard all the way down to the little snack bar where Tony and Nino leisurely lounge and wait for us, the report, the photos, and the video. We are a stream of color, slowly parading downward, stopping and taking photos of Ann and Mark, who seem to float down the steps.

Hours later, seated around the large wooden table with its white satin tablecloth, low lighting, and candles dribbling wax in tall puddles, Ann appears as if she and Mark are encased in a plastic bubble. We're all seated around them, joining in on the wedding night meal, laughing and eating, drinking the wine that keeps coming in fast delivery to our table. We are family now, bonded together. The conversations roll around the table.

"Danny, let me tell you something about having your freedom. You can have your cake and eat it too. It's not so much about the legal lockdown; it's about love, true love. The love and connection you already have, just like Ann and Mark. Look at them." Carolyn points to them, snuggled together. "Their journey and love for one another is incredible. God had a hand in their lives, without a doubt. Someone was surely doing a lot of praying for them. They've come full circle and now, back where they started, together but better. They had to be willing to walk through the open doors, following God's plan. Their love is what everyone wants, and you and Gerald already have it, too."

Kathy raises her glass, clinking to Linda's.

"Danny, you had us fooled," Kathy starts up. "You and Gerald are the best actors, and bringing your mom in on these love-affair shenanigans was just brilliant. I mean, you really pulled this off big time."

"Stephanie had us fooled, too; she played along with you guys so well. You saw how confused Tony was when you announced it was you and Gerald getting married on the bus. And the priest—he'll never stop talking about his first matrimonial ceremony with the Americans. He's still shaking his head. And did you see his face when you took Ann's hand and placed it in Mark's hand, saying she was the bride? His facial expressions were worth a million dollars. And between you and Mark together, ha, you guys would make the perfect television commercial for Restless Leg Syndrome." Kathy laughs, remembering today's events.

"Kathy, I didn't create all of this wedding hysteria to be left alone, tossed to the curb. It was mine and Gerald's greatest desire to be as one, to do everything jointly, merged tightly together, just like bread and butter, Jack and Jill, meringue on chocolate pie, Leonardo da Vinci and Michelangelo—and, well, you get the picture." Danny clanks his glass of red wine to Gerald's empty glass. Gerald reciprocates with a roll of his eyes, knowing it's going to be a long night as Danny is definitely in a celebratory mood.

"Let's stay another week here," Kathy throws the suggestion across the table with chocolate soufflé dribbling from her mouth. "This is my second time coming to Greece with Stephanie and Tony, and my twenty-nine or more tour in a row. I'm their perpetual traveler."

"I'm in," Lana echoes back to Kathy, raising her wineglass and clanking it once again to Patsy's. "I've lost count. I think this is my twentieth tour with Stephanie."

Across the table, Ann claps her hands together, puncturing the bubble and putting her and Mark back in the middle of our chaotic whirlwind of fun and laughter. I'm not sure what message passed between them, but Ann claps her hands again as a happy reaction to another fun evening as we continue to celebrate this joyous occasion.

The air is light and cool, and many conversations are ping-ponging back and forth, faster than I can keep up. Tony has three ears tonight. One is listening to Nino, and the other two are stretched over to us from his nearby table.

I watch as Mark reaches over to Ann and nonchalantly kisses her cheek, her eyes, her neck, her hands, and finally, her lips. They laugh together, getting lost in each other's eyes, forgetting about us momentarily. Today has been memorable, an event that will forever be engraved within our hearts and minds. And watching Ann, still floating and exhausted from the emotional surprise, the shock, and the overabundance of love from Mark and her new-found friends is —well, it's beautiful. They've found each other again, reconnected their hearts, and committed their love to one another. They know what it's like to be apart and endure the loneliness of separation or being with the wrong person. Now, they know how to laugh with each other and not take the little things so seriously, which is more important now than anything that had come before or after their wedding vows today.

"Are you ready to call it a night?" Mark yawns, giving Tony a wink. His crystal-blue eyes twinkle brighter than the stars above us.

"*Mamma Mia*, you must be tired, very tired," Tony leans over the table, picking up a spoon and dipping it into the lemon gelato with chunks of mixed fruit hidden within.

"Yes, we're exhausted," Mark confesses, pushing his and Ann's chairs backward as he thinks of making a fast getaway, but realizing he should give a speech of appreciation.

"I'd like to say a huge thank you for making this dream come true. I still can't believe how this all happened with Danny and Gerald taking the lead. Heck, when I asked Stephanie if we could renew our wedding vows in Italy or Greece, she said no problem, absolutely." Mark laughs, shaking his head, not believing the lengths we went to. "You guys were good, pulling off the most amazing production and giving us lifelong memories. We'll never forget you, and we love you all.

"And Danny, Gerald, and Patsy, you guys should go on Broadway, performing nightly with the big names. I'm telling you, there are none as talented as you. And, Carolyn, the everyday performances of singing your heart out. Thank you." Mark presses his right hand over his heart and blows a kiss to Carolyn with his left hand.

"I'm not forgetting you, Linda. You held out on us until the very end, finally sharing your mega-star voice. Thank you, my dear. And, will I ever forget our theme song or get it out of my head? *"Going to the Chapel"* is on constant replay," Mark compliments the singing duo with a dazzling smile.

"Anthe, my dear. You are the best wedding coordinator. Thank you. I'm still dizzy from all the twists and turns of a Greek ceremony." Mark blows more kisses. "Oh, Lana, your thoughtfulness will never be forgotten. Thank you for getting Ann the beautiful bridal bouquet."

"Mamma Mia, what a day," Tony says, listening to Mark's sincere words. *"Si, si,* yes, you must take the wife to the bed."

"Goodnight, my friends," Mark says, playfully scooping Ann up in his arms with her feet dangling in the air.

Ann throws her arms around Mark's neck and kisses him, one quick, playful smack on his cheek. They are highlighted before us as two lovers in a glass reliquary as the moon catches their hair, giving off strobe light effects with both of them shimmering with twinkles of gold dazzling all around.

Ann looks down at her hand and smiles. The moon showcases the stone as though laser beams are streaming down upon its brilliance. It's the ring that Mark gave her weeks ago when they legalized their vows in American. The gigantic solitaire diamond accentuates the precious jewels on the band purchased only yesterday.

"This is the most beautiful band I've ever seen, so many diamonds, and all the way around," Ann whispers in his ear.

"It becomes you." Mark squeezes her hand.

"Lordy! Lordy!" Danny says, stretching out every syllable. "You two better pump the brakes. There's too much hanky-panky going on in front of our virgin eyes." Danny is on the stage again, batting his eyes faster than ever.

"It is our honeymoon!" Mark is smiling enthusiastically. We see the hunger within his blueberry eyes.

"Heavens to Betsy! Goodnight, young lovers. You two need to get to bed before our eyes are traumatized forever." Danny giggles, and we join him.

"Does this mean the curtain is down and the show is over?" Danny quickly hollers, not wanting the cabaret to end. He reaches for his glass of wine and clanks it to Gerald's again, giving him a slow, sexy wink expressing his satisfaction at the happy ending.

"Oh, no. It's only the beginning," Mark shouts back, squeezing Ann's petite body tightly as she dangles from his arms. "Second time is a charm, and I'll never let this treasure go. When you find a lady like Ann, a true soulmate to share life with and create more memories, and going on more European tours with all of you—well, it doesn't get any better than this."

Mark loosens his hold around Ann, and she slowly slides down from his arms to stand on the wooden deck with her arm looped around his. Mark puts his arm around Ann's tiny waist, trying to lead her away to the honeymoon quarters.

"Okay, kiddos! Ya'll have fun on our honeymoon. You do know it's mine and Gerald's big night?" Danny reaches for his tall, sexy, Canadian lover, giving him a hard squeeze.

The spotlight is back on them for a brief second. We observe Danny's face portraying his feelings for Gerald, his fiancé. It's obvious that Gerald is, indeed, his sizzling hunk of burning love.

"Have fun, my friends. We'll talk more in the morning!" They both say in unison. Mark and Ann practically disappear before our eyes. They take off in a fast trot, almost running toward their room that overlooks the moonlit sea.

Now, thank God, the storybook is rewritten: once upon a time, there was a woman and a man who rediscovered each other and finally realized they'd turned into the wrong people, going off on wild rabbit trails, losing their way, until destiny intervened to reconnect their paths and ignite their love for each other. It was serendipity, a love affair too hot to ignore.

And as divine intervention would have it, they lived happily ever after with more love than before, relocating for a season to a dreamy lake house perched on a lagoon in East Texas, overlooking a parade of bobbing boats and fishermen. Afterward, still madly in love, they returned to the big city, and to keep the flame burning and their world full of excitement, they toss in an Italy tour with us every so often and host parties, bringing their new-found traveling buddies back together again.

ACKNOWLEDGMENTS

Thank God for the Americans' adventurous spirit and those who faithfully hop aboard my European tours every year and those never asking where we're going just as long as it's Italy or its neighboring country.

With a humorous laugh, I thank God for the endless Americans who continually ask the funniest questions that cause animated facial gestures of disbelief on Tony and I. You keep us laughing and on our toes.

Thank you, my American friends, for your endless devotion—twenty years—jetting back and forth to Italy and beyond with me and making lifelong memories together. Thank you for giving me these unbelievable stories that I will never forget. After all of these years traveling together, the vault is full, and I'm already eagerly anticipating writing the next book for the *Mamma Mia!* trilogy. Thank you for allowing me to lead and guide you throughout my beloved Italy and beyond. See you on the next adventure!

And, to the Queen of Authors, I am so grateful to Kathy Murphy, the creator of the largest "meeting and discussing" book club in the world, 780+ chapters of The Pulpwood Queen's Book Club, for choosing my book, *Mamma Mia, Americans Invade Italy!* as well as this one. She takes an author and introduces him/her into a world of enchantment, a world with hundreds of talented writers who live and breathe doing just that, writing and telling their stories. Thank you, Kathy. I love you dearly!

Thank you to my copyeditor, Carolyn Ring, who has worked hard to put this book into readers' hands—cover designer, formatter, editor, and where does it stop. Thank you for your hard work.

Thank you to my family who share me with so many others. I love you all! And a big thank you to my two gigantic poodles that have rested beside me on so many late nights of typing away on this manuscript. They know more about this book than you ever will.

Thank you to my devoted followers and dear readers who have supported my books throughout the years and who have joined me on this unbelievable adventure of taking you all over Italy and surrounding countries. Many of you have never stepped on foreign soil except by turning the pages of my books. My passion is just that, writing and sharing, and whisking you away to another world, a fairy-tale world of real life existence with the Americans causing hair-raising shock-waves. And the other passion is physically taking you to Italy and beyond on my coach, experiencing God's magnificent creation. Thank you for purchasing my books and writing your 'review' on Amazon.com - that helps more than you will ever know in the publishing world. And, thank you for your many emails, letters, advice, and unconditional love. I eagerly anticipate writing the next trilogy of Mamma Mia!

ABOUT THE AUTHOR

Stephanie Chance is the bestselling author of *Mamma Mia, Americans Invade Italy!* and an award-winning pick of the largest "meeting and discussing" book club in the world, 780+ chapters of The Pulpwood Queen's Book Club, receiving the official seal of approval for her *Mamma Mia!* trilogy of hair-raising adventures. Stephanie is beloved by millions of readers around the world for her 'tell-all' truths of the hilarious situations that Americans get in with her abroad; she's a comical, outgoing Italy tour guide with European genes stretching across the pond, leading Americans on two and three adventurous tours every year since May 2000.

As a paralegal, she worked sixteen years beside a renowned attorney in East Texas. Then, in a blink of the eye, she launched a "one-of-a-kind" shop unlike any other in the world, Decorate Ornate. This store is packed floor to ceiling with gorgeous home decor from remote places in Europe. In between her European tours, Stephanie returns to Europe in search of castle doors, religious relics, and fabulous finds. This May marks her 20th year zigzagging all over Italy and beyond in their Mercedes-Benz coach with the Americans hanging on tightly as she takes them to fairy-tale places.

Stephanie has been featured throughout Europe and the USA via television, radio and magazine, and been the keynote speaker around the globe. When not in Italy, you will find Stephanie in her treasure-chest shop Decorate Ornate, located on Main Street in Gladewater, the Antique Capital of East Texas.

Facebook.com/Stephanie Chance
Facebook.com/Decorate Ornate
Facebook.com/Decorate Ornate Italy Tours
www.DecorateOrnate.com
Email: ALNCHANCE@AOL.COM

Mamma Mia! Let's Go to Italy Together!

Tony, Stefania & Nino, the 'little' Bambino!